Shoot the Buffalo

Matt Briggs

clear cut press

Astoria, Oregon

© 2005 Clear Cut Press and Matt Briggs

Designed by Tae Won Yu
Copyedited by Allison Dubinsky

Printed and bound in Hong Kong by C & C Joint Printing Co., ltd.

SHOOT THE BUFFALO / Matt Briggs

ISBN-13: 978-0-9723234-7-5
ISBN-10: 0-9723234-7-3

Library of Congress Control Number: 2004107407

Clear Cut Press is grateful to its subscribers for their support.

Clear Cut Press
P.O. Box 623
Astoria, Oregon 97103
www.clearcutpress.com

Acknowledgments

I began this novel a long time ago and have many people to thank for helping this book along. Lisa Purdy has read and kicked around numerous drafts. Without her, *Shoot the Buffalo* would not exist. I appreciate Siobahn McNally at Donham Books in Northern Ireland for pirating an early draft of the book. Thanks to Anne Stadler and Richard Hugo House for a Hugo Gift Award for a portion of this novel. And thanks to Elizabeth Wales and Nancy Shawn at the Wales Literary Agency. I am also grateful to Matthew Stadler, Allison Dubinsky, Rich Jensen, and Clear Cut Press.

A portion of this book appeared in *The Raven Chronicles*.

For Fred Briggs

Contents

Shoot the Buffalo

Earthwork

One

Dad began to dig the dam behind the house the summer I was nine, the summer my sister Adrian died, the summer Uncle Oliver came to live in the attic. Dad planned to fill the gully with a twenty-foot-deep pond, but he was waiting until Oliver arrived to really get started on the excavation, but because no one had seen Oliver, and because Dad often started endlessly complicated schemes, Mom didn't believe that any quantity of water, a mud puddle, much less a pond, could collect behind the intermittent trickle seeping down the gully. Even though it rained all winter, the water didn't hang around on our hill. By the summer, our well went dry and the moss growing on the roof of the house turned as stiff as an old brush.

Dad constantly had something going on. He planned to hike for three months along the old Pacific Crest Trail from Canada to Mexico, packing his supplies on a llama.

A floppy wool Inca hat hung from a nail in the closet. Dad drew diagrams on diner napkins for a flying machine constructed with the 1940s Schwinn that hung upside down from the rafters in the storage shed and some plastic gallon water-bags he planned on inflating with hydrogen. When the well ran dry during the dry summers, we filled the gallon bags with drinking water at the trailer park spigot. Dad interviewed the farmers at the Busy Bee Diner while waiting for Mom to finish her shift. The farmers wore overalls and rain jackets. They drank coffee and talked with a drawl about feet of rainfall. They listened to Dad describe his final goal of turning the five acres of second-growth fir and feral pasture where we lived above Snoqualmie into a working farm. "Hell, son, what you have there is a stretch of timber. That hill up there is all clay and pine needles. Ain't going to grow nothing up there, except maybe radishes." But Dad didn't listen to them, because he wanted to be free of city life and people interested in his business. On Empire Way, where we had lived before in Seattle, Dad said he'd felt cramped with the police in the streets and the neighbors watching us.

Dad constantly researched a dozen schemes. Intricate diagrams covered the kitchen table. When he cleared the table, he just bunched the papers in his hand and threw them in the trash. An hour after dinner, a new layer of fresh plans spread over the tabletop, as constant as dust. The test of one of his ideas, Dad said, was if he still thought about the thing a couple of weeks after it had first occurred to him. His attempted plots almost always failed, which in the long run only allowed his fittest ideas to survive. He once attempted to harvest hydrogen from the creek to heat the house and fill three hundred gallon water-bags with lighter-than-air gas to make his flying Schwinn blimp. After a summer of running a current through the stream, he had collected enough hydrogen to fill a single red birthday balloon. With a flick of his match, the balloon exploded.

Dad never sat idle. He didn't stop until he'd smoked enough dope to put himself into a twitching coma. He vibrated with the energy he spent washing the dishes, shining the Dodge Dart with turtle wax, rubbing his hands together until the noise made Mom tell him, "Paul, go outside and do something." He converted the old root cellar into a profitable hothouse. It had seemed impossible that anything could be done with the damp, cracked cement basement of the farm's old hop shed. The cold space once reeked of the molding heap of fossilized potatoes, but Dad outfitted the subterranean room with halide lights, a forest of lush marijuana plants, a six-foot tank of water, algae, lilies, and orange carp. They brushed the pale roots of the water plants with their long mustaches. Slick tree frogs clung to the trunks of jade trees. In the damp paradise of warm vegetation, Dad smoked and his normally quick speech slowed to a drawl. He smiled with half-lidded eyes. "Hey, children." He looked around until he found us. "Can you go in the house, get me a glass of wine?"

With Mom working mornings, Dad relied on me. It was my duty to keep Adrian and Jake safe. I was responsible, because if no one looked after them they would end up as dead children, Mom said. Children were bitten by strange animals in the forest and the bites turned sour and festered and then the child died in bed. Children were washed away in overflowing creeks. I knew all of the things that could kill a child.

Our yard was a long way from the city yards with their well-trained lawns. Ours was full of unruly grass clumps. Each root ball lay distinct in the hard-packed clay soil. Our attempt at a lawn was a long way from the baseball diamonds behind the chain link fences and the swings with rubber seats that squealed out over a padding of wood chips. We had a single baseball mitt between the three of us kids. Without a baseball, a bat, or another mitt, it lay wedged in a corner of the toy box, where it became slightly soggy and then filled with a gray slime. Dad built a swing one summer, a wooden plank hanging from the leaning trunk of our black walnut tree. The very next summer, a two-inch carpet of thick green moss grew on the seat. Instead of hiking to town, we played on the vine maples, climbing hand over hand up into the twisted canopy of tangled branches fifteen feet over the forest floor of sword ferns and old leaves. I made sure no one fell out

of those trees. I made sure that Adrian and Jake got down
the road to the school bus stop, even when the road washed
out.

The paved road ended over two miles away, a half hour
walk down the hill. The bus stopped at the paved turn-
around. The highway crew turned the orange paving tractor
around at the dead end; only our road kept going beyond
it. On the hill, heavy rain moved the clay down the cut
bank. Trees and stones and even pieces of the road shifted
and moved. When it was raining really hard, Dad wouldn't
drive his car all of the way home. He left it on the other
side of the big gully ten minutes down the hill. The creek
bed passed under the road through a gigantic round
cement tube the highway department had laid down when
they first built the road. In the summer, the creek trickled
under the stones and seeped from underground to pass
through the cement tube and fell in a short waterfall on
the other side. In the winter, the creek grew so big it would
blow the road away. The gully filled with thick yellow
runoff and the cement tube wasn't big enough. Water piled
up behind the road embankment, leaving tidemarks of
flood scum on the trunks of the trees. Leaves hung from
the crooks of branches. Finally, the entire road bank melted
and the road, the gravel, and water traveled downhill. The
wind tore trees loose from the clay, peeling back the roots
from the side of the hill, uncovering big pink stones buried
like peanuts in fudge.

I kept poison berries out of Jake and Adrian's mouths. Mom showed me the berries we could eat. We could eat the tiny huckleberries that grew on the bushes that grew on rotting stumps and rotting tree trunks lying on the forest floor. We could eat the blueberries that grew in the heavy branches near the orchard. We could eat the plums and apricots and walnuts and acorns and apples and pears that grew in the orchard. I had to keep everything else away from Adrian and Jake. The forest was full of bright red berries that Adrian would always pile in heaps in her upturned skirt, and I would have to make her dump them out. If she ate one of these berries, Mom said, her insides would get cut up the same as if she'd eaten crushed glass; she would throw up blood and die. All the time I was watching her, she didn't eat a single poison thing.

Wild animals lived in the woods. Most of them were good animals. We saw an owl, once, sitting on a branch about fifteen feet above the forest floor, very still in the dark forest, and Jake and Adrian and I tiptoed past him. The cats found snakes and shrews and left their bodies on the porch. The shrews lay heaped on the planks, their mouths open, exposing their tiny white teeth. Their large, flattened hands covered their chests. The real, dangerous wild animals we never saw, except for their prints or their dung. Bears came into the orchard at night and left behind large piles of dung studded with cherry pits and apple seeds. At dusk, when even bigger animals, things we didn't know about, badgers, wolverines, and cougars, might find us, I hurried Jake and Adrian home. We rushed through the blue patches of light where the canopy of second-growth forest broke open and then, in the dark forest, already sticky with the spiderwebs strung out for the night, we ran as quickly as we could, bursting out of the line of fir trees above the house and dancing under the porch light, thankful for having gotten away from whatever animals slinked out of the hollow trees at dusk.

On frosty mornings, I tracked down Adrian and Jake's mittens, digging them out from the bottom of the toy box. I found their scarves folded on the top shelf of the closet. I made them put on their jackets before they could go outside.

Strange men kidnapped children. I kept an eye out for them, even though Mom remained vague about what they looked like. I figured that any adult man that noticed us kids fit the category of "Strange Man." Most men didn't even slow their trucks as they sped by us on the highway to town. We never ran into strange men in the forest, although sometimes a truck with hunters would pass while we walked down the road in the morning to school. The men, wearing their bright orange hats and carrying Styrofoam coffee cups, saw us but didn't smile or wave. On the way home from school, we could hear the distant crack of gunfire. Sometimes, strange men came down from the railroad tracks while we waited for the school bus. They asked me for cigarettes or an apple. These men had stubble on their faces and wore loose blue jeans with dirt stains worn into the knees and butts. They had backpacks with bedrolls and baseball caps. When I said, "I don't smoke," they always said something like, "Good for you," and then wandered down the road.

Knowing these things about wild animals and about bad weather and strange men didn't make any difference when the danger finally came. I was responsible for Adrian; still she died.

Each morning, I woke as soon as the light came over the rim of the hill, down through the cottonwoods and into my room. I had to get my chores done before I went to school, and I tried to reach the chicken coop before the rooster crowed. First, I peeled the old filter out of the coffee machine, tapping the grounds into an empty tin under the sink. Dad used the black soil as fertilizer. I took out a fresh filter and pressed the damp lintel against the bottom of the tray, careful it wouldn't come loose and fill the pot with grounds. Dad had shown me how to do it. "Wet the filter, but don't get the filter too damp because then it'll fold up and the grounds will get into the pot. You don't want that to happen again." I filled the pot with water. I poured the water into the machine and turned it on. Second, I put on my rubber boots and grabbed the chickens' water pitcher. I climbed up the muddy trail behind the house. During the night, spiders hung webs across the path, down from the gnarled rhododendrons over the moss-crusted apple trees. If I could find a loose branch at the bottom of the hill, I used that to sweep the cobwebs down. If not, I rushed up the trail with one hand thrust forward to catch the webs, but that never worked very well and I ended up at the top of the hill jumping around and just about losing my footing in the slick grass and mud, convinced a spider clung to my hair. After I brushed myself down, I walked across the pasture. The grass grew in thick patches, and the heavy blades held globules of condensed fog. By the time I had reached the chicken coop, the soggy lawn soaked my jean cuffs. If I moved quickly enough, the rooster would sit up, blinking and scratching at his head from his perch directly under the heat lamp. I closed the door behind me, to step into the murmuring and clucking of the hens and the sharp odor of the hay.

Adrian had adopted the albino hen, the only hen anyone could separate from the others. When the chicks were still just the size of my palm, after Dad had picked them up at the feed store, the albino chick lay like a discarded glove in the damp corner. The others jostled for the ring closest to the heat lamp. As the chicks pushed up to the bulb, they grew dopey and lost their place to the more desperate chicks. The weaker chicks were pushed back and couldn't get all the way up to the lamp. Smaller, and with a pink beak and red pupils, the albino chick never made it close to the lamp. I took her inside and Dad told me I'd have to throw it out. "Do you mean throw it away?" Adrian had asked. "You can't throw away a little chickie." She held the sickly bird in the palm of her hand, scratching its head and rocking back and forth. She kept it alive in a shoebox with a lamp and shredded newspaper and named it Francine. She named all of the other chicks, but as they grew up to become chickens, they all looked the same. Francine was the only hen's name anyone could recall.

"Hello, Francine," I said to the clucking hens. I took the feed down from the shelf and tossed it through the hexagonal chicken wire. I opened the latch and the hens brushed around my ankles. The rooster eyed me while I grabbed the brown eggs, still warm, from the floor. Most mornings, I gathered about a dozen and a half eggs, which amounted to more eggs than we could eat in a week. The hens didn't have nests. They laid their eggs wherever they happened to be. The eggs lay where they dropped. It was important to feed the hens, or they would begin to peck their own eggs and then we wouldn't get any. When I had the plastic pitcher stuffed with eggs, I closed the door and turned around, and I didn't feel as though I had earned two dollars in eggs, but that I had gone out and picked up a week's worth of food. Life could go on and on this way. The garden yielded more lettuce, radishes, and potatoes than we could eat. The orchard dropped more apples, pears, plums, and apricots on the ground in one season than we could eat in ten years. A carpet of heavy moss lived on the heaps of rotting fruit. The land more than provided for us even if the majority of the acreage sat under second-growth Douglas fir. There wasn't enough land for a working farm. It would never grow enough crops to sell for enough money to operate in the world. Mom and Dad still needed cash, and so they had jobs even though it was very easy to grow enough to eat. Although we didn't have enough money to buy new school shoes in October, the orchard filled with the excess of rotting pears.

After I fed the hens, I woke my brother and sister. I brushed Jake's face with a sheet of paper. He was seven and usually awake by then, waiting for me. I stepped back when he swatted my hand. He brushed Adrian's. She was five and lay extremely still in the morning and Jake almost had to shake the life back into her. I dressed them in hopefully clean clothes, but sometimes that was difficult, so I dressed them in practically clean clothes. Shirts passed if a stain could be explained by dropping something on yourself at breakfast. Clothing could not noticeably smell. Pants could have stains at the cuffs or knees and could smell from a distance of no more than three inches.

Finally, with everyone dressed, the chickens fed, and the coffee brewed, I would wake Dad. He lay slumbering in bed, alone, because Mom worked the graveyard shift at the Busy Bee Diner and left the house in the middle of the night and didn't get home until eleven. Dad worked the night shift and left the house at five o'clock. In the morning, it was just Dad. His arm usually stuck out of the sheets, his hand curled into a claw. The only thing that woke Dad up was when I said, "Dad, your coffee will burn." As soon as I said that, he grumbled and climbed out of the bed, pulling the sheets off and brushing his long hair out of his face and rubber-banding it back into a ponytail. He'd be so cranky without his coffee that he might tell me to go sit in the time-out chair just for following orders and waking him up. He'd sit down at the kitchen table and, after he drank his first cup of coffee and if it was a good morning, he'd make breakfast. Scrambled eggs with melted cheddar, bread coated with gobs of butter toasted in the skillet, and bacon fried into shriveled brown strips.

Dad had begun to dig into the hill above our house. A seasonal creek had eroded a muddy cleft into the clay. Dad called streams like these *quickets,* or his favorite word, a *freshet.* He loved small streams and would drink from them, holding the entire flow of the freshet in the scoop of his hands. This freshet started in a boulder field way above our house under the summit of the hill. The entire circumference of my known world was bound by that trickling creek, from its source, to the gravel bar where the creek dumped into the Snoqualmie River. The creek started where a collection of boulders had come to rest thousands of years ago. When the glaciers retreated away from the moraines that became the foothills of the Cascade Mountains, they left behind gigantic smooth stones. "Why did the glaciers leave?" Jake asked. "They don't like the heat," Dad said. "They could come back someday. They operate on geological time, though, which is no concern of ours." Dad was obsessed with the opinions of other people even though he desired for himself the same inhuman, creeping, fuck-all reassurance of a glacier, as if his own actions were inevitable. He spent most of his time hiding where he could do what he wanted without scrutiny.

Dad wanted to heap soil across the gully and dam his freshet and fill the ravine behind our house with water and trout and, in the summer, water for our garden and, in the winter, a place to skate. He believed deeply in the cleansing power of labor. He declared that the dammed creek would provide us with water and that the water was wealth.

"How much is this project going to cost?" Mom asked. "Major earthwork building projects require a CAT and gasoline," she said, "and late fees when you don't return the CAT on time as your project just becomes a big hole in the ground."

"Nothing, Gayle," Dad said. "The goal of this project is to do it myself." He held up his hands, covered with fresh blisters and dirty Band-Aids. "With these two hands."

One night after Mom came home, we could hear Dad in the gully throwing dirt out of his pit—a scrape and grunt and then a scrape and a grunt again. Mom said to us, "Let's go spy on your father." We walked down to the county road and then up the hill and climbed into the forest and made our way down the way-trail until we stood in the shadow of our rhododendrons. Adrian held my hand and Jake knelt down in the leaves. Years and years worth of leaves heaped under the boughs. The dry leaves crunched and Mom shushed us. We watched Dad working down in the gully. He didn't stop. His face held a slight smile and his eyes stared inward as he kept up a steady rhythm, a sharp thrust into the soil, planting his foot on the upper edge of the shovel blade and then levering his arm so that a tall square heap of clay split out of the earth. He cocked back under the weight of the clay and then flung it at the slope and started all over again. "What do you think you're doing?" Mom shouted. Dad stopped and looked around at the forest, not seeing us until Adrian ran down the hill.

She dropped herself down, both feet at a time, and caught herself with her hands. It seemed like she rapidly hopped down the hill, when really she was more or less tumbling. She wore her typical outfit of a pair of blue jeans and a dress. Mom followed after her, but Adrian moved as quickly as if she had really fallen. Adrian had never had her hair cut and it was still blond, the way my hair had been until I turned seven. She hardly ever washed her hair, so it bushed around her face wrapped with stray leaves, thin twigs, long strands of grass stalks, and the loose sprigs of pine needles. When she got to the bottom of the hill, she must have heard Mom about to catch up with her and lay down and rolled on her side the rest of the way. When she stood, her dress was plastered to her skin, covered with mud, slugs, beetles, and leaves. She just brushed them off.

Dad stopped his shoveling to watch her and Mom climb down into the pond.

"You are completely changing the way this place looks," Mom said.

"This hill wouldn't even be here if it weren't for the glaciers."

"Glaciers are a natural process."

"I am a natural process," Dad said. "I'm working to make our dreams come true. Our dreams need water, just like a houseplant."

Mom had just killed yet another plant in the living room. The only plant in the house sat in the front window and was usually in the last stages of a desperate, short life. This plant had seemed to thrive and then, suddenly, aphids had infested it and, within a week, it had turned brown.

"You are defacing the natural beauty of the hillside. You're destroying our home."

"I'm going to cut some trees down, too," Dad said. "We need light."

"I'm worried," Mom said, "because you don't know what you're doing. Do you think this dam will hold if it should actually fill with water? A dam that you built by hand? Even dams built by engineers don't always hold.

What if that dam breaks? It'll wash our house away. What kind of dream is that, honey?"

Dad dropped the shovel. "Can't you just believe in one thing I'm working on?"

"I know you'll finish what you start here. I'm not worried about whether or not you can accomplish what you want to accomplish. But it's a dam holding two tons of water in a gully above our house. This is dangerous, Paul."

"If a beaver can do it, I can do it."

"When is the last time you just sat down, or we played cards or whatever? I'm worried about you. When is the last time you played?"

"This is play for me," Dad said. If a man could physically dig a hole to China without hesitating to pierce the hard granite crust of the Earth, without incinerating himself in the liquid nickel core of the Earth, that would be Dad. She put her hand on his face, and he reached up to take it off but held his hand against her hand. He gently took her hand down. "I'll come inside and wash off in a minute."

"How long is a minute?"

"Sixty seconds."

"How long is a second?"

"One Mississippi. That long."

To hold back the dam, Dad built an intricate wall of fitted granite stones he had carted out of the mountains and mosaics of the colored gravel he had dug up from the hillside. They descended in patterns across the surface of the dam. When she saw the steady accumulation of granite and stone and his careful arrangement of bracken ferns, sword ferns, and bamboo, Mom stood in the muddy grass in front of the dam under the maple trees and looked up the gorge. "You know, Paul, I think you can do it. I think we can turn this place into the place we wanted." Mom became excited by the dam. She repainted the outside of the house and cleaned out all of the accumulated junk and washed the floors with boiling water and made sure that Jake and I kept our toys in our toy box. At night, when Dad was working outside, the house filled with burning candles and we ate soufflé made from eggs our chickens had laid in our chicken coop and beans from our garden that I had planted, watered, and watched climb the string, then picked and thrown into freezer bags. Dad washed his hands at the sink and sat down and asked us to stop eating. "I'm not going to say grace," he said, "because that is a crock of shit. But thank you, anyway."

Two

In late June, Dad brought Uncle Oliver home. When Dad pulled up, Jake and I were across the street knocking over elephant ears, these seven-foot-tall bamboo weeds that grew in the ditches all around the fields and roads of Snoqualmie. Dad parked the Dodge Dart and Oliver, much skinnier than Dad, and carrying everything he owned in an olive duffel bag like a negative image of Santa Claus, walked briskly up the driveway, threw his bag onto the roof of the house, and grabbed the gutter to pull himself after it. "Oliver," Dad bellowed, "you're going to pull the gutter off the house."

"You sound like a father," Oliver yelled down to Dad. "Oops, sorry, forgot. You are one." Teetering on the steep, mossy slope of our old roof shakes, he noticed Jake and I standing in the elephant ears. He waved, crawled around to the attic entrance, and disappeared into the door with the bag on his back like an ant with an egg. And, in a little while, because we hadn't expected him and hadn't been keeping an eye out for him, we forgot about him.

When Mom came home from work, we sat down at the dinner table to eat peaches she'd canned the previous summer, potatoes from the back garden, and hamburger Dad had bought reluctantly at the store. Meat, milk, and cigarettes were the only things that kept my parents tied to the grocery store. They had tried to belong to a co-op, but didn't like the meat prices. I don't know if Dad had planned on telling Mom about Oliver before Oliver started to sing. His voice sounded faintly through the floor-boards. His song went, "Oranges and Lemons said the bells of Saint Clemens." As soon as he started, Mom asked, "Do you hear that?" His voice sounded faintly through the roof beams and the ceiling tiles. Sometimes, he stopped singing and then it was quiet. After he sang a couple of songs, he began to accompany himself with some sort of metallic percussion instrument, clanging knives, spoons, tin cans.

Dad drained the sink and tapped the drain screen in the trash. "That's my brother," Dad said. "Oliver."

"Why didn't you let me know he was coming?"

"Does he need to apply for a Green Card to the Republic of Gayle?"

"Why isn't he sitting down to dinner with the rest of us? Where is that singing coming from?"

"The attic."

"Your brother, whom I have never met, is singing in my attic. Is he sober?" Mom asked.

"When will he come down?" Adrian asked.

"I don't like the idea of a vet in our attic," Mom said. "There isn't enough room to stand in there. It's weird, don't you think, for a guy to spend six years in the army— most of that overseas in Korea, Japan, and Vietnam—and then he comes back home and the first thing he does is find the smallest possible space to hide in?"

"It's pretty big up there. It doesn't look like it, but you can walk around," Dad said. "It's probably the biggest room in the house. Warm, too. The heat goes right up there."

"What did he do over there?"

"You said it was fine if he stayed with us for a while. You read his letters. What am I suppose to do now?"

"I would have liked some warning, that's all," Mom said. "The house is a mess. I'm a mess."

"He's family, so any attempt to impress him, I think, would just look snooty to him. He's a very down-to-earth person. You'll see. And besides, we need his help around the place. I wanted to build a rockery to keep the mudslide from coming into the house. Do you want our house buried under mud?"

Mom poured herself another cup of coffee. While she had the pot in her hand, a drip fell from the machine and hissed on the burn plate. "What did he do over there?"

"I don't know. He says he was a chaplain's assistant. He says a lot of things about himself."

"I can't have a killer or a Jesus freak in my house."

"Gayle, he's my brother. I thought we agreed that part of the idea of moving here was so that we could have a more open social environment for the kids. Less protective. Open. Organic. If Oliver had a place of his own, he'd let us stay there until we found a place. Not only are we all brothers in the family of man," Dad raised his finger, "but he's my actual brother."

"I really don't know this guy. And you haven't seen him in six years. Listen to that. He sounds like a raving lunatic."

We could hear him singing something in the attic, a slow, mournful song with some instrument that sounded like a maraca of crushed glass. "My beautifully delightful morning morass," or something like that.

"Gayle, it's going to be a long time before we are where we need to be to make this place work. Maybe Oliver can help?"

"How long are you thinking of letting him stay?"

"Just for a couple of weeks, if that's what you want. Just until he gets adjusted and finds a job and a place to live. But honey, I thought we were trying to reinvent America. You always say, *one family at a time*. If we can't have a Vietnam vet in our family, then how can we ever succeed? If we are going to turn this farm around, we have to have his help. I can think of three projects I could use him on right now. He's the cheapest labor you're going to find, I might add. And he is my brother. If you can't trust your own brother, who can you trust?"

Oliver stayed in the attic for twelve days. Each morning, Adrian asked Dad, "Is my uncle coming out today?" Dad said, "I don't know. Why don't you ask him? Tell him to wear his boots if he does."

Adrian put on her red rubber boots and walked to the steep clay bank behind the house. A gigantic cottonwood and its underground matrix of roots, runners, and baby cottonwood trees held the whole clay hill back from our house. The short path to the upper field cut through the patio between our house and the root cellar, then up a makeshift ladder of roots. Daddy longlegs, wolf spiders, and banana slugs lived in the ivy blanketing the thick trunk. Adrian brushed the leaves with a fallen branch to clear away the spiders and slugs. She grabbed a vine to lean out over the steep embankment and dark pool of seepage to get closer to the little attic door where my uncle hid. "Uncle Oliver?" she cried. "Why are you hiding?" He didn't come out.

Sometime during the time Oliver hid in the attic, an animal came out of the forest to slaughter our hens. Whatever it was left tracks in the muddy path to the vegetable garden. In one place, I found a single fuzzy print. I'd seen bobcat prints before. They looked like a big housecat's paws, with four pads. I'd seen coyote prints. They looked like a small dog, with their nails cutting into a depression. But these prints were too blurry and didn't have the round shape of either bobcat or coyote, house cat or stray dog. Whatever it was hadn't broken through the wire fence. Whatever it was had pulled out the chicken's stomachs and spread the brown feathers and blood in the lawn.

"We're going to call the police," Mom said. "A person did this. What animal would deliberately spread the guts of our pets in the lawn?"

"Gayle, you can't call the pigs out here. We're not exactly growing a cash crop of petunias," Dad said. "They're not going to do anything about a dozen chickens, anyway. And what could they do? Handcuff a weasel or whatever it was?"

We found the rooster wandering in the mossy orchard. He didn't make a sound as I leaned down to pick him up. Through his feathers, his skin felt cold and his spine stiffened. I carried him through the woods, petting him on his rigid neck. His eyes were as glassy as the plastic eyes sewn onto Jim Fuzz, Adrian's sock toy. We collected the pieces of the chickens we could find. I wore gardening gloves covered in dirt clods, which gradually became coated in blood and feathers. I threw the pieces into a garbage bag and buried the bag in a deep hole Dad dug late in the day.

Dad stood in the yard that night and looked up into the dark woods. He held a flashlight. The dark forest swallowed the beam except for the trunks closest to the house. The round dimpled pattern flickered across the bark and then disappeared, catching boughs, sword ferns, fallen branches. The forest sent out flocks of tiny white moths. They flashed in the ray. The next morning, when the rooster didn't crow, Dad, Jake, and I went looking for the place where the animal had come from. We didn't have any idea where it had returned. Dad thought it had come from a burrow under an old stump. Jake thought it had crawled out of a cave. "I don't know," I said. "It depends on what it was." But we didn't know. We didn't have a map. We didn't have a rifle, either. We carried Orange Crush, apples, and sandwiches, and we began to follow the tracks. About a mile along the way-trail, toward the top of the mountain, we found Francine's fly-covered cadaver. Farther up the hill, we came into a stand of crowded, dark fir trees. A musky odor hung close to the boughs. We came out into a forest clearing where a tall fir tree had fallen over. A lean-to tent lay propped against the side of the log. A man sat on a stool by a fire drinking coffee. He stood up, abruptly, when he saw us. He didn't say anything for a long while. He just looked at us without any expression and then he scratched his arm. "Morning."

"Hello," Dad said. "Are you out hunting?"

"Yes, I am," the man said. He wore an Army jacket. His red beard had begun to turn white. His teeth were yellow where the edge stuck into his gums. They were thin, skinny teeth, like a rabbit's. The whitish red whiskers, instead of ending where his beard stopped, just continued short and fainter across his face. He had very thick peach fuzz, fur really, covering his entire face. He was very tall and skinny, and his legs bowed.

"What are you hunting?"

"Bear," the man said. "And I'm always on the lookout for a twelve-star buck. I saw one back here about a year ago."

"I own a farm about a mile and half, two miles down this hill. My chickens were slaughtered yesterday by something. Don't know what kills chickens, do you?"

"Shit," the man said. "Everything kills chickens. Pack of coyotes. Wild dogs. Neighborhood dogs. A chicken is a sitting target for just about anything that works up a hunger."

"Name's Paul Bohm. These are my two boys, Aldous and Jake."

"Pleased to meet you. Ernie Badden," the man said.

"Most people call me Badden."

Dad took a look around Badden's camp, the burnt cans of ravioli in the fire pit, the neat, packed earth under his tarp, the rolled-up mosquito netting, the trenching tool, his green pack, and two tin garbage cans. "You live up here?" Dad asked.

"When I'm hunting, I pretty much live wherever I am. I don't have a home like most folks."

"Sure a lot of stuff to be out hiking."

"I'm not hiking. I'm hunting. It takes me all day to move five miles with this gear."

"This is Weyerhaeuser land, you know."

"They don't bother me. I don't bother them. I have an understanding with them. To be honest with you," Badden said, "I'm hunting something big. I'm hunting the biggest mammal in the Cascade Mountains. Problem is, you can't find something like that on the move. You got to find its home. Only way to find its home is to speculate how the beast lives and then to live like the beast."

"What would that be?" Dad asked.

"North American Primate. Sasquatch." Badden said. He didn't say anything for a second, just darting his eyes at Dad's face and then Jake and mine. "You now think, or rather know, I'm nuts. I agree with you. Thing is that I've done my legwork. I know that there are two possibilities about native primates in North America. Either they do not exist, which is the most likely. Or *they do exist*. If they do, I'm going to be the one to find them. My guess is they survive on grubs and slugs and bark and that's why they've been so hard to peg."

"And ravioli," Dad said.

"I'm just getting started," Badden said. "I'm not on my diet of grubs and slugs and bark just yet. Everyone is looking for an animal that kills deer and so on, the way you would expect some person trapped up in the mountain to do, when in reality, the big old man can live on an undisturbed square mile of forest, just like our ancestors. If the food was plentiful, our old-time forefather didn't do that much traveling and could spend his entire life in a very limited geographical area. So to find him, I'm moving up and down the western ridge of the Cascades manually looking for Bigfoot in every nook and cranny."

"Well, good luck to you."

We left Badden in the forest and headed back down. About three hundred yards below Badden's camp, we found two more mutilated chicken fragments covered in flies.

Badden was the first hunter I'd ever actually seen up close. Occasionally, we found empty beer cans and spent shotgun casings. In the autumn, sometimes hunters drove their campers onto the logging roads. Mom told us to stay near the house. She believed that these hunters, with their quilted jackets and fur caps, shot at anything that moved.

When we returned home, Dad packed his backpack.

"Did you find it?" Mom asked.

"No," Dad said.

He didn't tell her about Badden, but he did begin to pack his backpack. "Where are you going?" Adrian asked him.

"Hiking," Dad said.

"Can I come?"

"You can come as soon as Oliver comes out of the attic."

When Dad left, Adrian packed a cardboard box full of

her tin tea service, Jim Fuzz, and a plate of brownies she and Mom had baked in the range. The hot oven filled the house with the odor of syrupy chocolate.

"I'm going to get him out," she told me. Adrian called from the bottom of the mud bank. "Uncle Oliver?" She wedged the box onto a clay ledge. She climbed up to a higher spot and pulled the box after her. She wiggled her way up to the top of the bank, but because she had the tray to take up with her, she didn't sweep away any of the spiders or slugs. "Oliver?"

Jake and I tiptoed on top of the toilet tank and peered out through the narrow bathroom window. Dad had added the loose addition to the main house right before we had moved in because the main house didn't have indoor plumbing or a septic system. When we were both standing on the toilet, we felt the walls shift. "We're going to fall," Jake whispered.

Adrian looked up at the attic when Jake spoke. She almost fell when she attempted to brush her hair from her eyes. She hissed, "Go away. You'll scare him."

We ducked down and heard a crash. Adrian started to cry. When we looked again, we saw Adrian squatting at the base of the cottonwood, holding onto the ivy vines. The box lay at the bottom of the ditch and her tin tea service lay scattered over the back patio. Jim Fuzz lay headfirst in the muddy water. Mom ran outside. She had worn her cut-offs to honor the first day of the exposed sun. Her legs were white from the long, overcast winter. Her cutoffs, made from the pair of jeans she had when she was pregnant with Adrian, were very loose. She kneeled down into the collapsed pile of Adrian's things. "It's okay, honey. Why didn't you ask for help getting this up there?"

"He'll never come out." Adrian howled. She saw something on her hand in the ivy and screamed. "Spider!"

"Honey, don't let go." Mom tossed Jim Fuzz to free her hands. He hurled through the air and bounced against the house and splashed into the ditch, then sank. Adrian slid down the clay bank. Blue mud slicked her sundress to her stomach. Oliver came out then. He jumped from the roof of the house and scooped Adrian up. He had the beginnings of a beard and the start of the hair he wouldn't cut for years and years, not until Dad finally kicked him out of the attic.

After twelve days of thinking about my uncle, he seemed more important than any of Dad's friends who came to the house and smoked grass and drank at the kitchen table and talked about music. Oliver had just grabbed Adrian, where I wouldn't have been able to even cushion her fall. He slid down the slope on his feet, with Adrian curled up in his arms, just the way that she had held Jim Fuzz. Oliver landed in front of Mom and handed my sister over to her. Adrian held onto Oliver's beard. Oliver screeched when Mom tried to pull her hand free.

"It's okay," he said.

"I'm sorry," Mom said. "She just wanted to see what you looked like. No one has seen you." Mom tried to hold Adrian, but she was coated in blue mud and slid free.

"What does she think?" He was shorter than Mom. His face, although it didn't look like an old man's face with thick wrinkles and a large nose and shaggy white eyebrows, did have severe crow's-feet and a lot of wrinkles for someone just a few years older than Dad. Acne scars pitted his cheeks. He held his face in profile, with his chin up, to let Mom examine him.

"You don't look like the mad hermit I think she was expecting."

"I'm not mad. And I'm most definitely not a hermit. I'm just trying to get all of the military bullshit out of my system. I'm on a strict diet of stale bread, red wine, and Zen. But man cannot live on Buddha alone."

"Sounds like substitute bullshit to me," Mom said.

As they walked around to the front of the house, Jake and I ran to meet Oliver. I tried to find Jim Fuzz in all of Adrian's stuff, but his spongy yarn body must have soaked up the ditch water and sunk into the drain field. He would slowly run through the sluggish stream that gurgled under the house, trickled below the street, and oozed into a clump of blackberries and alder down the hill.

Oliver sat in the sun on the porch. "This to me seems like a good place. Perfect. There isn't any noise pollution. There are strawberry fields within a five-minute walk and fruit orchards and potatoes. The only reason a person would need to leave would be to go to the library." Mom smiled and sat next to him and Adrian lay between them, pulling on Oliver's beard. With every yank, he squealed, "Stop!" so Adrian pulled even harder.

Three

Dad returned from the Cascade Mountains with photographs of the Sasquatch. Rain dripped from the eaves while Dad's coat dripped water onto the tiles of the kitchen floor. Adrian connected one bulging puddle to the next with the tip of her slipper. Dad leaned back to suck his joint. The twisted paper stuck out of his mouth like a white tongue. He pinched his fingers and nodded his head to accentuate his story. Mom slurped her coffee while Oliver accepted the roach from the tweezers of Dad's fingernails. Dad told us he'd seen fresh tracks in the old snow above the last clearcut, before the tree line fell away to the stunted pines under the Cascade's granite caps.

"In the hard snow, I found tracks as long as shovels, as wide as my forearm. I could make out the toes and the lines in the thing's foot. I almost shit my pants." Dad rocked back and forth in his chair.

Oliver laughed so hard that he leaned over into his gut. He thumped the flat of his hand on the table, jostling the coffee.

"What?" Dad asked.

"Sasquatches," Oliver said, "sound remarkably like squashes."

Jake stared at Dad as he squeezed his eyes shut. Jake pressed himself against the wall. "What happened, Dad? What next?"

"I pulled out my camera." Dad hissed out a cloud of smoke. "I grabbed my camera and my hatchet. My hands shook so badly I'll be surprised if the pictures aren't blurry." Dad slapped the roll of film onto the table where Adrian grabbed it.

"Don't open it, Adrian. You'll expose the evidence."

That Dad was able to produce photographic evidence, even if it was just a canister of undeveloped film, to me verified his entire story.

"I followed the tracks through the forest. I thought the snowman could be anywhere. I thought he could be in the snow under me, the very snow I walked on. I thought the monster could be in the trees, like the shadows, that it would just step right out of the darkness in a stand of pine, reach its hands out and pull my head into its mouth and eat." Dad laughed. His face wrinkled around his eyes. "It was the smell that finally convinced me that it was out there. It smelled like old wool socks someone had been wearing for months without changing."

Later, when we tried to go to sleep, Jake kept me awake asking questions. "How big do you think it is? Do you think it has a language? Do you think we'll be able to see it sometime?"

"I'm sleeping."

"There aren't any monsters," Adrian said.

In the sharp shadows that fell against our wall, cast by the floodlight in the pasture up the hill, I saw the fingers of the abominable snowman reaching through the walls, its fingers long and twisting like a fistful of snakes. The shadowy, cold hands pulled Jake and Adrian and me out into the dripping forest. Pine needles coated our hair.

Jake and Adrian said they had seen a ghost come out of the forest. Jake said he was a man wearing a duck hunter cap and a red plaid shirt. The first time they saw him, he stood in the middle of the living room floor, standing over Dad. "He took something from Dad's mouth," Adrian said. They seemed so convinced that I believed them, but I didn't tell Mom or anyone else because I hadn't seen him.

Oliver didn't know about the red plaid man, but he knew everything about the Sasquatch. Before we fell asleep, he came in to reassure us about the abominable snowmen. "Yeti," he told us, "do not have sex. Through subliminal scents and whispering, they entice the male human to take children into remote forest ambush grounds. When the adult male human becomes frustrated with the toddling speed of his children's legs, he abandons the child in the woods. A paternal Yeti sees his chance. He grabs this unsuspecting child and deposits the ignorant adolescent into the depths of a mountain lake. Like a cocoon, the hiding place transforms the young Homo sapiens. The child grows into adulthood in the lake, and bursts from the sack at nineteen, transformed. By this time, his back hair, encouraged to grow in the hormone-filled sack, curls around his waist. He is hairy. He is Sasquatch. He is Yeti.

"Biologically, the first duty of the Sasquatch is to sneak through the woods, lurk in the bushes of a remote municipality's most isolated residences, and whisper to the men and women. Childless families have children. Sedentary fathers take up jogging, then hiking. Fathers, who otherwise spaced out in front of the TV with a case of beer, rouse their children and jog through the woods. Soon, they leave the children behind and the kids are kidnapped, secreted in mountain lakes, and the process continues."

Jake had wrapped his sheets around himself. "And?"

Oliver said, "I lived at the bottom of a lake in a Sasquatch-satchel for twelve years. I have the back hair to prove it." He rolled back into his chair and slapped his hands onto his knees.

"No," Jake said. "Tell us about the man who was kidnapped and married a girl Sasquatch."

"No, I have to go," Oliver said, "Leave me alone, I've got some work to do."

Adrian fell asleep as soon as Oliver left. I listened to Jake toss and turn. I listened to the TV in the living room, trying to hear voices under it, trying to tell if the voices came from the television or from outside. But the mumbling gradually pulled me into a slumber of unbroken dreams about hair-covered men moving at the edge of a dark forest. Their long figures stepped into the pale light and faded again into cedar trees.

When Dad said he wanted to take Oliver into the mountains, Mom said, "I don't think so." Dad's hands had new scabs and he walked with a limp from a blister on his back heel. Mom said, "Paul, it's the Fourth of July. Your brother has just come out of the attic. You have just come out of the mountains. If anyone is doing anything with anyone, it is the six of us doing something together. A picnic, you know? Watermelon and corn on the cob?"

"I don't believe in any of the patriotic bullshit," Dad said.

But two hours later we were in the car with a watermelon and a brown bag full of ears of corn on the way to the Olympic Mountains. I wanted to go to Seattle the way we always did to see the fireworks, but we went past Seattle. And we were going to keep going and end up in the middle of nowhere, where we couldn't even hear fireworks. On some Fourths, we walked down to Snoqualmie and watched the parade. The loggers wore their suspenders and cut pants and carried old band saws, oiled and sharpened and glittering in the sun. The firemen rode on the battered fire truck that coughed bluish clouds of exhaust. The Boy Scouts marched behind their standard, a tall staff with a wooden Indian totem of a bear with a mane of banners. On the Fourths that Dad had to work, Mom took us to Seattle. We sat on the waterfront pier leaning into the pebbly cement rail between Puget Sound and the wide Waterfront Boulevard. Crowds of other families waited until it turned dark and Ivar Hagland's clam house exploded tons of gigantic, drifting fireworks over the dark bay. If I had my choice, this was my preferred thing to do, because I could see how the other families dressed and talked. Unlike on the trip into the department store to buy shoes, people wouldn't stare at Jake, Adrian, and me. We were just other people in the crowd.

It wasn't easy to get us going, the six of us squeezed into a single Dodge Dart, three adults in front and the three kids in the back. "I have the window seat," Jake said. "I have the other window seat," Adrian said quickly enough that it sounded like an echo. But before they could do anything, I sat in the Dodge and closed the door. Jake's face pressed up to the glass. "Go away," I said. He rapped on the window with his knuckles. He repeatedly tried to open the door, clicking the door lever over and over again. "The other door is open," I said. Adrian wouldn't climb in, so Jake tried to get her through the door to stick her in the middle. No one liked to ride in the middle of the backseat, because they'd have to put their feet around the axle bulge. The bucket-shaped bump vibrated and, after a long drive, became hot enough to raise a blister. I had my spot staked out. When Dad came, Jake and Adrian complained to him. Thankfully, he wasn't interested and said, "Why don't you two get into the car?" If they had just jumped into the car, everything would have been settled, but instead of Dad starting the car, he went back into the house to get Mom's backpack. Mom said, "I'm not getting into the middle of this. You three need to settle this your way. Don't hit each other, or no one will sit in back. The three of you will sit in the trunk." As soon as Mom went back into the house, I said, "It seems pretty settled to me." Oliver carried out a sack of groceries for our picnic. As soon as Jake and Adrian explained to him that they had called windows, he leaned into the back passenger door.

He smelled like aftershave and tobacco and weed and he said, "Hi, Aldous, how are you doing?"

"I'm not moving," I said.

He said, "Aldous, are you aware of the rules? If you break the rules, it's anarchy, isn't it?"

"I'm not moving," I said.

"Do you think calling the window is a stupid rule? Because I think dissidence is called for when someone comes up with a stupid rule."

"It is stupid," I said.

"How do you think the seating should be arranged?"

"I don't know."

"By seniority?"

"What do you mean?"

"People should choose based on their age."

"Yes."

"Would you like it if the youngest chose first?"

"That's not how it works. The oldest gets first pick."

"Does everyone here think that's fair?"

"No," Adrian said.

"I agree. That wouldn't be fair at all. Do you think I should flip a coin and if it's heads, then the oldest gets to choose first, and tails, youngest?"

"I'm already sitting here," I said.

"What do you want, the Calling Rules or Seniority Rule?"

"I don't want any rules. I'm already sitting here."

"How about I flip a coin?"

"No."

He flipped the coin and picked it up. "Tails."

"I don't believe you. Let me see," I said.

He showed it to me; it was tails.

"I'm not moving."

"I have to enforce the laws of our society," Oliver said.

He snaked his arm toward me and I steeled myself to get tickled or to be pushed. But he snaked his arm around my body and then scooped me out of the backseat, bumping my head on the Dodge's ceiling, and dropped me into the grass. As soon as my head cleared the Dodge, Jake and Adrian took their seats at the windows. "It's my turn," I yelled. "It is my turn to sit on the side."

"You can sit at a window on the way back," Oliver said.

I didn't want to go anywhere now because we weren't going to Seattle to see the fireworks like we did when Dad worked. My feet would get burned off on the red-hot bulge in the middle of the Dart. Adrian would jam her elbow into my ribcage. Jake would fall asleep and put his stinking head on my shoulder. I wouldn't be able to lean on the door. I'd have to sit with my feet folded under my butt until they fell asleep and, when I tried to walk again, they would tingle and pain would shoot up my legs.

When Dad took the driver's seat, Mom held the door open for Oliver. "After you," she said.

"No," Oliver said. "Girls in the middle. Boys in the middle on the way back."

"I already called windows," Adrian said.

On Highway 101, we drove through a fog until we reached the narrow highway toward Lake Quinault. Dad floored the Dart around eighteen-wheelers whose headlights cast globes of glowing mist. For a second, Dad drove in the radiant white vapor and then sped up the hill toward the next truck. The drivers stared into the road and didn't look at us. Above the mist, we drove through the early morning forest. Driving along the black pebble beaches

on Lake Quinault, the sun finally burned through the morning haze.

We drove by the water. Trees grew on the other bank.
The windows were down and air that smelled like wind
and lake water streamed in. The voices of the adults sounded
hollow and far away on the other side of the adult wall. I
fell asleep again. When I woke, Mom leaned into the backseat, pressing a cool soda onto my forehead. The car sat on
the shoulder in the shade of some alders that grew in the
river-scarred forest on the bank of the Quinault River. Oliver
and Dad sat on the hood drinking cups of water and smoking and laughing.

"Are you thirsty?"

"No," I croaked. I was thirsty and hungry. I didn't want
to be here. My legs had fallen asleep in the back of the Dodge,
crammed under the backpack between Jake and Adrian. Mom
turned her back on us, not even noticing how uncomfortable
I was. I didn't say anything now, though, because I'd said no;
I tried to wedge my foot into the springs under her seat. She
didn't even notice.

When the car stopped in the gravel parking lot, the
engine ticked. Oliver and Dad hunched over their boots,
laced the cords, wrapped their pant legs into their socks,
and tucked shoelaces into their boot tops. I copied them,
but the fabric of my pant legs knotted in a hard line around
my calves. Oliver smiled at me, and then he dropped the
cigarette from the corner of his mouth into the gravel.

"We're late," Dad said, and he started to walk toward the trailhead.

"Wait a minute," Oliver said. "I want to take a picture of us." He pulled his camera from his backpack and fiddled with it. When someone took my picture, I smiled, a little bit wide, a staged smile. Oliver tapped the shutter and then positioned the camera against his open eye. I could only see his squint. "Cheese," he said. "Say 'Gouda, Munster, Edam.'"

"Good Monster, damn," we said.

Oliver clicked the camera. "Say Limburger."

"Nobody is getting blisters on this trip," Mom said.

"Everybody gets blisters," Oliver said. "Everybody gets their butt wet." For miles, the path zigzagged across the gullies formed in the clay valley walls by the streams running from the ridges down to the Quinault River. As we approached a ravine, the trail sloped along the embankment, back and forth down to the stream. The trail crossed the gushing stream over a tumble of slimy logs and mossy stones. The heavy spring rain sluiced muddy runoff and melted snow down the crevasses into the green-brown Quinault River, which we rarely saw, but could hear sometimes, groaning through the mossy Sitka spruce trunks. At the first bloated stream, Jake and Adrian hesitated. "Come on," Oliver said. Ascending the other side of the ravine, the trail cut into the forest undergrowth, red decomposing wood, rocks ground smooth under old glaciers.

Adrian shook her head. "We aren't supposed to get wet."

"We're in the woods," Oliver said. "We're going to get wet."

"Okay," Jake said. He walked into the water, not even stepping on the logs. He tripped and landed in the gravel on the other bank.

"Help me," Adrian squealed. She stood in the stream. Her pant legs turned dark blue. Oliver picked her up and tossed her onto his shoulders. She squealed again. When he tried to set her down on the other side of the stream, she said, "Let me stay here. I'm not heavy." She held the hair on the back of his neck with both hands.

"Get down from your uncle's shoulders," Mom said.

"We have to catch up with Paul," Oliver said. "She's not heavy. And she can walk as soon as we catch up."

"See Mom, I'm light." Adrian smiled at us. "What took you so long? Come on," she said to me. She climbed onto Oliver's neck. "He stinks," she said, and then we started hiking again.

We walked for miles that way, Jake stumbling through the streams, Oliver staggering along with Adrian on his shoulders. I leaned into the path and my breath hissed. The pit of my stomach rubbed into my chest. My weight pulled me back toward the valley floor. Gravity caught me as if I were water in a stream rushing downhill, over rocks, under fallen trees into the river. My skin began to grow hot and started to steam in the cool air. We moved forward faster and faster. I didn't look into the forest around the trail. The pain of lifting my legs up the hill started to feel good. We made better time, but we didn't catch up with Dad. Out of the corner of my eye, I watched for movement in the woods, for shadows to betray a Sasquatch in disguise, as a tree branch or as a granite boulder.

When we finally caught up with them, Oliver and Mom sat on the bank of a small stream. Long strands of wild grass fell over the side of the bank and twirled in the clear water. A birch grove grew along the stream, the white and silver bark peeling off in long stripes. Adrian slept on Oliver's jacket in a patch of sunlight coming down through the trees. Jake threw himself down and looked up through the leaves into the canopy of fir branches rushing way above the birches. In the forest, the first layer gave way to another and another. We didn't see the sky at all.

"I'm glad you finally caught up with us," Oliver said.

"Where's Dad?" I asked.

"Forget about him," Mom said.

"Did you see anything on the way here?" Oliver asked. "I thought I heard someone following us. For a second I thought it might be you, but then your mother said that was ridiculous because for one thing, you guys don't walk that fast and, second of all, it sounded like an elephant or something. Did you see any elk?"

"You heard that, too?" Jake said. "I thought it might be something."

"What?" Oliver asked. "What could it be?" But we didn't hear anything when we stopped on the side of the trail, just the dripping of water from the boughs, the distant trilling of a bird, and beyond that the roar of the Quinault River.

When I complained about coming out here instead of going to Seattle to celebrate the Fourth of July, Oliver said, "What is there to celebrate? The states freed themselves from British rule so that they could be free to create Manifest Destiny and spread mini-malls from sea to shining sea, killing every man, woman, and child that happened to live in their way."

Mom walked along for a minute, adjusting her backpack. "Oliver, we aren't celebrating the anniversary of the birth of the nation, we are celebrating Independence Day, the beginning of summer."

"Who in the hell is Uncle Sam, anyway? I don't believe we ever had an elected official named Uncle Sam."

"I think of the Fourth of July as a good celebration," Mom said. "It's not like Thanksgiving. You may be soured by the whole patriotic thing, but I think of the Fourth of July as more like a folk celebration."

"You mean you think it's a pagan thing?" Oliver asked.

"When you get right down to it, yeah. Uncle Sam is a randy old man. He has that very tall, thick top hat. And what's with the Sams on stilts, elongated legs? The summer solstice, all that."

"Where are our fireworks?" Adrian asked. "I want to go see the fireworks." Dad had brought a package of sparklers. "These are the best ones," Adrian said. We lit the sparklers and they threw out hot filaments of metal. We wandered away from the light of the bonfire so they would work better. I put the spare rods in my back pockets. Mom, Oliver, Adrian, Jake, and I walked through the forest with the sparklers. Dad stayed behind at our campsite. The trees jumped up around us, gigantic sharp shadows that overlapped because we were all equal sources of light. We kept walking farther and farther out; then I realized it was just Jake and Adrian and me. Then Adrian was far away from Jake and me and her sparkler went out. "Help!" she called out. I found her standing in the middle of a stand of maple trees. She had both arms at her sides. She took my hand and I held the sputtering light; then we walked through the forest, even though I wasn't sure where we were going. She could tell right away. "Where are we going?"

"We'll know when we get there."

Even though we had just come through the woods, in the strange, hard light of the sparklers, nothing seemed familiar. Adrian and I kept walking and changing sparklers until we found ourselves in a clearing. The limbs of the trees twisted into the knotted canopy of crossing branches at the edge of the meadow.

Jake came out of the forest behind us. "I'm out of sparklers."

"We need the last one to get us home," I said. "Look, we can see the stars here." We lay in the middle of the field and looked at the sky. It swam with the light of the individual specks of light and, in some places, they were so dense that the stars crowded in on one another. A light came out of the forest, flashing like a strobe light, and then we heard something thrashing. The light grew, a throbbing blue glow. And then Mom ran through the clearing. She didn't have any clothes on and held in one hand a sputtering sparkler. She crashed through the bushes on the other side of the clearing, and the whole clearing fell back into the darkness under the stars. Then more light came. I thought it might be Mom again. The light flashed and then Oliver, carrying a sparkler in each hand, ran into the pasture. He stopped when he saw us. He kneeled down and said, "Come on!" He took off after Mom's light.

"Where are they running to?" Adrian said.

"I wish we were in Seattle, watching the real fireworks," I said. We lay under the stars that held their familiar positions. Dad had told us what they were called, but Jake and I, although we often asked each other what they were, could never remember the names.

"You're stupid," Adrian said.

"Why?"

"Look," she said.

"I don't see anything."

"You can see stars. They're better than fireworks because

they're always there." The three of us lay there for a long time. I realized, listening to the three of them breathing, that not only had I been responsible for watching out for them, but they were watching me, as well. Finally Adrian said, "Come on, it's time to go home."

We made our way back downhill and, when we came back, Dad sat in front of the fire listening to his tapes and drinking a beer. "Children, come here and feel how big this fire is!" Dad sat impossibly close to the flames. Steam rose from his clothes.

Rain started to fall. The heavy drops rattled the leaves. "Did you feel that?" Dad asked.

He walked away from the bonfire. "We need to put everything in the tents. Where's your mother?"

"We haven't seen her," Jake said.

We moved everything inside, and when we finally sat down in the tent, Oliver and Mom came back. Their hair and faces were soaked, but their clothes were dry. Oliver and Mom sat in the tent with us and passed a rolled joint back and forth with Dad.

Dad served everyone slices of cake. He poured Jake, Adrian, and me glasses of milk. As we ate, I tried to understand what they were saying, but Mom and Oliver and Dad were talking about something I couldn't follow, and it didn't help that they kept stopping suddenly and laughing until they started to choke. Oliver built up the fire even though it filled the campsite with too much heat. Beer cans lay around the fire. Jake and I played German Whist in our tent while Dad and Mom and Oliver sat in the dripping water right by the fire. "Hey," Oliver said. "Come on and join the party." We sat next to the fire. Dad passed the joint to Oliver. He sucked on it, pinching his lips and closing his eyes. Then he tried to pass it to Jake, but Dad passed it off to Mom.

"Good time?" Dad wheezed through a mouth full of smoke to Mom.

"Sure," Mom said.

Oliver flipped through the songs, pressing fast forward and filling the campsite with the squiggly sound of rushing tape. He halted songs in the middle of words and put on new tapes. He turned to sing a lyric and wagged his butt.

I got to keep moving, I got to keep moving
Blues falling down like hail, Blues falling down like hail
Blues falling down like hail.
And the days keep on minding me
There's a hellhound on my trail.

He slid a tape into the machine. The recorded album had a spitting needle, and then the static of worn vinyl filled the air. Dad and Oliver suddenly started dancing in slow circles, holding each other as though the other was a woman. Mom laughed and grabbed Jake. They jittered and Adrian jumped back and forth, oscillating like a monkey push puppet. I swayed back and forth.

"I don't know how to dance," I said.

"No one can explain it to you, Aldous." Mom frowned at me and twirled across the space with Jake twined in her arms.

Oliver held Dad by the small of the back. I jumped back and forth and held onto Mom and Jake's hands. We jumped up and down. Jake's hair flapped. Mom's ponytails snapped and as Dad leaned back, I could see down his throat through the passage defined by the loop of his white teeth into the pink fleshy passage falling into a small black hole deep inside his neck.

He snapped his head back and drew a roach to his mouth. He coughed and sucked air through the joint's burning nub. Smoke spilled out of Dad's mouth. Layers of blue fog shifted through the forest in flat hazy fields. As I jumped up and down, my head slipped through the layers. Jake stopped jumping and crab-walked across the ground. Dad turned the volume of the music up, filling the forest with a throbbing acoustic guitar and the wispy holler of an old voice.

I stepped into the darkness away from the bonfire. The hot, smoky air was gone; instead, I was surrounded by the cool cedar smell of the quiet forest. Cold splatters of rain soaked into splotches on my clothes. In the distance, under the roar of water falling on the broad maple leaves, I could hear the sound of howling. It sounded like someone was joking and leaning back and howling, though it was far away and sounded more like moaning. The noise filtered through the rain and made me think of someone's mouth opening and forcing out the scream until his vocal box ached, until his tongue started to dry, until the sound had been completely sent out of his body.

I jumped back toward the sweltering, smoky heat. Oliver sang, "I can't get me no. No. No. No."

I was afraid that I wouldn't be able to eat enough. What we didn't eat would be eaten by our parents in the long evening after dinner. The odor of peppery meat unwrapped from foil caused my stomach to flutter. I wanted to eat as much as possible, and so when I actually ate I became stuffed and bloated without satisfying my hunger. I lay in the tent holding the watermelon hardness of my stomach. I wanted to burp or shift the weight so that I could still eat the steak and potato salad, maybe a bite of chocolate cake.

I offered to put the food away, so that tomorrow I could eat some of this for lunch, maybe eat the cake at breakfast, waking as early as possible and pulling the backpack into the forest and cutting three thick slices for Jake, Adrian, and myself. Oliver and Dad, though, had just started to eat. They stopped periodically to take a gurgling hit from the old brass coffee urn Dad had converted into a hookah. They placed the stem of the long metal utensil into their mouth with a dentist's precision and took a long drag. "I can't believe this food," Oliver said. "This is the best meal I've ever eaten. Better than the best. Bestemostest."

While hiking, Dad often stopped and changed his shirt. A heavy, oily sweat poured from his pores. His hair slicked down and then went all crazy where he brushed the sweat away from his eyes with the flat of his palm. He kept moving as quickly as possible, just dumping water. We tried to keep up with him, which required us to jog every now and then. He would start to get farther and farther away up the trail and then we would jog. In a way, it was like we were trailing behind him, attached to some kind of cord.

Occasionally, he would stop and change his shirt and we could catch up, or he would change his shirt and climb up onto the side of the trail and smoke so that when we came up, he sat in a warm, hazy cloud of smoke and Mom and Oliver sat there as well, their hands folded out on their knees as they drank water. We would want to rest with everyone else, but Dad would hop up and say, "We got to keep moving; it is a long way to the Enchanted Valley."

Later, as the daylight faded toward dark, we came out into the meadow where the Enchanted Valley Chalet stood. The Chalet was a lodge built to provide shelter for hikers in the upper part of the valley when the weather turned suddenly. The valley faced the Pacific Ocean and storms could sweep in from the sea and flood the valley with snow or rain on days that seemed like they would be clear and sunny forever. Dad lay bare-chested in a patch of sun on the mossy ground. Elk floated through the pale light, their antlers reaching into the sky like skeletal hands. Inside the lodge, a huge fire cast shadows and bright light over the walls. We ate and I fell asleep dreaming of the trail and the twisting roots and Sasquatches walking through the mists carrying captured children like bags of laundry.

My bones ached to the marrow. My shoulders had blisters from the backpack straps. My belt had rubbed my back raw. In that distance, I was lulled into the forward movement, away from the car, which felt connected to the highways and the cities and then, finally, Dad's job at the Red Diner in Seattle and Mom's job along the highway. The car and then the roads were connected to Port Angeles and Grandma and my parents' pasts before they met each other and before they had us kids. Out there, it felt as though Dad had finally escaped any scrutiny at all.

The morning sunlight fell through the open door. A distant clicking sounded outside. I didn't want to get out of my sleeping bag, but I pulled myself out onto the worn boards of the lodge floor to wake up Jake and Adrian.

Adrian's shallow breath hissed in and out. Oliver and Mom's backpacks lay against the wall with their sleeping bags rolled and stuffed behind them.

Dad had built a huge fire in the outdoor pit, prodding sizzling bacon with a long stick. His black skillet lay on a burnt stump.

"Look who's up," Mom said. She leaned against a tree, reading a book. Oliver lay on his back, his elbows behind his head, doing sit-ups and grunting with each rise.

"Me," I said. My voice sounded too loud against the quiet activity of my uncle and mother and father. Above us, the mountains looked blue. White, marshmallow-shaped clouds rolled along, way up in the sky. I sat by the fire, feeling the warm flames as they crackled in thin, gassy pulses.

"Aldous," Dad said. "Could you get me some more wood?"

"Sure," I said. I watched Oliver feel his muscles after exercising. He looked into the distance, over the trees toward the mountains. Then he leaned down and put on his shirt. He looked at Mom after he drew the shirt over his stomach and tucked it into his belt. I wandered into the thick underbrush to find kindling and firewood, but Oliver and Mom didn't stop horsing around.

When I got back, Dad handed me a plate with scrambled eggs and bacon and some pieces of half-burnt toast caked with soft butter. "Here," he said. Oliver sat on the log next to me.

"So who's going to go with me to the pass to look at the glacier?" Dad asked. "Oliver?"

"I'll go with you," I said.

"You can't keep up," Dad told me.

"I don't feel like it today, Paul," Oliver said.

"Come on," Dad said. "Just you and me and the mountains. We don't have to take backpacks. We can race up to the glacier, run our hands over that hard ice, and be back before dusk."

"I don't think I'm in the mood for racing."

"I brought you all the way out here so that you could see some things," Dad said. "You can just lounge around at home. When in Rome . . ."

"Eat until you drop," Oliver said. "I'm tired. Let's eat breakfast and then think about it. Forget it. I thought about it. I thought I might lie in the middle of this meadow and get a sunburn, that's what I thought."

"How long would it take us to get to the glacier?" Mom asked.

"It would take Oliver and me a couple of hours to go up there. I think it would be too much of a trip for the kids."

"We came out here to be together as a family," Mom said. "Don't take off now."

"We'll be together later. I just want to go for a little while."

"Am I supposed to just pine away while you two go mountain climbing?"

"You want me to stay here? On a day like this?" Dad expanded his arms to include the sky.

"I want you to spend time with us."

"I'm staying," Oliver said. "Why would you want to be anywhere else? What are you going to see up at the top of the mountains anyway?"

"Don't you want to touch the ice where the river starts?"

"I do," I said.

"You can see it from here," Oliver said.

"You can see the moon from here, but you can't touch it. I want to put my hand on it," Dad said.

"I would like to," I said.

But Dad was looking up to the top of the valley. He had a sort of glazed-over look, a film, covering his eyes. He had several days of beard. His hair was visibly thick, each strand the width of a toothbrush bristle. Underneath his harsh hair, though, Dad had a clear, deeply ruddy skin with an almost applelike reddish glow, burnished-looking. The morning light and the reflection of the Jackson glacier, a bluish color, glinted not only off his eyes, but off the contours of his sharp nose and smooth cheeks, and would have reflected off his chin and jaw if he didn't have so much stubble.

Adrian stood in the door. She ran down the steps and tumbled into the mossy turf around the lodge. She rolled and then placed her palms into the springy grass, then stood and ran and wrapped her arms around Mom's leg.

"I've got to get ready," Dad said. "There's more food for Jake and Adrian."

Dad packed his backpack. He rolled his shirts into tight logs and stuffed them to the bottom of the pack. "Can I help?" Jake asked.

"You can't go with him," I told Jake. "You can't keep up."

"I'm finished," Dad said. He leaned over the backpack and rolled it onto his shoulders. "This is it. You coming?" Oliver shook his head no. "I'll be back later."

"Why can't I go too?" I asked, finally.

"I thought you wanted me to spend time with you, Gayle. It will take me three hours by myself. It will take five or six with the kid."

Mom said, "Paul, you take Aldous with you."

Dad looked at me. "You'll have to keep up."

"Yes," I said.

"I want to go too," Adrian said. "And Jake has to come."

"I can't do that," Dad said.

"You're their father. You should be able to do that."

"I came up here for a vacation to celebrate Oliver's freedom with Oliver, not to babysit in the middle of the forest. Forget it, Aldous. Stay here." And then Dad left.

Jake walked behind him to the end of the field. I watched him walking behind Dad as they passed into the shadows of the hemlocks. Jake walked back and sat in the clearing. He looked small in the distance. When he stood, I could

see how small he was in comparison to the tree trunks.
Even though the mountains and the glacier at the end of
the valley were far away, they seemed much closer because
of their immense size.

Adrian leaned into the fire to grab a rasher of popping,
spitting bacon off the skillet. Her fingers grazed the greasy
layer coating the pan and then she held a sliver of fatty
meat. She screamed and flung the bacon into the meadow.
Muttering *ouch ouch ouch*, she licked the grease off her
fingers and started to cry.

"Aldous, why weren't you watching her?" Mom grabbed
her around the waist and held her to her chest as though
Adrian was a gigantic doll. I always had to watch her, and she
was always doing something stupid. If I didn't have to watch
her, maybe Dad would have been able to take me with him.

Adrian lay with her head against Mom's shoulder while
Jake and I sat on the log by the fire and coughed in the
smoke. When she looked up at us, coughing and eating our
bacon, she started to scream again.

"I didn't think things would turn out like this," Mom
told Oliver. "I think the only thing I've learned from all of
this is, don't give up control. Never do anything that makes
you do what you don't want to do."

"Paul hasn't forgotten that."

I scraped the fatty parts of the bacon into the fire and
set my plate on the other plates. I looked around the
meadow as Mom spoke, looking at the places she might go

without us. She couldn't go anywhere. And I didn't know what she meant that she wanted another life, because she seemed pretty happy most of the time. But Mom said things like this sometimes and when she said them, it made me feel she was going to leave me behind, as if I was somehow part of this life she wanted to leave behind.

"Paul doesn't know how out of it he is yet."

"Tell me, Gayle, what is it you'd like to do?"

"I don't know," she said. "I just know what I don't like to do."

Mom looked into the fire and held Adrian. Her shoulders shook. Finally, Adrian squirmed away from Mom. "I'm fine now," she said.

After we had finished breakfast and washed the dishes in the stream, Oliver asked me if I could look after Adrian and Jake. "Your mother and I are going to go for a walk."

"Can I come?" I asked.

"No. Watch Adrian."

At this point I wanted to lock Adrian and Jake up in a big cage hanging from the ceiling of the chalet, or leash them to a tree. I didn't understand why it was always my responsibility to watch over them while everyone went off and had fun.

Mom stood up and brushed her bottom. "You know, I don't have to go with you, Oliver," she said.

"You don't have to do anything," he said. "But I think you would like to see the river, wouldn't you?"

"What do you mean?"

"Come on," he said.

"I can go with him," I said, "if you don't want to."

"Let me," Adrian said. She stood up and grabbed Mom's ankles.

"No, you stay with your brother," Mom said.

"Yeah, stay with Aldous," Oliver said.

"No," I said. "No. I resign. I'm no longer responsible for Adrian and Jake. I'm going on strike."

"Aldous, we'll go for a walk later," Mom said.

Jake, who had been running from the other side of the field, now stood panting by the fire and then flung himself on the ground. "I'm bushed," he said.

I poked him in the ribs and he rolled over and socked me.

"Stop it and watch Adrian, you two," Mom said.

"I'll watch Adrian," I said. "But I get to go swimming in the river later."

After they left, we sat in the field building cities out of river stones and stopped when we heard a crashing noise.

"What's that?" Jake asked.

"I don't know," I said. Around us, the trees made noises like chattering teeth, like drums, like animals and people moving. The branches shook as wind started blowing up the valley. I looked up and the marshmallow clouds had moved on. A hazy halo clung to the sun and everything else looked blue. Adrian twirled around in the middle of the field. "I'm wind. I'm the wind."

"You're passing wind," I said.

"What?" she asked.

"You're a fart," Jake said.

"Kids," Mom yelled from the lodge later that morning, after we had found a colony of ants under a rock and picked it up to watch them haul their eggs into the little holes. Mom had changed her blue jeans and now she wore shorts. I had packed a pair of blue and white striped shorts that used to be Dad's. The braiding around the pockets and along the edge of the legs had pulled loose and several stray lengths trailed down the back of my thighs. I liked them because I thought I looked older in them. At least twelve.

"Can I put on my shorts, too?" I yelled.

I stood on the wooden steps of the lodge in my bare feet and changed into my shorts. The wood was hot under my feet. I could feel the warm grains. Then, I followed Oliver across the pasture through the cool, muddy path under the hemlock to the river. The river rushed under the hemlock tree, pausing in deep green pools. In the shallows by the path, I slipped into the water, holding onto the river's rounded rocks. Jake splashed into the water behind me. Oliver sat on the bank above us and stared into the forest across the river. "Did you hear that?" he asked us.

"Yeah," Jake said. Jake stood up on the bank and crouched. "I heard it."

"You don't think there are people out here with guns?" Oliver asked.

"No," Jake said.

"You're trying to scare us," I said. "There's nothing to be afraid of. We're in nature."

He smiled at me. "Nothing to fear." Then he made a wild face as though he had just sunk his teeth into the live wire of a cattle fence. He jumped over one of the green pools and slammed belly-first into the water, kicking up white sprays. We watched him swim downstream underwater. When he surfaced, Jake and I splashed water on him.

He dunked Jake in the water and brought him up laughing and coughing up the river. Then I felt one of his cold, strong hands grip my legs and drag me into the water. The surface rushed above me and the murky ice-cold greenness swept around me. I felt the water slip through my mouth and I breathed it down in painful gasps as if I had swallowed fist-sized marbles. I found myself on the surface of the river, the hemlock boughs dripping into the water, my face tilting in and out of the water. I stood up on the shallow rocks, my knees shaking. I climbed into the soft moss under the trees. The dry fronds pushed into my back like shag carpet. Under the ferns, I found a pair of underwear. They were like Mom's underpants. "Look," I said. I held up the pink fabric with the blue stripes, the kind of underwear that Mom always piled on the counter at the laundromat as we folded laundry.

Large drops of rain pelted down on the dry riverbank stones, kicking up dust for a second, and then everything was wet. We ran back to the lodge, past the smoking fire pit, and inside, where Adrian and Mom drank hot chocolate and our dry clothes waited. We muttered *cold cold cold* and stood warming our goosebump-tight skin in the heat of the fire.

When I woke up around dawn to the sound of rain falling against the roof of the lodge, I noticed that Mom's sleeping bag was empty. The door had blown open. Rain swept into the room, banging the door against the frame. A thick mist clung to the trees and the sky. The cold, wet air filled the room.

"Morning, kids," Dad said.

He dropped dry logs into the fireplace and lit paper. Jake made a mumbling noise in his sleep. The fire filled the room with a light, but instead of warmth, I could smell the damp fabric of Dad's backpack. He sat by the fire and blew air against the old ashes and the smoking kindling until the heat began to fill the room.

I sat up in my sleeping bag, keeping the warm insides wrapped around me. "I am not in charge," I said. "Everyone makes me do everything and I am not in charge."

"You want something to eat?" Dad asked me.

"I am hungry and cold and I want to go home."

Dad leaned over his backpack and pulled out his hand

ax and his cooking stove. He set the ax down by the fire
and started the cooking stove. Its blue flame cast sharp
shadows in the corners of the room. I watched the flames
and Dad rocking back and forth staring into the fire. He
poured the steaming coffee into a cup. "Want some?"

"No."

"Then go back to sleep."

I covered my head with the sleeping bag. I peeked
through the arc of my forearm and the wood floor.

Dad picked up the ax. He held it in his hand, feeling
the weight of it by dropping it into his other hand. He
looked into the fire, and then he dropped the ax on the floor
with a loud *thwack*. He stood and leaned back his head as
he swallowed the coffee. The door stood open. Outside, the
rain fell in thick clouds. Then he closed the door.

I lay in my sleeping bag, feeling my ribs pressing into
the hardwood floor. I fell asleep listening to the fire snap
the wood.

Adrian woke us up. She cried, "Where is everybody?"

"I'm right here," Jake said.

"Dad left," I said. "And Mom and Oliver left last night,
I think."

"Where did they go?" Adrian asked Jake. He looked at me.

"Why would I know?" I said.

I didn't know what to do, but finally we put on our
coats and we stood on the stairs to the lodge. We couldn't

tell what time it was because the clouds hung over the tree-tops and a steady rain fell into the meadow. Water dripped from the blueberry bushes and stalks of wild grass.

Jake said, "We're supposed to stay here."

"No, we're not," I said. "If nobody comes back, we'd better go after them. I'm sick of staying here."

"Now?" Jake said.

"No. We'll go later." Dad had left his backpack, but I didn't want to touch it. The few times I'd touched it when I was growing up, he'd say, "Stop," and then he'd lift the backpack up and begin to take everything out and then put it back into the backpack. "You didn't take anything out of here, did you?" Dad would ask. Then he would look through everything again. "A backpack is a man's key to survival. Without it, a man hasn't got a chance of making it in the wild. Everything that I keep in this backpack may one day save my life."

In the backpack I shared with Jake, we had packed sixteen Disney comic books and several changes of clothes. I had packed an old pillow because I hated sleeping on my bunched-up jacket. We didn't have any food or can openers or emergency candles.

"I'm not touching Dad's backpack," I told Jake. "Are you?"

"But he has food," Jake said.

"I'll tell. I don't want him to think I went into his back-pack."

"I'm hungry," Adrian said.

"Mom and Dad can't leave us here," I said. "If they are just going to take us out here and leave us, we should just go. Let's go."

"Where?" Jake kneeled down to roll up his sleeping bag. "Where are we going to go?"

"We're going to catch up with Mom and Oliver. Then they can open Dad's backpack and take the food out. They can't get in trouble with Dad."

"We can't do that," Jake said.

"We're *going* to do that. They can't just leave us here."

After we had put on our jackets, we stepped into the rain. Everything was gray and I didn't know what time it was. Heavy streams fell from the eaves of the chalet into gravelly spots where the rain had worn right down into the dirt.

"Come on," I said.

"Maybe we'll see a Sasquatch," Adrian said.

"Why did you say that?" Jake asked. "Can we go back inside and just wait until someone comes back?"

"No way." I imagined Mom and Oliver and Dad coming back to the empty lodge. The fire would lay black and cold in the hearth. They would wish they had just stayed at the chalet with us. Already the rain had started to soak through our coats. I stepped around the puddles in the trail. Jake followed me. He held Adrian's hand. Behind us, the lodge leaned into the clouds of rain. The masses of water floated down around the wooden building, covering everything. The trees rose up into the rain. Through the windows, I could see the fire Dad had built. The windows glowed orange.

"How far away are they?" Jake asked.

"Just up ahead, I think," I said.

We walked for a long time. Under the trees along the trail, the rain didn't seem so bad. Water splattered out of boughs, but our wet jackets didn't feel cold. Water soaked through my boots. Mud caked my ankles.

I tried to keep from stepping into the streams of water, but it was hard to know when a branch would fill up and then tip its water down on me. Muck filled my socks, and I reached back and pushed Jake. I held Adrian's hand and she slowly stopped talking to me.

After a long time of walking through the mist and the rain, Adrian hissed, "Stop. Can't you hear him?" We stood in the middle of the trail. In the rain, the middle of the trail became an active stream. In places, rapids actually ran down the trail and we walked in the shallow water along the side of the trail. If we tried to walk in the bushes, it began to hurt, because even though our jeans were already wet, the bushes had so much water that they turned our jeans silver and the fresh water felt really cold on our thighs. So we walked in the less brushy middle area between the edge of the trail and the deep, running stream in the middle of the trail. Adrian pulled herself over the bank on the side of the trail and ran into the forest. "He's over there. He's not the Sasquatch; it's the man in the red plaid shirt."

"Stop!" I yelled after Adrian. "Do you know where you're going?" But I was afraid she had seen someone in the trees and I didn't want her finding some hunter or mountain man or even ghost out in the forest when Mom and Dad and Oliver were supposed to find us and feed us. Jake ran behind me. It surprised me sometimes how quickly Adrian could run. She was small enough that she could roll under the fallen logs. Jake and I had to stop and climb onto the bark, grabbing onto shelf fungus and old branches. When we stood up on the log, we were out of the bushes into the plush forest floor moss and I could see Adrian a hundred yards ahead of us or so. There wasn't anything beyond her. Finally, she stopped and leaned down on her knees, sending out clouds of white breath vapor. By the time Jake and I caught up with her, my skin was crawling from the water my jacket and jeans had caught running through the blueberry bushes. Water dripped freely inside my shirt. I felt my muscles begin to contract and then I got a really bad cramp in my leg. My foot went all tingly and I grunted and walked around in a slow circle and muttered to Adrian, "Look at how we are now. We are not supposed to be wet."

"What did you see?" Jake asked her.

"I don't care what she saw, because we're soaked now." I leaned back and let the rain coming down into the clearing wash over my body. Sometimes, when I was really wet in the rain, the best thing to do was just to let it wash over me and not to fight it, but to just allow myself to be wet and try to keep moving.

"How are we going to get back now?" I said.

"Your compass," Jake said. "We just came from that way, anyway." He pointed off in a direction that did not seem right to me. I looked around the clearing, trying to see the trail, but all I could see were other clearings like this one, and other trees, and then the gradual wall of mist and rain and dripping water and hanging moss. For my last birthday, I had received a compass on a black plastic wrist-band. Sometimes it stuck, and, standing there, under the spruce in the middle of the Hoh Rainforest, a thin film of moisture had slipped inside. I tapped on the surface of it and then roughly adjusted it for latitude. Dad had set the plastic yellow marker, but I wasn't sure if it had slid during the run through the forest. I pointed in a direction and said, "That's north."

"Which way is the cabin?" Jake leaned down to look at the mossy logs and bushes. "Maybe we can track our way back?"

"We came down and the cabin is up," Adrian said.

———

I looked up *hypothermia* later, able to dig something up in a book about survival, the kind of book that had diagrams of potable herbs and shrubs and bark recipes. There just isn't very much information about hypothermia, even though it is the primary killer of hikers who lose their way in the forest. Clothing is very important for survival and of all of the clothes a lost hiker should not be caught lost in, cotton pretty much tops the list. Cotton takes up water like a blotter, and all of the books inform the outdoor survivalist not to wear cotton when he is expecting to get damp. Anyone can expect to get damp, but no one expects to get lost. Denim may be great for around camp, but it will accelerate heat loss if the hiker is caught overnight in a drizzle. The law of conduction: heat moves from a warm body to a colder one. Jake, Adrian, and I were bodies floating through the drizzling fog of cold air.

The stages of hypothermia are as follows:

1. *A person feels cold and has to exercise to warm up.* Within an hour of leaving the Enchanted Valley Chalet, I felt cold because my clothes were soaked. I was packed in a cold object and my warm body was transferring its warmness to the cold and the cold was transferring its coldness to my warm. I hiked down the trail, keeping warm, but gradually I began to get tired.

2. *He starts to shiver and feels numb.* At first the water dripping down my legs felt uncomfortable and cold, and then I no longer felt the dripping water.

3. *Shivering becomes more intense and uncontrollable.* Chattering teeth feel funny. The place where my jaw joined my skull felt slightly swollen, then the entire length of my jaw felt a little hollow and the entire jawbone clicked up and down, forcing my lower teeth up. If I closed my upper jaw, my teeth made a slight motion. Sometimes, sitting bored in school, I would position my leg so that it would shake by itself. I would sit at my desk with my leg shaking and wonder what part of me was making my leg shake. I wasn't so calculating as my teeth began to chatter and I kept my jaws apart that I couldn't hear the noise, the noise that to me indicated how cold I had become.

4. *Shivering becomes violent. There is difficulty in speaking. Thinking becomes sluggish and the mind starts to wander.* The forest, which had seemed vast enough that it could hide Mom and Oliver and Dad and any animal that could fit in between the gigantic conical trunks, gradually began to become smaller and warmer. The rain became steam. I thought for a second that I could hear Mom and Oliver. My skin crawled and then blushed.

5. *Shivering decreases and muscles start to stiffen.* I thought that we had finally found the trail and started following along it, then went back to try to convince Jake and Adrian that they had to keep going, that it was dangerous to keep stopping to stare at the trees, that we had to keep going or we would get hypothermia. Jake had a drooping eyelid and smiled at me. "Hippopotamus."

6. *The victim becomes irrational, loses contact with the environment, and drifts into stupor.* The rain no longer seemed like something dangerous. It felt like slowly dripping warmth from a molten sky. "Back the way we came," I said.

I just started walking, maybe in the direction I had pointed. Under the trees, I couldn't remember where we had come from. The day had been dark in the middle of the meadow, but here it was almost like night. Even though we were under the trees, thick drops fell from the branches and clouds of mist settled on our already soaked jackets.

After walking for a long time, shivering and feeling my hands grow heavy and numb, I felt the forest grow warmer. The ferns, which had seemed damp, leaned down and brushed my face with their thick arms and spread cool water on my hot face.

Jake stopped. "I need a rest," he said.

"No, we need to find the trail," I said.

"Let's sit for a second," Jake said.

"Sleep," Adrian said. She climbed onto the moss under a squat cedar tree. Its moss-covered bark dripped water, but the moss felt as soft as my grandmother's overstuffed bed. Adrian lay down, and Jake sat next to her. He leaned against the tree. The gray light filtering through the canopy fell around us.

"Let's take a break," Jake said.

"How long?" I said.

"Five minutes."

"Okay." I lay down next to Adrian. The moss felt soft around me, and warm. I rolled back into it. The ice-cold water didn't fall out of the sky here. It was so dry. Under the leafy ferns, I saw moths. They flew from the shadows of the plants and fluttered around us and over us. Millions of white moths, like bits of paper, shifted through the air. They coated the undersides of the leaves. I watched them as I began to fall asleep. Clouds of mist fell down through the boughs of hanging fir trees. Jake's face lay near mine. I smelled the thick loamy smell of earthworms. Above me, the thin clusters of evergreen needles rose into the mist. I felt comfortable. Little white moths flashed under the hanging boughs of needles like the white nubs of marijuana cigarettes. The white shapes of them, small angular wedges, settled on my face.

7. *Victim does not respond to the spoken word. Falls into unconsciousness. Most reflexes cease to function and heartbeat becomes erratic.* Adrian sat up and stroked my hair. She smiled lazily at me. "We shouldn't sleep here. We should sleep in bed."

"We can get up," I said. "We can get up later."

"Promise?"

"I promise," I said.

I heard a mumbling then that gradually increased until I sat up. Around us stood a circle of hairy men. They wore long shaggy cloaks of hanging moss. Their eyes didn't have any whites, but were all black and glittered in the bluish light shining down through the boughs. They shuffled around us and spoke a soft song. They all stepped forward, toward us. Then they stepped back and faded into the trees. Adrian folded her hands under her head and lay in the moss. I watched a black millipede, a million legs marching a slick worm body over her hood, and I wanted to reach out and brush it away, but I couldn't move. If I thought hard enough, maybe it would fall off her, but it kept marching.

8. *Heart and lung control centers of the brain stop functioning. The accident is complete.* I fell into a sleep as deep as a cold well of water and mud listening to the Sasquatch song.

I woke in a white room. It was empty, and other beds lined the side of the room, like a hallway. A window looked out over a parking lot. A streetlight shone down on an empty parking lot and moths danced up into the light like rain going backwards.

I pushed myself up by my hands, then I levered my feet under me and stood shakily on both legs. I took a step, and my muscles constricted. Then I took another, and felt a little better. Blood rushed to my head. I opened the door to find myself in a hallway, also empty. A few chairs sat next to the door. A woman in a nurse's costume sat at a desk and, beyond her, I could see a door that looked out into the night.

I moved down the wall, keeping my hand on it for support. A nurse looked up from the desk. "Hi," she said. She shuffled out from behind the desk and sat me on one of the chairs. "How are you?" she asked.

"Fine," I said.

She smiled and felt my face with the flat of her palm. "You feel fine," she said. She kissed me on my forehead. "Come on, get back in bed and let me call your folks."

Mom, Dad, and Oliver came to pick me up. Dad and Oliver stood outside the room. Mom came in and looked around the room before she sat down. She smelled like soap and cigarettes and wore a thick sweater that I didn't recognize. She finally looked at me and leaned down and brushed the hair away from my eyes. "We came to get you," she said.

Jake and Adrian and I had fallen asleep in the forest, but Adrian didn't wake up. When they found us asleep like victims of the fairies, the rescue team raced us to the hospital in Port Angeles. Jake woke up on the way there, but I didn't. They filled me full of electrolytes. They kept me sleeping until I woke up in the hospital. But Adrian was as cold as the trees, as the ferns, as the damp earth where I had led her.

Cheap Haircuts

Four

Master Sergeant McGrath stepped into the bunk room. I woke from a slumbering dream under damp Sitka spruce boughs to find myself under my wool barracks blanket. My two roommates still slept as McGrath walked across the linoleum tiles and leaned over my desk, smoothing the surface with one of his gloved hands. My number two pencil rolled along its hexagonal axis over the white pressboard surface, pocked and gouged from the hundreds of pharmacy tech students who had studied here before me. It ticked on the buffed floor and rolled against his thick rubber sole. Master Sergeant McGrath wore flight boots caked with an enamel gloss so thick the leather always seemed freshly spit-shined. In the three weeks that I had been at Fort Sam Houston, a dried palm of mess hall lettuce had browned and hardened onto his back heel. He brushed back the drapes and looked out at the first light coming through the stand of magnolia and palm trees that grew in between the cinder block barracks. The rangers ran laps around the parade field. They sang "Tiny Bubbles." Under their hoarse voices, someone marked the cadence with a guttural bark, *left left left.*

Under his breath, Sergeant McGrath sang with the Rangers. His discordant voice echoed faintly against the painted cement block walls. I carefully pulled the covers over my head the way I had as a kid protecting myself from the Sasquatch. I hadn't learned much in the eight weeks of basic training, but I had learned always to avoid singing sergeants. I curled into a ball under the dog hair blanket. The wire frame of the military bunk squealed and Sergeant McGrath let the drapes slip back. He coughed. "You bald-headed chicken fuckers awake yet?"

My two roommates and I jumped out of our bunks and stood at attention. With my hands pressed tightly into the elastic band of my khaki underwear, I stood steady and relieved to have my sleeplessness taken up by a familiar routine. "You three have been volunteered to buff the barracks today and tomorrow. Just because y'all are in class, don't think I can't get you out doing some PT before breakfast." He opened the door and, as he walked down the hallway, he called out behind him, "Report to me after class. At-ease." When he slammed the door to the breeze-way, my shoulders slumped.

Grumbling and moaning, my two roommates climbed back into their bunks and pulled their blankets over their heads. In a minute, they dozed off. I tried to sleep the last hour before muster, but my thoughts kept shifting back to the one place I didn't want to think about, to the copper hurricane lanterns that hung over the tables in the Red Diner where my father had worked in downtown Seattle, to the creaking structure of Seattle's Public Market that smelled of water-sprayed tomatoes, zucchinis, and artichokes and the open-air salmon market, to Snoqualmie. I'd become used to these long gaps of thought because, in the Army, I spent most of the time waiting in lines, just standing in tight formations staring at the hat band of the soldier in front of me, until a sergeant rushed me through the tasks; each step standardized so that even things as different as first aid (patching up holes in someone) and marksmanship (putting holes in someone) followed the same customary procedures.

Lying in bed between the first calls of the Rangers and First Formation, I thought of my Uncle Oliver; he was closer here in the Army. Although he killed himself in 1980, he remained in a soldier's familiar turn of phrase, or the way a drill sergeant laced his boots. I saw Oliver's frown as he examined my bedroom cleaned by my nine-year-old standards in the command sergeant major's scowl as he inspected the barracks. Drill sergeants mimicked

Oliver as they barked out marching songs. The constant pressure of the sergeants reminded me of Oliver's fetish for polished boots. The only really pleasant memory I had from basic training occurred when my training unit lay on the Brigade parade ground with our pairs of boots. We polished them again and again until we saw the reflection of the sky and clouds in the curve of our toes and heels.

Before I enlisted, when my hair still hung into my eyes, I had watched the Army's TV ads, noting soldiers' body language, the common movements of a group snapping together a communications device.

I had felt like a spy among my classmates in middle and high school; I'd perfected the Generra-sweatshirt-over-501's style that would allow me to sit at the back of class among the other students without being noticed, but every morning, I woke in the house where my father smoked marijuana in his sparsely furnished bedroom. I showered and put on my jacket that I kept outside so that it wouldn't gather the thick odor of old dope smoke. I'd learned to be aware of this odor in sixth grade, when one of the stoners pinned me against the plywood play-shelter wall. His thin mustache shook as he accused me of being a pothead.

"You're so fucking gone you don't talk to nobody. We can all smell it on you. If you don't bring us a gram we're going to crack your skull open." The next day, I didn't go to school, and when I did go back, I wore a freshly washed jacket.

From then on, I carefully kept my clothes smelling like wood smoke, like anything but the rich tar of burnt hemp.

I drifted through school in the back of the class, carefully turning in my homework and reading books while the other kids talked. After coming home one day to find my father sitting in the same chair that he'd been sitting in that morning when I left for school, I called back the Army recruiter who'd been calling the house. I hadn't eaten anything besides rice and margarine for three days.

The recruiter came out to the house in a gold Nissan, crushed on the left side. He drove me to the Mar-T Cafe in North Bend, where he fed me and three other high school boys and told us about the military. He had grown up in Puyallup, an old farming town in the Green River valley. He had the face of Barbie's Ken, a bowl of blond locks and smooth orange skin. He had once been a powerlifter for the Army, but hadn't lifted weights for a long time, and his muscles had slowly turned back into fat. He still wore his old clothes, and the buttons on his white dress shirt pulled tight to the grommet under the indentation of his belly button. "Army life is perfect," he said. "You meet the finest people on earth, and you're paid to go into the woods and camp and shoot rifles. You even get to throw grenades. Afterward, you travel on Uncle Sam's ticket. You could end up living in Berlin or Paris or Athens. Picture yourself," he said to me. He leaned over and pinched my arm. "You wake up early, because you're excited to finally be out of basic training and you've just been stationed in Greece. You shower in the completely clean barracks, put on your civilian clothes and go down to the market and there you are," he leaned back, "in Greece."

Before the Army cut our hair, the trainees stood around the gravel lots outside the Fort Bliss Retention Center and the voices spoke about hot rods they had lowered, about how they just needed a good hit, the bud they grew back in Louisiana, and man how you could come through the swamp and there would be a massive stalk of ganja taller than the tree your father'd planted for you when you were born. I needed a fucking ax to chop that fucker down. Where the hell you from? Oklahoma. Michigan. Seattle. Jamaica fucking New York City. We'd been scooped out of the suburbs and the neighborhoods and the forests; we had been shipped from distant cities; and now we stood in line at basic training waiting for one of the few moments that I remembered having seen in the movies: the moment when the recruit's hair is cut. By cutting our hair and by removing our clothes they seemed to have erased our pasts.

We waited in a line, listening to the cackle of the electric shears sing down the hallway. Each of us held four dollars in our left hands. Sergeants walked down the rank to make sure we held the money properly, face up, each George

Washington staring down the row of loose camouflage pants. They made sure we were all the same. When the buzz of shears paused, we stepped forward. Bald barbers in smocks mowed through our scalps and seized our money. Everyone had to pay. Bald recruits had to pay. Boys with locks they had been growing since their childhood had to have their heads sheared clean. The hair looped from our fleeced scalps onto the white and green linoleum until a hundred misshapen wigs carpeted the floor. The barbers grabbed the money with one hand, buzzed with the other, and wiped the stubble from our heads with our crinkled dollar bills. They heaped the cash onto a stack and barked, "Next!"

The drill sergeant detailed me to sweep up before I could have my turn. I swept up clumps of whiskers, knots of short black curls, bunches of clear blond strands, bushels of brown tufts, unwashed and reeking fibrous cuttings, and hair scented with Drakkar or Ben Gay. I pushed all that old hair into a garbage bag. When I pressed my fingers into the stringy mass, it compressed and a clear oil oozed onto the top strands, pasting them into a shell. The smell that rose from the bag was like the odor inside a discarded hat.

We stood stiffly in the formation outside, rubbing our clean heads. The bristles hissed under our palms. Everyone's head looked the same, a wispy sparkle of follicles on bald skulls. We joked, "Hey, I like your outfit; where can I get one?" We learned how to talk to each other. We talked about the barbers, saying, He's fucked. I can't believe this. Shut the hell up. Each incident piled onto the next and we referred to them immediately like common history. We didn't talk about the life we had before or the life we would have afterward. Our lives consisted of the last five minutes, and I was no longer a spy slipping out from the marijuana haze of my father's house.

I spent nine weeks learning how to be in the Army, how to be like everyone else. Everyone else spent time learning how to be like me. The uniformity of the Army costume and the fact that we had spent the last nine weeks isolated in the world of basic training gave us a common background. We were a superficial brotherhood united by a single haircut.

I had insisted on going into a field that had the strictest test admission requirements. I ended up as a pharmacy tech training in Texas, by way of an elaborate system of requested job classifications and kickback schemes that ran like the comic book ads for *Grit Magazine*; sign up five soldiers and get a nine-inch portable Sony TV. So I said "journalism" and my recruiter swept his nicotine-stained hand over his greasy, golden locks and saw that TV downgraded to a Texas Instruments solar calculator and hard-sold the pharmacy tech job. "You'll get to train at Fort Sam Houston."

"In Texas? The state?"

"They have a twelve-women to one-man ratio."

"I don't want to deal with drugs."

"You'll be a pharmacist. You get a white lab coat. You measure things on scales. People respect that."

After basic training, on the bus from the airplane, the driver said, "Look at those lights, welcome to Heaven on Earth," and then she gathered a growl from the bottom of her stomach. "This is party town!" The soldiers on the bus leaned their shaved heads back and howled.

The bus sped under the parade field floodlights and circled to a stop in a parking lot beside a cluster of cinder block barracks. Women swept hair away from their sunglasses, snuffed their cigarettes against the bunker walls, and threw the butts into gravel-filled coffee tins. They whistled as the sergeants ushered us down the narrow bus steps. I stood with my bags in the long row of soldiers; each of us held his duffel filled with identical Army issue. My legs felt soft from the long flight and bus ride. A group of men in blue jeans and T-shirts paced back and forth on the sidewalk behind the sergeants. They laughed and spit trails of brown chewing tobacco onto the pavement.

"Listen up. Welcome to Fort Sam." I stood immobile in the ranks. The anonymity of the uniform kept my face hidden in the column of other uniforms. The civilian clothes and uniforms, the men and women mixed together, and their loud voices forced my hands to unfold and fan over my thighs. I was eighteen, and I didn't know how to party all the time. I thought any party would be like the weeklong binges my father and uncle had held in Snoqualmie, a frenzy of drinking and smoking that often stripped the cupboards bare.

A sergeant paced in front of us. He yelled, "Hey y'all. Welcome to Fort Sam. Name's Cadre Sergeant McGrath. We're going to get you bedding, billets, some sleep. So stand fast."

We recognized his trickery in the words *stand fast*. The words didn't fit the list of familiar commands. If we moved, we would find our hands pressed into the warm asphalt, the pebbles and tar imprinted in jagged relief on the balls of our palms as we counted out fifty push-ups.

He turned away from us as if he had finished with us, and one of the soldiers in jeans yelled at him, "Give them the command, Arnie." He wore a loose red shirt with the sleeves rolled tight to his forearms. A gold bracelet glittered just over his wrist. He crossed his arms and slid his long fingers in the front pockets of his jeans and said something to a blond soldier with a notch in his nose.

"Watch yourself, Chavez," Sergeant McGrath said. He turned back to us.

"I said stand fast." We didn't move.

"A command," Chavez said. "They're just out of basic. They don't have any brains left." He checked his bracelet like a watch, turned, slapped the notch-nosed soldier on the shoulder, and they walked into the breezeway between the barracks.

"At-ease," McGrath barked. We relaxed. The words fit the limited range of commands we had learned: *At-Tention, Parade-Rest, At-Ease.* Someone looped his left foot out of the line and someone else sat. We knew the rules. Everyone did what he was told. Soon enough we would be like the soldiers in blue jeans around us. Soon we would be the way we had been before the barbers sheared the excess growth of our hair, before I had clumped the hair into a knotted black plastic sack. I could feel people wanting to throw away their similar Army-tailored selves and be themselves. I would no longer be like any of them.

Five

In October, the Fort Sam Houston heat drained the green out of the leaves of the magnolia trees until they hung as dry and pale as potato chips. Stray brown paper bags, yellowed paper cups, and shreds of khaki T-shirts blew against the physical training field's fence where they eventually bleached under the sun. McGrath yelled cadence over the whistle of crickets, through the clouds of red dust kicked up by our shuffling feet. Sweat plastered his gray PT uniform to his stomach, water rolled from under his slightly too long hair, and drops quivered in his squiggly gray beard hairs. I waited for him to break us. I needed him to move us out of the sun so we could cool off before someone passed out. And if it wasn't too soon, that someone would probably be me. Granules of red sand, split seedpods, strands of thorny weeds coated my neck. I wanted to puke. I wanted to turn my stomach lining inside out.

Everything around me blasted white and, *whoops*, I thought, *a heat stroke*, but I'm too fit to have heat stroke. My hand reached out for empty air and dug through the layer of loose grit on the training field ground. My twelve weeks training in the middle of summer in the middle of the Fort Bliss desert felt wasted.

"Down! All of you down!" McGrath hollered as he poured canteen water over his head.

I'd already hit the ground. I felt the warm hardness on my back, and I lifted my legs slightly from the dirt and readjusted myself. If I had a stroke, then at least I'd get a rest.

Everyone else dropped onto the field of fried grass root-balls and fuzzy cactus knots. McGrath called, "Assume leg-up position!" We answered, "Assume leg-up position!" I squinted into the sky watching the distant fighter jets scratch contrails into the blue above San Antonio. Our leg-ups kicked up even more dust. I yelled my cadence even though tiny bits of sand coated my throat. I barely heard my voice. I let myself sweat. I didn't wipe it away. I marked time until my muscles burned and then I shifted to find fresher muscles. Around me, the trainees from northern bases and the trainees returned from civilian life started to cough and began not to move, not because they were protesting but because they couldn't. I watched Sandy Comstock, a little too heavy in the waist. She was a tall blonde who was older than the rest of us and had just returned to active duty and training from a civilian office job in Houston. At first, sweat had slicked her T-shirt to her back. But now, salt stains ringed the gray fabric flapping on her dry back. I wanted her to pass out, soon, because as soon as someone broke down, we would all have to sit in the shade while the MPs and medics came to haul her fried, spent body to the clinic. McGrath would never be allowed on a PT field again.

McGrath had passed beyond the purely functional role of making sure we got our exercise. He didn't care if we were in shape. McGrath wanted to know something about us. He wanted to know who would pass out or burn out with heat stroke before we complained. He wanted to know who would complain. In basic, the drill sergeants caught my platoon the first time, and when someone said, "That's it, I need to go sit down," they let him sit down, and the rest of us were worked over until we lay twitching and coughing on the field. The second time, no one broke rank unless they fell out from heat exhaustion. McGrath tested the makeup of our unit. Whoever spoke up would suffer the consequences of breaking rank, but then everyone else could cool off in the shade. I wasn't exactly considering this position as I rolled around in the dusty field. I didn't want anyone to notice me. I waited, instead, for someone to have a frothing, dry-tongued sunstroke. Oliver would've taken the role of weakling. He'd have taken a fake, full, spastic sunstroke, jigging out in glory, using it really to object to the principles of the test and also to get the free ride to a clean bed and a ward full of nurses.

"Fall-in. Attention!" We jumped to our feet. "At-ease. Down!" We dropped. "Not quick enough. Back up. Fall-in. Attention!" The up and down routine, aside from the pain after we'd done push-ups until we couldn't move our arms, and leg-ups until we couldn't move our legs, quickly sorted the unit like sifted gravel. The slow-moving soldiers gradually stood while everyone else fell.

"Stay together. If you're standing while everyone else is sitting, you have fallen out. If you are sitting while everyone else is standing, you are wrong. If another soldier falls out, we are all going to be out here until dawn. We'll have ourselves an all-nighter. I can get a deuce and a half to light this mother up."

"Sergeant?" I found myself saying before I thought about it. Nine weeks of Fort Bliss, of marching across sand, of running through sand with four hours sleep, of sleeping in sand dunes, and I found myself speaking without thinking. I was saying something I shouldn't be saying to a cadre sergeant.

"Private, did I indicate that anyone could speak?"

"No, Sergeant."

"So keep your mouth shut."

"Yes, Sergeant," and I just about did keep my mouth shut, and then these words were coming out: "Several of the soldiers are about to fall out from sunstroke."

"The point, Private?" McGrath smiled at me and shook his head. "Because I'm glad one of you spoke up, I really am."

"It would be a real problem for them if they fell out and had to report to the clinic with sunstroke and heat exhaustion after PT, when Army regulations specifically forbid them from standing in direct sunlight for more than fifteen minutes, Sergeant. The Base Commander would be very offended at their flaunting of his orders, Sergeant."

I waited for my punishment. The soldiers around me made slight noises indicating I'd blown it, they were going to get it, they would get me if they survived whatever I'd brought down on them, and as soon as they recovered they were going to beat my skin blue with soap until my arms looked like rotten bananas. McGrath dumped the dregs of his canteen over his chest. "Okay, shit-breaths, time for a five-minute break. Get in the shade and dump some canteen water out, before y'all look like crispy fried chicken thighs."

"But Private Bohm, why don't you just take two laps around this track for your lip? You've got five minutes."

Five minutes was a ten-minute mile, a shuffling jog, but I'd already drained my muscles. When I started to jog, each shuffling step forward required a conscious lifting of my feet, lifting of my thighs, tipping forward, and setting everything back down. I moved a gigantic, melting, clay doll of myself around the track. I didn't mind too much, though, because running had become an escape from basic training.

I knew what would happen while I ran. I had some control over what I thought about while I ran. I no longer thought about Seattle. Adrian dissolved into a faint musty memory of a toy box, and the cold mud on the Quinault trail became alien in the context of the dusty parade ground at Fort Sam.

I threw myself down on the grass under the line of hardened trees. I sprinkled water on my hot, dry skin. I lay back and closed my eyes. Chavez leaned forward and brushed me on the shoulder. "Good job, Bohm," he said.

"I want y'all to meet in the mess hall for dinner before y'all can sign out for the evening," McGrath said to the unit.

We had somehow gone from being tormented by him, to him allowing us off-base.

"You'll be back in bed by eleven hundred. The rules are simple as long as we speak-a the same language. You suck my cock and don't try to stick your dick in my brown eye. Tonight, I let you go out until nine. Next weekend, y'all go out Saturday. Week three, if everyone has behaved themselves, which as far as I can tell means you haven't got caught, because we all know none of you is civilized, we'll pretend you're all, like, A-dult soldiers and you can come and go as you please."

"Sergeant McGrath?" Specialist Chavez asked. "I need to say something." Chavez jumped up from a group of soldiers sitting in the shade. He'd been talking to Sandy Comstock.

She knew Chavez from community college in Dallas. Just
about all of the other trainees had just graduated from
high school the previous summer, completed basic at more
or less the same time, and were going through training for
the Army Reserves. Comstock and Chavez, both special-
ists, made a big show of going out to the NCO club. The
first weekend, Comstock had crept off base to visit her
parents in Dallas and brought back her car, a dark blue
Ford Escort with a hot pink stripe down the driver's side.
Chavez, as a reenlisted soldier, was a few months, a year
tops, from going to NCO training and becoming a sergeant. He was experienced enough to know how far to
push the boundaries with McGrath. As old hands at military life, Comstock and Chavez had already endured the
punitive trainee induction rules and didn't want to go
through them again.

Chavez slowly picked the long strands of sun-bleached
grass from his legs until everyone watched him. "Sergeant,
I was thinking for the convenience of people who might
have plans at around six o'clock, you know, soldiers who
might want to miss dinner at the mess hall, that it might
be better if we hang the check-out list from your door or
something."

"Do I look like I am made of rubber, Specialist?"

"Excuse me, Sergeant?"

"Do I look like I am made of rubber?"

"No, Sergeant."

"Well I am fucking made of black, Indian rubber, Specialist, because it sure as hell looks like whatever you say bounces off me and sticks to you. You don't even know when your off-base privileges begin. An off-base pass is an optional benefit of your belonging to the United States Army. You can't just come and go as you please; this isn't some goddamn youth hostel. You are a soldier. A soldier is not a thinking, feeling human being. A soldier is a machine. The USA is not going to let its hard-earned machines—that's all your asses—off-base until it knows each and every one will come back. So I want you sorry lame-ass party-going smack-injecting freaks to sign out before y'all go out and do whatever it is y'all do."

"That's bullshit, Sergeant. You should just let us sign out. Otherwise the people who don't want to hang out around here will just leave without getting passes."

"What Army were you brought up in?"

"Sergeant, I'm just being realistic."

Sergeant McGrath dumped the rest of the bottle of water over his skull, and then put his soft cap back on. "On account of your Bolivian Army lip, Chavez, I want you to run the two-mile PT test and I want you to do it until you remember that this is the US Army. Bohm, you make sure he keeps good time."

I stood up and wanted to sit right back down again. My legs shook. "Sergeant?"

"Private Viscount, does that phonebook-sized, Dick Tracy watch you've been lugging around tell the temperature?" Viscount ran to the front of the formation and squinted at the rest of us under his large, rounded prescription goggles. He usually hid his eyes behind faintly tinted aviator glasses, but during PT he left his glasses in his locker. He was the only soldier who still wore his dog tags, the key to his locker, and the plastic dog tag liner that ostensibly kept the tags from tangling in his chest hair.

"Yes, Sergeant. It's ninety-three degrees and we're at four hundred feet elevation."

"That seems like a reasonable temperature and reasonable elevation for you to break some PT records, don't you think, Chavez?"

"Sure does, Sergeant."

"Sergeant?" I asked. My legs twitched and my feet ached.

"Bohm? Speak up. You don't mind throwing out your shit breath when it suits you. Get your ass on the track. Eight times is two miles. I'll be under the shade drinking your water, unless of course you don't drink the same kind of water as the rest of us."

We began to run. At first I felt a little relief in the movement of air, but then we ran back into a thick dust rose we'd kicked up on the first run around the track. We came around the edge of the track into the cooler air, away from the heat trapped against the trees and the blistered paint of the old hangar. Sweat poured over my eyebrows and trickled into my eyes. I blinked until I could see Chavez's shadow in front of me. I kept my front stride just in his shadow. I didn't say anything. Instead, as I let my thoughts mechanically take over, I half dreamed about floating in the raft in my father's trout pond, the greenish slips of trout rising to the surface to nudge circling maple leaves and then descending back toward the murky bottom as the leaves twirled around in the cool water. I coughed as the San Antonio dust wrung my throat dry. I was still behind Chavez.

My face began to burn. My T-shirt slicked to my stomach. The fabric didn't hold any water, so the hot, dry air quickly dried even that. My skin felt as bristly as a towel that had stiffened dry in the sun. Everyone else lay sprawled and panting in the shade.

Chavez said to me, "You don't need to keep running." He was just a step ahead of me. "What're you trying to prove?" Chavez started in on me on the last lap. "Do you think you can make it now? You were about to pass out two laps ago. You sure don't look any better now."

I fell behind Chavez and followed him around the last lap. I heard him grunt with each step. "You're a fucking shit, Bohm." I felt connected to him, because as I pushed myself forward, I pushed him. Through all of these weeks of training, no one had noticed me. Everyone was busy keeping his head down and just trying to make it through the training. The heavy cloud of dust kicked up by the runners hung over the field. He came in about a quarter of a lap in front of me. When I came in, finally, everyone was standing in formation and smiling at Chavez as he rolled around in the dust in front of them. "At-ease," he hollered. Chavez lifted his hand, and when I was slow to offer my hand back, he socked me in the shoulder. "Man, you made me run too hard. After an hour and a half in the sun. Do you ever stop?"

I stood limply in the last row. My muscles shook and I felt my stomach knot and my legs charley-horse.

"Sign out at six o'clock sharp. You're all going to have to hang around for dinner, because the Nurse General has a few words to say about birth control and sexual practices that you will all want to know so that you can keep your dickhead intact as long as I have. But if you don't come and try some of the delicious mess-hall cake I reserved for our event, and you are caught off-base without a pass, we will do whatever we can do, including sending you back to basic training."

"Can you do that for us?" Viscount asked.

"Don't get your hopes up, Private."

After everyone signed out for the evening, everyone gathered in the breezeway. And then everyone left with the few trainees who had returned from nearby hometowns with their cars. The cars filled the parking lot with headlights.

Men, the air thick with musk, gathered in packs on the tarmac. Women in short sundresses, their hair unraveled from their daytime buns, found rides. Chavez stood in the breezeway smoking a cigarette. He wore a red satin shirt and his gold bracelet. He smiled at me and said, "Bohm, come here."

He shook my hand, a firm shake, and then turned me around to point out a crowd of girls, Sandy Comstock and PFC Wahl and some other female soldiers. Sandy and PFC Wahl looked at me and smiled.

"There's going to be a party tonight," Chavez said.

"What about the curfew?" I asked.

PFC Wahl wore a yellow sundress with large blue poppies on it. She reached down to adjust her sandals. Janet had pale, waxy skin that appeared almost translucent on the surface of her arms or side of her neck. A matrix of veins lay under the clear skin around her eyes.

"What do you think?" Chavez asked.

"Of what?"

"Of Wahl?"

"What about her?"

"I can see you eyeing her. Dude, I bet she can feel your eyes on her like they were two mosquitoes. You don't know how to check out a woman all surreptitious. This isn't the place or time for that Neanderthal shit. Go ahead and look, but remember, no one should see you looking."

PFC Wahl turned her back, shifting her weight back on her heel.

"See, that's how you do it. So that's your taste. You like them fat asses. You like meat on their bones."

"I don't know how I like them."

"So come on to this party and find some simple shit out for yourself. So how do you like Janet?"

"I don't know."

"Yeah, I know what you mean. I haven't even decided myself yet. But I'll let you know as soon as I come to some sort of conclusion. So what about it, Bohm?"

"We aren't allowed off-base yet."

"Man, this isn't basic. They don't control me. I'm inviting your ass to my party. The polite thing is to say yes."

"Yes. Thank you. But I don't know."

"There's going to be beer."

"I've got something to do."

"Like what? Look dude, I'm inviting you to a party. There's going to be beer. There's going to be females. Beer and females, means drunk bitches. What in the hell do you have to do that could compete with that?"

"Where is it going to be at?"

"We haven't found a place yet."

"It's late already."

He leaned forward and whispered. "There's going to be dope, fine Californian bud."

"Forget it," I said. "Thanks for the offer, but I've already got plans. Maybe another time."

"Dude, what's your hell?"

I raised my hand and started to walk away. "I'll see you later." I walked across the dusty PT field. It was dark. The stars shone, just visible now, in the deep part of the sky. A turquoise blue edged the horizon. The streetlights had kicked on over the residential streets of the officer's quarters, big houses set back from the road with gigantic green lawns and their sprinklers going rat-chat-chat. Chavez and his friend Taylor chased me down. Taylor had a long nose with a large triangular bump right below his eyebrows. Otherwise he looked like an impeccable blond Boy Scout.

"Where in the fuck," Chavez asked, "are you going?"

"I don't want to go to a party. Maybe some other time."

"I just want to make it clear to you that if McGrath finds out about this party, everyone's going to know who told him."

"I'm not going to tell McGrath about your party. I've got plans," I said and they turned around and I heard someone say something and they laughed.

I crossed the dark parade field where we had physical training, climbed up onto the bleachers, lay down and looked up into the hazy evening sky. A warm breeze carried the smell of the scorched grass. I no longer saw myself as a soldier. Without my uniform on, I was the person I had been before I came here. My blood was a deep, moldy dope green. Everyone loaded into the cars, and soon everyone was gone and I sat alone on the bleachers, staring over the dusty field toward the dark greenness of the officer's houses under the heavy, old shade trees.

After our first night at the military base for basic, during in-processing, a full week before the training had actually started, the sergeants ushered us out of the barracks and onto the field, where we raggedly marched in our civilian clothes into a long building. The first odor that trickled around us as we stepped into the polished hallways was the overpowering reek of mothballs. At the door, a specialist handed us gigantic burlap bags. We filtered into the building and took off our clothes and were given green underwear and green socks and camouflage uniforms and black boots and green hats. The barbers processed us, and we stepped, still smelling of formaldehyde and rubber, out onto the dusty field on the other side of the barracks.

We all smelled the same, a heavy odor of mothballs that didn't entirely go away until the end of basic training, after the color had faded from the Fort Bliss sun. I had believed that this harsh odor was something only found in my grandmother's armoire. The long week we stayed at my grandparent's house right after Adrian died, I had hidden in the closet among the white folds of taffeta and the Battenburg lace sleeves, so that I wouldn't have to go downstairs and face Oliver, my parents, and Jake. After an hour of lying on the floor of the closet, my lungs had begun to ache from the mothballs.

The formaldehyde-stiffened uniform was called a Battle Dress Uniform, shortened to BDU. All we did while we wore them was march and pick up trash, stand in ordered formations, and take a beating from the drill sergeant. We didn't do much battling. BDUs didn't burn. When we first received our uniforms, wild stray threads spilled from the careless seams, from the pockets, from under the buttonholes. I held a Bic lighter to the threads and the thread curled back to the fabric, but the surface couldn't burn. I held the lighter to my arm and I felt the hair on my forearm hiss and singe. As we stood in a long line burning the stray threads from our BDUs, the drill sergeant told us how the fabric would survive a flame thrower. "Your ass will be a shit pile of black ashes and some sorry shit'll scrape your ass off the BDUs, so your replacement will have something to cover his ass."

I couldn't escape from Snoqualmie. A few days before, I even thought I saw Oliver in a uniform swaggering out of the Academy of Health Sciences. He wore a soft cap and boots so polished they sparkled in the early morning light. He stood under a palm tree and smoked, and when I started to walk toward him, I saw the Sergeant First Class tarnished stripes on his hat. The man was old enough to be my uncle, scrawny and his uniform wrinkled as though he had just put it on. "Can I help you, son?" the man said in a flat, nonregional military accent— -the mix of Southern rhythm and phrases worn down by Northern flat vowels and vocal speed. "I thought you might know my uncle," I said.

"Is he stationed here? What's his name and rank?"

"Sergeant Oliver Bohm," I said. "I'm not sure where he is." My uncle remained in my head. I can barely remember when I didn't know about him, when he was just another one of the things my father talked about. I wondered, if he had stayed in the military, if he'd still be around filling his boots in some dead-end post.

"Don't know anyone by that name and rank," the sergeant said. "No one."

Six

Monday, in front of the formation, McGrath unwrapped a menthol throat lozenge. He held it up and looked through the transparent blue candy and then sucked it into his mouth. "How did y'all like your weekend? From what I hear, it was a wild weekend. What do you say, Private Viscount? Wild weekend?"

"I did alright, Sergeant."

"As well as you, Specialist Chavez? If Private Viscount did alright, you must have done outstanding."

"Stayed in, Sergeant. I'm in school."

"Private Viscount, I'm glad to hear you did alright. Somebody did alright. So, just to find out how alright y'all did, I've decided y'all should have a random pee-pee test. Sounds like a great way to open the week. Doesn't it, Private Viscount?"

"What are you testing for, Sergeant?"

"Do you have any suggestions?"

"Geez. I don't know."

"I'd like to come out here with a spinal tap and drive a tube right into your tailbone like I'm drawing syrup from a sugar maple. Like I was a mosquito. Do you think that would be a good idea, PFC Wahl?"

"If it's your idea, Sergeant, then it's a good idea, Sergeant."

He stopped in front of her and looked at her for a long while. He sucked on his throat lozenge, his neck muscles rolled, and then he smiled at her. "Good."

"Does the idea that your brain fluid is as bad as the San Antonio sewer system seem far-fetched to you, PFC Wahl?"

She shifted back onto her boots and raised the tips of her toes from the pavement.

"Are you going to answer me? Do you think I won't order you with even a hint of suspicion into a medical clinic to get your spine drained? Because if I find something that shouldn't be there dripping out of your medulla oblongata, I'll juice your skull, coat a sheet of butcher paper, and sell your blotter acid ass to the damn drug-fiend Navy corpsmen so fast you'll think you sneezed."

McGrath crushed his lozenge in his teeth. He chuckled. "Good Lord JC, I crack myself up sometimes. Specialist Chavez, march them into the CQ and line this sorry crew up. You know the drill."

"Yes, Sergeant."

As we marched in, McGrath took his hat off and strolled behind us down the hallway. A female cadre sergeant waited for us. She was a short, thin woman with an almost completely round head. Her scalp hair had been cut so short it looked like a patch of cheesecloth. The back of her neck looked as wrinkled as a vacuum hose attachment. She ran the tips of her fingers over the back of her neck, along the ribbed skin, pausing to place her pointer finger into the folds. "How do, Sergeant?"

"Cup detail," he said. "Could be worse, Sergeant Willis."

Sergeant Willis laughed a short, truncated hack. "Come on, girls."

"I'm a private first class," Sandy said.

"And a girl, or we'd just line all of you all against the wall and you'd all donate at once. No skin off my nose if that is how you want to do it, girlie? But girls get special treatment. Girls get privacy."

"Sergeant, may I suggest that they do it that way?" Chavez asked.

"Specialist, are you attempting to address me?" Sergeant Willis said. "I'm going to milk this crew and get to lunch on time. I'm expecting you to maintain a schedule and follow proper procedure. Sergeant McGrath, where did you find this sorry excuse for a soldier?"

"They just turn up, Sergeant. I don't have to look for them."

"When is the last time you shaved, Specialist?"

"Sergeant Willis," McGrath said, "I can always take a little time out of my schedule to observe you drill your soldiers if you think that would be helpful to me. Once a soldier has more than fifteen years of experience, he usually needs a much younger and wiser professional to remind him how things work in the Army. I'm sure I can pick up a few tips on how to run a tight ship. A few things I might not have seen before in those apparently wasted fifteen years of experience. You best leave their hygiene to me."

"You're welcome, anytime, Sergeant. Anytime." She cracked her neck and rotated her chin in a figure eight and went into the bathroom.

McGrath set his hat on his desk and sat down and poured himself a cup from his thermos. He looked up at Chavez. "Get everyone in order, Specialist. And see that you shave before you put on a uniform."

Chavez walked up and down the line. He held his hand behind his back and barked. "Females to the right of the hall. Males to the left."

He smartly marched us into the barracks and lined us up—two males and two females—from one end of the barracks to the other. As he issued the frosted plastic cups with yellow caps, he smiled and said, "A random cup for you, and a random cup for you and a random . . ."

"A random cup—my ass—for you, Private Bohm." He slapped the cup into my chest. "Now, why would McGrath choose today? Next weekend when the curfew gets lifted would make more sense. Unless, Bohm?"

"I didn't tell him anything if that's what you are getting at."

"Why would you think I was getting at that—unless, well—unless you ratted?"

He turned and went into the bathroom.

"Did you say something to McGrath?" someone asked me. But then Sergeant Willis walked down the hallway and everyone fell in. We waited as each pair went into the bathroom. In basic training, we would have been heel to toe in parade rest, our backs arched, everyone silent and listening to the drill sergeant slowly walk up and down the line. Now, soldiers squawked their rubber-soled boots on the freshly buffed floor, leaving black smudges. Soldiers talked in loud whispers. Females set dates for the upcoming weekend with the guys who had cars. The line listed in a haphazard column down the hallway, through the common waiting room, past the banging dryers in the laundry room.

After we had our cups, McGrath strolled down the line. "Which one of you weasels is dirty? What kind of smack have you been feeding your veins since you arrived in party town? Putting your needle skills to good use?"

"No, Sergeant," we said.

"You may think you're back on the block where you can get away with living your degenerate lifestyle, but the military's a class outfit and we don't want any needle freaks, homosexuals, transsexuals, bisexuals, asexuals, or what-have-you here. When we test you, I'll know. There's always a couple of you who think you can get away with fooling old Master Sergeant McGrath. You'll hold out. You'll sit there quivering with a bladder full of rancid piss and try to slip that old greasy charm on your friendly Sergeant. But the US Army did not train me to allow freaks or degenerates into its unbroken green ranks. Nobody gets past me without the full check. I can wait. I've got all day. I am not a heroin addict. I don't need to pay a visit to the Man, because I am the Man. So drink up. Guzzle that water."

We slowly marched down the line. Specialist Chavez supervised the male bathroom operations. He leaned against the stalls as we lined up at the urinals. "Get pissing," he said and laughed.

Nothing would come out of me. I shook my penis, but nothing would come out. I forced my stomach down. I socked my bladder. I gave myself a kidney punch. Everything trickled to a stop as Chavez coughed. "Can I have a little privacy?" I asked.

"He's the asshole responsible for this mess."

"Asshole."

"I'm not and I can't go."

"Let me fill it for you," Chavez said. "It's the least I can do."

"No."

"Why no?"

"It's my test."

"Oh, you want to pass on your own merits? Or is it that you don't trust that mine is clean?"

"It's my test."

"Answer my question, Bohm."

"You're an asshole, Bohm," someone said.

"I didn't say anything."

"Go ahead. Fill the cup."

Chavez raised his chin and looked at himself in the mirror, then glanced at the two other privates who had just buttoned their flies and stood in front of the stalls with full urine cups raised. He barked out from the bottom of his stomach, "You're not resting in here, are you Bohm? You're not going to piss me off on my watch. Go out and tell Master Sergeant McGrath what you're trying to get away with."

"Sure."

"Come on, Private Bohm. You can say 'Yes, Specialist.'"

"Yes, Specialist Chavez."

"Go on, discuss this with McGrath."

McGrath stood up at his desk when I came out of the bathroom without a full cup.

"What's giving you trouble, son?" He closed the door. "Is there something you want to tell me? No one except me can hear you and I understand the difficulty of telling someone else. Come on. Come clean. It'll be in your best interest. It's hard and I understand that, admitting that you have a problem, but look here, son, if you can't pass this cup test, then you have a problem. A problem like that is bigger than you or me. You need some help. We can do this as two clear-headed reasonable people. You admit your problem. I get you the help you need. Or we can do this like two muddle-headed military fools and you continue trying to fool yourself and make trouble for everybody. So what's it going to be?"

"I just can't go to the bathroom."

"Bohm, what kind of narcotic tar have you got clogging your dick?"

"I don't have anything to hide," I said. "I just can't go with Chavez watching."

"There aren't any fags in the military, son," McGrath said. "Are you one of those fairies trying to infiltrate the male bootie of this god-fearing army?"

"No."

"Fucking shit. Say, 'No, Sergeant.' Where did you come from?"

"Fort Bliss, Sergeant."

"Didn't they punish you enough there?"

"They did, Sergeant."

"Then go out and drink some water and fill that cup, Private."

"Yes, Sergeant." I opened the door.

The line of my classmates stood still against the wall now, quietly readjusting their weight onto the balls of their feet, slipping into parade rest, preparing to slip into front-leaning rest position. They all looked the same, camouflaged arms folded behind their backs. "Keep that door open, Private," McGrath yelled after me as I walked down the now orderly hallway. "If any of you bald-headed chicken-fuckers—excuse me ladies, in your case I should say bald-headed chicken-fucked—don't cough, vomit, shit, or piss up some urine, I'll send you to the MPs right now, so help me JC. I don't have all day. Sergeant Willis doesn't have all day. Get ready to go and then go."

I drank water. I filled the paper cup with ice-cold water and sloshed it into my mouth. I drank until the wax coating the cup started to flake into the water and the cup turned into a ball of pulp between my fingers. My stomach began to feel as heavy and cold as the watermelons Oliver used to float in the trout pond behind the house. By the time I finished drinking, almost all of the other students had filtered down the hallway.

Chavez returned from the lab. They had to pack and certify the package at the desk where McGrath sat. He watched Chavez wipe the cups clean with a rag they kept in an aluminum basin of diluted bleach, and then set them into their individual cardboard packing cells. "What took you so long, Chavez? Did you have to pull out some of your druggie friends' urine?" McGrath stood up and told those of us remaining to wait, and then he went outside to smoke. He shook his head at the three of us who remained. I waited in the hallway with performance anxiety, looking at the green and black tiles and the poor painting job. The soldiers shuffled out, leaving only PFC Wahl, Viscount, and me. Wahl held herself against the wall, tapping her foot. I paced back and forth, waiting for the water I had sloshing in my stomach system to gurgle out.

"I can go now, Sergeant," Viscount said. He hurried into the bathroom and Chavez walked slowly after him. PFC Wahl pulled a tattered *Newsweek* off one of the waiting tables and rolled her eyes at McGrath. "I've been drinking water, but you know how it is when you try to go—if I had known about the test I would have drunk some coffee or something." Her almost-black hair had loosened from her French braids. Strands of crooked hair fell over her pale neck. She half smiled at me and turned back to the magazine. She chewed on her lip and lightly tapped her boot.

Watching her fidget and twitch made me want to go to the bathroom, but when McGrath asked me, I was concentrating on PFC Wahl's single hand fanned along the wilted back of the magazine, her short nails slightly ragged along their edges, holding a faint sparkle of worn gloss.

"Are you two going to piss, or are we going to have to draw up an Article 9?" Sergeant McGrath said.

Now I really had to go, but it was like I couldn't on general principle.

"PFC Wahl?"

"I've tried and tried, Sergeant McGrath, but I just can't go." She made a forlorn face and then wrinkled her forehead. "Nothing ties it up as much as when you have to go. If we were driving across country and there weren't any women's rooms for as far as I could see, then I'd have to go." She read my name stitched over my left pocket. "Bohm, what's your first name?"

"Aldous. Excuse me," I said. "Sergeant, I have to go."

Chavez followed me into the bathroom. "Man, he's caught you now. They really test this. You'll get an article and then they'll send you to some treatment program and you'll never like getting high again."

"I haven't done anything."

"I can help you."

"It's nice of you to offer your own urine, but I've got some of my own that I need to spare."

"My own? That's classic," Chavez smiled. "I would like to be able to help you, but if you want to be that way, suit yourself."

As I filled the cup, Chavez pulled a box out of the bathroom garbage bucket, and then started to dump the urine from the cups into the urinal next to me. He smiled at me. "You had your chance. You'd best wait until I've emptied all of these."

I gave the cup to the Master Sergeant. He looked at me. "What took you so long? Hoping you could digest some of the China White you've been smoking since you arrived at Fort Sam?"

"No, Sergeant."

"We'll find out. You pill-popping pharmacy techs, bunch of fucking druggies."

Janet still paced pack and forth. McGrath looked up at her after he filled in my information in the checklist. "You can go, soldier. You wouldn't be dirty, would you? A fine upstanding young woman? A private first class after only four months of service. Why did we even call you in?"

"I'm sorry I couldn't go, Sergeant," she said. As she walked outside, she swayed her hips. Once we stood on the other side of the courtyard, she said to me, "I have really got to pee. Why didn't you hold out?"

"I had to go."

"They'll catch you. They're really going to test it. You'll get busted."

"I'm not dirty."

"Sure."

"I'm clean. Alpine scent clean."

"Why did you wait so long?"

"I can't go with people staring at my thing."

She laughed. She ran her hand along the back of her neck and then turned to look back at where they were loading the cups into a cardboard box. They carried the crate of urine cups out to a truck. Janet was a little taller than me, and with her wide hips and long legs she seemed sort of puffy because she kept things in the cargo pockets of her BDUs. I could see a paperback in one hip pocket. Most of the female soldiers ironed their pockets so they didn't stick out at all. She walked into the women's section of the barracks. The door with the sign, "No Male Entry" swung closed.

I woke early to sneak off-base and catch the bus to town. I wanted to escape all of the strangers I suddenly found myself living among. The buildings on the base were stucco; palm trees grew in the lush lawn. Beyond the gates, dead brittle tufts of white grass bristled in every yard. The yellow veneer of paint blistered to sun-bleached wood. Stucco houses crumbled to the underlying brick. Everywhere, hand-painted signs advertised *Barbacoa.* I thought it was some sort of refreshing alcoholic drink. Only later did I learn that *Barbacoa* was Spanish for "barbecue." In downtown San Antonio, I stood across the street from the Alamo. A sign above the Alamo read, "The Center for Texan Culture." I thought it was the place where regulations were set for ten-gallon hat height, chili viscosity, and rattlesnake boot design.

I played video games in an arcade full of soldiers like me, thin runner's legs, too-short hair, baggy gray sweatpants, and white T-shirts. Under the electronic hiss of rubber tires peeling out, I heard two girls picking through the soldiers. They stood in the space behind the video machine. "Too skinny," one voice said. "Much too skinny."

"Too ugly," the other voice said.

I looked behind the machine and my turbo-powered race car tipped against a cement divider and exploded. One of the girls looked at me. Her hair hung in floes past her eyes and jutted in black shiny arcs down her back. She stared at me, and she looked at her friend, a short girl who laughed.

I scooped the quarters off the machine and rubbed them between my fingers. The hard metal clicked and grated. I squinted in the heat on the street and pushed myself through a pack of men in gray suits. Each man wore a sticker on his pocket with his name written in a thick marker pen. I followed the men down the steps into the Riverwalk and the heat near the river rushed around my body like smoke.

I turned and went back to the arcade. I saw the girl with black hair standing outside. She wore shorts and her brown legs were skinny and her knees stuck out like balled socks, but she had breasts that tugged upward on her shirt. She looked down the street to where I stood and started to walk quickly away.

I followed her around a turn and down a flight of steps. She stopped and glanced behind her again. Then she kept walking beside the river. She walked ahead of me. When she stopped and leaned against the wall, I stopped and looked down into the slowly moving green water. The river fell over a waterfall and trickled down a canal into a large grate. We came to a place where children swam and dove. The children carried plastic forks, and when they came up dripping from the water, they shook the corpses of sucker-fish at the ends of the prongs. Seagulls circled through the air and landed on the cement walk, squawking and gobbling the fish the children flung them. The girl stopped and sat on a bench. She nodded to one of the boys swimming in the water. He smiled at her.

I walked past them. "Hi," she said.

"Oh, hi," I said.

I stopped and stood looking into the water at the children swimming around. I felt her hand press flat onto my back and I turned around quickly. She pulled her hand back as though she had just slipped it into a hole full of slugs. "What do you need?" she asked.

I didn't really know what I needed and the frankness of the question upset me. Had things just progressed, her allowing me to follow her, her speaking to me, I probably would have followed the chain of events. I had followed her from the arcade on the off-chance that she might talk to me. Now that she had, I found my mouth stiff.

A boy with a fork pulled himself out of the river. Water streamed down his chest and dripped onto the bricks. He wiped the water from his face by rubbing the palm of his hand over his hair. His hair slicked back like a 1930s gangster's. He held the fork in the other hand, pointed down as though he could stab somebody with it. "What do you want?" he asked me. His voice was high and squeaked a little.

"Nothing," I said and I started to walk away.

"Hey come back, Señor Freak-o."

I walked through the neighborhood near the Riverwalk. I sat on a long stairway rising into a house; wooden Victorian eaves rose into the hot sun. Palm trees swayed in the steamy breeze. I sat there trying to think about anything but the girl I had followed down to the Riverwalk. I had wanted to talk to her, but the possibilities of what could happen once I began to speak frightened me. What I needed was to talk and for someone to listen.

I saw myself, then, as she must have seen me, my shaved, thuggish military head, the loose white T-shirt, my oddly emaciated basic training body. Any words that came out of me would seem foreign and a strange attempt at coming on to her. And then what would I do?

On the way back to the bus, I passed a yard where a boy sat at a card table with a pitcher of water and a pair of scissors. He had written a sign, "Cheap Haircuts, 5 dollars." I smiled at him, but he stared into the middle of the street.

After this incident, I started to find that the female soldiers' uniforms, which had seemed to hold no promise of curves or hints of shape under them, had now become revealing. I stood in morning formation looking down the line at the female soldiers. I tapped my foot to keep my head in line.

In basic training, a female unit had lived in the barracks across the highway. As the platoon lined up for morning drill, we faced away from them. The drill sergeants prowled back and forth, punishing soldiers who glanced behind them by ordering the offender to drop and knock out fifty push-ups. I had thought it odd that anyone looked at the women. What did they see under the loose camouflage blouse, the baggy unflattering pants? The women in utility uniforms had looked the same as men to me, a single ugly unisex antisex.

I found my eyes following the arc of white necks to the roll of French-braided hair, down the drape of the uniform over a female soldier's shoulder blades, down to the buttons on the wrinkled camouflage fabric on a female back pocket. I wasn't thinking about what I thought I should be thinking about. I sometimes felt guilty when I realized I hadn't thought about Snoqualmie or Adrian's death for hours. I suppose to actually feel an obligation to think about her was a sure sign I wasn't thinking about her. I felt bad about feeling as if I had to remember her. This is not to say there wasn't a base of perpetual anxiety that *someone would find out*. Somehow, someone might recall what I had done. This had never happened, even as a child, except in the weeks after her death when we all only thought about what I had done. San Antonio and the dusty parking lot where we mustered under the swaying palm trees. It seemed to me now that I actually stood in formation in the Army and that the silt odor of the Snoqualmie River would remain safely pushed back in my memory. It almost seemed that way, and then a rainy day washed over Fort Sam and the puddles on the sidewalk reminded me of the last of the summer rainstorm dripping from the eaves of my grandparents' house in Port Angeles where we stayed after Jake and I'd come out of the hospital.

The Guide to Moths

Seven

The rain collected in the buckle halfway down my grandmother's walk. The ground had sunk, lowering the square cement flagstones into a shallow V-shaped depression. The day the summer storm had hit the coast, my grandfather had planned to cut the grass. The push mower still sat under the corrugated fiberglass carport, propped up against the side of the house. He hadn't cut the lawn, then it had rained and now the grass had grown fresh, light green shoots in the steady rain following the storm. My grandfather kept his front lawn in a civilized and well-groomed carpet, free of moss and dandelions. He always cut the lawn edges sharp. The flowerbeds held small river stones. A ring of mushrooms grew close to the front fence. Loose, windblown sheets of the daily paper no one had remembered to pick up lay caught on the base of the fence posts. When the deputy sheriff came, he parked his white

Ford pickup truck across the street from the front gate and stomped his thick-soled boots through the collected water in the walkway and up onto the porch. He knocked soundly on the front door screen, then he knocked on the side of the house itself, sending the rap of his heavy knuckles through the house timbers. I watched him turn his head slightly away from the front window where I sat holding an empty soda can.

Mom, Dad, and Oliver sat in the room. They had hardly spoken all morning. Mom drank coffee and paged through a *Reader's Digest*. Dad and Oliver stared at the floor. They were dressed in dark suits they must have bought while I was in the hospital. I stood up and was about to ask if I should let the deputy in, then decided not even to ask. I just let him into the slate-tiled front hall. He smelled like sweet cherry cough drops. He had unwashed, overgrown hair that hung over his collar. His shaggy mustache was in need of trimming. "Afternoon," he said to me. "Your folks in?"

I nodded and let him come into the hallway. His smell filled the hallway and, behind him, raindrops flecked the slate tiles. I hadn't been directly outside since we'd been in the forest. My skin felt warm and soft from the bed and the bath and the long day sitting on the couch. The cold wind coming in made me think about how warm my skin had been under the trees where I had fallen asleep. A clammy heat filled my arms and legs. I felt dry now except for this gust of outside air and cigarette smoke that came in with the deputy. Dad cleared his throat and stood up and said, "What can we do for you?" Dad didn't like policemen and that manifested itself, in this case, by his refusal to meet the deputy in the eye, by Dad quickly walking across the room and moving behind him and introducing everyone in the room. "This is Aldous and Jake and this is Oliver and this is Gayle Bohm, my wife." Dad offered the deputy a cup of coffee. Oliver and Mom sat on the couch together, and during the introduction it occurred to them that maybe they should be on opposite sides of the room from each other.

"I do need a cup of coffee," he said. "Much appreciated." He sat down in the place where I'd been sitting and he looked out the front window. Only the deputy sheriff didn't even look at his good view over the front lawn, the slope down the hill toward the Strait of Juan de Fuca. He held a file and he took out a notepad from his breast pocket and a ballpoint pen. "It is pretty amazing the kinds of things that can happen to a person if they don't have sense," he said. "If I had the authority, I'd make it a crime to leave the house if you didn't have any sense."

Dad remained standing in the entry. He leaned up against the wall. Oliver stood next to him and Mom came back with the deputy's coffee, two sugar cubes and a water glass with a finger of cream in it. The cream looked yellow in the glass. "I forgot to ask how you like your coffee."

"This is fine, thank you," the deputy said. He set the glass of cream down. He dropped the two sugar cubes into the coffee and took a sip. He grabbed the glass of cream and drank it right down, then put it back again on the side of the table.

"I just wanted to let you know," the deputy said, "what the official report of your daughter's death says. The record doesn't indicate that a crime occurred." He read from his file. "On July 14th, 1976, Adrian Bohm, age 5, Jake Bohm, age 7, and Aldous Bohm, age 9, were separated from their parents and uncle. Due to extreme weather conditions, the three children lost consciousness. They were admitted to the Port Angeles Medical Center July 16th with hypothermia. Adrian Bohm died due to a heart attack due to her condition on July 16th at 10:32 PM. Jake Bohm and Aldous Bohm were released from medical care on July 17th. The autopsy report confirmed that Adrian Bohm, age 5, died from hypothermia."

When he finished, he took a couple of sips of his coffee and then said, "I'm sorry about Adrian Bohm's death. Do you have anything to add to this?"

"Such as?" Dad asked.

He shook his head. "I wish I could quantify for you how senseless your daughter's death was. It must hurt a tremendous amount knowing that she doesn't have to be dead. There must be a great deal of pain in knowing that if you'd spent even one minute considering the danger, she would still be breathing and playing today. I know it'd be real hard to live with myself knowing I was guilty as if I'd killed her with my own two hands. If you don't have anything to add, I'll be going." The deputy sheriff picked up his notebook and set down his mug. "I am obliged for the coffee."

On his way out, I told him, "I shouldn't have led them outside. I know about the rain. My mom told me."

The deputy sheriff was putting on his hat. One hand tucked his hair up under the band. "You're just a little kid. What do you know about keeping dry? It's not your fault." He turned around and walked back toward his truck.

Dad came back from the funeral home with Adrian's body in a box. They had burned her and that was what we had left, her ashes in a box. Grandma asked if she could see it. She wore a black blouse and skirt and dark brown shoes. "Where are you going to put her?"

Mom didn't say anything, but took the box and handed it back to Dad. "Can you put this in the trunk?"

"Are you leaving now?"

"Yeah, Mom." Mom leaned in and kissed Grandma on the cheek. She hugged Jake and me.

As we started to leave, Grandma asked, "Are you coming back tonight?"

"We've imposed on you enough," Mom said.

"Gayle, I don't think you're ready to go. After what you have put yourself through. Don't you think you should spend some more time thinking about it? The minister is real interested in talking to you."

Mom turned around on the walkway and climbed into the car. "I didn't know you were going to go so soon," Grandma said to me.

"I didn't mean to do it. I didn't mean to kill her," I said.

"No one wanted to see her dead, Aldous. Things happen that are beyond anyone's control." My grandmother held me against her. She smelled like baby powder and a faint hint of something alcoholic, antiseptic, and sweet. I could feel the small bones moving in her shoulder where she held me and stroked my back.

Oliver sat against the window in the back with us. On the ride home, I stared out the window at the dark tracts of forest growing right up to the road. I had left Adrian behind in the mole holes, in the wormy black earth at the bottom of a mud puddle. I had left her behind in the dark green space of the fern core, the swampy roots of cedar trees, and she still floated there, stuck away from us in the damp darkness behind the rain. My parents and Oliver passed a small joint back and forth that grew smaller and smaller and smaller. They started to laugh by the time we reached Tacoma. The laughter wasn't so much *ha ha* laughter as an internal explosion of breath in the base of their throats, something caught in their chests that couldn't get out. We stopped to eat at a place near the Tacoma Narrows Bridge. As I waited for my hamburger to come with a small bag of potato chips on the side, they started to talk about what they were going to do next weekend. When we finally arrived at home, Mom went to her room and shut the door, leaving Dad and Oliver in the living room. They stopped talking and just sat and stared outside.

That night Mom said it would be the best thing if Oliver moved, considering everything that had happened. "I should move too," I said. "I should just live somewhere else. Maybe I should go with Oliver."

"Look. I'm the one who was slighted here," Dad said. "We are all at fault here. No one needs to move out because of what happened."

"Slighted?" Mom said. "We both have a dead daughter."

"Gayle is right; I should go," Oliver said. I wanted to jump then into the middle of the kitchen and throw the coffeepot on the floor and scream at them all and tell them that I had done it. I had killed her. It was me and I should go to jail with all of the other murderers even though I didn't think that would happen. But they were all sad and silent and I couldn't make myself jump, so I slipped out of my chair and went to bed and only later did Mom come into the room to tap me on my shoulder and tell me to brush my teeth.

Jake wouldn't talk to me until much later, when it was very dark in the rest of the house and no one was talking in Dad and Mom's room and even Oliver upstairs in the attic didn't make a sound. Jake asked me, "Why did you take us outside when we were in the mountains?"

"I was mad," I whispered to him. "Mom and Oliver and Dad had left us all alone without any food. You didn't have a better idea, did you?"

"I didn't want to go outside."

"What would you have done?"

"I would not have gone outside into the rain."

"We go outside when it is raining all of the time."

"We're not supposed to."

"Do you think I did it on purpose?"

"You were mad," Jake said. "I'm not saying it's your fault."

"What are you saying, then?" I jumped out of bed and crouched on the bottom bunk near his face. He barely moved in the bed, pulling the sheets a little over his head. "What are you saying, Jake?"

"You went outside, into the rain, on purpose, is all I'm saying."

I grabbed him and he fought back. We wrestled and I found that he was sweating in bed and hot and slick and we struggled, gasping because we didn't want to wake Mom or Dad and get in trouble. Jake's breath smelled. He got his hands past my hands and his fingers were on my face and his thumbs pressed into my eyeballs. "Are you trying to kill me now?" Jake hissed and his breath smelled like cheese.

"I didn't," I said. "I didn't mean it. You should take it back."

"Adrian is gone," Jake said. He relaxed his hands.

"I didn't do it."

"Who did?"

"I didn't mean it," I said and crawled back in bed and turned away from Jake and lay there listening to him climb into the bottom bunk. I could hear him crying in the dark. The light came over the lip of the hill, burning down through the branches and fog and through the windowpane coated with mold and lined with the fuzzy packets of moth cocoons. I slapped my feet on the cool linoleum and got the coffee going, opening the tray and finding it empty because we had just returned from Port Angeles. I took out a new filter. My fingertips rubbed the cotton lintel making the top of my gums go electric. I filled the pot from the tap, listening to the glass carafe ring as the water whisked up. I poured the water into the machine and turned it on. It burbled as I put on my socks and rubber boots and grabbed the plastic pitcher to pour more water for the chickens.

Behind the house, I could hear tree frogs murmuring in the shadows. It was hardly light. At the base of the steps behind the house, I broke a branch off a bush and ran up the slope waving the branch to catch the spiderwebs. Stray leaves fluttered behind me. I walked across the pasture, getting the cuffs of my jeans soaked. I opened the chicken coop door, startling the rooster, who rolled off his perch and strutted one way, then the next, while I gathered the dropped eggs. I said "Hello, Francine," even though Francine was long dead now. The chickens drowsily clucked. I pulled one corner of the feed bag because it was placed high up on a shelf, and it dropped down into my arms, almost knocking me over. I grabbed a handful of grain, cool and dusty in the bag, and scattered it over the chickens. They jumped up and began to dance around, looking for the fresh food. It was as though the grain was some sort of magic powder that revived them. On my tiptoes I put the feed bag back onto its shelf, and then hurried away with the plastic pitcher full of cooling eggs.

By the time I slid back down the steps to the front door of the house, the sun came down against the side of the coop and the rooster began to crow. Back in the house, I was half awake and thinking ahead of myself, going through the familiar rituals of waking up. I woke Jake and this was the first time I wasn't able to wake Adrian. Jake grabbed my hand when I leaned down to shake him awake, and he rolled out of bed and leaned into Adrian's bunk to wake her up. Her bed was made. The sheets were tight from the way Oliver had folded the sheets in hospital corners. Jake's hand scrabbled over the sheets and then he leaned back to look at me to see if I had noticed what he did. I pretended not to see.

We listened to Oliver pack his things in the attic. We could hear him stamping around. Finally, he climbed down the ladder and around the house with everything in his duffel on his back.

"Do you need a ride?" Dad asked.

"I'll walk," Oliver said. "Here, this is for you," he said. He handed me an old birthday card envelope. It had Oliver's name written in spidery handwriting across the front. "For Dear Oliver." He walked down the muddy driveway. He left the same as he had arrived.

Mom lay on the bed with her face in the mattress and didn't move. Dad sat at the table with both of his arms lying there as though they were something he was serving up.

I found a photograph of us at the Quinault trailhead inside the envelope. At first it seemed mostly just a flat thing that didn't really look like Adrian and Jake and Dad and Mom and me. The colors didn't look like the valley where we'd been. The green looked more brown than the thick lime coated with fresh rain. The black mud looked grayish in the photograph. And we all looked washed-out and pale and I could tell what we were thinking. Adrian was in midgesture pulling up her skirt, and she was looking out into the forest, which bothered me because I would have liked to see her looking at the camera and at me. I realized Oliver's shadow fell over the gravel right up to our shoes. The photograph really didn't capture any of our thoughts then. Looking at it, I wanted it to mean more than it did.

Dad asked me, "Would you like to dig some more on the dam with me?" I slid the photograph back into the envelope and put it into my room and hurried outside to help him.

I had an old shovel. We hefted the damp mud up and threw it onto the heap and, after a while, the ache in my gut was replaced by the burning cleanness of blistered palms and sore biceps.

Mom and Dad spent most evenings together. They hardly spoke, getting ready for dinner with a brief exchange of monosyllables. One evening, after silently eating macaroni and cheese at the kitchen table, all of us together briefly, Dad finished, leaving his half-eaten bowl of noodles on the table. Jake asked, "Why can't Oliver stay with us, like before?"

Dad scowled. "He sure was comfortable upstairs."

"What is that supposed to mean?"

"Gayle, I've known Oliver all my life. I knew what he was like."

"Jake," Mom said. "I don't think it would be a good idea for him to be here after Adrian has left us. Do you?"

"There's more room," Jake said. "He should be here. How's he going to help remember Adrian if he's in Seattle? Nobody is weeding the peas."

"You can always weed the peas," Dad said.

"Nothing is like it was."

Jake was obsessed with keeping the memory of Adrian alive. When he stayed with Grandma in Port Angeles, Jake found an old hat box in the attic. He brought it home and packed it with stuffed animals, Adrian's favorite dress, wrappers of her favorite candy bar, and photographs of her.

Each evening, before he went to bed, he opened the box and examined each of the objects. But already we were forgetting about her. The objects seemed strangely changed, swapped into a random bin of things at some stranger's yard sale.

"We don't need Oliver's help," Mom finally said. "We can remember her ourselves."

Jake always left half of the food in his bowl because the other half was for Adrian. He spent the first day we came home from Grandma's looking for Jim Fuzz. "See, Jim Fuzz has gone after her," Jake said. "He'll find her and bring her back."

"Jim Fuzz," Dad said, "is a stuffed animal. Let's be realistic about this. She's dead, Jake."

"I don't think Adrian's death is an opportunity for you to teach valuable life lessons," Mom said.

Jake said, "If you are so mad at Oliver, why did you see him in Seattle?"

"I'm going to take a class at the college," Mom said.

"You're seeing Oliver?" Dad asked. "This man you accuse of murder? This man you said should rot in hell for eternity, not that you believe in that kind of thing, eternal punishment or hell; but hypothetically, he should be damned for the rest of his life. This man who was my brother and with whom—"

"—I didn't accuse anyone of murder. And especially not Oliver."

"I am not the only one who left the kids behind in the woods," Dad said.

"Oliver is just as affected by this as we are."

"That wasn't his little girl."

"No," Mom said, "but he is a sensitive person."

"I'm sensitive. And she was my little girl. And you're my wife."

"That doesn't mean I'm your property." Mom grabbed her jacket and sat out on the front porch with the door open to smoke.

"If you're going to smoke one of those cancer sticks, would you close the door?"

"You smoke."

"I smoke an herb that I have grown myself. Plants. No company is stuffing extra toxins into my smoke."

Jake set his fork down in the middle of his plate. "If we can find Jim Fuzz, we can find her," he said. He slid out of his chair, tucked it under the table, went to his bunk, and pulled his quilt over his head. Dad left the table, leaving me to look at the macaroni harden in the bowls for a long time, waiting for someone to say something, but nobody did and finally I collected the dirty plates. I filled the sink with water as hot as I could make it and scrubbed them clean. I breathed in the steam and clenched my fists in the water until they turned red.

What scared me later, lying in bed, listening to the September wind rattle the cottonwood branches and the tiny sound of the record player in the distant living room, was that I could disappear like Adrian. My physical existence would be reduced to a half dresser of worn, brown corduroy pants. I woke late at night listening to the tick and hum of the propane heater. I eased out of my top bunk, carefully climbing over my brother's bunk, and crept into the living room. I slid open the desk drawer and found the thick black marker Mom used to write addresses on Christmas gift boxes. I wrote my name on the fanned edges of as many of my parent's books as I could. I took out six or seven at a time, and wrote my name in big block letters: ALDOUS. I sat on the floor hunched over the stack of buckled paperbacks and unraveling hardbound art books, writing as quickly as I could, ALDOUS, ALDOUS, ALDOUS.

Eight

Oliver slept in a bed that became the wall when he wasn't using it. Jake and I didn't know that the first time Mom took us to his place. When she took us, she parked the Dodge near a city baseball field and walked us along the sidewalk that smelled of the rotting lettuce and spilled beer in the alleys. Seagulls fought for crusts of moldy bread. When one got hold of a rind it took off and the flock screeched after it. We walked past the dark, warm door of a tavern. The drizzle-slicked asphalt reflected the bar's neon comet. Mom turned up a flight of stairs even though smut coated the porcelain tiles, and to me it didn't look like anyone could live in a building like that. We walked down a thin red carpet in a hallway coated with layers of thick, baby blue paint that smoothed the molding edges like caramel-coated apple. Mom inserted a key into the door at the end of the hall with a swift flick of her fingers. She jangled the key out from her chain, marked with a twist of faded red string. She led us into Oliver's apartment, a single room with bay windows overlooking a vacant lot, a busy street, and then the large, blank brick wall of the Egyptian Theater where we had gone to see *Fantasia*. The theater's brick wall sat straight but went from the alley to the roof in undulating waves. Beyond all of that, beyond even the wisp of smog on the smooth sheet of Elliott Bay and then the blue line of islands, over the front of clouds, the Olympic Mountains stuck up their peaks. The Hoh Rainforest lay beyond their completely white and sharp caps.

I looked around Oliver's apartment and I didn't see a bed. I had to ask him, "Where do you sleep?" I stood in the middle of the room looking to see if he slept in a sleeping bag or something like that. For some reason the idea of him sleeping in a sleeping bag in a room seemed right. It seemed like he would come back at any time; that this wasn't even his home but a place to camp out until he came back. There was no place for Mom to stay if she came here and left us with Dad in Snoqualmie.

Oliver took my hand and led me into the closet, wiggling through the curtain of his jean jacket and Army jacket, over a pile of glossy magazines spilling out as I tried to step past them. Women smiled from the covers with jawbreaker red lips. Thick incense odor filled the narrow space. One wall in the closet was all bed. "This is my bedroom," Oliver said. "Comfy, eh?"

The room had a single desk and two chairs and several large pillows and a potted jade tree and that was it. Books and plates and newspapers covered the desk. Jake sat on a pillow while Mom fixed tea in the kitchen. "Do you want a cup of tea?" Mom called out from the kitchen.

"I don't want a cup of tea," Jake said.

"I was asking Oliver," Mom said. "There's coffee."

"Do you think I want coffee?" Jake asked.

Oliver hugged Mom and she squirmed away from him and looked at me. "Do you want tea?" she asked me.

"No," I said and then Oliver grabbed me and began to hug me and then we went after Jake. "Give your long lost uncle a hug."

"Leave me alone," Jake said.

Mom came out of the kitchen. "Oliver had a lime," Mom said. "So I made you some limeade." She held a pitcher with a few wizened ice cubes bobbing around. The water looked reddish rather than yellow. Mom also had two tiny glasses made of thick glass with the word CUERVO printed on the side. She set the glasses on the floor and then filled them and set the pitcher down next to them. Oliver sat down cross-legged on the floor with this tea and he smiled at us. "It's nice of your Mom to bring you by, finally. I missed you both."

I took a sip of the limeade and it tasted sweet with a twist of rusty drainpipe, and despite the floating pulp of something that might be a lime, it didn't taste like limeade.

"Thanks, Mom," I said.

"If you like this, you can have mine," Jake said and he poured the rest of his glass back into the pitcher.

Mom and Oliver drank their tea. Strands of spiderwebs hung from the corners of the ceiling and I watched a daddy longlegs tumble along the edge of the ceiling and the wall.

"How's your Dad?" Oliver asked us.

"He's doing better," Mom said.

"How are you doing with how he's doing?"

"Same," she said.

"You want to see where I sleep?" Oliver asked Jake.

"No."

"I'll show you." He pulled one wall down and it transformed into a bed, legs coming out and the bed was made. The edges were neatly folded into each other. "Now for the grand tour of my home. Face west." Jake and I stood with Oliver and looked in the direction he waved his arm and then we turned as he turned. "Face north. Face east. Face south. Thank you for participating in the grand tour of the illustrious residence of Oliver Bohm, former sergeant in the United States Army."

"Let's go," Mom said. She stood up and shook out her legs from sitting on the floor. She stamped her sandals and the sound sounded hollow in the nearly empty room.

Oliver grabbed his jean jacket. Jake brushed the dust from his butt. "I'm going to need some pop to wash the taste of that stuff you gave us out of my mouth."

"Jake," Mom said. "You keep your brother company."

Jake looked at me.

"We'll be back," Mom said.

"But what are we supposed to do?" Jake asked.

"Wait," Mom said, "until we come back." The door closed. We listened to another door close down at the end of the hallway. We were alone.

We started with Oliver's wall bed. We pulled it down smoothly into the room, exposing the green wool Army surplus blankets and the tight balls of the blue striped pillowcases. Cigarette butts fell on the floor. Behind the bed, rows of paperbacks lay stacked in the shelves like cordwood. Their spines faced the wall. The paperbacks had yellow and blue and red painted leaves. A rusty aspirin tin lay on a shelf next to the books. ASPIRIN was punched into the tin with large spiky letters like the words on a saloon, and a woman blew a cloud with her cheeks puffed up. The air curled away from her pursed lips. White pills that looked like the top edge of a screw and pink, heart-shaped pills like Valentine's Day candy filled the tin. I wanted to eat the candy but then I would have to share with Jake so I put them back.

"What's that you have?" Jake asked me.

"Aspirin," I said.

"Let me see."

"It's just aspirin," I said. "Let's see what Oliver has in the kitchen."

Standing on the discolored tile floor, the black tiles scratched and worn and no longer black and the white tiles stained and scuffed and no longer white, I could put my palms flat on both sides of the room. A package of saltine crackers wrapped in a plastic bag and twisted off with a piece of wire sat on a narrow table with enough room for a single chair against one wall. The fridge took up almost another wall; and a sink and drain board with a window overlooking a rooftop and the same view down First Hill toward Puget Sound took up the other wall. Everything smelled faintly of bleach, and except for the two mugs sitting in the sink, one chipped and one cracked and both holding soapy water, the room didn't have any clutter or crumbs or anything. A stream of water fell from the pitted chrome faucet where it rolled into a black groove worn into the white basin and then pooled in the rusty drain. The fridge clicked open, dropping the door onto one broken, loose hinge. I held the door up while Jake examined the insides of the fridge. A faint green growth coated a tub of cottage cheese. An open bottle of Coca-Cola containing unidentifiable, transparent fluid sat on the top rack. A Crock-Pot with a glass lid contained bulky, fuzzy white growths. "Soup?" Jake asked.

"I'm eating his candy," he said. "They leave us here; his candy is mine."

I tried to jump after Jake, but the door to the fridge came loose and fell on the floor, gouging a hole in the not-white, not-black tile. As the door ripped the linoleum, it made a huge noise as the chrome and metal plating hit the floor. The chrome bar that held the drinks popped out and flew into the main room, jangling across the floor and under Oliver's Murphy bed.

Jake had the tin in one hand, the lid open, and his fingers were up to his lips as if he pinched them. "This doesn't taste like candy," he said. "Try one."

"We won't eat any more of them," I said. I took it and it tasted like a piece of sugary charcoal cut with glass cleaner.

"I'm not putting another one of those in my mouth," Jake said.

We put the door to the fridge back together and tried to fix the scuff, but found by wiping the floor it started to get clean and made it look worse, so I got the rag dirty by dusting the top of the cabinets and then we just blended the scuff. We put up Oliver's bed and then began to examine his cupboards, his chest of drawers, every shelf, all of the things, but we didn't find anything.

My breathing started to become heavier. Or I knew I was breathing whereas before I didn't need to think about it. It sounded like a freight moving uphill. I knew the sound from the Milwaukee-Seattle railroad Dad sometimes hiked. Before crossing the trestles, we listened for the sound of the coming freight trains. I balanced on the bright rail, the rim worn to a burnished edge by the rolling steel wheels. The screech of shearing metal came from the way down the grade. The bass huff began in my hipbones. I felt that tingling now in my legs. Oliver's apartment had that gradual increase in the metal noise of a far-off train. "Why are you huffing and puffing?"

"I'm going to blow the house down." Jake found the magazines in the closet. "There are naked women in the closet," Jake said. He thrust a slippery armload of glossy magazines at me. The covers had foxed and pitted from sitting in a stack in the closet. Stray magazines slipped to the floor, their pages fanning and the centerfolds uncoiling like tails.

The door swung open, and Oliver stood in the doorway with Mom behind him. Mom said, "Pack it up, kids, because we have to go see goddamn Paul. Pull up your pants, Aldous, and stash the magazine in your knapsack. We've got to go."

Dad still had another three hours to work. We waited for him at a diner where men drank dark cups of cold coffee from old porcelain mugs. The booths had red vinyl cushions and counters edged with chrome. The women who ate in the diner seemed to all be dressed in plastic yellow, red, and blue coats; their skin drooped, white and stark against the primary colors of their coats. I wondered what they had in their tattered department store bags—

the Bon Marché, Nordstrom, Frederick & Nelson's, Woolworth's. To me, these were bag ladies. I didn't associate the title with the older, transient women we ran into near alleys, women pushing carts, who looked themselves like ripped and torn bags. In the diner, the women ate ice cream sundaes with whipped cream and nuts.

The diner, Ben Paris, sat in a triangular building. When I asked Mom while we were waiting for Dad what she and Oliver were doing for all those hours, she told me that they were visiting some friends of his. I didn't believe her. I had never seen Oliver's friends. I did not believe that he had them. Instead, I thought they went somewhere together, to a movie, without Jake and me.

"I don't believe you, Mom," I said.

"Good kid, good, you're learning something then."

I drew lines from the pools of water condensing at the base of my water glass. I looked down on the space between Westlake and Pike Street. A few iron benches and scraggly trees sat in the shadows between the buildings. Even in the late summer evening, it was blue. The light hadn't faded yet, and the electric glow of the Coke sign hadn't started. A man danced with the pigeons. His old ragged overcoat turned in spirals like a dervish. He lifted the flaps of his coat and the pigeons scattered and landed on his arms. They flashed their silver wings. Around the base of the man, bread crumbs caught the streetlight.

"Look," I said.

"I've seen him," Mom said.

But Jake hadn't. He crowded into the booth next to me and looked out at the man. The streetlights flashed on, and the lights in the diner became brighter; the glass grew opaque. Jake leaned into the window with his hand over his eyes so that he could see outside.

"Let's go," Mom said.

When Dad was off, he hugged Mom and smiled at Jake and me. "Nice to see you," he said. "What did you do today?" he asked.

"Not much. Hung around with the kids," she said.

"Aldous and I played with Oliver's wall bed," Jake said.

"Wall bed?" Dad asked.

"Mom said it was called a Murphy bed, but it was a wall bed."

"Did she?"

We drove though the city, across the floating bridge, and rolled around the buckle, then across Mercer Island, and finally to a foggy land where the only movement through the windshield was the white flow of the fog line. We passed through Issaquah and Preston, and then the familiar shifts of the road up the hill, finally parking in the driveway. And the tick tick of the car after it stopped, and the smell of the house, cedar and firs, wood smoke, meant home and sleep.

I woke later to Dad in the kitchen arguing with Mom. She was whispering, but he talked in a loud voice. "He might as well come and live with us. He needs time. Things haven't been going that well with him."

"No," Mom said. "He's doing just fine."

"Are you going to move in with him?"

"He hasn't asked me."

"If he asks you, will you?"

"This is absurd. Before today, I hadn't seen him in weeks. The last time I saw him, I was with you."

"Gayle, if you don't tell me—"

"What? You're going to kill the other two kids?"

"Ah, so you've spoken at last." I heard the sharp ring of the keys and then the cool sigh of the refrigerator opening. "I'm going out."

"It's three o'clock in the morning."

"I'm gone," Dad said.

The next morning, Dad called us from the other side of the mountains. Mom paced the rooms of the house muttering to herself, "What has he done this time? What has he done?" Jake and I groggily pulled on our pants and lay back in the bed with our clothes on. I watched the shadow of Mom falling into the kitchen from the living room. I wanted to say, "Jake and I will go get him, go back to sleep." I would drink coffee and drive the car over the mountains, wearing Mom's high heels so that I could reach the gas pedal. I would find Dad on some back road, next to his car ditched in the dark woods, and bring him home where he could sleep, dry and warm.

Mom made coffee using hot water from the tap and crystals in an old jar from the cupboard. She dumped milk and coffee into a thermos. Jake and I sat in the backseat. The naugahyde felt like extremely cold skin when we first sat in the car. Jake and I didn't have to argue over the window seat. We both sat in back and I slid my hand along the ribs between the two passenger seats. In front, the green light of the dash lights caught Mom's hair as it unraveled down her arms. She knocked the strands back as she took turns faster than she should have. We were on the road to the Pass, and soon would drive over the lip of the mountains. Mom didn't say anything. I thought she was mad, but there wasn't a way to tell, except that she wouldn't talk to us.

"Mom, are you okay?" Jake asked.

"I guess not," Jake said.

Jake laid his head back into the seat. He folded his arms across his chest and closed his eyes. He opened them and gave me a dirty look. He closed his eyes again.

In the dark, we drove over the Pass; the trees rose into the starry sky. The black shape of Guy Peak loomed into the Milky Way. We drove, small and light, under the shapes of distant objects. I believed we were on our way to a land I didn't know anything about. "Where are we going?" I asked Mom.

"To pick up your stupid father," she finally said.

Mom pulled off the road and we drove through the trees, along a two-lane road. A few cars passed us the other way; their headlights were pale in the early light. The glare caught in our car and lit everything. Jake's face turned white.

Finally, we came to a small town with dark storefronts. Dad stood outside a telephone booth with his hands in his pockets. He watched us. He wore a beard and held his hands up into the air. "Hello," he said. "Hello, Gayle, I didn't think you were coming." Dad played the part he had played before. Perhaps he enjoyed stranding himself to see if Mom would still rescue him.

"I shouldn't have come."

"I need to eat."

"Where?"

"A bar."

"It's seven in the morning," she said.

"A truck stop? A Denny's? Gayle, I don't know."

"Do you have money?"

"No."

We ate breakfast at a diner full of old men drinking coffee; we sat down and Mom gave us a look that must have been meant to shut us up, but Dad ordered coffee from the waitress and Jake quickly said, "A pop, root beer."

"The kids don't want anything," Mom said to Dad. "Water," she said to the waitress.

"I want a burger," Dad said.

"It's breakfast time anytime, but lunch eleven to three. What'll it be?"

"What time is it?"

"Ten twenty."

"No chance of a burger?"

"No chance."

"Eggs and hash browns."

The waitress scrawled something on the pad. She looked at Mom, and left.

"Mom, Mom," Jake said. He set his head on the table, and rolled his chin back and forth on the palm of his hand.

"Jake, please," Dad said.

"What are you doing here?" Mom said.

"I should ask you," Dad said.

The waitress returned with an oval platter heaped with gelatinous eggs and a mat of fried hash browns.

"Want ketchup or anything?" The waitress set three small glasses of water on the table and topped Dad's coffee.

"Excuse me, lady?" Jake said.

"Jake," Mom said. "Leave her alone."

Mom said to Dad, "Where's the car?"

"At the head of the Cle Elum River. It crashed." He smiled when he said that and he held her hand. He smiled at her with hash browns in his mouth. We could see them between his teeth. He laughed and closed his lips. He swallowed and smiled at Jake.

Jake turned to Mom and said, "Can I have your water?"

"No."

"Aldous, can I have your water?"

"Yeah."

"Thank you," he said. "Thir-sty," he said. He grabbed my glass and slurped the water into his mouth. He tilted the cup up to his nose and threw the glass back so that the ice cubes bounced on his lips, "Ah," he said.

Then Mom said, "The kids and I are going to start driving east, and we aren't going to stop at the Rockies or the Mississippi. We will drive until you aren't in the picture anymore. I will get another shitty job and maybe find another shitheaded man. Okay? Is that how you would like it?"

"Mom," Jake said, "Can I have your water?"

"Just a minute, Jake."

"Gayle?" Dad said.

"Why do you want him to move back into this house? After what has happened?"

"I just lost my daughter. I don't have to lose my brother too," Dad said.

"What about me?"

"What about you?" Dad asked.

"Okay. You win," Mom said. "He can move back in. If we live through this summer, maybe we can do something about it." Mom stood up and leaned against the table. "Finish your eggs, I'll drive you home. You have to go to work tonight." Dad brushed his beard with his hands and scooped a forkful of eggs into his mouth. Jake raised his eyebrows and spit an ice cube back into his empty glass.

Nine

"Beasts live in the forest," Oliver said. "They come into our world to hide among us in disguise. These animals look exactly like houses, peaked roofs, shingles, eaves, porches, mother-in-law apartments, all of it. These beasts maneuver out of the trees and plant down beside the road, looking for all the world like a fixer-upper, cheap, you know, but it's just a show so that people will come to live in them, not knowing.

"Suddenly, the house beast gets a hair up its ass, and sets out, just taking off with all the people's stuff crammed in its guts. The beast rips out of its foundation, unhooks the electrical wires, jerks out the pipes and crawls back into the forest, dumping out the furniture, the family portraits, the family heirloom grand piano. I'm sure you've seen a place where a house like this has been. In that gaping founda-tion, one of these beasts has lived, listening to the people go about their daily business. These people were unaware that every word they said was being heard, and would ultimately be used by this beast. But that's what it fed on. It lived off the captive family's words. It would get a little indigestion after a bad joke, get stuffed and a little drunk after a bullshit card game with the cronies. But when it came down to it, the beast really liked an argument. It filled the house with its hostile breath, the vapors altering the mood of the people inside, raising their blood pressure, making them pissed. Really utterly mad. They started with bickering at breakfast, carried over from a night of insomnia, tossing and turning because they were already peeved at something somebody had said during the day, you know, 'John, would you please brush your teeth after you eat an onion sandwich?' John lies in bed, having spent thirty minutes brushing his teeth. Morning, John gets up and throws the milk at his wife. 'You smell like milk, bitch.' You get the picture. And a murdered family, one that just gets nuts and kills itself, is a real bonus to the beast. Every beast that's been around has scored a family murder. The men start to drip frothy red bubbles out of their nostrils and they butcher their sleeping wives and carve the hearts out of their children and in horror at their own brutality, they cut out their own shit-filled innards.

"I've lived to tell about seeing one of these monsters moving. In the dark trees by the Raging River, one night coming back from a late day fishing upstream toward

Preston, in the pale blue dusk, I saw a house walking upright, through a stand of old cedars. A yellow light spilled out of the windows. Bare floors tilted in the forward stride of the long sumo-wrestler legs. Its toes pressed into the damp earth. Naked lightbulbs swayed inside the empty rooms. It was a vacant two-room house-beast. The building didn't make much noise. I could hear, as if nothing was happening, a distant airplane, the rush of water over stones in the river, the rattling of a car on the Preston-Fall City Road. I lay in the cover of the sword ferns, their spiny leaves tickling my face, drifting spores up my nose. I had to sneeze. But, if I sneezed, I'd get a two-yard-long sumo-wrestler foot planted on my face. A heavy creak of wood resonated through the forest. The house lowered its roofline under a cedar tree's drooping branches and was gone. I sneezed and got the hell out of there.

"I recalled the time your Dad and I returned home when we were kids, and where our house had been, an empty foundation stood. Our sister, Joyce, sat crying in the driveway. 'My record player was in there,' she said. It had been. But everything was gone. Our house had been one of these monsters and had just picked up and left with all our stuff in its guts."

"Where do these creatures come from?" I asked. Oliver held me onto the bed. Jake snored in the bottom bunk.

"Gigantic . . . prehistoric . . . flightless . . . birds. They evolved. They had to. At first, they just sort of looked like houses, and no one lived in them. But the FBSS, Flightless Bird Slaying Society, found them out. They had to become trickier to survive, breed, mature, mutate, and breed again."

"Houses don't have sex."

"True. However, my friend, birds do."

"No, they don't."

"And why not? Wouldn't you have sex if you had the chance? Hell yes, you would. Birds got to have sex. Where you think they come from? New Fucking Jersey?"

"How can you tell it's a house?"

"Centuries of fucking evolution have made that impossible. Literally. Evolution. Survival of the best damned fuckers. Hence, the need for there to be sex and lots of it. The ones that could be detected have been killed by the FBSS. It is a moot point these days. Nobody can tell."

I was ten years old and full of moot questions.

Most marriages cannot survive the death of a child. My parents moved Uncle Oliver permanently into the attic, and hoped that his doing the irrational thing at the right time would save them, as the saying goes, the wrong thing at the right time. With Oliver in the house, the tiny structure covered with peeling brown paint, tottering on rotting posts and pillars, became the central place in our world. Mom said that when she was at work, she wondered what Dad and Oliver were up to at home. Even Seattle seemed like a place on the outskirts of what was ours. Everything in *The Seattle P.I.*, everything that happened on TV, happened outside what was really important.

I remembered Adrian clearly, sitting on the toy box with Jim Fuzz propped up next to her while she looked at the pictures in her Mother Goose board book. I knew her hair fell over her face all the time because she had always looked at things by bringing her head as close to them as possible. But now Adrian was gone. And having the toy box and the book with the scratch-and-sniff sticker of a skunk Adrian had rubbed to its fuzzy white paper did not change that. Adrian was gone, and Oliver was there instead.

Now that Oliver had returned I kept waiting for him to ask for the last photograph of Adrian back. I kept it in Oliver's old birthday envelope stuck into the endpaper of my copy of *Uncle Remus*. The photograph had always seemed a momentous thing because, in it, I imagined all of the evidence of what was going to happen could be found. I leaned toward both Jake and Adrian, almost pushing Jake into Adrian. And she had her skirt pulled up and one hand in the pocket of her jeans. I could see the skin on her stomach, already brown from the sun from lying on the boulder behind the house. Mom smiled at Oliver and leaned slightly, her hands falling back just as if she might have gestured at him. Come on, she might have just said, but her mouth was just closed and pursed. Dad stood behind the line of us, fiddling with something in his backpack.

Even though I thought I should return it to Oliver, I kept the picture and didn't tell him I still had it.

Oliver inflated a raft and we all floated around in the small pond at the bottom of the clay hollow. In the brown water, it felt like boating around at the bottom of a coffee cup.

Dad hoped to fill the hole he had dug in the ground with water. "When this is full," he told us, "everything will be all right."

When it finally filled in June, the freshet resumed its course down the dry crick bed under the dam. The sound came back again. Gradually, the memory of the silence filtered away and the dam seemed as though it had always been there. I could feel the weight of the water caught in the clay hillside and it did feel like wealth. The clear pool held hundreds of cubic feet of water. We couldn't see the bottom because, through the dim water, the light came through the branches, slicing down through the green clouds of dark water and reflections. This blockage of water was Dad's masterpiece.

Between the city and our house, the trip ran along miles of highway paved with cement blocks and edged with reflectors, through the town of Snoqualmie with dark storefronts, past the only light, past the red neon sign flickering *Rainier* at the Mount Si Tavern, past the few old timers standing out on the sidewalk drinking cans of Olympia, through a heavy fog in the dairy fields, and then off the asphalt-paved road up the hill where the asphalt ran out and then the tar ran out and then eventually the gravel ran out and the car bumped and slid on the muddy ruts. Now, though, everything felt beyond our house. We weren't hiding from everything else. It was hiding from us. Gas prices caused inflation and grocery prices rose. It didn't matter, because we had water and canned vegetables. A war occupied the TV news somewhere. It didn't matter, because we only had a black-and-white TV and were only allowed to watch black-and-white movies, *King Kong, Tarzan,* and *Animal Crackers.*

It was hot and I dove into the pond, so cold it fried the heat out of my joints. The school of trout raced away from me. Normally, I could see them drift toward the top of the pool and tip their noses at the surface of the water. Or they struck leaves and insects, sending rings over the surface.

In the morning, the sky hung down in a flat sheet of gray. In the front yard, a shadowy beast sat in a pile of windfall apples. Without the rattle of falling water on the roof shakes, without the gurgle of runoff spilling out of the gutter pipes, I could hear the sound of the animal. A noise like Oliver guzzling wine rose from its maw as it nuzzled an armload of rotting fruit. Late apples from the feral orchard littered the yard. The bear lifted up a furry side, then dropped the flesh, making a wave pass down its fat sides. It had a whitish snout and eyes that reflected the cloudy blue light from the sky.

I crept down the front steps and it turned to face me. It shifted onto its back and a yawn spilled out of its head that smelled like old bananas. I wanted to touch its fur. The creature blinked at me, rolled to its four feet, and staggered away between the twisted fruit trees, shambling into the shadows under the hanging cedar tree boughs.

After I saw the bear, I sat on the steps until Jake woke. He and I followed the tracks and smashed elephant ears into the fruit orchard. The long grass among the trees had been pressed down as though an asphalt roller had steamed around the trunks. Cracked apple cores lay in heaps under the trees. Some had been squashed. We followed matted grass and broken twigs into the forest. We tracked the beast until we came to a copse of cedar trees, and among the roots of the trees, we smelled a rancid odor. The beast had vomited a slick pool of half-digested apples. Jake looked at me, his eyebrows rose, and then he laughed. "It looks like the monster's been playing with Oliver."

When Mom woke, we told her about the monster. She didn't believe us, because she didn't know about the man in the red plaid shirt, or the howls in the forest at night. She didn't know that the shapes of the forest crept from under the sword ferns, out of the musty holes in the clay banks, and peered through our windows while everyone slept. Real Sasquatches climbed through the dark canopy of maple, cedar, and fir trees.

When we told Mom about the monster in the orchard, she just shook her head and stood in the mess of the previous night's party. Oliver's birthday weekend had lasted forever; Oliver and Dad wouldn't stop. Finally, they had collapsed around three o'clock Monday morning, falling where they danced. Records fanned across the living room floor, empty Oly cans lined the ledges, mugs with brown stains dripping from their lips covered the coffee table, and ashtrays overflowed with roaches and the orange plugs of cigarette butts. "How about a walk?" Mom asked us. "Your Dad's gonna clean all this up."

We walked the five miles to the Snoqualmie Falls and then we walked downriver to the confluence of the Tolt. The Snoqualmie River roiled next to us, flowing toward Duvall. Breaking through the low clouds, the sun opened to a cold, blue sky. Fresh grass filled the fields we passed and the river flowed dark with green clay. We sat on a small hill overlooking the river and lay back to look at the sky, at the clouds, at everything, and fell asleep in the warm sun. Mom woke us with a cool hand on our foreheads. "You two sure are tired," she said.

"One more minute of sleep," Jake said.

"You'll get sleep tonight," Mom said.

As we sat on the knoll, I became aware of how different Mom seemed outside the house. She smiled at Jake's jokes. She pointed out small things as we watched the clouds move toward the mountains. At the edge of a mud puddle, she found the miniature skull of a shrew, delicate and round, like half a bird's egg. We stopped at the edge of a marshy pond and snapped a cattail out of the reeds. "Here," she said and handed it to me. I carried the skull and the cattail and held them in my lap while we looked at the clouds and listened to Jake snore.

I nudged him. "You're snoring."

"What?" Jake sat up quickly. He rubbed his hand through his hair. "What did I say? I wasn't talking, was I?"

When we came home, the door opened to the carpet vacuumed into orderly rows, the books tightly packed into the shelves. Someone had carted out the beer cans, the wine bottles, the Nalley's potato chip bags. Someone had polished the coffee table, wiped the residue of smoke away from the windowsills and off the windowpanes. The house smelled like the chili stewing on the stove and the earthy fern-scent of curing hemp. Dad and Oliver sat at the kitchen table ripping the leaves away from the stalks.

"Coffee?" Dad asked Mom. She smiled.

Sunday night, Jake and I always played in our bedroom. We built Lego starships. We fenced with block swords and the blade snapped whenever we knocked them together. Jake broke my sword with a swipe of his hand and then thrust the pointed end of his sword into my stomach. It felt like someone had jabbed an actual knife into my guts and I looked at Jake's face, his grin, the jaunty wave of his hand as he declared my death. I buried his face into the toy box. He tried to bite my arms as we struggled, then I had his head under the lid and I closed it. He started to howl, and his muffled shrieks filled the bedroom.

"Child-men, stop!" Oliver stood at the door looking at us. He smiled. He kept smiling, even when we stopped fighting. He smiled at us, and squatted down. He lost his balance and fell backward into the kitchen. He sprawled out and squirmed. "Paul, it is most definitely a hit. I'm peaking already. Jesus."

Mom said, "He's just playing." Then she saw me holding Jake's face into the toy box. She hit Oliver in the head with the back of her fingers. "What have you been doing? Have you given them something?"

"No." He rubbed his head. "Man. Hair feels good."

"What was it?"

"Fuerto Man-coy?" Oliver asked.

"Orange juice," Dad said. He handed Oliver a mug, and Oliver slurped it down. "Tang," Dad said, "Tang's the thing."

"Tang's the thing," Oliver echoed with a gurgling voice. "What did you give the kids?"

"We were fighting, Mom," Jake said. "Aldous was trying to kill me."

"Then stop," she said.

"Where's the fucking lute? We must go to the root cellar," Oliver said.

Dad and Oliver put on their jackets. Dad smiled at Oliver. "You're really gone."

Jake brushed himself off and went into the living room to sit by Mom. I picked up the blocks and made an executioner's ax and practiced chopping my head off.

I woke when I heard the rattle of gunshots outside. I lay in the bottom bunk, hearing the tapping raindrops hit the window, along the roof, waiting to hear the gunshots again. The analog clock seemed motionless.

I wriggled out of the bed and slapped my feet on the linoleum floor. A block skittered under the toy box. I brushed my teeth and washed my face. A leak had sprouted in the bathroom ceiling, and water trickled into the corner, down the wall, and across the floor. The ship, I thought, was sinking. I packed my lunch, forcing the sandwich, the orange, into my lunch box. Another sound cracked outside. I hoped Mom was awake, but she and Dad lay in the dark bedroom. Dad's arm lay over her side like an uprooted tree.

The rain came down so quickly that it soaked my jacket. My hood drooped over my eyes, so I held the flap open with one hand and kept walking down the hill toward the stand of cedar trees that kept the school bus stop dry. I looked forward to getting into the spot because the air was warm and the musk of the trees made it feel like a safe, good place. Along the loose gravel shoulder of the road, I couldn't see anything. I started to feel the cold water spreading into my sweater. I'd have cold wet spots in my clothes all day. I couldn't see into the dark trees behind me. And then, through the crash of water coming down through the maple tree leaves, I heard a sound like a car backfiring. Coming down the steep slope toward the bus stop, I found a collection of soft plastic buckshot shells on the ground. When I stopped to grab them, I saw a shape, the slight movement of some branches, and then nothing. The wet copper caps of the shot felt warm.

I ran then, not caring that my tennis-shoe heels kicked long trails of grit onto the backs of my jeans. Lunch bag-colored leaves stuffed the ditches. Spots of whitish mold crept over them. The water drowned everything. The cedar trees, bloated and loose, drooped over the road. Everything dripped moisture. Rain settled from the clouds, constantly drifting to the earth. It welled out of holes in permeated clay and ran downhill. I practically swam through the air, full of rotting vegetation and rain, until I stepped into the warm brown stand of trees at the bus stop and listened to the stream carrying all of that water into creeks and into streams and finally out of the creek mouth into the Snoqualmie.

A crack appeared in Dad's dam. It was like a cake that only sat on half the plate. A large uneven break bled mud down the hillside. Dad patched it and smoothed the surface, but Mom wondered if the whole dam was just slowly dissolving behind the weight of all that water. Mom said, "A crack like that is an indication of structural failure."

"I fixed it, Gayle," Dad said. "Have faith in me."

———

First her stuffed bear disappeared, the one she used to lie on and look at books with, the one with the eyes Mom had replaced with black, rough buttons from the old minidress she no longer wore because she said she couldn't fit into it. The bear had always sat on top of her chest under the window, and when it disappeared, I realized it had been gone for a while. I wasn't sure how long, but one morning I woke up and the sun came down through the ivy and blackberries behind the house, through our window, and I didn't see its familiar shadow spread out over the floor. I got up then and realized it was gone. That was the initial shock; a kind of loss of what I took for granted. And then I noticed that other things were gone. I opened her toy box and it had her dolls and doll clothes and the erector set that she never played with. Jake and I always wondered why Mom had given it to her instead of to us. Can we play with your erector set? No, she always said, and that saying no to the one thing of hers that we wanted to play with I think became better to her than any actual toy could ever be.

"Jake." I woke him up. "Jake?"

He slipped down from his bunk and shivered on the cold floor. He wasn't awake but looked around and then leaned down to wake up Adrian, something he did every morning. "She isn't there," I said. And he sat down on her cold, made-up bed. "Jake, where are Adrian's things?"

He didn't exactly look like the guilty party. Maybe he was, but he did seem sort of unaware of what I was talking about.

"In her toy box," he said. "In her place in the closet. Where she left them."

"Her bear is missing," I said.

He looked at the window and then he started to cry. "She took it. She wanted it."

"What do you mean?"

"She must have taken it. Who else would take that bear?"

I wanted to tell him that she was dead, that someone else must have taken it. She was dead and someone else must have taken it *that was not Adrian,* but he was crying and he had just woken up and I didn't want to tell him again that she was dead.

Her stuffed giraffe vanished. The plush Humpty Dumpty made a jailbreak. Her wooden blocks, her sailboat, the pile of pink and red dresses suddenly weren't there one morning. "Who's taking her stuff?" I asked Jake. "Adrian wants her things."

"If she wants her things, why doesn't she move back into the house?"

"Because you told me she was dead."

"She is dead."

"Oliver says the dead don't live in the houses of the living," Jake said. I couldn't argue with that.

Her erector set disappeared before I had the nerve to play with it. One morning, I woke up and her toy box had vanished in the night. No trace remained of Adrian except her made-up bed. No trace remained except the reminder that she no longer slept in our room. I waited for Mom to notice that Adrian's things had vanished, but she didn't notice anything. After a while, the absence of Adrian's things was just part of how things were in our room.

I watched as Oliver slipped further and further away that autumn. He became seized with an action and followed it to an obsessive conclusion. When he decided to study, Oliver couldn't sleep for a week. He sat up late at night in the kitchen reading textbooks, anthologies, encyclopedias. He sat in a stiff-backed chair at the kitchen table with a book in his lap, a coffeepot at his left elbow, and he worked his way from the top to the bottom of the stack of library books. "I want a library brain," he said. "I want to think the thoughts of paper." After he finished each of the books, he went to the attic to sleep.

Oliver's obsession with pushing himself reminded me of my impulse to grab, with both hands, the high-voltage wire we called the cattle killer that ran along the field behind our house. The three cows on the other side of the fence kept the grass manicured and neat up to the white-washed boards. Above the cows, I could see the clouds as they moved toward the Cascade Mountains. Mom called the huge blue spaces between the anvil heads Dutchman's trousers. Our yard, in contrast to the pasture, was filled with bushes, raspberry bushes, blackberry and blueberry bushes, and an old stump with a gigantic huckleberry bush growing on the top. Our neighbor's pasture seemed like a great simplification to me. If I lay down in the thick, wild grass in our yard, I might not even see the sky.

The cattle killer scared the hell out of me. Dad had worn a trail along the edge of the wire where he headed uphill. Sometimes, I walked with him, keeping my eye on the taut wire. It had singed and wilted the grass that tried to grow up against it. At one point, the trail turned under the fence and headed across the field. Here, we had to crawl under the fence and pass within inches of the wire. Occasionally, I would touch it, and my bones would turn into iron, my muscles would flex; then it would end and everything would turn blue and my entire body would feel full of electricity.

The cows never touched the wire. Sometimes, I would try to get them to accidentally brush against it. I would feed them the softest, juiciest grass I could find, grass that lay like damp velvet in my hand. Then I would lay some on the wire. The cows would just look at the grass and then stagger away. To me, Oliver seemed fascinated with some internal version of the cattle killer. He played with putting his hand on the wire, and sometimes he had to grab it, no matter what it did to him or to us.

———

After we went to the library, I didn't see Oliver for three days. When I did, he started the cycle again. He walked with me to my bus stop, carrying the books he had read in his backpack. On the way, we passed Badden carrying a rifle. "What's this?" Oliver asked.

Badden wore work boots, blue jeans, and a thick green Army jacket decorated with Army patches. "I'm hunting," Badden said. He held up his rifle, a shaft of blue metal with a highly polished wooden handgrip and stock. He smiled at the rifle. He looked up quickly at us, to see if we were smiling as well, but we weren't.

"She's a beauty, don't you think? If I'm close enough I can fire a round through the passenger door of a GMC pickup truck, through the thighs of the person in the passenger seat, through the driver's thighs, and through the driver's side door, unless I hit a seat belt or something, and then the round probably wouldn't make it clear through the truck. This is the kind of weapon we should have had over there. MI6 is a damn toy. Used to shoot birds in the backyard as a boy with a higher gauge than one of those."

"First Cavalry?" Oliver asked.

"Were you?" the man asked. He dropped his rifle into one hand and clasped Oliver's hand by the thumb. "Good to see you, man."

"Naw. I wasn't." Oliver said. "Now, get the fuck off my hill with your weapon. There are kids playing in these woods. I don't want you firing any rounds through the passenger door, through our thighs, and then out the other door, unless you hit a seat belt or something."

"Look, I'm out hunting bear. I've got a friend who lives up this way and he told me about them. Will Minipis? Know him?"

"I don't want you killing any of the bears in my woods."

Badden looked at me. He had stubble on his face. "I don't want to deal with this; I'm just hunting. I have a right to hunt here."

"This is a neighborhood. Go hunt on Queen Anne Hill if you want to kill someone. Just blow the shit out of some rich bastards. But leave us alone."

"All right, man. Got you."

Oliver and I left him behind. I found that in the interchange I had put my hand in Oliver's hand. I looked back at the hunter and I saw him look at my uncle, then glance down at me and stare into my eyes. I gripped Oliver's fingers. I thought sometimes that Oliver didn't know I was there, but then before I went outside to play he'd say, without looking up, "Shoelace is untied."

———

Oliver and Dad had mysteriously disappeared when Mom, Jake, and I heard the gunshots down the street. The gunshots echoed, the mountains amplifying the short bursts. Mom's voice came from the kitchen "Boys? Stay here." Jake and I were in the bedroom, elbow-deep in the box of blocks.

I went to the doorway of the kitchen, edging my foot out into the black-and-white linoleum to wait for her to say something. She didn't see me. She stood at the drapes, holding them back with the tops of her fingers as though she were brushing something from her forehead. Without looking at us, she opened the door and left it open. The sound of outside filled the house, the papery rustle of leaves and the tap of water dripping from the gutter into the barrel.

Mom walked down the driveway kicking gravel in front of her. Her arms were crossed. Jake ran after Mom. I grabbed him. "You go back," I said. The flat snap of the shots stopped Mom. She ran down the road. We ran after her.

Badden leaned into his rifle. He fired into the tree. Smoke puffed from the nozzle like a massive pipe. He stood at the bottom of the road's embankment. A dark shape dropped from a tall maple. Two bear cubs scrambled up into the tree, their heavy paws sticking to the wood. Mom stood at the edge of the road and yelled. The man released his hand from the front grip and glanced up at us. For a moment, he held the rifle cocked onto his hip. Then he leaned back into the rifle. His index finger drew back softly and the bodies fell from the tree as though he had gently pulled them down with the hook of his index finger. A second later, the gunshot echoed and cracked again.

Badden dropped the rifle. It bounced with a metallic clack. "Shut the hell up woman," he said. He leaned down to his rucksack and freed a knife as long as his forearm. He flashed it up and held it in the air, where I could make out the serrated back. I thought of running my finger over it, the sharp nubs like the teeth of a comb. "Get out of here," he said.

Mom stopped yelling. She stood far above him. From where I stood, the crown of his head came to her knees His face slackened. The tight line of his mouth drew into a slight smile. Mom swallowed. "Children play in these woods," she said.

"I'm not hunting your kid," the man said. He looked up at me. For a second our eyes met. He said to Mom, "You can just get them the hell away." Then he turned his back to us and sliced into the bear. I wanted to see him as he pulled his tools from the rucksack and set them out, knives, twine, garbage sacks. I wanted to see him cut the fur from the flesh, and cut the limbs, legs, and arms into meat.

———

We waited two days for Oliver and Dad to come home. That afternoon, Mom locked all the doors to the house. She left the windows cracked open and we sat in the living room waiting for the familiar rattle of the car as it crushed the gravel in the driveway. But they didn't come. Jake and I paged through magazines on the floor while Mom looked out the window. The sky outside darkened. Rain fell. Mom lit up her cigarettes. She crushed the butts in the ashtray.

A huge eighteen-wheeler rolled up in the driveway. Dad and Oliver jumped from the cab. A large man sat in the cabin. He threw open the door, then he leaned back in the seat like he was gathering power. Dad and Oliver walked past me into the house. The man in the truck leaned out and grunted as he stepped down each of the steps. His hands folded around the chrome railing running up the side of the semi's exhaust pipe. Thick plates of hardened skin defined the joints in his hands. His back rolled under a tight red-and-black plaid shirt. He wore a baseball cap with the words, *Keep On.* "Hey-hey," he said to me.

Dad and Oliver stood in the kitchen, a constant motion of arms setting a frying pan on the oven, dumping coffee grounds into the pot, the snap of tin cans opening. "Sit down, John," Oliver said to the truck driver. Mom leaned against the doorway to our bedroom. She tapped her finger on her hip.

"It's good to see you, honey," Dad said. "After what we've been through, if old John hadn't picked us up, we'd still be on the North Fork of the Skagit. John, this is my wife, Gayle."

"Pleased," John said. He unfolded his arms and extended his crustlike fingers to Mom, who ignored him.

"Where's the car?" she asked.

John blew out his breath and folded his arms across his huge stomach. His sides stuck out beyond the seat edges, and the chair back pressed into his back like a rake dropped in the mud. Jake and I stood in the bedroom. Jake filled his cheeks up and offered me his hand and, as I reached toward his hand, he pulled it back and smoothed his hair down. I watched the truck driver roll his eyes up and down as he watched Mom cross the room. Dad opened cupboard doors behind her, as if he didn't see her. Oliver opened the refrigerator door and dropped an ice tray on the counter as if he didn't see her either.

"Coffee for all," barked Oliver. He handed a cup to John, who said, "Much obliged," as though he was in some sort of Western. Oliver turned back to the stove.

"Where's the car, Paul?" Mom asked again. She stood in front of Dad.

"It's just in a ditch for a while," Dad said.

"In a ditch, bitch," Oliver said. He rolled hamburger in his hands and flattened it into patties. "Burger?" Oliver said.

Dad started to laugh. They laughed while Dad finished cutting up the lettuce and Oliver dropped the meat into the frying pan and the grease snapped.

Mom sat at the table with John. He held up the coffee to my mom. "Good coffee."

"Sure it is," she said. Mom propped her hand under her chin. "So John, did you see where the car was?"

"No. No ma'am, can't say that I did."

"Three fur burgers all up," Oliver said. Dad started to laugh. He laughed and had to prop himself up against the sink. He bent over and his laughter echoed in the room. Oliver watched him as he laughed and he smiled. When Dad stopped, Oliver winked at him, and then they both started to bust up.

Mom bit her lips. She held them with her bite until her lips started to turn bright red. Her face turned white. Jake and I stood in the doorway watching her. John reached out one of his massive hands and then he had his hand on her shoulder. He whispered something to her.

"Shut up," she said to him. "You don't know that about us."

"Sorry, my mistake, ma'am," he said.

Mom stood. She tottered for a moment, but steadied herself with a quick hand against the edge of the table. She slowly walked into the living room. We didn't have doors in our house, except the bathroom door and the doors outside, or I think she would have slammed one.

Dad stopped laughing. "Oops," he said. "Burgers to go." He pulled out an entire kitchen drawer and set it on the counter. He dropped a bunch of baggies onto the counter and flipped the burgers onto pieces of toast, garnishing them with swipes of a knife.

"Let's go," Dad said to Oliver.

"It's a bummer here," Oliver said to John. "Where you headed to?"

"No place that fellows like you would want to go," John said. He stood up in a steady heave until he leaned above the table.

I thought maybe everything would calm down now. Oliver and Dad's drunk routine went along like this. As things got bigger and bigger, the one-upmanship led to: I can stand on my tiptoes taller than you can stand; I can stand taller on this stool; I can stand on this chair; I can stand on the goddamn peak of the roof, you motherfucka. After that they had to calm down. Dad would sit down, put his head down and cover it with his hands; that was it, time to settle down. Oliver would go outside, and when he came back, he would be quiet and make himself some coffee. I looked forward to this peace. As wild as things got, everything almost always went back to the way it was supposed to be.

This time, the tension that settled was outside. It was a tension I wasn't even aware of until it was relieved. The branches in the trees outside splintered. The grass uprooted itself, root-balls, night crawlers, gravel, and the deep white tap stems pulled themselves up. The dam burst, dissolving into mud like a bread crust left in the sink. The deep cavern of water Dad had stored in the hillside to see us through the summer gave out and began to resume its trip downhill. First, it had to move through the dam, which it did, and then through the rhododendrons and ferns planted on the dam, which it also did, and then it moved through the storage shed, the mowed grass, the driveway, the mailbox, the road, and through the forest gathering up dirt, mud, gravel, and leaving behind only blue clay. Everything else just melted. The water left. It made a sound like a long summer rainfall condensed into three minutes. It made a sound like all of the baths Mom had ever taken in her entire life condensed down to three min-utes. Three minutes of the roar inside a seashell and it was gone. There wasn't any sound at all for a long time, until we heard the gradual noise of the leaves moving in the wind and the faint trickle of the freshet running back again in its old place, wrapping through the potholes and car-nage left by the evacuating water. We all went outside and looked at the trail of wreckage left by the burst dam. Dad and Oliver followed the water downhill and Dad shouted after it, "Come back you damn pond," and then they started running downhill and disappeared into the fir trees on the other side of the road. The trucker looked at us and he was about to say something, but what could he say? He started several times and finally all he could come up with was, "I don't expect they're going to catch up with that water."

"They're resourceful," Mom said. "I'm sure they'll find something."

"Need a lift somewhere?" He was a trucker, after all, and all he could do was move himself and other stuff from one place to another. For a second, I think Mom would have gone with him. But his truck wasn't shiny and red. It was worn and dented and she smiled. "No. I've got to clean this mess up before I can go on my way."

"Suit yourself, ma'am." He nodded at us and then went back to his truck. "Listen, if these two fellas give you any trouble, you just call me, okay?" Then he opened the door. "Thanks for the coffee, ma'am."

We listened to the truck fire to life in the driveway and then it was gone.

We were left alone with Mom in the house. Mom turned on the TV to go to a news program, but she turned the channels until she came to a Jerry Lewis movie. He fumbled around a plastic room. Every time he stood, or tried to walk, he would fall. He groveled on the floor and made a face. A couple sat in the room with him. Instead of doing anything, they kept talking as if Jerry wasn't with them. Mom laughed. She chuckled so hard that Jake and I looked at her and then examined the man throwing himself down on the floor and wincing. Jake sat next to her and laid his head on her shoulder. The color in the plastic room on the black-and-white TV was the stark black and white of ink on paper. Jerry Lewis lost his balance, unable to cope in a world made of plastic. The couple chatted about something, it didn't matter what, because the talk filled our house with their voices and Mom's laughter.

Ten

Dad once hydroplaned across the freeway, over the oncoming lanes, and landed in the ditch. Oliver screamed, "Hole in one!" Jake and I thought that was hilarious. I laughed so hard I forgot my bruised shoulders. I even forgot the way the oncoming cars had jerked around us. When anything horrible happened, Oliver would make jokes and make us laugh until the shock had passed, an emotional sleight of hand that kept the ball moving long enough that I don't think any of us realized how miserable my uncle was until he killed himself. Oliver buffered catastrophe so well that we became blind to the long mornings when Dad and he snored on the living room carpet, to the chipped dishes that were never replaced, to our family's gradual decay.

With his long hair reeking of incense and his hands that always brushed me, Oliver seemed like the guru of love.

My parents spaced out hugs like a weekly allowance. Oliver would grab my shoulders when I said something funny, whereas Mom would frown and set her coffee cup down.

Jake and I relied on the noise of his late-night pacing, the repeated creak and tick of the attic floorboards. We became accustomed to the perpetual grit of coffee grounds scattered around the sink faucet. He wasn't a visitor; he was necessary to the family. After he came to live in our attic, Mom stopped waking up in the middle of the night to lock the windows, pushing against the locks until her elbows turned white and folded up, until she knew everyone in the house was safe. By the autumn of 1976, my uncle's role in the family seemed as integral to its existence as Mom or Dad's. Life progressed like a perfect blues, every line of every day repeated with heavy variation through the progression of the same basic phrase. *Woke up this morning with the blues all about my head.* My uncle balanced my parents. His attraction to Mom kept Dad interested in her, and Dad's love for my uncle kept Mom interested in him and, together, the three of them may have kept going on and on. Even when Mom or Dad tired of the ongoing progression, the other two would make the necessary adjustments in pitch, and keep the AAB AAB AAB uninterrupted. They improvised this song, incorporating even their failed attempts at escape into the ongoing rhythm of our family.

I believed that all friends should be like Dad and my uncle. They clung to each other after Oliver moved in, so much so that Mom called Dad, Oliver's wife. One morning on the way to school, I passed Dad and Oliver on the couch, twisted into each other's arms. The ashtray spilled soft dust across the floor, and green bottles lay in stacked crowds on the coffee table and the fireplace mantel, and records fanned from the stereo. I picked my way over the clutter and looked back at Dad's head resting on the slowly rising and falling pillow of my uncle's chest.

I thought of Oliver as my own best friend, as well. The sound of my uncle's voice as we played hide-and-seek in the late spring convinced me that he was the only person in the world worth spending time with. Everyone else would have to wait when he was available. We began to play after I had cut thin strips in paper cups from top to bottom and Oliver had placed white votive candles in the base of the cups. The candles shone through the paper slits. I moved through the dark shadows of the ferns, listening to Oliver count the hide-and-seek numbers. He said each word in English, German, French, Spanish, and Latin. He would count to twenty before he began the hunt.

I saw Jake's red T-shirt moving in the ferns ahead of me. White moths dipped through the spring air in jerky paths. At Oliver's *seven*, I stood and ran into the forest, falling over branches and bushes. During the fall to the ground, the sharp edges of leaves brushed my arms. My hands sank into cold, liquid mud.

"Acht." I moved using smell, touch, sound, like the bats that whisked through Dad's trash-burning bonfire. I was up and out of the grassy smell of ferns and under the cedar trees. It was a little lighter there, and I saw Oliver turning slowly in the circle of candles at home base. He covered his eyes with both hands.

This was Oliver's favorite game because he said it taught us to live without sight in a dangerous situation. We became objects responding to our sense of touch. The formal rules did not help us in this game. It was him, hunting us down through the forest, finding us buried in the sharp cedar tree boughs, the long needles slipping in scratchy fingers down our backs. It was a game where we learned to swallow down on heavy breathing. We learned silence, and patience, while Oliver howled and then stalked us silently through the trees. Oliver smiled and said hide-and-seek was the chess match of the senses.

In the dark forest, other things moved toward us between the shadowy spaces of branches, over the outlines of fir trees, over the smell of mud puddles full of earth-worms. "Jake, Aldous, come on down," Oliver shouted. "Nuevo!" I climbed the trunk of an apple tree, and I perched in the branches, holding my breath while the leaves rattled. I breathed out when their rustling stopped. Moving through the darkness, the creatures that were more dangerous than even my uncle slipped into muddy holes and hollow trees.

I listened to Jake thrashing through the forest. I could tell exactly where he was, because the bushes snapped and the leaves sounded like a coffee tin full of shaking gravel. If I could tell where he was, Oliver could easily tell. When Jake stopped forcing himself through the forest, he hid in the crab apple tree. I could hear the branches knocking back and forth like cow bells. I was quietly hidden in my tree, soundless and invisible.

"Twenty," Oliver finally said. I saw him standing in the circle of candles, jumping up and down. He howled. He jumped out of the light. "Where are you hiding?" His voice floated through the forest.

I waited for a long time and gradually became aware that I had been left in the tree. I thought Oliver was just waiting for me, and I wouldn't fall for that. So I listened to the stiff orchard branches creak in the draft coming up the hill. Wind rarely blew against the hillside, but in the evening, the warm valley air moved up through the trees and the cool air in the creek valleys came downhill—according to Dad—and for a little while in the evening, the forest began to make its noise. The ferns crackled and the maple leaves shook. As I sat in the branches of the cherry tree, the wind moved the tree trunks, and I couldn't tell if Oliver was out there or not. They had left me in the forest.

I climbed down from the tree and scuttled on all fours under the massive sword ferns on the steep slope going up from the orchard and into the second growth. The stuttering flame of a Bic lighter flickered through the branches. It came out of the rhododendron at the top of the hill over the pond at the edge of the overgrown field. The rhododendron had a warren of cat runs and an old wooden bench Jake and I had discovered when we had first worked up the nerve to enter the bush. We went in there once and said we'd never go back in there again. It was full of spiderwebs and we saw a wood spider the size of a baseball mitt.

I crawled and inched my way up the hill. I could smell the familiar smoke of marijuana. At the base of the dam, in the bamboo, I found a small dress from one of Adrian's dress-up dolls. I wondered if Oliver was really trying to scare Jake and me, if the entire hide-and-seek game was really some sort of scheme to scare the crap out of us. I wanted to yell out for Jake, but then Oliver would be able to find me. Jake and Oliver came down the hill then. I saw the flash of Oliver's white T-shirt. They reeked of pot smoke, and even though everyone in our house smelled like pot smoke to varying degrees, they really reeked. Jake was crying, and when he saw me standing in the blue dusk light in front of the bamboo, he said, as if we had never been playing hide-and-seek, "It's you." They had been doing something without me, and enough time had passed that

they had forgotten we were right in the middle of a game.
"I was hiding," I said.

"Oliver was looking for Adrian," Jake said. "She's hiding
too."

"Did you find her?" I asked.

"I did," Oliver said. "I found her, but she said she didn't
want to be found."

I held the dress, the last thing I had that had belonged
to Adrian. I folded it and tucked it under my shirt behind
my back.

"When she's ready to come out," Jake said. "She will."

When I wanted to learn the proper way to pursue the first
girl I loved, I didn't approach Mom or Dad; I talked to
Oliver. I thought it was natural that I would approach
him for this advice. He seemed to have more luck than
my parents. After all, they had ended up with each other.

I went to see him in October. To reach the attic, I had
to climb a ladder Oliver had built from two by fours. The
ladder leaned over the ditch behind our house; slime and
algae draped from the wooden rungs. The greenish mush
pasted to my hands as I climbed onto the tar roof of the
bathroom. Wiping my hands off on my blue jeans, I called
into the attic, "Oliver?" The small door opened in the side
of the house where a window had once been. My uncle had

hung a section of an old carpet and then a curtain of beads from the old window frame. Inside, Persian carpets Oliver had stolen from a roadside rummage sale coated the walls. While Mom and Dad had pawed through the battered chairs, the cardboard boxes full of old records, Oliver had covered the Dodge Dart's license plate with a piece of notebook paper. When Dad had started the car, Oliver had jumped into the backseat with the carpets wrapped around his body. "Step on it," he had said. Dad had pulled away while Mom looked into the rearview mirror. "It looks like you can keep them," she had said.

"Come in." Smoke flowed out from the lip of the entry as I pushed through the rugs and beads. Over the carpets, drawings plastered the walls. His attic smelled like the incense he always burned from a brass brazier hanging over the doorway. The brazier was corroded black, and dragon feet gripped the dish rim. A child-sized chair sat in front of a large fruit crate propping up a typewriter. Manuscript pages layered over the drawings. Oliver sat on a pile of pillows by the room's only window. He read from a stack of paperback books: *The Floating Opera, Crime & Punishment, Easy Success in Corporate America.* I pulled a foam cushion from the crate. "Are you busy?"

Since kindergarten, I had been in love with one girl, the daughter of the local grocer. I knew I would love her always. I love Gina Lansing. Gina & Aldous. A & G, kissing, kissing, kissing; whenever I saw her in the school hallway, I would stare down into the pale linoleum tiles, speckled with black pits. I would look at her as she walked away and I could feel my nerves scrubbing my stomach like steel wool. I sat down on the couch cushion. "I am," I said, "in love."

"I'd get over it as soon as possible," Oliver said. He brushed his beard with one hand and looked out the window into the forest.

"I can't. I see her everyday."

"Start a fight with her," Oliver said.

"What?"

"Kick her down during recess," he said, "and drag her out behind the gym and have your way with her."

"I want her to like me."

"She will."

He sat against the round attic window. His hair spiraled in mad fibrous arcs from the back of his head. He rolled a joint into a tight stick. "Anything else?"

"No thanks." Dismissed, I tried to climb down from the attic, but one of the two by four planks pulled free from the ladder. I held the greenish plank in my hands as my body pitched into open air. I plunged into the ditch of brackish water that funneled runoff down the clay hill. The long, lime-colored fibers of algae coated my jeans. When I crawled up the muddy bank and lay in the ferns, Oliver leaned out of the attic. "You didn't find a pipe while you were rummaging around in there?"

―――――

The first grade, and by default every other grade in elementary school, was controlled by the children of the lumbermen who worked for the mill in Snoqualmie. During recess, they controlled the swing set. The swing set was constructed of eight-inch steel pipes and climbed twenty feet into the air. At night, the crows came out of the cornfields that grew along the banks of the river and perched along the rim of the set. After school, I could see the shadows of crows sailing over the playground and digging up worms or bits of lost sandwiches. I couldn't believe how different the naked swing set looked without the children using it. During the day, the swings screeched back and forth, each rubber seat filled with a singing girl pumping her legs and flinging her hair toward the sky. Over the mechanical scream of the swing chains, the kids sung about the people they hated.

I believed that Gina wasn't like the kids who stood in line. These kids came from the backwoods above the mill and their parents worked long hours in the mill or some-where up the forks of the Snoqualmie felling timber. These children wore second-generation plaid shirts and blue jeans so faded and patched that when I called Lance's pants "Frankenstein's jeans," he didn't beat me up, but smiled and said he sort of liked that.

Because Gina's father managed the local Associated Grocer's affiliate, everyone thought she was rich. On the mill's payday, the mothers would shove their carts up and down the aisles of the store. They gave a large chunk of their paycheck to Mr. Lansing, who worked the cash register on payday because he liked to gossip with the mothers. My parents hardly ever went shopping on the mill's payday because the valley women would stop and look at my parents and whisper about Dad. They didn't know what he did for a living, but they all knew what he grew in the root cellar in the hill above our house, because, on the Saturday after payday, they sometimes showed up on our step asking about my brother or me. Dad would invite them in for a cup of coffee and sell them a rolled bag of weed.

Maybe I felt Gina and I had something in common, because between her father and my dad, we took a good deal of the Mill's net pay. Only it was obvious from the small three-room house where I lived that my parents weren't rich. Gina lived in an old house with three stories and a big garden, right in the middle of town.

Gina wore a powder-blue velour shirt with a single silver button just below the neck, and she wore her hair in long, dark arcs down the side of her face that made me want to climb out of the monkey bars and pull her off the swing set and dance with her across the play yard, throwing our hands in front of us and snapping up our knees like a couple from an old movie. She packed her lunch in sophisticated brown paper bags while I carried an aluminum lunch box that smelled like last spring's tuna sandwiches.

I hadn't yet learned the word "nerd," or even heard the word much, because everyone who talked about me stood in the line for the swing set. In the pictures of me from the fourth grade, my hair was actually shaped around the outline of a Corningware salad bowl that Mom still owns. Thinking I was witty, I called the lumber kids "The Swing Set" to the few children who would play with me from day to day. The Swing Set approved boys for all the girls without one. No one assigned my best friend Willie—actually my only friend—a girlfriend, but they assigned a girl named Angie to me, and her way of dealing with this calamity was to begin to draw circles and hearts with my name on the arms and chests of the basketball and hockey players on her Pee-Chee.

Angie wore a pageboy in a time when everyone in Snoqualmie had long hair. She wore plaid dresses and black buckled shoes in a time when girls wore pleated skirts or bell-bottom jeans. Already in the fall of 1977, bell-bottoms were on their way out in most places, but in Snoqualmie they were the hot new fashion item. I think they gained popularity as soon as they hit the thrift stores. The Swing Set's parents splurged and replaced the tattered remains of the fourth grader's hand-me-down stovepipe legs with new, used bell-bottoms. Angie didn't conform to the fashions found in magazines or on the backs of the children at school. She didn't conform to Snoqualmie style, where essentially anything found on the hips of John Fogerty could be called chic. Where I grew up, the names of bygone guitar gods, Page, Clapton, Beck, were passed around like the holy names of heroes from a war we had never heard of and didn't know the stakes of. Joe Walsh's career after the Eagles was carried on single-handedly by the rundown logging communities in the Cascade Mountains.

Angie would laugh while she read during the quiet reading time. I was a slow reader. I hadn't picked up the process of putting speech to the letters until the end of the first grade, and found myself behind everyone else in the fourth grade. Angie's pace as a fourth-grade reader infuriated me. She laughed as though whatever she was reading was so funny that she couldn't hold it in. The thing that really irritated me about her laughing was that the author wasn't going to hear her laughing. She could write a letter and spare everyone else the agony of having to listen to her. She laughed, holding the book in one hand, legs draped almost to the floor, one black shoe tapping on the ground. She flicked her black bangs out of her eyes. She held back her laughter and looked at me as though she would read with me any day.

I waited for her after school one day and followed her home. When we passed the corner, putting us out of sight from the school, I said to her, "Hey, dog nose."

Angie turned around and smiled and said, "I knew you were following me."

"Look," I said, "We have to talk."

"We don't have to say anything."

"I can't be your boyfriend," I said. "I love another."

"No, you don't."

"Yes, I do."

Angie started to cry. "You don't. Why do you follow me and then make me cry?" She dropped her Tupperware lunch box onto the gravel shoulder. It bounced, came unfastened, and the clear plastic thermos and sandwich box tumbled into the rushing ditch water. "My lunch box!" Angie screamed. I wanted to say, Let me get it for you, but I didn't want her to think I liked her, so I just stood on the bank as she jumped after it. She had paused for a second before plunging into the black runoff with her white leggings and shiny penny loafers. The Tupperware sandwich box floated in an eddy, but her thermos zipped down a drainpipe and I don't know if she ever found it.

I found myself sometimes looking at Angie, even though she never looked at me after the Tupperware incident. I thought that because the other children had selected Angie for me, they saw her and me as mirror images of each other; they saw us as people who belonged to each other. The only common ground Angie and I shared was that we didn't fit in.

My friend Willie Minipis and I had met in the goat pasture above my house, on the side of Mitchell Hill. From the pasture, I saw the tops of the trees all the way down to the valley floor. Beyond the granite face of Mount Si, the Cascade Mountains had held the first of the season's snow. Willie threw a dirt clod at me. I threw a stone at him.

He hit me with the next dirt clod and the hard pack of dirt loosened on the side of my head, releasing fine granules into my scalp. I felt my skin blotch red and then harden. Round particles of dirt slid under my shirt, along my spine, and filled my underwear. I charged uphill at him, to close the quarters and hopefully beat him down. As I ran uphill, throwing my arms into the bed of the pasture, tearing the green chlorophyll of the grass stalks, Willie laughed and laughed. He folded his hands on his stomach; his curled figure rolled downhill at me and knocked me over. He continued rolling and laughing until he stood and wiped his eyes. "Man, you're stupid. Dumb."

I lay back into the slope of tangled grass. Above us, clouds raced toward the south, exploding into fuzzed spires above their buzzed-off bottoms. "You're lucky," I said. I meant it. He was lucky it was uphill and not downhill, because I would have tackled him and we would have rolled, me throwing sharp elbows into his ribs and rubbing his nose into the ground until I felt his arms go limp and his body go soft under me.

"My name is Willie Minipis. I'm from California. Know where that is?" he said.

"It's south."

"So is Mexico. I've been to Mexico. Have you?"

"I've been to the top of Mount Si and I saw everything from up there."

"You didn't see my butt."

At school, I started to play with Willie almost every day. I played with him because the children of the loggers wouldn't talk to me. Willie wore corduroy every day. He had long, dirty blond hair tangled into a ponytail. He was so skinny, his legs didn't throw a shadow. He would run after me, and I would have to stop because he would stagger ahead of me and collapse his hands to his knees, panting. He would reach out a huge hand and grab my face. "Stop," he would say, falling over me and pushing my face into the grass.

Sometimes, I would play without Willie and he would find me. I would play alone behind the school gym and he would run around the side of the building, tackle me and throw me to the ground. "Hey hey hey," he would say, each word hitting a higher note. Or I would sit in the library and hide from him and he would show up at the window, his large Muppet hands shadowing his face. I couldn't escape him.

Willie always had problems that he had to tell me about in full detail. The zipper to his corduroys broke or he lost the key to his house. He hated the dog his parents bought him for his birthday and he wanted me to come over to his house, take the dog out to the woods by my house, and leave it tethered to a tree in the wilderness. "You want me to murder your dog?"

"No, just leave her out there until she's gone or until something comes and gets her."

So I took Willie's dog, Misty. It was a black Labrador that was about the same size I was, and it was probably the worst-smelling animal alive. I imagined that a dog covered in maggots would smell better. A rich, thick cloud of stink surrounded Misty, a magnified stench of rotting bananas combined with the odor rising from the thirty-year-old outhouse at my grandparents' house. After school, I dragged Misty up to my house. She kept tugging on the leash and throwing herself to the ground. Every time a car came, I would step to the shoulder and pretend she was smelling the bushes. When I finally reached my yard, Jake ran out and started hugging the dog. "What's his name?" I didn't understand how Jake couldn't notice the stench. He squatted next to it, his arms wrapped around the matted fur.

"Willie," I said.

"Willie, I love you," Jake said. He held the dog by its face. My brother was about half the size of the dog. It rolled its eyes and stuck out its large pink tongue and licked my brother. Jake made a face as though he had swallowed a bitter pickle. He coughed. "He loves me."

"He's a she," I said.

"And her name's Willie?" Jake smiled even though his eyes started to fill with tears.

"I didn't name her."

"Where'd you get her?"

"A friend wanted me to leave Willie in the forest to get eaten by the Sasquatches."

"Can we keep Willie? If they just want to throw her away, then we can keep her. Mom will let us."

"Can't you smell Willie?"

"No," he said even though his face had now turned red and tears dripped from his cheeks.

Jake held the dog until Willie's father drove up that night while we ate dinner. He knocked on the door and I could hear my name coming from his lips as my parents stood at the door and finally Mom came inside and said, "I'm sorry Jake, but the dog belongs to Mr. Minipis."

"We can't give Willie to them. They would let her get eaten by the Sasquatches," Jake said.

"Her name is Misty and she belongs to them," Mom said. She knelt in front of Jake and took him into her arms while Dad tugged the dog outside by its collar. Jake started to cry.

"Aldous," Mom said. "Why did you steal Misty? Do you want a dog?"

"I didn't steal her," I said. "She followed me home."

"We can get a dog if you want one."

"I don't want a dog," I said. "They smell."

Even though I wanted to make Willie pay somehow for having lied to his parents about my having taken the dog, I understood this impulse of self-preservation and didn't hold it against him. I just wanted to get even, and I still wanted to play with him because I didn't want to return to the library.

I wanted more control over my own identity. I didn't want to be identified with Willie or Angie. My first move had to be, number one, to blend in by finding clothes like the other children wore. After that I didn't know what I wanted to do. I told Mom that I needed pants with big bottoms. "Bell-bottoms?" Mom asked.

"Whatever they are called, I want them. I also need brown paper bags for my lunches."

"We just got you that lunch box," she said.

"It smells like rotten tuna," I said.

When my teacher called me Aldous I told her, "I'll answer to Zack."

"Aldous, don't be hostile."

"Who? Who are you talking to?"

"Aldous, please."

"Zack," I said, even though I knew it would never stick. I joined the Boy Scouts so that I could wear the uniform to school on uniform day. On the first Monday of the month, I sat in a class filled with other kids dressed like me. I wanted to impress Gina with my normality. I would be more normal than everyone else. I would be the best at normality.

My Scout uniform brought me Oliver's attention. He sewed the patches into the correct places, showing me how to measure them and lay them out so that they wouldn't curl. He taught me how to crease the sleeves through the uniform, the fabric taut and harsh under the starch Oliver sprayed on the blue cloth.

My chance came with Gina, finally, when she and I ended up on the same team to decorate the lunchroom for Thanksgiving. The Recess Lady supervised us. She stood in the middle of the room and told us to cut out leaves. So we sat at a table and constructed leaves out of orange and brown construction paper. I sat next to Gina. She didn't move, so I figured that I at least wasn't repulsive.

"Those are some nice leaves." I nodded at her leaves, a pile of ovals. I had already accumulated a pile of perfectly formed maple leaves. "Are those alder?" I asked.

Gina looked at me. This was a verified register of my existence. I had, I thought, swerved out of invisible nerddom into recognizable cool. I straightened the fold of my Cub Scout shirt tucked into my bell-bottoms.

"No," she said, "They look like circles. Yours are much better than mine."

"Yeah," I said. "But not all leaves are maple leaves. Some trees have oval leaves. I'm not sure which kind, or where they grow, but I'm sure they're beautiful trees. Your leaves, even if they don't look like anything found in nature, do look like something that should be in nature."

"Okay," she said, raising her eyebrows. She stopped cutting leaves and joined the kids taping brown crêpe paper to the walls. She left to get some glue and I quickly cut triangles into the edges of her ovals to make them maple trees.

In March, when it started to get lighter in the evenings, Oliver would tell me about love. "Let me tell how you should get this girl you need," he said to me. "Bring that pitcher of Kool-Aid up to the attic and we'll talk."

We sat in the fading light, looking down on the road while a few cars drove by with their headlights on, lighting up the darkness between the trunks of the forest. The soft flickering nub of Oliver's joint cast shadows over his face.

"I think you need more guts," Oliver said. "How long has it been?"

I told him.

"Since kindergarten, Aldous?" he asked.

"Zack," I said.

"Who?"

"Call me Zack."

"Aldous, this is a problem. Maybe you don't really need her? Is that it?"

"I love her."

"How do you know that?"

"I just do."

"How? Do you wake up at night wanting this woman, this girl? Because if you do, I sympathize. Sometimes, when I've just met a woman I like, she's all I can think about. All I can think about is how much I would like to see her and know that we are alone together. But I know I can't trust myself with her. Might do something rash. There's this check-out girl at the Food Mart. Every time I'm in there, I find myself staring at her wrists. Nothing too sexy got me—no folds of cleavage, no butt cheeks pressed in blue jeans. It's this woman's wrists that have me. I'm there getting my change, and her wrists turn as she cups my change, drops the coins still warm into my hands. Pop. She's got me. I go outside thinking, hoping that I've forgotten something. I'll buy another carton of milk to feel her brush the palm of my hand with a quarter, even though Paul will make me drink the entire carton if I come home with more milk. It's that moment. I'm back in there buying a pack of gum. Know what I mean?"

"Yes."

"Those thin girl wrists have got me. What do you think about?"

"When?"

"When you look at her body, Aldous."

"Her eyes."

"Eyes. Yeah. Eyes," my uncle said slowly. He leaned back against the wall. He looked out the window and said, "Don't you want to just lay her back and fuck her until you scream?"

"When I see her in the hallway, I think about what it would be like just me and her in a quiet place, me looking at her," I said.

"Why would you think something like that? Don't you think about kissing her?"

"No."

"Why not?" Oliver flicked the ashes from the end of the joint to the ground. A few burned into his shirt and he grumbled as he brushed away the gray flakes. He looked out the window. We sat in the darkness looking into the branches of treetops across the street. "Aldous, why?"

"I don't know how to kiss her," I said.

"You don't need to know how," he said. "Will you get out of here? I have things to do."

At soccer one evening, I jumped for a flying ball and it crashed into my face. I felt the sky blacken for a second, then I woke on the ground with Angie wrapping her hands around me. She was crying. I looked up into her eyes and saw her chin folded back and her eyelids half-closed and a stream of water swelling out of her tear ducts. It was far better than the patient, "Are you all right?" Mom would have performed. Angie didn't care. I could be dead, and then she would happy because she held the corpse of her love.

The coach clicked his fingers in front of my eyes. "Aldous, why don't you and your girlfriend just rest over there under that tree?"

The class bully, Greg, stood behind him. "Need any help, coach?" Greg hunkered down next to me. He shook his head. "Pretty tough blow, to flatten you like that."

"She's not my girlfriend," I started to say, but my mouth didn't work. All that came out was a vague, "not . . . not . . ." Angie dragged me across the ball field and held my head in her lap. I writhed under her care, looking past her chin into the blue sky until Mom rescued me. I finally gained motor control. But Angie walked me off the field, holding my hand and petting the skin on my forearm with her other hand. "You'll be okay."

At school the next day, the swing rocked back and forth with children singing the love and marriage song. They sang as I came outside, a love song for Angie and me. Their voices filled the playground. I went into the play shelter, but I could still hear the chorus echoing against the dusty asphalt. I turned around and went to the library.

I began playing chess, isolating myself in the library with the children who never went outside. They wore black polyester polo shirts, which made their arms flash, stark and ivory, as they leaned over the board to move the pieces. Their lips were swollen red from chewing on them as they pondered their next move. In the library, the chess masters lined up on a long desk meant for newspapers.

"Welcome," a wizened child said. "Have you played before?"

"I know how," I said.

"So you do," the child said. "So you do." He pounced on me with the four-move checkmate, moving as quickly as I moved. I snapped my piece down and he had his down after me. Snap, snap, snap, snap, checkmate. "That'll be all."

I was a fourth grade nerd and snob. I wasn't even able to fit in with the lowest of the geeks, nerds, or twerps. I missed my friends, but I didn't want to be seen with them, because then people would know that they were my friends. I was afraid to have Angie as a girlfriend, when in actuality I was afraid to have any girl that was breathing and real as a girlfriend. Angie lived in a trailer park near the only laundromat in Snoqualmie. When Mom took our clothes there to wash, I would walk around the main drive through the trailers. Old cedar trees had been left from before anyone had ever logged. A green hair grew over the asphalt. I walked on the flat surface and looked up into the branches. I couldn't believe she lived at the laundromat. Her mother was the librarian, and sometimes I would have to wait in the car when Oliver and I went to the library, because Angie sat at the only desk in the library drawing pictures.

———

I spent all of my time thinking about the midnight hunting expeditions Oliver started taking me on in the first week of April. Oliver took me outside with a butterfly net and an incandescent lamp. We hunted for moths; we planned to fill a mason jar with their bodies. The lamps cast a bluish light into the shadows of the cedar forest. We sat in the darkness, under the hanging boughs in the spiny leaves of the cedar. Out of the black, moths circled the light. They poured from the sky in jerky paths and waving lines. Small dark moths spit headfirst into the fluorescent light and spilled into the jar. Other moths landed on the bulb and their wings caught on fire in blue flames.

Oliver brought his Indian knife set with him. He had bought it while in Vietnam. He kept it in a special locked box upstairs. The box had water buffalo and a blue woman dancing with her hands turned backwards. When he opened the box, exposing the knife box's bed of faded red velvet, the biggest knife looked like the number seven. It sat in a leather scabbard attached to a belt that also had two other knives attached to it. Oliver said the invincible Indian Gurkhas used the knife. When we went hunting for moths, Oliver always took the belt of knives.

Once we were in the forest, he pulled the curved knife out and charged, screaming into the forest. "Come on, you fucking moths!" He stood with his legs apart and then he swung the knife into a small maple tree, almost cutting it down. But the blade stuck into the wood. He yanked on it and, finally, it pulled free. He leaned over it, running his hand over the edge. Looking up at me, he smiled. "I didn't break it."

We collected piles of moths. We collected forests of bark-colored moths, reams of paper-colored moths, we collected so many moths that I thought we could open a business and have a corner on the moth market. I learned all about moths. I pinned them to an old photo album and, under each insect, I wrote in careful, ten-year-old handwriting, the common name, the Latin name, and the real name Oliver and I had made up: Spandywag, Cold Hopper, Mug of Coffee, Swank Weasel Bat, Flap Jack o' Soar. We named and catalogued them all.

My naming grew out of hand and I started naming everything. I found the power of naming helped identify and explain how things worked. Many nights, when Oliver wouldn't capture moths with me, I would go outside with a flashlight and identify everything. I made lists of names. I named everything in wider and wider circles from our door. As soon as I named the tree in our front yard, I could locate it on my map and I knew where it was, and if I knew where it was, I knew where I was and I could never get lost again.

Species, genus, kingdoms didn't exist. One tree with pine needles was much different from another tree with pine needles. I named each plant and patch of ground cover around our house, because everything in the world around our house had its own life. The cedar tree that grew stories above our house supported ants that crawled across the ridges of bark toward the canopy of leaves. Four birds lived in the branches of the tree.

I drew maps with appendixes to identify everything. I felt like one of the explorers of the South Seas, coming on island after island. You can only name so many things after yourself and your mother and your father and your brother and everyone else you know. Unlike Jake, who couldn't see individual things in his world, I saw everything. Jake's drawings of forests were green splashes of color. My drawings were of the window I looked out of, the telephone wires running down to the telephone poles on the street, everything, until I grew bored of recording the world and my paper looked like I had scribbled wild circles in meaningless patterns.

Oliver laughed when he pinned the moth wings to the black paper. "You like this one?" he said. I paged through the *Encyclopedia of Moths* to the picture of a similar creature. "I like the twisting tongues of moths. The way they stream in a circle and can unravel, and taste anything," Oliver said.

"Uh huh," I agreed. "This one?"

"A Cheese Ragglanock?" he said.

"Mump Monger," I said.

"No, Snot Guster."

"The Snag Hag?"

"Scaly Wart of Paradise," he said.

Years later, when I was packing out of Dad's house and moving all the things I wanted to keep but would never see again, I found the old book with the names of the world around my house. I found the book with moth names and the crushed balls of ancient moths. I hadn't preserved them and their wings had dried and powdered away. The corpses rolled into tight little balls. The pages of thick construction paper curled back. I threw the catalogue of those midnight expeditions into a black plastic sack and threw the black plastic sack into a dumpster.

The Sergeant's Tea

Eleven

Janet owned her elbows. When she ran, she thrust them out for people to see. She jammed them into people who stumbled her way. A light green sheen coated her elbows and smoothed the slight bumps, moles, and creased folds around the dimples at the joint between her upper and lower arms. If someone actually owned up to their elbows, I suppose, they'd claim everything else.

I apologized for my body as if it wasn't appropriate, as if it was a sweatshirt and jeans in a marble-floored waiting room to a black-tie restaurant. Even though basic training had stripped off pounds of body fat, when I stood my shoulders slumped at an awkward angle. I tried to pull my spine straight. I slumped. I stood straight. I fidgeted.

Janet didn't even apologize for her kneecaps. They didn't have the gnarled, twisted skin and the nodules of fat that hang from almost everyone else's knees. Janet had two knee lobes and a firm layer of fatty muscle on her inside thigh. An indented line ran right inside her gray flannel military shorts. It was strange to me that she didn't apologize for her elbows or her knees or her thighs. On a Snoqualmie playground, any lack of apology equaled vanity. Janet didn't seem vain, just unapologetic. The monkey-bar regulations of a Snoqualmie playground, I guess, didn't apply to everything.

There were pretty females in the unit. Janet wasn't exactly one of them. I heard her voice before I saw her. She often waited for someone to finish jabbering on and then would say something off-the-cuff, posed as a compliment, but at the same time completely undercutting whatever the person had just said. Chavez told a long story about how he got a low price on his stereo from a loser in Houston. "Have you ever been in a fistfight?" Janet asked. When he finished telling a long story about a fistfight, Janet said, "It takes real talent to win a fistfight." Her voice held a slight squawk and when she spoke, it often split. To me her voice sounded like a put-on child voice. Right then, standing in formation, Janet talked to Sandy about the makeup giveaway gift at the mall. I wanted her to run around and ask me something. I stood so that my shadow fell across her leg and shoe, over her neatly rolled socks and dirty running shoes. I tried to pull my spine straight.

In the early morning, soldiers on disciplinary detail swept the courtyard in the middle of the Academy of Health Sciences. They sprayed down the cement plaza and watered the tall plants with brass nozzle hoses. A soldier, his hands covered in latex gloves, waved a metallic wand, pumping the contents from a yellow carton of Miracle-Gro. The tall palms and rubber trees dripped water into the conglomerate pebble planters. Sitting on the lip of one of the wide pots, I felt the thick growth crowd around me as it arched toward the square of pale light. The rising sun fell against the western wall, cool shadows spread up the sides of the courtyard walls.

"Bohm, could you come over here and be a sweetie and talk to me?" Sandy Comstock stood under the tall rubber tree. I could tell from her slight smile as she watched me that she knew I'd been carefully watching Janet. Which in turn meant she'd been carefully watching me. I thought I'd attained some kind of invisibility. If I hadn't, then how many things about myself had I given away? The oily odor of the chemical fertilizer mixed with the water vapor around us. She had long, thin fingers with wrinkled skin bunched around her knuckles. When she talked, she placed her pointer finger along her moving jaw. "So would you like to go with Janet, Rico, and me on a little weekend expedition?"

Comstock kept her car three blocks away because McGrath had caught a trainee stepping out of his GTO. He'd assigned the soldier to a midnight guard-duty shift. The MPs had towed the GTO while the trainee slept at the CQ desk. In the morning, while we stood at formation, McGrath had called out for the trainee. Could you point out your car, soldier? Sergeant, I don't have a car. Private, how right you are. You aren't allowed to have a car until the tenth week. Chavez, march them to class. It was as if the teacher confiscated his second grader's cap gun.

"Chavez and I don't get along," I said. I glanced up into the plants. I thought I saw a large insect scurry into the folds of the trunk. Why did she want me around?

"No. He likes you."

"Chavez said to you, 'I like Aldous Bohm'?"

"It's not like we talk about you. He's never said anything about you or anything. Why do you think we talk about you?" Sandy assumed a mock male manner, speaking deep in the back of her throat. She slapped me on my chest. "Oh, that Bohm is such an asshole, and on and on, and then, yeah, let's invite him on a picnic trip."

"I didn't mean it like that."

"So what about it?"

"It's not like I have something to do," I said.

"Good. I'm glad you can fit us in. Tell me, smart-ass, about Janet."

"What about Janet?"

"I thought so."

"You thought what?"

"Are you new? Don't they make girls out there wherever you're from? Alaska? Oregon? The Klondike? Someplace with Kodiak bears and mountain lions and volcanoes, and all that wild stuff?"

"Washington state."

"Like I said, *wherever*. Where did you go to basic training?"

"Fort Bliss. Am I filling out a résumé?"

"No. You already have the job." She smiled and pushed me on my shoulder. "Janet talks about you."

I didn't say anything. I was supposed to ask, "What does she say about me?" But I didn't say anything.

"I think Janet likes you."

"She *likes* me like Chavez *likes* me?"

"She likes you likes you."

"How could she like me? She doesn't know who I am."

"How come you like her? You don't know who she is."

"I didn't say I liked Janet."

"Okay then, I'll tell her that. I'll tell her you don't like her."

"Don't do that."

"What should I tell her, then?"

"Don't tell her anything."

"What will I tell her when she asks?"

"Is this the third grade? If Janet wants to talk to me, she'll talk to me."

"You're right. This isn't the third grade. You've got it all figured out. So I guess you wouldn't like to do something with me and Chavez and Janet this weekend?"

As she talked to me, I tried to see if she did anything that gave her away. I couldn't figure out why she would even talk to me. I realized then everything she was doing, twisting her hair, not looking me in the eyes or staring directly into my eyes, everything gave her away as a liar. I didn't see why she would lie to me or even what she gained by lying to me.

"Do you know, when I was seven, I had heart surgery." She looked up into the plant and turned around slowly. "I almost died."

"I didn't know that."

"Well, I did. They almost didn't let me into the Army because of it, but I'm only in the reserves, so I guess it didn't matter. Has anything like that ever happened to you?"

"I guess."

"I was in the hospital for a week and the nurse said that if I didn't spend three hours every night quietly reading, I would die. I wanted to watch my programs, but she said that I would have to just sit in the bed and read a book. I read *Treasure Island*. Have you ever read it? I read it to stay alive, but after the first hour of reading I forgot all about why I was sitting in that bed. For all I knew, I was sitting in the bed to read that book. And then they operated and I lived."

"I think I only saw the movie."

"That would make a good movie," she said. "The little girl who has to read to save her life. It would be very poignant." Comstock peered into my eyes.

"I think I've only seen the movie of *Treasure Island*."

"Would you like to see the scar? It's still really ugly. Chavez says I should have it sanded, but I like it." Comstock unbuttoned the front of her khakis and pulled the avocado-colored Army-issue down. She wore a purple bra, and the scar ran along the edge of her breast, then curled down into the shadows under her shirt. I stared at the soft curve of her breasts.

"That's some scar," I said.

She buttoned up her BDUs. "I almost died. But then I got better because of Jim and Long John Silver."

She looked away from me for a moment. Her eyelashes hung over her pupils and her face relaxed and I thought she had turned off the internal motors that modulated her facial expressions; she was just a person with a plain face for that second, blankly staring into her thoughts.

"Why are you two hiding in the bushes?" Janet said. She sat next to me. "Is Sandy showing you her scar?"

"No," Comstock said. "I was just asking Aldous if he'd like to go with us this weekend."

The machinery in Comstock's face worked again. I didn't understand what she had been talking to me about. I didn't know if she'd been serious about *Treasure Island* or if she was just performing in order to find something out about Janet.

"And he said he'd be delighted to come with us, didn't you, Aldous?"

"Sure," I said again.

"You know, it's against the rules to go off-base. It's breaking a direct order. You could get an Article Fifteen. Are you up for that?"

"I am. I am up for that."

Early Saturday morning, before my roommates woke, I slipped down the hallways and out into the empty lot. McGrath walked across the parking lot and he stopped when he saw me standing in the breezeway. "Good morning to see the city, don't you think? Private?"

"I was on my way to breakfast; just on my way to eat."

"I like to see that, a private with enough fire to get up and grab the day by the tail."

"I was thinking about going to the library and typing a letter to my Mom. She has bad eyesight and my handwriting is so bad."

"Get running, Bohm, before you piss me off. And Bohm, we all know the library doesn't open until ten thirty. Mistake one. Do not ever volunteer information."

Sandy passed a corroded VW bus driven by a dreadlocked white guy wearing a white cowboy hat. Layers of bumper stickers covered the back of the bus: *Mondale, Meat Is Murder, US Out of El Salvador.*

"Is that a genuine hippie?" Chavez asked in a thick, cowboy drawl. "Or one of them ranch hands? Very confusing to me. Cowboys herd cattle to slaughter and hippies don't eat meat, so how could it be a hippie-cowboy?"

Janet landed into a hippie routine. She pronounced *man* with three syllables. Instead of man, she said ma-ay-an; the second syllable climbed up into her nose. Sandy tried to join in, but she said man flat and simple like she was talking about someone who was male. Chavez and Janet rolled their eyes.

"We are on our way to peace and the promised land, man!" Chavez said.

"What are you, an Okie?" Janet asked.

"Straight out of the dust bowl of the soul," Chavez said. "I remember back in sixty-seven I was living on the commune, man. When I had a heavy vision. I was cooking some toast and I think I snorted some bread mold."

"Toast is toasted," Sandy said.

"Stuck in a straight world, man. When I toast, toast, I cook my toast."

"We cook meat. We bake pastries. We toast toast."

"I cook. I bake. I toast, man," Chavez said.

"Sometimes, I wake up and walk outside and look around at all the little hills around us and I begin to believe that the whole world is as flat as this, that the entire world just rolls on and on and on. I grew up in Boulder, Colorado, and always the world just ended a little ways away. And now, I look around me, and it just goes on and on. Don't you think that's a little scary?"

"Yeah right, Sandy. Now Aldous, don't you think these two ladies are hot?" Chavez turned around to look at Janet and then winked at me.

I didn't say anything. But Janet jammed her pointer finger into the soft flesh under my ribs. "Go ahead and answer the gentleman." She sat against the back window. Her backpack lay between us on the bench seat.

"I don't know." I said. I cleared my throat and looked out the window at the passing suburbs. "So we're going to see something other than San Antonio?"

"We are going a long way from San Antonio. You'll like the place we're going."

Comstock drove on the freeway, zipping past cars, and Chavez kept a volley of Depeche Mode tapes circulating through the deck. I felt more and more distant riding in the car, because Chavez talked about someone named Rafael, a friend Comstock and he had in common, and how at a club one time Rafael had split open his pants, right on the dance floor. "You know how it is, you lean back to bust a move. This dude throws himself back and he's got these Levis on so tight you can see his snake."

"Oh gross," Comstock said.

"And then his crotch splits open and you can see his underwear. Lucky he wore his underwear, or he'd have flashed all the ladies."

"You know he asked me out last summer, right before I was getting shipped to basic? He knew I was leaving so he asks me out," Sandy said.

"A little of that departure-date soldier action," Chavez said.

"Slight rewind," Janet said, "Did you say 'Lucky he wore his underwear?' Do I sense a common male practice here?"

"Naw," Chavez said. "I get cheesy if I don't have on a pair of boxers."

Janet looked at me.

"What?" I said. "I put on my underwear this morning." I unzipped my fly and showed her the fabric. I wore my khaki, Army-issue briefs.

"Oh, excellent, a demonstration," Janet said. "Here's a boy who wears his Army issue under his normal clothes."

"How can you do that?" Chavez asked. "They itch. And you spend all the time that you're in civilian clothes really in secret military uniform. Everyone else is naked under their clothes. Bohm is really in uniform under his clothes. You can take the uniform off him; you can take the Levis off him. You can take every article of clothing off him, but you can't take the uniform out of him. Born green, dude."

The car bumped over the rough freeway. Around us, the last of the suburbs of San Antonio fell away to a sparse forest. The clouds rose in tall pillars on the horizon, providing the only break in the countryside. I imagined that the early settlers of the plains had nothing to look at except the sky until they began to learn the minute variations in the land. Everything seemed uniform on first examination and then, the longer I learned it, the more variations it picked up. Oliver had once told me about an ancient tribe that tortured criminals by making them face a flat rock surface. They tied them to a plank of wood and left them staring at the wall in order to turn their brains back on themselves. Supposedly, the agony of looking at a uniform plane without any contrast to latch their attention on turned their thoughts back on themselves like a malfunctioning robot. Dad often punished Jake and me by turning our heads into the corner of the kitchen. I would stare into the monotonous pea-green wallpaper for hours, but the longer I stared, the more familiar and intimate the surface became, until each square inch revealed the flaky membrane of a mosquito wing left from one of Oliver's killing sprees or a long thread of spiderweb or the buckle in the long seam between two strips of paper.

A thin wall separated what was going through my head and the vocals of Martin Gore. No one spoke. We were in the silent part of traveling where everyone drifted. The passengers fell in and out of sleep. The driver lulled in the steady rhythm of the yellow line. Janet stared out the window. I lay my hand on her backpack, feeling the wide nylon weave. I felt the shapes inside, a loose lumpy bulk I thought was a towel, an angular book, and more things, hard edges and squashy masses. The road had started to climb now into sparse trees. We stopped at a grocery store in a small town in the mountains. Around the town, the mountain ridges held fresh snow. Chavez sat on the hood of the car, smoking his Camels, while we bought food for a picnic.

"Smoke?"

"I don't."

"So you getting along well with Sandy? She sure is a trip."

"She's okay."

"So have you?"

"What?"

"Hooked up?" Chavez dropped his cigarette on the ground. He cupped another one under his hand and snapped a match. "Come on, tell me."

"What do you want to know?"

"Whatever, dude. I mean, she seems like a freak to me."

"Like a what?"

"You're a good little boy, aren't you, Bohm? I'm not Mr. Suave, you know. I understand how it is for guys like you. But, guy, this is AIT. Things are easier here. A girl like Janet wouldn't look at me twice in Houston. I wouldn't even bother with her. I mean she's alright and all that. Few hos get through basic training without at least looking fit. That's all that is pretty much required, isn't it? A college girl like Wahl, this is the best she's ever going to look. She knows it. Four years from now she'll be used to a completely different class of male. Someone who can talk and who's going to get a really great job and doesn't give a rat's ass about his own ass. Right at this moment, she's got to learn some things. I'm happy to teach. She doesn't care about any of this. Now for you, Sandy is excellent starter material. Take it from me, you can't go wrong with Sandy. She is a completely sufficient slab of ass."

I wasn't sure I heard Chavez correctly. As he talked he glanced at me to check if I nodded or smiled, and I just did because that was what he checked me for. Mostly he held a glassy-eyed stare toward the horizon as he talked. When he paused to take a breath his tongue came out and licked a spot on his lower lip. I wondered if he spoke in some kind of code I didn't comprehend. I couldn't ask him, what in hell are you talking about? He'd know I didn't understand and he wouldn't tell me anything else.

Janet and Comstock came out of the store with a bag of groceries. Janet smiled at me. "So, you two boys getting along?"

"Sure," Chavez said. "Aldous here's been telling me about his sex life."

"The torrid affair of Private Bohm's sex life," Janet said. "Let me guess. Cheap motel hookers along the strip and the shocking revelation of his fascination with white nylon underpants?"

"What? Why did you say that?"

"Nailed," Janet said.

Comstock, Chavez, and Janet laughed as they fastened their seat belts. I stumbled into the backseat. They started talking about a volleyball game they had played Friday and how they used to spend summers inner-tubing and how good it was because you'd get drunk and float along in the cold water in the burning afternoon; you could go to the bank and puke and then you were back out in all of that water. "Dude, it's been a long time since I did that," Chavez said. "How about you, Bohm?"

"I've never done that."

"You must not have rivers out there. When I was in Germany, they had rivers, real, old rivers." I smiled as he started to talk about the Danube. "Texas definitely doesn't have anything like that."

We turned off the highway and drove for a while along a narrow road that circled through the steep gullies and ridgetops. Finally, we came to a roadside park that overlooked a waterfall and bluff. To get to the best place on the bluff, we had to climb over an ancient barbed wire fence. Chavez jumped over it and I stepped gingerly on the wire and helped Janet and Comstock. "Such a gentleman," Comstock said. "I could never have managed."

Sitting on the bluff, eating lunch, Chavez and Comstock and Janet talked about the Army and Texas. I tried to make a few jokes. I asked about the Center for Texan Culture, the institute across the street from the Alamo, but Chavez shook his head. "Dude, there isn't anything like that." And then, "Dude, whatever."

After lunch, Comstock and Chavez said they wanted to go swimming. They went down the hill to swim in the stream. The creek trickled through steep cliffs, but the slopes of tall grass and gnarled trees made it easy to get down to the gravel bank. Comstock and Janet stripped their clothes off. I looked away.

"What is your problem?" Chavez said to me. "Your problem is that you're from an uptight background, isn't it, Bohm? Your daddy got home at five thirty, on the dot. He wore a hat and when he came home, he took off his jacket, hung his hat on a hook near the front door, and loosened, but did not take that tie off. He kissed your momma on her cheek. Everyone sat down and ate meatloaf and string beans and glasses of milk. 'How was your day, son?' your daddy would ask you at dinner."

"I can't help it if my house was like the majority of American homes," I said. "What can I do?" At any moment I thought they would be able to see this wasn't true. I would do something to mess it up.

"The majority of American homes? You sound like a census taker." Chavez pinched his voice and forced the sound through his nose. "Bohm, your cheeks are so tightly clenched, you use dental floss to wipe your ass."

I stripped and dove into the water, to keep myself busy but also to avoid being seen naked. The cool water gushed around me and then I was at the stony bottom, thrusting my hands against the rock. The gravel bit and chewed my hands and it felt good. I stood up in the marshy reeds on the other side of the rapids. The muck suspended my feet in mushy dirt almost as fluid as the river.

Chavez swam past me. "Now you can raise your naked chick sightings by two." He drifted downstream.

Chavez and Janet laughed and over the rush of water

and the ring of the stream in my ears their voices sounded muffled. I ran my index finger over my ear trying to pop out the water, and I swallowed, but everything sounded far downstream.

Chavez climbed out of the river onto a gigantic rock slab. He smiled at the sky. "Dude, this is the fucking life!" He jumped and yelled headfirst into the rapids. I swam out into the rapids and held onto the underwater rock face. Through the clear, faintly yellow water, the shadowy bodies of Janet, Comstock, and Chavez played tag. Janet had a faint farmer's tan from basic training, and her breasts in the water didn't look any different from a boy's chest. Chavez climbed up past me onto the rock. "What are you doing?"

"Soaking up the sun," I said.

"Then you need to get out of the freezing-ass water," Chavez said. He dove into the river and through the cloud of bubbles he sent up, he grabbed Janet's foot. She grabbed his foot and they struggled around in circles until they ended up in the shallows. Chavez broke out of the water and ran up onto the back. Janet followed him. Water ran down her shoulders from her hair and dripped from the tips of her breasts. "You almost drowned me."

"Why aren't you coming out?" Janet asked me.

"I will in a minute."

"Are you being a perve?" She dove into the water. When she surfaced beside me a slick arm brushed my leg. I back-paddled out into the middle of the river.

Janet wiped the water off her face and looked for me. "Where are you going? Why don't you come out of the water?"

"I'll come out in a minute," I said.

She swam toward me. "I'll pull you out."

"In a minute."

"Were you looking at our naked bodies?"

"No."

"Do you have a problem with naked people?"

I stood in the mucky far shore. She came up out of the water next to me. "Where's the ground?"

"It's mud," I said.

She stood up next to me. I could feel her warm breath. The faint peach fuzz on her face lay flattened by the river water. She smiled. "Well, well," she said. "I've got you now, perve."

"We're going to leave your naked asses in the river," Chavez yelled.

"We have to go," Janet said. "Daddy's calling."

We hurried back after swimming and no one said anything. We listened to songs on the radio, songs broken by an announcer in Houston and then the San Antonio station. "We've got to hurry," Chavez said. "I don't want to be late."

"Late for what?"

"Can we drop you off at the gate?" Chavez asked.

"Sure," I said. "Aren't you guys going to go back to the barracks?"

"Later," Chavez said. "We'll come back when we have to." They dropped me off at the gate and the MP stepped out of the gatehouse. I watched the Escort drive down to the intersection, signal left and turn right.

Twelve

The following Friday, I ran into Janet in the breezeway even though I knew she was supposed to be gone already with Chavez and Sandy, but there she was. As she edged past me, I grazed the front of her shin with the tip of my tennis shoe. My shoes had once been white and now looked tan on first glance and on second looked green in places. I should have thrown them out. I brushed the tip of these shoes against Janet's shin. She wore dark tights, a pleated navy blue dress, and regulation French braids. Tiny hairs fell behind her ears, down onto the sloping muscle curving from the back of her neck into her shoulder blades.

"Ouch," she said. By the time she spoke I had jumped down the stairs to the walkway bordered by the short, neatly edged grass. Water sprinkler sockets sprayed arcs of mist. The area around the cinder block barracks was damp and cool and sparkling with red-yellow-blue drops. The moat of damp grass kept everyone either in the breezeway or out in the parking lot. I turned around, feeling the water dampen my discolored tennis shoes. Drops clung to the thick black hair growing on my shins. While I hadn't been a runner before training, by the time I got to Fort Sam, I needed to run. I slipped into the click and clatter of motion. If I didn't move, I thought about Snoqualmie.

Janet wore tiny silver earrings. They matched the tiny veins of silver in her blue dress. The dress had a texture like a crumpled bag. When she turned to speak to me, I looked at her earrings and she smiled.

"Excuse me," I said. "I'm sorry." I stood now at the bottom of the stairs down on the walkway surrounded by the fizzing sprinklers.

"Where are you going?" Janet asked.

"I'm going running."

"I can see that. Where are you running?"

"What are you doing?"

"I was going to go out, but the car left already," she said. "I took too long getting ready."

"Sandy and Chavez left you behind?"

"Yeah."

"I'm sorry," I said.

"No need to be sorry for me. I take too long."

By this time my socks were soaked. "Hey," I said as if this had just occurred to me, "you can go with me."

"I'm not going running."

"We can do something else," I said. "What would you like to do?"

"Take me to dinner."

"I'll have to change."

"Yeah, you will," she said. "And buy some new shoes."

I took a shower and was convinced that she would leave without me. I dressed and showered and then ironed the new clothes I'd picked up from the PX. I'd bought a pair of stonewashed denim jeans, tight-fitting around my waist, that flared like circus strongman pants around my thighs. I had a thin snakeskin belt with a bright silver buckle. I wore a black turtleneck, a vest, and tasseled deck shoes.

My shoes didn't have traction. I took long sliding steps on the linoleum. I rushed, slid, and rushed because I thought Janet had already gone. But Jason Viscount sat in the breeze-way. "Nice duds," he said. He wore his BDUs, a crease running over his knees and down into his polished boots. He nodded his head and grinned as he looked at my clothes. "My father says you can tell the caliber of a man by his shoes."

"Viscount, do you even own a pair of civilian shoes?"

"I'm not going to buy any clothes now that they've given me all of these clothes. Anyway, I don't know what I want to wear yet. I don't want to wear what I wore to basic training. That was who I was then. I don't want to wear what they have in the PX. That's not who I am now."

"What do you do when you go off-base?"

"Off-base. What's out there?"

"There's an entire city out there."

"San Antonio. Big-time city," he said. "Where are you going, all gussied up?"

I didn't want to tell him. Maybe it would be bragging to tell him because I was going out with a girl. Maybe he'd take a look at Janet and think, Well, there he is going out with a whatever-he-thought-Janet-was, and it hadn't occurred to me before that people would see me in relation to how they saw Janet. I didn't know how they saw her. Janet came out of the barracks with a freshly applied layer of makeup. She smiled at me. I stood away from Viscount and didn't say anything to him. "Are you going to call a cab?"

I told the dispatcher the intersection and he cleared his throat. "Private, it's a five-dollar minimum tip from that location to anywhere. When that cab comes, you have five dollars in cash ready or it isn't going anywhere. If you aren't there when the cab comes, we'll call the MPs." When the cab arrived, I opened the door for Janet. The interior was warm and smelled faintly like cigar smoke and salt and vinegar potato chips. The driver said, "How are y'all doing tonight?" He flicked the meter and it began to unreel. Salsa came from the stereo. The driver looked at us through the rearview mirror and said, "The dispatcher told you a ten-dollar minimum tip for a downtown trip?"

Janet sat forward then and whispered to me, "We

should just run for it when we get to a stoplight downtown. Ten dollars." She sat with her hands folded and her
fingers intertwined. She looked out the window at the
dusky skyline and the suburban yards lit by the streetlights.
I sat with my hands open on my knees so that any sweat
that came out on my palms would evaporate. I cleared my
throat and Janet glanced at me and smiled.

The cab idled at a stoplight. The black light box swung
from a line strung over the middle of the street. The humid
air down by the river simmered on the asphalt. The hot air
spun up in long, rolling waves, rippling the pocked cross-
walk markings. "We should just hop out now," I said to
Janet. "This is highway robbery."

Janet opened her door, letting in the thick, musty heat.
"I didn't actually—"

The cabbie flicked the locks, and all of the doors, even
the one swinging out into the oncoming traffic, clacked
locked. I tried to grab Janet and pull her back into the cab.
"He's trying to lock us in," she said.

"The fare?" the cabbie asked.

She pulled me and we fell through the heat onto the
yellow line between the cab and the oncoming traffic.

"Look both ways," I said.

We ran across the empty lanes as the light changed from
red to green. "What did you say?" Janet asked me. The

truck behind the cab honked its horn and the cab driver yelled but we couldn't hear what he was saying. "I should've left something," I said. Janet ran ahead of me. Men in suit jackets and bolo ties and boots escorted women in dresses. Fleshy necks stuffed the sidewalks. They had graying hair and beaten leathery skin. Older couples stood on the bridge looking down at the dark, trickling flow of the San Antonio River. Janet and I scurried through them, down into the humid canyon where the river flowed; it was much hotter down along the river than up on the street. Candles burned in sconces on the buildings. Women fanned themselves with conference brochures. Janet ducked into a garden store full of wooden, hand-carved painted figures, cowboys with long faces and handlebar mustaches, Mexicans with bandoliers and sombreros, mules carrying bags under a rope net, and a gigantic Daniel Boone towering over the cash register. We stood under the sole fan, dripping and wheezing.

"Next time, I call for the cab," she said.

I listened to Janet's breathing in the heat. She took in a deep breath and her shoulders rocked forward and she leaned forward as she breathed out. "What am I doing?" she asked me when she saw me watching her.

"You're breathing funny," I said.

"I'm just breathing," she said. "The air feels good in my chest if I breathe it all in. You should try it."

I leaned forward and tried to breathe and she put her

hands on my back and chest and leaned close enough to me that I could smell the coconut odor of her shampoo. "Come on. Breathe in. Don't stop. Keep drawing in the air." Her hands kneaded my chest as I drew air in, and then once I had it, I kept it in because I didn't want her to take her fingers back. "Let out your breath," she said. I let it out. "See, much better."

"I heard about a place where we can get drinks," she said.

"I don't know about—"

"—they don't card anyone."

The fan wasn't working. My face was getting redder and thick, salty drops rolled off my eyebrows. We found a place under the shade of willow on a cement bench overlooking the river. Above us, we could see the last of the day, the cloudless distant blue sky. Late afternoon light glanced off the office towers' glass and chrome edges. It was too hot for most people. The Riverwalk was empty. Janet and I sat until we stopped sweating and started to dry and the sun went down. At dusk, people began to come down from the street to walk along the river.

"Don't you feel different here than at home?" Janet asked me.

"How do you mean?" I did feel different. I felt more like everyone else, even though that was beginning to wear off. I was pretty sure that Janet meant something else.

"I thought I might feel like an adult after basic training—that going to basic training would make me a woman," Janet said. "When I was in basic I sure thought that. I thought as soon as I got out, nobody would mistake me for a girl. Nobody'd even bother telling me I wasn't old enough to know what I wanted to do. But I'm still pretty much a kid. We're not old enough to just order a drink or rent a car. I even get carded trying to go to the movies. In a way, it's sort of a perfect place to be because I don't have to do anything. It's just temporary, us being here, and I like that, no sense of consequence. I wish everything could always be temporary. If you like it you can do it again, and if you don't like it, you can just wait until it changes."

"Don't you worry that something you just thought would be fun," I asked, "might end up being permanent? Like what if when you jumped out of the cab, you got hit by a car?"

"You said," she began to laugh, " 'look both ways.' I did. How could I get hit, if I have you looking after me? You didn't want me to get hit."

"Of course I didn't want you to get hit."

"You're looking out for me."

"Are you sure you want to go to this place and try to get drinks?"

"You're having one too. I'll look out for you."

———

"Good evening? Can I start you two off with anything from the bar?" the waiter asked us without so much as appearing to appraise our ages.

"Gin and tonic," Janet said.

"I'll have a beer," I said.

"What kind?"

"He'll have a Corona with lime," Janet said.

"I'll have a Corona," I said.

We'd found a table on the patio of the place Janet had mentioned, an Italian restaurant. I wiped the sweat from my face with the paper napkin on the table. They crumbled a little, leaving a white fuzz in my stubble. We sat there for a while, watching the crowd walk past the patio. A busboy placed two water glasses down and then poured the water. I drank my glass of water.

"Where are you from?" I asked.

"It really doesn't matter where anyone is from."

"I'd like to know."

The waiter came back with our drinks and hurried on to another table. Janet took a sip and then said, "Holy moley, this is strong. I found my new home away from home." She took another drink and then crushed a chunk of ice in her teeth. "Everyone is from someplace," Janet said, "and I'm really not into talking about where you're from or your family or anything about you really, if that's all right with you. I'm homesick enough without talking about it, without dwelling on it. I like being here drinking my gin and tonic with you."

"What are you going to do when you leave?" I asked.

"I don't have the faintest idea," she said.

Janet had long eyelashes, a slope of wrinkles under her eyelids, tan skin, and brown moles. Her hair was thin and straight and she had it tucked behind one ear and the other side fell freely. She had on coral-colored lipstick, slightly the wrong color for her skin. I didn't know what to say to her. She wouldn't let me talk to her about her past or my past. I didn't know about anything else.

We read the menus and when the waiter came back, she ordered fettuccini, which is what I wanted to order, so I ordered spaghetti. When I looked up, I realized she was looking at me, and I brushed my face and wanted to ask what she was looking at. She smiled at me.

"I'm from Seattle," I said. "Well, not really from Seattle, a little town—"

"Let's not talk about that," she said.

"I'm going to Germany—"

"I don't want to know where you're going," she said. "I didn't get carded," she said. "I care about that. You've got nice legs. I care about that, otherwise what is there? This is all over in four months."

When we finished eating, she asked me, "What do you want to do now?" She looked as if she expected me to say something and I didn't know what and then she looked at me like, "Well?" and when I still didn't know what she wanted from me, she said, "Get a cab, I know where a party is going on. There'll be beer. You can get drunk."

The cab was dark except for the glow of the console and silent except for the whir of the air conditioner and the tires on the pavement. The driver didn't say anything to us as he drove from the middle of town crowded with people out toward the Loop. Janet smiled at me and moved closer to me and then lay her head on my shoulder. I didn't put my hand on her shoulder, although I wanted to lean into her. I wanted to ask her what I should do. But then she might realize how I was taking this and then she would return to looking out the window. I didn't want her to move. I didn't want to jeopardize anything by moving myself. I also didn't want to arrive at the Super 8 where the party was going on. I looked at our reflection in the cab glass, just her lying against my shoulder and the streetlights going past, slow from a distance and then moving more rapidly down the side of the glass and finally racing down to the very edge.

The cab left us on the curb in front of the Super 8 parking lot. A gigantic mud puddle covered one end of the lot and the rest was full of cars. "Shall we go in?" Janet asked me. A cold breeze ran down the highway and over the mud puddle, sending silver ripples over the surface, and then moving air went through Janet's hair.

I should have said something suave like, "Yeah, we should go in. I'll get a room." But instead I shrugged and followed Janet around the edge of the mud puddle and up the back steps. We found a fire escape door propped open with a crushed beer can. I followed her down the silent hallway. Our feet made a whirring noise on the carpet and the fluorescent lights buzzed and then we went up another flight of stairs. Outside on a balcony there was street noise, cars on the pavement, a distant honking horn, and then back into the quiet, warm hallway. She stopped suddenly in front of a door and then turned around and went back to the first door in the hallway. I could hear a faint dance bass beat and the floor vibrated a little, not even enough that I noticed on the first time down the hallway, but feeling it now it seemed pretty clear something was going on behind the door. Janet knocked three times and paused and knocked three more times. The door opened. Cigarette smoke, dance music, and the babble of a hundred people kissing and dancing and singing and trying to talk between all of the other noise blasted out into the hallway. The door closed behind us and we were in a hallway stuffed with sweating bodies, people I recognized and many I didn't. I followed Janet through the kitchen, the sink stuffed with ice and gold tin cans, the counters covered with empty cans and bottles and a few taller clear vodka and gin bottles. Janet disappeared into the living room where people danced and the floor felt as if it was waving and shaking and I rotated and flung myself through them. I found myself on a balcony with Viscount and Sandy. She frowned when she saw me. "Where have you been? Did you just get here? Did you come with Janet or did she come here by herself? Viscount said you went with her. Is that true?" Sandy kept fussing with her strap and then she told Viscount that she wanted to get out of the military somehow, that she couldn't stand it anymore, that maybe if she joined a religious cult they would be able to get her out of the military. "What do you think?"

"I thought you're only in the reserves," I said. "Don't worry about it."

"I know I'm only in the reserves," she said. "But the thing is I think it's weird how my parents spent all of this time and money on me and now when I get home I'll have to get a job. What do you think I'm qualified to do?"

"You can do anything you set your heart to," Viscount said.

"Are you serious?"

"Just put mind to matter," he said.

"This is serious stuff," Sandy said. "Don't spout that cracked bullshit."

"What do you think I should do, Aldous? Do you think I could get a job as a pharmacist? My mother thinks this training will lead to something like that. But I wonder. Can you picture me in a white lab coat working at the Fred Meyer or in the mall at some drugstore and I'll have a brown paper bag lunch and sit on the bench outside near the fountain just like I did when I worked at Radio Shack. *That* was a horrible job."

Chavez appeared out of the people and clouds of smoke and socked me in the shoulder. "Who invited you, man? Who told you about the party?" He turned around and looked around the room. "I don't see any of your friends here." He turned back. "Oh, you don't have any friends."

"I came with—"

"Just kidding, man, you're welcome. Come on, let's party." He grabbed me by the back of the neck and stepped into the closet by the door and took a brass pipe out of his pocket. "We're going to smoke us a little bowl, you and me." He produced a baggie with cracked leaves, stray tiny seeds, and stems. He pulled out a pinch of it and stuffed it into the pipe bowl with his thumb. He handed it to me and gave me the lighter. "You do know what to do, don't you?" he asked me in the closet as I just held it all, and I said, "I think so," and then he showed me by miming and I put it up to my lips and drew air into the pipe and lit the wad of dope and it flamed and then turned red and sparking and a dense cloud of smoke flushed into my mouth and seared my lungs and I tried not to cough. I grunted it down into my stomach and Chavez smiled at me and took the burning embers and sucked the smoke in himself and I started to burn and cough and he said, "We are all on the same sheet of music now."

Chavez's friend Taylor stuffed himself into the closet. He leaned down and pushed us back against the wall. "Dude, you need to watch where you are going."

"I saw you duck in here. I need another hit." When he had the pipe in his hand he looked at Chavez and then saw me crammed into the very back of the closet. "Oh shit, it's the snitch."

"He's a little bit stoned right now," Chavez said. "So watch the paranoia."

"No shit?"

"That's the shit."

Taylor sucked in a lungful and then held the pipe out and grunted and coughed and he handed the pipe along to Chavez who took another hit and then offered it to me and thought better of it.

"I am so fucking horny, dude. I am dry, man. My dick is cracked and thirsty like the motherfucking Sahara desert. You know that girl?" Taylor asked.

"What girl?"

"She said, dude, that I could go fuck myself. She said she could swallow five guys like me. She said I can swallow a room of limp dick assholes like you. What does that mean?"

"What girl?"

"Comstock."

"Sandy?"

"Yeah, Sandy."

"She's crazy. You just leave that shit alone."

"Dude," Taylor said. "If something doesn't turn up, a man has got to do what a man has got to do."

Chavez turned and looked at me. "You all right, little buddy?"

I nodded, and he and Taylor left me in the closet. I listened to the music outside and the people laughing and something crashing. There was something oddly familiar about the sensation, and I thought how odd it was that I had avoided taking a toke or even really taking a drink all of the years I'd been in my father's house. It had been right there under the coffee table in his tin drink tray and I could've just helped myself, but it had seemed like his thing and not something I would ever want to try. I lost the sense of sound for a second, but then it came back. I looked out the thin crack of the closet door at the bodies moving up and down the hallway, their shadows falling against the white closet wall, and I didn't want to move, but gradually the intense throbbing feeling began to disappear and I sort of liked the absorption of the ghostly floating feeling it gave to my body, and then I slipped out through the crowd of people in the hallway. People smiled at me. I tried to find Janet.

I opened the door to the next suite. The music came through the wall. In this room couples sat on the bed, kissing, and I almost laughed because this was a make-out room. I had only heard about make-out rooms. I made it to the balcony and looked back into the room. There was Janet kissing Chavez. I didn't see Sandy. I said, "Sorry." The hallway was quiet, and I thought about the activity going on behind the other doors, really there was no way of knowing what all of the activity was going on behind those doors. How had this happened? Janet had her head tilted at a slight angle and her jaw moved slightly and her eyelashes lay on the smooth under-rim of her eye. She hadn't opened her eyes but had turned with Chavez. I could see the back of his neck. He had a boil, a slick spot of skin in the black hairs at the nape of his neck. Janet's ragged fingernails pressed into his neck skin. I didn't know what to think. I didn't have any full-blown plan so much as an idea that if I'd stayed with Janet, I'd have her fingers on my neck right then. I also had the idea that maybe she'd come here with the plan of finding Chavez and that any interest she might have had in me had been tossed at dinner. And anyway I looked at it, really I just wanted to pull Chavez away from her.

In the hallway Sandy spilled the beer on me. She had cans in both hands. She took a three-swallow drink from one can and then shook it and took another drink and then dropped it and held her pointer finger at the ceiling and then said to me, "You look lost."

"I'm trying to find—"

"—do you want to get out of here?"

She handed me the other can. "Yes," I said.

"The door's right over there," she said. "Will you open that can for me?"

I opened the can for her and she took it back and then handed it back to me. "You can have a drink. That's rude of me to make you do all of the work and then not let you have a drink."

"I'm not thirsty."

"Not thirsty. Everyone is thirsty. Look around you," she said. "Everyone is drinking."

I tried to push past her and then she pushed up against me and sloshed some beer on me. "Hold me," she said.

"You've had a lot to drink," I said.

"Get over Janet," Sandy said. "I don't even know why you like her." She took a drink. "Why don't you and I go someplace? You can forget about Janet. She isn't for you."

"Sandy, you should go home," I said.

"I can't go home. Home is Houston. Will you take me to Houston?"

"I don't drive," I said. I took her beer. "I don't think you need another one of these."

"That's mine."

I pushed through a crowd of dancers and then stood in the hallway. I looked around, and when I looked back into the living room, I saw Taylor handing a Corona to Sandy. She lay against the wall and brushed her hair out of her face. I thought I should go back and grab her and take her out of the party, and I looked around and everyone had hooded eyes and seemed sleepy even though they danced and talked and laughed and they all deserved to be together.

I drank her beer and then in the bathroom grabbed two more and drank those. Everyone had two beers in their hands and drank and danced and talked and I pushed through the bodies. The TV was on in one of the bedrooms and everyone watched it. But the TV didn't make sense; it sort of rolled along but didn't make sense. The colors moved and flickered. The horizontal moved out of the TV. The blue light fell against people's faces. I walked down the stairs and passed a couple of men wearing blue jackets with yellow patches sewn onto the balls of their shoulders. They carried short, heavy yellow sticks and at the top of the stairwell stopped to look at me. I wanted to ask them, "What are you looking at? I'm not even here."

"Yes?"

"Did you come down from upstairs?"

"No. I'm from room 212."

"Do you have your key?" They stopped on the stairs.

"My wife has it," I said. And then a crash came from upstairs and they jumped up the stairs.

Viscount came down the back stairs and said, "Party pooper. Everyone's going to get busted." We walked across the parking lot. The sprinklers ran and left the pavement slick and black with puddles. Unraveling cigarette butts floated in the water. A black-and-white painted Jeep and a Caprice Classic police cruiser pulled through the puddle, splashing water. We turned to walk the other way, but they shined their floodlight on us. I kept walking to get out of the puddle. I climbed onto a cement garden wall.

"You punks stop right there."

"We were just going to catch a cab," Viscount said.

"Did you just come out of that Super 8?"

"We did not," Viscount said. "We came from the Days Inn where my mother is staying and now we are going to that pay phone—" he pointed at the pay phone, "—to catch a cab." He started to walk.

"I'm going to give you a direct order, soldier. Attention."

"I don't have to follow orders from some rent-a-cop," Viscount said.

"Soldier, as an officer, I hold an E-5. I can tell from your damn raw attitude that I seriously outrank you. Do you want to challenge my authority? Attention."

I resisted the urge to jump to attention.

"What base are you from?"

"We don't have to answer that. We are on our way home."

"You have to answer that. I'll take the two of you downtown right now if you don't listen to what I have to say. If you don't listen, I'll arrest the two of you."

I could only see the light of the flashlights just around us and then the streetlights. Then cabs started to arrive and I could see that the party was moving on around us and the police didn't seem that interested. They seemed as if they really believed they had caught the people they were looking for.

They had us turn around, and I saw Sandy and Chavez and Taylor and some other people hop into a cab and disappear.

They searched us and said it might be a good idea to just take us downtown and drug test us just to be careful, but that they'd called a cab and would see that we got back to base safely.

A cab arrived and we got in and rode the long way back to the base. The police car followed us and when we got to the base, the police car veered away.

We paid for the cab and I went into the empty barracks and lay down in bed and looked at the cinder block walls and finally fell asleep. When I woke I had a gigantic headache and I went to breakfast and it was fairly empty. My two roommates snored in their beds.

Thirteen

Saturday morning nobody made any noise. No one scuffed the waxed linoleum. The washing machines sat empty. The bored night CQ had even folded someone's clothes and covered them with their olive laundry bag. At lunch, the trainees slowly walked to the mess hall in small groups, talking in modulated, soft tones. They ate egg burritos and drank tomato juice. They said, "Man, why do you have to make all that noise eating?" They hurried back to the barracks, waving the bright sunlight out of their eyes. In the evening, after I returned from the library, just about everybody slowly trickled off-base. There wasn't any talk of any party, just movie times and restaurant menus.

On Sunday, Chavez played volleyball in the sandy field between the barracks. He drank a fluorescent sports drink. Everything had returned somewhat to normal. Everyone returned to their normal places. Except no one had seen

Sandy after the Friday night party. She didn't report for Monday morning muster. McGrath checked his watch. "Makeup is not part of the uniform, PFC Wahl."

"Yes, Sergeant."

"Go pull PFC Comstock out into the light."

"I don't think she came back after the weekend," Janet said.

"Has anyone seen her?" McGrath called out. I thought she might be sick, or maybe she'd gone to Houston. It also didn't really matter to me, because Sandy had fed me the lines about Janet liking me when it was clear that Janet liked Chavez and unclear to me what Sandy wanted with me. Whatever I had thought I felt about Janet was maybe just a matter of her having paid any attention to me at all in the first place. It didn't matter now. No one said anything. McGrath called us to attention and marched us to class.

Monday night, I went to read in the courtyard in the Academy of Health Sciences. After a day of classes, nobody went back to the school complex. I had the entire place to myself, except for a few instructors finishing up class work. Finally they left as well, hurrying out with their graded papers and garrison caps over their scalps.

Eight giant cement planters held seven giant rubber trees. Ferns and dangling vines hung out of them. They circled a fountain that sprayed over an elaborate abstract copper sculpture of mixed planes, pools, sloped cascades, and interlocked waterfalls. The noise of the gurgling water and flung streams sounded like a Cascade Mountain creek coming down through a granite gully, cedar trunks, patches of moss, and clear-cut tangles. The fountain kicked up a slight mist, keeping the air cool. As I tried to read, I ran the same loops about Adrian's death. Hiking with Dad once in the spring, we left early in the morning, early enough that the dew hadn't dried from the ferns and salmonberries. The undersides of their silver leaves were slick with water. First the front of my thighs became soaked and then the back of my legs and finally my clothes slicked to my body. I hurried to keep up with Dad. The bushes felt freezing and then suddenly everything went warm and I started to get tired. I wanted to lie down for a minute and Dad said to me then that I had to keep moving because that was the only way to keep warm. If you are wet in the woods, he said, you need to get dry. Finally we stopped under the boughs of a cedar tree and he stripped my pants off and gave me a pair of his shorts that were too large for me, and then he pushed me along in front of him and then I was tired because I was going too fast but I didn't want to sleep. I just wanted to stop. I knew when I took Adrian out into the rain that she shouldn't get wet.

I huddled on one of the plastic pieces of furniture strewn between the planters and the fountains. Large plastic crescents and lozenge-shaped tables and squiggly benches lay like discarded toy blocks.

I didn't notice Janet entering the courtyard until I heard her slosh into the fountain. She stood in the pool up to her knees, with her sandals in one hand and her dress pulled up with the other. She walked through the water and stepped onto the courtyard tiles, flicking water from the ends of her toes. Tiny drips speckled my face and the book I was reading.

"Stop," I said. "This is a library book."

Four floors of balconies ran around the courtyard. At the very top, I could see up into the sky where puffy white clouds rolled. Janet walked toward me, leaving her wet sole-shaped prints like parentheses on the cement floor, where they turned dark and then began to fade dry.

I turned back to my book, but I couldn't read now. "What are you doing?" I wanted her to leave me alone. I wanted her to somehow erase what had happened Friday night. How could she explain what had happened? "Well, this happened and this happened"? "Chavez puckered up and I puckered right back"? She didn't have to explain anything to me, but if she liked Chavez how could she like me as well? If she kissed Chavez, then her only interest in me somehow had to do with Chavez. I kept my face in the book. I couldn't read it, but I wasn't going to look at her.

"I'm reading," I said.

"What are you reading?"

"I came here to be alone," I said.

"We are alone."

"Alone, by myself," I said.

"How can you stand to be here when you don't have to be here now?" she asked. I didn't have an answer. I turned the page, losing my place, but I wanted to maintain the illusion that I was reading and progressing in the story and found her presence annoying but not annoying enough to make me stop reading. I flicked to the next page.

"What are you waiting for?"

"I'm not waiting for anything, I'm reading," I said. "An activity in and of itself."

"In and of itself? Is *that* in your book?"

It occurred to me then that she was actually looking for me. Why would she come here if she didn't like it here? Unless she had looked for me everywhere else. Had she used up Chavez already? I wanted to ask her, "How is Chavez?" or even better, "How was Chavez?" But I also didn't want her to get pissed off and leave. I didn't say anything.

"Read out loud to me."

"No," I said.

She grabbed the book and said, "I'm going to find the sex scene." She turned the book inside out so the spine rolled back and my heart went wild. My book. It was more than just my book. I (and not Janet) had checked it out from the library. She shook the spine. She held the book so it went floppy as she put her sandals back on, stepping into the soles. She walked in a circle around the planter and the white plastic bench. "There doesn't appear to be a single dirty scene. Why are you reading this?" She walked around the rubber tree plant again. On the far side of the giant pot she started to run, and ran outside.

I ran out after her. A battalion of medics marched down the middle of the street. The standard, navy blue with long yarnlike gold tassels and the seal of the unit, undulated with the shuffling forward march of the battalion. Their boots clicked on the asphalt. Every toe was brilliant and polished in the late-day sunlight. Each boot moved forward. The whole parade moved forward. They sang *Jody Jody / When I get back / I'm going to kick old Jody's ass.* The battle medics had been on field maneuvers for two weeks and Fort Sam Houston had been quiet, but now they were back and in the morning barked out their PT songs. Janet had made it in front of the formation and stood on the other side with my book. She waved it and then walked across the PT field, the marching medics advancing in front of me.

I walked behind the marching soldiers and then down the bank alongside the road down to the PT field. Janet had crossed the entire field. She stood under a lamp near the ordered streets of the officers' neighborhood—wide, quiet asphalt streets with large old shade trees, watered

lawns, and names and rank insignias on the mailboxes.
The ground still held heat from the day. It rose in squiggly
lines, distorting the four story complex of the Academy of
Health Sciences, the columns of marching soldiers, and
quiet officer housing. The sound of the cadence scattered
in the rising air. I heard the crickets around me, then
marching songs. When I arrived on the other side of the
field, Janet was already down the block. The sidewalk was
cool under the trees and the roots of the old trees had
buckled the cement. Toys lay in the yard. Birds sang in the
trees in the officers' yards. Adrian had always wanted to
know the names of the birds singing the songs. She had
also pretended to know the tunes they were singing. Dad
would tell her the name of the species: "That's a woodcock," and she would say, "It sounds like a woodcock is
happy." I followed Janet. She headed toward the library
and movie theater and I wondered if she was trying to take
back my book to the library. I cut down an alley and walked
toward her, but she turned and jogged up the steps of the
movie theater. "Did you lose something?" She had my
book tucked into the crook of her arm.

White terra-cotta art deco flourishes hung over the movie
theater's stucco walls. *Peggy Sue Got Married.* Kathleen
Turner smiled from a keyhole floating in a Magritte sky.
We walked on the heavy ceramic tiles in the lobby painted
with palm trees. The thick odor of boiled coconut oil used
to pop popcorn filled the brightly lit lobby. Faint filaments

of cobwebs hung from the chandelier, a contraption of chrome candlesticks and smoky lights mostly burned out. Janet said, "Two tickets, please," to the bored-looking teenager behind the counter. Janet handed them to the ticket taker, who refused them and waved us past the dusty velvet rope and down into the theater where the trailer for the next movie flashed across the screen.

I sat down with Janet toward the back of the theater. I watched the blue light of the film fall over her face. She smiled and looked at me, her eyes black and blue glittering wells, reflecting the light coming down. I watched her watch the movie. At one point she stood and set the book down on her chair. She smiled at me and tucked a long lock of hair behind her ear. She placed her hand on the back of my neck and her fingers on my forehead as she said, "I'll be right back." She left. After a little bit, I thought, Maybe she won't come back. At least she left my book. I watched the movie, but I wasn't really watching the movie because I worried that Janet had left me in the theater. What did that say about how she thought about me, especially if she had not only kissed Chavez on Friday, just the day before last, but what if she'd also had sex with him? She wasn't coming back. She took me and left me in *Peggy Sue Got Married*. Maybe after dinner she was giving me a second chance. I'd done something wrong. It wasn't that bad of a movie that it would be a punishment. She walked back the way she came, having whatever suspicion she had about

me. Maybe I should get up and leave and catch her before
she got too far or just to let her know I didn't fall for her
trick. But then what if she really did have to go to the bathroom or to get popcorn? I'd leave. She'd come back and
find the empty seat, not even the book she'd taken. I didn't
want her to feel bad. So I waited and watched the movie.
Fabian, charge me, Fabian. I felt her body, the odor of per-
fume, the slight popcorn odor still on her fingertips. Janet
sat down and brushed my arm. She took my hand. I had
my hand in her hand; her hand felt, first of all, warm and
smooth and firm, but then on closer thought also felt like
a bundle of individual little wires leaking a slightly acidic
fluid. It was her hand inside mine. I gripped her hand just
slightly, not enough, I hope, to make her think I was
affirming anything, but hard enough for her to know I
liked having my hand in her hand. I'd rather have her hand
in my hand, but she'd grabbed my hand first. Another nice
benefit of having the hand contact was that I knew when
she found a scene tense, although this wasn't exactly a sus-
pense movie. She pulled my hand tighter when the slight-
est thing went into doubt, like when Peggy Sue slept with
the beatnik who wanted her to become his farmwife.

   The movie chairs had wooden armrests and thick, life-
preserver style cushions. Janet sat next to me and I could
feel her breathe, and when she laughed, I could feel the
seat rock slightly, hear the screws jingle as she laughed. She
used a protective laugh, not freely letting herself just laugh

a deep belly laugh, but clucked and chortled in her throat. When she laughed, I didn't laugh because I was watching her. She said, without looking away from the screen, "Don't look at me."

"I'm not looking at you."

The movie ended. The credits began to roll up and the lights came on low on the sides of the theater, casting dappled light down the walls. The other moviegoers rose to their feet, almost all women in pink and beige and lime green sundresses and white leather sandals, all dressed the same, carrying matching handbags. They had short, flared hair. They smiled at each other, blinking as they stared at the real three-dimensional people they were surrounded by. Janet said, "That was a good movie."

"Sure was," I said.

We cut into the line of women. They smelled like carnations and rose water. We walked under the dusty chandelier and outside onto the sidewalk. It was dark outside now except for a faint, smudgy, dark blue sky with glittering stars just now beginning to poke through. Janet smiled at me. "Let's take the bus downtown."

We walked over to the bus stop and stood under the shelter. We didn't say anything about the movie or anything really, both still a little drowsy from sitting in the theater. I wanted to tell her I'd liked watching her watch the movie, but how did I say that to her without creeping her out? I didn't want her to think I was obsessed with her.

Normal boys merely liked girls they'd just met; they didn't love them. Normal boys thought about other girls.

I wanted to know about her and Chavez. I just stood near the bus shelter with my hands in my pockets. She stood really close to me. "Do you think those were military wives?"

"Oh yeah," I said. "They all looked identical."

"It seems like a nice life when you come out of a theater, but they were all alone. Did you see that? They were just there with the other Army wives."

"Maybe their husbands didn't want to come with them?"

"Military husbands don't see chick flicks."

"Regulations," I said. "They might be military women and have military husbands at home."

"It must be lonely to be a military wife."

The bus came then, grumbling and rattling, and then stopped with a squeal. It was dimly lit inside. The light brightened when the door opened. The driver checked the rearview mirror as we climbed in and paid. The bus was mostly empty. We rode in the bus out of the military base and then through the neighborhood past the base.

"What happened with you and Chavez?" I asked.

She stopped and looked at her reflection in the bus window. Her face was just the dark outline of her hair.

"Nothing happened with me and Chavez."

"I forgot my book in the theater," I said. What is meant

by the word *nothing*? It could mean that we had sex and he cried and I cried and we professed our deep and lifelong love to each other and then woke up and decided we didn't mean it and it is nothing to me but had been something. *Nothing* really meant, forget about Chavez, when really I was thinking if he got to kiss her, at least, then it was my turn.

"Come on, you can get a new one or pick it up later."

"It's a library book." I stood up and was a little dizzy and then I pulled the cord and at the next stop jumped out of the bus. I stood on the sidewalk and looked at Janet.

"Are you coming?"

"I'm going downtown."

I kept walking, but for some reason the thought that I'd misplaced the book worried me. I had some sort of super-ability to lose things. I'd lost the book. I'd been the last, or one of the last people to see Sandy. I'd lost Adrian. I walked under the palm trees, feeling a wave of sensation in my arms and legs. I stared up through the fibrous trunk and palm fronds at the starry sky. The emotion was so strong, it felt sort of joyfully painful and satisfying. I wanted to laugh at myself because it was just a book, however, I felt there was something destructive about me. I enjoyed feeling like that. Maybe I'd done everything on purpose. I thought about getting lost in the Quinault rainforest and about what Adrian would be like now had I not lost her. I was only nineteen years old and I'd lost everything in my life. I went back through the base gate and cut across the parade field.

I lay down for a minute and looked up at the stars. There was an electrically charged sensation, a tingling at the back of my neck as I thought, *I am completely cursed.* I sat up as the feeling began to fade, and it was as if I had been listening to the rush of my own blood. Going hiking sometimes, it took almost an hour of walking through the woods before I no longer heard the sound of the radio in my ears, fragments of radio songs. "For Those About to Rock, We Salute You." Slowly I no longer heard the music but just the sound of my blood in my veins and the wind in the fir boughs. I realize I'd been listening to white noise. I thought it was telling me how important I was in relation to Adrian, Jake, Oliver, even Sandy and Janet. But really I was in the middle of a field. The grass felt cool against my thighs. I could see an airplane over the San Antonio horizon. Above everything, the scattered, twinkling stars had been scattered and twinkling before I had even looked at them and would be scattered and twinkling even after I stopped looking at them. Although I felt as if I was the only one looking back and holding Adrian in my memory, how often in her life had she thought about me? She thought about me a lot, I'm sure, but not every hour. The cold ground had drawn the warmth out of my legs and back. My skin felt as cool as stone.

On the way back to the theater I thought I saw Sandy walking by herself on the other side of the parade field. "Hey," I yelled. But in the cold breezy air it sounded to me as if I were shouting inside a closet. The woman, tall and slightly stooped like Sandy, turned down one of the officers' streets lined with tall, leafless elms. I ran across the field and then down the street and found the woman on the stairs up to her house. She heard me sprinting down the street and turned to look at me and quickly got her door open and then slammed it shut.

I found Janet sitting on the theater steps with my book in her lap.

"Where have you been?" she asked. And then she saw the dust on my shoulders and I tried to smile, but it felt put on. "What is it? It's only a book."

"You don't want to talk to me about it."

"All right." She handed me the book and I began to walk back toward the barracks. "I was only kidding." Janet followed me. "What's wrong?"

"Why do you think something is wrong with me?"

"What's bothering you? Did I do something?"

"No," I said, even though I didn't want to say it. "You didn't do anything."

On Tuesday, Sandy Comstock was announced AWOL. She was officially gone then, although she hadn't been in class and no one had seen her at the barracks since the party.

They started whispering her name in line for coffee during the first break on Wednesday. "Sandy Comstock.

Yeah. I know some people that went to basic training with her. They said they could see it coming." It became common knowledge by the end of the day that the MPs had found her wandering the Loop, the highway that circled the downtown core of the city, half-insane, holding a backpack full of stuffed animals, Strawberry Shortcake dolls, a panda, and ballerinas. She suddenly gained a strange notoriety through her absence. We began to sift through the evidence, nodding as we weighed the knowledge that her madness had been there all along. Someone recalled that, once, she had stood in line, waited until she got right before the cashier, and then hurried away and sat down at her desk, an incident no weirder than the half-dozen odd things that other trainees had done at seven o'clock in the morning, half-asleep from a long evening of studying and watching basketball on TV. But these things, her habit of picking the dry skin off her elbow and chewing on the hardened flesh, confirmed that she wasn't like the rest of us.

Instead of asking, "What happened to her? Why did this happen to her?" people assumed that she had it coming. She was a slut. Taylor, who often played volleyball with Chavez before dinner, talked about the party and how she had fucked five guys at once. "You're making that up," Viscount said. "Yeah, it sounds like a porno movie or something," Taylor said. "She was on this bed and she was just thrashing. I mean, everyone was drunk. I don't even remember who was doing it with her, but anybody could,

I mean anybody. The funky smell. You don't think about that when you see a porno, but fuck, all of that cum reeks."

"She had it coming to her," Chavez said in the breeze-way. "You went to basic training with her, you know what she was like. She had to carry that postage stamp around with her all the time. What was on it?"

"A wooden duck decoy," Janet said.

"Yeah, that's weird. She was a slut."

"Don't call her that," Janet said.

"You don't think a woman who bangs five guys at once is a slut?"

"Depends on how you mean banged. I don't think she was the one banging. I think she was banged by five rapists."

"She goes crazy," Chavez said, "so she isn't responsible for shit, is that how it works? She asked us. Christ, she begged us. We didn't do anything to hurt her and I don't think that drove her crazy. If that drove her crazy, she might have gone nuts eating her dinner one night. Stop looking at me like that. She was one crazy bitch."

Fourteen

Cadre Sergeant McGrath carried a long silver tube dangling behind him like an architect's drawing case. "It's a Swedish-built 84MM Miniman recoilless gun." Viscount punched his thin wire-framed glasses up onto the bridge of his nose. He had read every Tom Clancy novel and knew the statistics of almost every piece of military hardware used by the USSR since 1946.

"It's a thermos, you idiot," Chavez chortled behind him. "He carries his whiskey in it."

"Specialist Chavez?"

"Yes, Sergeant?"

"Why aren't you in front of your formation?"

"I'm observing the workings of the ranks from the interior, Sergeant."

"Assume your position."

"Yes, Sergeant."

"What day is it?"

"Friday, Sergeant."

"What does that mean, Specialist Chavez?"

"It means the weekend, time for the enlisted man to rest, polish his boots, meditate on the manual and, come Sunday, to pray, pray, pray."

"That may be your prerogative, Chavez, but I'll take it without the smirk. I'm sure some of you have other plans more to your liking than a suck-butt like Chavez. Am I right? But word has come back to me from the kind men and women who work at the San Antonio police force that some of y'all are getting into big trouble in your spare time. So this weekend, all of y'all will only be allowed off-base if and when you, one, sign out as usual, and, two, if a little time-honored tradition for troubled classes is honored. I will have a few words with Specialist Chavez and a few of you each Friday afternoon. If all goes well, then you will all be given off-base passes for the weekend. Which means, if and when you are arrested off-base for freebasing in the Super 8 parking lot, you won't get charged with being AWOL in addition to the rest of the mess. If Chavez doesn't come by to enjoy a few minutes of pleasant conversation and if he can't find several volunteers, then we'll have a sparkly barracks to enjoy come Monday morning. Can I expect to see you at two this afternoon, Specialist?"

"Yes, Sergeant."

"And bring along some of your friends, Chavez. I would

like to get to know what kind of trouble you druggie pharmacy techs are getting into this weekend."

"Yes, Sergeant."

"I already know who I can trust and who I can't. Just because you have just come out of basic training, where you've just spent eight weeks perfecting the art of what you can get away with, you aren't fooling me. You may as well not try. If you expect to go out this weekend and do whatever it is you do back on the block, gangbang middleschoolers or what have you, I will have the MPs bring you back and you'll spend the weekend cleaning bathrooms. The base has plenty of accommodations for you. All I ask is that you don't get caught. Otherwise, I really don't give a fuck. Because there are hardly three of you worth the bus tickets Uncle Sam paid to bring your pimple-farming asses here from the airport.

"March them to class, Specialist, and be sure you bring them back this afternoon, show up with some company, or y'all, that means every last one of you, are going to know what the mess hall looks like Saturday night."

At break, Chavez stood up on his plastic chair. "Okay, y'all, I don't want to keep any of you who have something to do after class hanging out with me and McWrath, so if you have plans after class, why don't you stand over by the tree."

Everyone moved to the tree, but he started calling out names as we started moving.

"Damn it, I knew you'd do that."

"That's because it's exactly what you'd do," someone said.

"Doesn't anyone want to be on my good side?"

"How much are you going to pay us for the privilege?"

"Bohm, what are you doing this afternoon."

"Seeing a movie."

"Who's seeing a movie with Bohm?"

No one said anything. I looked at Janet. "I am," she said.

"Well, well," he looked at me, "Good, that's two people who can change their plans. Who else?"

"I can go," Viscount said. "I don't have anything else to do."

"Jason," Chavez said. "Why don't you join our good friends Wahl and Bohm for a nice after-lunch aperitif with Sergeant McLaugh?"

A greenish love seat lay under the window, the cushions peeled back to the foam-matting insides. The old couch swallowed Chavez and Viscount. Chavez climbed up onto the armrest. I sat on an old wooden stool that had once been painted red, then green, and was now blue. The paint had worn back down to the wood. Janet sat with her legs crossed and her hands on her knees on a fold-up gray chair. She didn't really say anything to me when I came into the room; she just nodded and then went back to looking out the window. McGrath wore his uniform, even though he'd asked us to come as we were.

"What's this?" Chavez asked him. "You even shined your boots."

"I always shine my boots," McGrath said. He sorted through the teacups on his sideboard. He had a very tall tin teapot that ended in a short, conical cap with squares and circles cut into it. It rested on an electric burner plate. The steam floated over the cement blocks and pooled across the ceiling.

"I see," Chavez said. "Then you've been letting that piece of lettuce grow mold on your heel for the last six weeks?"

"At least when I was four years into the military, I knew how to shine my boots. When I was in basic training, they didn't even give us boots with finished leather. They threw suede boots out of the back of a deuce-and-a-half, no matter what size, and within eight weeks you couldn't tell the difference between one of our boots and patent leather."

"And my granny had to walk fifteen miles to school, through the snow and it was uphill both ways. Yeah, we've heard it, Sergeant McGrath, the old folks always had it harder when they were our age. And every year, everything gets easier. In my lifetime, children don't have to roll down car windows, or walk up stairs, or use a dictionary. We're all just blobs of freaky Jell-O brand gelatin."

"I think you've pretty much nailed it right on the head. Does anyone here like sugar and, if so, how much? Don't move your freaky Jell-O brand gelatin arms or legs, because I can spoon it in for you."

McGrath sat on his desk, covered with layers of aging paper. He had a Shell Oil poster on his wall from July 1981 with a photo of a beach. The upper half had faded while the other half was still a glossy golden shore of sea foam and sand. He looked at each of us while we sipped his tea. "Tea," he said, "is better for this kind of thing than coffee. My Momma used to have her old friends over to her house and they'd sit around the coffee table. She'd serve biscuits and they'd drink their coffee and talk about quilting and about church and who was getting promoted on the base. After about an hour of politely sipping my Momma's coffee and nibbling on sugar cookies, they'd be so strung out that you'd never know which one would burst out singing first. Momma and her best friend would always race into singing this old song that I hated. I'd be sitting at the kitchen table doing my homework and I'd have to go hide in my bedroom. 'What is it?' Momma would yell after me. 'Don't you like me having a good time?' And I'd slam my door and sit down and stuff in the foam plugs my father had given me for the times he took me out to the rifle range and I'd read and read and maybe an hour later . . . "

"Excuse me, Sergeant," Chavez said. "I've finished my tea. Very good. Didn't know tea could be so good. I thank you very much, but if you don't mind, I'd like to be going now."

"Sit down, Chavez," McGrath said. He stood, slapped up the pot and high-poured a dose of brownish tea into Chavez's cup and then flipped in two sugar cubes. "Listen up. It may sound like I'm rambling here, but I'm getting somewhere and that's why we're all here, because if I don't get y'all to the same somewhere tonight, then I sure as hell will get you to the same somewhere by Sunday night, after you've buffed the floors that I've just scuffed with your back teeth. Now, where was I?"

"You were at a shooting range," Viscount said.

"I was?"

"You'd just put in earplugs," Janet said. "You're at home. Your Mom's flipped out on coffee."

"So, one time Momma came and knocked on my door and it was maybe another hour later. 'Come out,' she said. I didn't open the door, but I could tell from the way she said, 'Come on out,' that if I didn't open the door I'd be in trouble, so I opened the door and she grabbed me by my hand and said, 'Come on, everyone's dancing.' In the living room, Dad's bottle of whiskey was out and they were still drinking coffee and dancing. That may seem pretty silly to y'all, I mean, kids whose mothers were acid freaks and hippies, but these were the women who ran the Baptist church on base and here was Mrs. Johnson bugging out on the couch, with three buttons of her blouse undone and her bra straps showing. And Mrs. Johnson wasn't a little woman. No, she wasn't. Mrs. Johnson was married to

Command Sergeant Johnson, and he weighed four hundred pounds. They were a matching set, and they'd sit in the front pew of the church on Sunday like their own private herd of cattle, and you could almost hear her going over the list and making a little frown and check mark when someone was missing at church. And here she was, with the pale flesh of her breasts sloshing like a cup of tapioca against the rim of her lace bra. I was just about sick and my Momma made me dance with her and the whole time I'm thinking, 'Who is in control of this? Because it sure isn't me because I'm only a child and everyone who's supposed to be in control is crazy.'"

"Damn good story, McGrath, I'm very glad you invited us over. I think this is an excellent tradition—"

"Sit down, Chavez," McGrath stood up off his desk and sat down on the coffee table between us. He looked out of his open window at the parade field. In the dusk, a formation of Army Rangers had just spread out in neat rows to do PT. As they started their jumping jacks, they'd raise their arms for the count and, just as their hands tapped their hips, the sound of their cadence came across the field and into the room. McGrath didn't have the light on. His skin was faintly blue and he rubbed his eyes, then looked slowly at all of us. "Do you know how long it's been since something like this has happened on my watch?"

"What?" Viscount said. "What happened?"

"No one told you?" McGrath said. "Jesus. Don't you people talk with each other? Bohm, tell Viscount what happened."

"I don't know, Sergeant. Did Sandy Comstock go AWOL?"

"Comstock turned up Wednesday night at the Sea Breeze Motel. She told the MPs that she had been stealing MI6 bullet casings. She had six of them in her locker."

"Had she been?" Chavez said.

"She had. She also had the assembly for the insides of an MI6, which is a felony, and she would've served time in Levenworth, the works, if she didn't also happen to be a nut. It turns out that while she had been at a party held by our class leader, Specialist Chavez . . ."

"Whatever you're going to say ain't true," Chavez said. "I don't know who told you this or how it even started, but it isn't true."

"How do you know what I'm going to say?"

"People talk."

"No they don't," Viscount said.

"They don't talk to freaks like you," Chavez said.

"Who's the freak?" McGrath said.

"From what I understand, she was the freak." Chavez stood and brushed himself off with the flat of his hand and sat on the other armrest. "I'm about ready to go."

"Would you like a little tea, to calm down? I've got herbal tea. Would you like lemon zinger, chamomile, raspberry zucker?"

"I don't want any tea. I'm not responsible for her flipping out."

"What are you responsible for, Chavez? You stepped up and took the position of class leader. Now, you may see it as an opportunity to nail every single eighteen-year-old that causes old Mr. Hambone to take notice, but I can assure you that no one intended it to be used that way. The Army trains leaders, not rapists. And you used this little position, this little monkey-ass position to gangbang one of my soldiers and then leave her for dead in a motel on the strip. Didn't you think I'd find out about it? When the shit hits the fan, it doesn't end up in a little neat pile that you can poop-and-scoop." McGrath stood in the middle of the room. I became aware, then, that the sweet odor of hard alcohol drifted away from him.

"If you found out about it, then why did you need an audience for it? Why didn't you just pull me aside and crack my skull open in the time-honored tradition of the United States Army?"

"This is the new Army. They don't let us do that any-more, or I can assure you, we wouldn't be here. And anyway, you're right—*you* didn't do anything. Maybe you didn't do anything to her. One thing is for sure, you didn't do a thing to stop it."

"I haven't done anything that I'm not supposed to do. The reason you didn't try to crack my skull open is because your buddies, your other cadre sergeants think you're a soft old man, and they really don't care what happens off-base if it doesn't come back to them."

"It's not as easy as that."

"It is as easy as that, in case you haven't noticed, Sergeant McGrath. To roll down the window, you press the button. To get from point A to point B, you buy a ticket, get on the plane and you're there. To get laid, all you got to do is pull down your shorts, you don't have to unbutton anything."

"I'm talking about five of my soldiers raping one of my other soldiers; I'm not talking air travel and I'm not talking about the latest modern convenience."

"She was begging for someone to fuck her. They were drunk. They are men. They are soldiers. She was drunk. She's a woman. I remember her at the party, and shit, was she ever asking for it. She wore this tight white leather skirt. You don't go to a drinking party in something like that. Everyone, except a girl who wants to get balled, knows that. What were those guys supposed to do?"

"Christ," McGrath said. He drew the word out and sputtered to a stop. "The reason I'm here is because I don't want something like this happening again. I'm revoking your position."

"I figured that much," Chavez said.

"What happened to Comstock? Where is she?" Janet asked.

"She's in the hospital now," McGrath said. "I had this sort of basic trust in you kids. Year after year, the leaders led well enough. That's all I ask, lead well enough, I don't ask that they inspire anyone with their dedication, but I also ask that they don't let their students rape each other. An adult expects a little civilization to stick around for the next generation."

After the tea, it was beginning to get dark. A steady rain fell. I started to walk quickly into the rain. I kept retracing two points: Janet had slept with, or at the very least exchanged bodily fluid with Chavez that same night; and I could have saved Sandy if I'd been paying attention. "Aldous, where are you going?" Janet yelled after me.

She turned around again and started to run after me. Her boots splashed in the overflowing ditch water. She ran across the street. A truck sped by, spraying the water it kicked up. She followed me. I ran under the palm trees and the magnolias until I came to the bus stop. I stopped and sat down.

"How come you haven't been talking to me this last week?" she asked me.

"I want to be alone," I said.

Janet rolled her tongue over her bottom lip. She breathed out in what I thought was showy excess.

"I can't believe what those thugs did to Sandy. To think I kissed Chavez. I kissed him that night."

I folded my hands in my lap and examined the numbers on my wristwatch.

She scooted to the far side of the bench. The water flung itself against the glass of the bus stop and sheets fell like an artificial waterfall over the front of the stop. A bus came and stopped. It honked its horn. Janet ducked out into the torrent. Its headlight turned the drops white where they passed through it. She stood on the bottom step. The bus smelled like coffee and the breath of the people inside, peppermint and garlic, and they looked at Janet as she shook her head at the driver. "We don't need to go anywhere. Thank you for stopping anyway."

"Those aren't houses," the driver said. "They're for people who are waiting for the bus. Here it is. If you're not waiting for the bus, you should move on."

"We'll leave," she said. "Come on. We have to go."

"Why do you want to go somewhere with me?" Cold water trickled behind my ears. "I as good as did that to her, you know. I'm as guilty as Chavez and Taylor."

"That's a little melodramatic."

"What?"

"Okay. A lot melodramatic."

"I saw Taylor giving Sandy a beer. I could have done something. I saw her get into the car with those guys. I could have stopped them."

"You could have."

"I did that to Sandy."

"Oh my God. Were you there?"

"No."

"Were you there?"

"You think I was there? I was with Viscount, I wasn't there."

"Was Viscount there?"

"We weren't there."

"Then you weren't there and there was nothing you could have done to stop it."

Another bus stopped outside the shelter. Janet ran out into the rain. Without her standing there, I could hear myself breathing, the long drag of air into my lungs and then the hiss of escaping air. I looked at the black marker graffiti in the back of the stop. Janet came back then and I was aware of how she filled the bus stop. I had to shift my weight against the wall so that I wouldn't lean into her breathing. She had come back. I was surprised to find myself relieved.

As the bus rolled away back into the heavy rain Janet sat down on the bench next to me and put her arm around me. "I thought I'd meet a certain kind of guy in the Army," she said. "To be plain. I wanted to meet a certain kind of guy in the military." Janet wiped the water out of her hair with the flat of her palm. She said, "I didn't sleep with Chavez. It would have been never worked out, Chavez and me.

Because I can't imagine what a future would be like with
him. I thought that was what I wanted. I thought he would
be a sort of disposable guy. Clearly, that was a mistake.
With you, though, I can imagine spending time. I can
imagine where you're from. I think we probably have a lot in
common. Are your parents divorced?"

"Yes."

"We grew up in the same generic suburb, Maple Leaf or
Rolling Hills or something like that. We all did, right? We
ate the same 7-Eleven nachos. It's not like Chavez isn't like
that, but some people actually like Whitesnake and
nachos. Did you like 7-Eleven nachos"

"No?" I said.

"I could see, like, you and me doing something in the
future when we both have real jobs. With you, I can imagine
things like that."

"A future," I said. Plans were always things other people
had.

"I have this image of you and me sitting on a park bench
and you're wearing your work clothes, a tie and jacket
and shiny black shoes, and I have my work skirt on and
we're eating food in takeaway boxes. We've just met after
work. I don't know. Don't you ever think about what you'll
be like in the future?"

I didn't want to tell her no. I had been trying not to
think about what life had been like and listening to her

grasping at what I might be like in five years made me wonder just how accurate she was. Janet thought she knew about where I'd grown up. She thought she knew what would happen to me. I couldn't help but consider that at some point I would not be thinking about the past every waking moment, and then what? And then what did I want to do?

I looked at Janet staring into the air in front of her and she didn't hear the rain falling against the bus shelter or feel the cold water overflowing the gutter. She didn't know what I did to my sister. If she did, would she still be grasping for an image of me in five years near her, on a park bench with takeaway boxes?

Shoot the Buffalo

Fifteen

I was a tenderfoot in the Cub Scouts, stuck to the ground and stuck to my parents. I built torsion-powered rockets out of balsa wood, hollowed so the twisted rubber would hurl the missile down a wire track. Everyone in the Cub Scouts raced rockets. We drew diagrams, color patterns, schematics. My spacecraft glittered under silver paint, applied in three layers of sticky enamel. The other Scouts rubbed decals of the US flag onto their rocket hulls. I painted black circles, dark swirls, the silhouettes of old men with Rasta beards. I never won. I might win the second heat, race into the third heat, but I never won.

The boys of The Swing Set and their logging-men dads stood in clumps at the base of the scoreboard, a huge roll of white butcher paper with our names written at one end, exponentially decreasing to the triangle of winners and the last spot where the lone winner's name would be placed.

Mr. Laxton, the scoutmaster, walked through the crowd of dads, slapping backs and laughing. His son, Lance, would win the competition because he always won the competition and, according to Oliver, the other dads wanted to stay on Mr. Laxton's good side so that their sons had a chance of coming in second or third. First prize was fifty dollars. Second prize was dinner for four at Stuart Anderson's Black Angus Steak House. Third prize was five free supermalt milkshakes at King of Dairy.

Mr. Laxton wore his khaki Eagle Scout uniform, dry-cleaned, steam-pressed, and decorated with so many jostling honor beads and ribbons that he had to wear a different uniform at camp. He called his other uniform his "working uniform"—"Without all the froufrou to distract me from the task at hand." Mr. Laxton wore a startlingly huge mustache, groomed and waxed so that it stuck out on either side of his face. He stood on a podium about to address us. We were Cub Scouts and a handful of Boy Scouts and, among the entire pack, we didn't have enough awards to match the left pocket of Mr. Laxton's ceremonial uniform. Mr. Laxton twisted the left bar of his mustache tight and let it recoil into his face. He spoke about our moral obligation to learn the rules of good scouting. "It's a big world out there and it takes civilized young men to hold it together."

Oliver wore a jean jacket, a skippers' hat, and cowboy boots to the pack meetings. Once, Mr. Laxton had asked

Oliver why he didn't have a uniform. "Because I'm grown," Oliver had said.

The rocket races were held in the elementary school gym, a brick building built in 1911 that dominated the prefab classroom modules sitting behind it. The lockers in the basement, where we weren't allowed, had a salty, old-shoe smell. People only went in the basement during Halloween when it became part of the Haunted House. Strobe lights glinted over the damp cement floors and, in the smell of old athletic sweat, one of the logging men flapped six sewn-on arms like a gigantic spider. He danced up and down the steps and we screamed, spilled through the locker room, up the stairs, past a wall of disembodied screaming and gibbering human heads.

The gym floor's ancient wood had been stripped and polished, and waxed until it was now covered with a brittle layer of clear polish. Our shoes clicked on the wood like fingernails tapping a marble countertop. Windows towered up three stories into the scaffolding of the ceiling and, in the morning during PE class, the sun would spill through the air and linger in the floating particles of dust. The shouting of the Cub Scouts and their dads as the rockets whirred down the wire tracks filled the gym with a tinny din, as if we were yelling inside an aluminum can. The races ended and another tier of winners was added, while the losers slipped into the knots of boys standing along the bleachers. The losers' names weren't recorded in the chart. They just dropped off. They were eliminated. I carried my loser rocket over to the Ronald McDonald tankard and the coffee urn. Oliver sat on the bottom bleacher with Mrs. Laxton. She swept a hand over her face and smiled at me. She was my den mother, so she had watched me build the rocket and paint it. When I had finished painting it, she held up the dark rocket and said, "This might be too much paint. But it is interesting. What made you think of this?"

"I don't know," I said.

"You're so creative," she said. "You must get that from your uncle."

"Yeah, I guess," I said.

"I'm sure you do." She stared intently into my face as though she were trying to decipher some secret glyph.

Oliver grabbed the loser rocket out of her hand. He held the rocket in his lap as though it was a penis and twirled the tip. "I don't think this made a very good rocket, Aldous, babe," Oliver said in a corny voice. He looked at Mrs. Laxton and she bit her lip and looked across the gym at her husband. But he was talking to one of the scoutmasters whose son stood beside him, crying and holding up his rocket, and didn't notice that Oliver and his wife were talking. I'm sure if he had noticed, he would have walked across the gym, grabbed his wife with one hand and his mustache with the other and taken her home.

I dropped a nickel into Mrs. Laxton's collection plate and poured myself a cup of orangeade from the Ronald McDonald tankard. His red nose had been rubbed until the yellow plastic showed underneath. I leaned into the bleachers and sat with the other boys from my den. The six of us sat in the shadows above the light. The indistinct, blue-uniformed Scouts knotted on the floor. We had all lost in the first three rounds and it would be hours before the final races were decided, so we had time to kill. The boys in my den still thought of me as the new kid, even though I had been going to Mrs. Laxton's house since last fall. They all went to the same church on Sundays and they saw each other four extra times a month. I dwelled on how far this put me behind. I couldn't hear what they were saying beside me. I could only hear their whispers. Keith and Dayle caught the bus with me at the same stop. They stood in awe of Mr. Laxton's son Lance and Lance's best friend, Greg. Greg was about to undergo the ceremony of the Arrow of Light. He would become a Boy Scout and then he would no longer come to the den meetings.

Greg didn't compete in the races. He bet on them and carried money in a hollowed-out Scout manual. For him, the real money wasn't in who won, because Lance always won. But anyone could win second place. Greg sat in the shadows until the final three heats, when he stalked the sidelines and tapped the shoulders of the bettors. He talked out of the side of his mouth when he did this. He asked me, "So, who do you think's going to take second?"

"I'm not," I said.

"Of course you're not, you're a loser."

Oliver and Mrs. Laxton walked along the sidelines of the racetrack. She wore a long white skirt and jacket with a bow around her neck. Her hair fell in arcs from her face and along her shoulders.

"Mrs. Laxton Report," Greg said.

"What do you mean?"

"Your uncle bag her yet?"

"What?"

"Come on, don't pretend to be a numbnuts with me," Greg said. "We all know your uncle's shooting to snake her."

After the races had finished, after Greg, Keith, and Dayle left, I sat back on the edge of the bleachers watching Oliver and Mr. Laxton roll up the track. In front of the gym doors, Mr. Laxton's huge truck sat idling while they loaded the track and the scoreboard, with Lance's name written at the far end in the winner's slot.

The room felt gigantic without the noise of the race, without the whispering people in the rafters. The polished wood softened the glare of the floodlights. I climbed up the bleachers to the top and looked down through the rafters and the hanging lights at Mr. Laxton and Oliver. I realized then that Mr. Laxton was telling Oliver something that was making Oliver mad. When Oliver got mad, he always pulled his cap off his head and twisted it in his hands. His face turned slightly red, and I could see, even from the ceiling of the gym, veins starting to spread in Oliver's neck.

Mr. Laxton leaned against the truck and then twirled his mustache in one hand, a familiar gesture for me from the dozens of Western movies I had seen, even though it seemed more like shtick from *The Apple Dumpling Gang* than *Showdown at the OK Corral*. I felt, squeezed into the rafters of the gym, that this was an appropriate space for me. I spent my time hiding just behind the periphery of other people's vision. Something was happening and I just let it happen. I didn't go down to find out what was happening. I didn't know how to help.

Finally, the truck had been loaded and Mr. Laxton closed the doors. The lights turned off. They made a noise as though a giant had taken a plodding step in the middle of the basketball court; then the light disappeared. The outside streetlight dimly fell into the room but otherwise, I couldn't really see anything. I started making my way down the steps, crawling on all fours, the palms of my hands sliding over the rounded metal bolts and the waxy wood.

When I opened the emergency exit, I stepped into Mr. Laxton and he placed his hand on my shoulder. Mr. Laxton smelled like soap. His hand gripped my neck muscle and I felt as though he could pick me up. The knot of his hand dug into the flesh at the base of my neck. "So, Aldous," he said to me and I was washed in the odor of Certs. I thought that maybe someone had once told him that he smelled nasty and now he made up for it by drenching himself in pleasing aromas. "What were you doing up there in the dark?" I could see his hand reach up and brush across his mustache and this made me think whatever I had been doing had been something faintly dirty.

"Snaring the old lockers," I said.

"Snaring?"

"Ask my uncle, because I don't think I can explain it very good. He knows all the words."

He blinked and made a half-turn away from me. "Aldous, maybe you can clarify something for me?" I didn't respond because it looked like he was going to keep going no matter what I said. "I've been asking around, and it doesn't look like your family belongs to any of the local congregations. Correct?"

"I don't know," I said.

"Have you ever gone to service?" I think he could tell from my blank look that I wasn't even sure what service was; I had never been inside a church.

"I'm getting a bit concerned here. I am," Mr. Laxton finally said.

"I didn't do anything," I said.

"I am not accusing you of anything, except maybe ignorance, but that isn't your fault. It certainly isn't."

"I didn't," I said. I was confused about what he meant by ignorance. When The Swing Set wanted to call someone stupid, they said, "You're ignorant, dumb as dirt." But I was pretty sure I wasn't stupid.

"You didn't what?" He sat on the bleacher bench. He held my arms; I felt small compared to him. My parents seemed large to me, but compared to other people they sometimes seemed smaller. My uncle stood up to Mr. Laxton's shoulder and Dad came up to most men's noses. Most people looked just a little over the crown of Dad's head. Mr. Laxton was a very large man. His hand wrapped around my torso and pressed my arms into my rib cage. Inside the close sphere of his body, I could smell something below the wash of Irish Spring and Certs. It was like mildew, permeating his clothes and skin.

"Aldous," he said, "What didn't you do?"

"I don't know," I said.

"So, Ralph, corrupting my nephew?" Oliver asked. He leaned against the dark brick wall of the gym and lit up a cigarette. In the sudden spark of light, I could see Mr. Laxton standing up above me. His medals sparkled in the flash.

"I was just having a word with Aldous. As a matter of curiosity, Oliver, I was wondering where the boys went to service?"

"It's none of your fucking business," Oliver said.

Mr. Laxton grasped Oliver by the shoulders and said, "You're right. It's no concern of mine." I realized again, as his hand closed around Oliver's shoulder, just how large he was. At times, I wonder how subjective my memory of these events is. In my memory, Mr. Laxton seemed a giant, distorted like a medieval painting in which the important subjects grew big and bigger depending on their significance.

We watched Mr. Laxton walk away and then Oliver said, "Come on." Oliver tossed me a rocket. It had a little American flag and tiny aerodynamic ridges cut along the fuselage. It was Lance Laxton's winning rocket.

"What is this?"

"Industrial secrets," he said.

My den mother wanted me to call her Amelia, but I called her Mrs. Laxton. It didn't occur to me that my uncle and her were doing anything, maybe because my uncle was so close to Mom. It seemed natural for him to spend time talking to Mrs. Laxton on the phone. It seemed natural that she would sit on the sidelines of the competition and talk to him. I found it strange, later, that anyone related to me or Dad would have anything worthwhile to offer a woman, especially a married woman in a secure position among Snoqualmie's high-pressure PTA. I suppose that she was sexy for the 1970s. Her skin was pale and she had a constellation of bright red freckles under her eyes. She wore loose, brownish clothes and when she reached for her pack of Virginia Slims, the undersides of her arms jiggled. I attempted to conceal my stare through her wide armholes at her black bra, which held the allure of late-night movies, of the sound of the tinkling piano coming past the cedar-paneled entrance to a lounge, of an entire adult world that I knew like I knew the names of the planets. Mercury, Venus, Mars, Vagina, Cocktail, Orgasm.

Oliver always drove me to den meetings at the Laxton house. He dressed up before he went. For Oliver, this meant that he would take a bath, shave, and put on a clean white dress shirt he had bought when he had tried to work as a waiter at the University Bar and Grill. While she was scrubbing out the grease stains, Mom had spent one evening watching reruns of *I Love Lucy*.

Mom had been sliding downhill for as long as I could remember. She had long ago stopped tilling the vegetable patch behind our house, stopped repairing the fence where the animal had broken through and murdered the chickens. When Jake and I started school, her paintings went into the storage shed above Dad's growing room and she started working at the truck stops and diners between Preston and the Snoqualmie Pass. The yard turned to weed. The raspberries jumped the vegetable patch; within a season, the entire garden had turned into a thicket of raspberry, blackberry, and feral strawberry vines. The smoothly mowed lawn collected into thick-rooted clumps over sterile black ground.

My typical image of Mom in 1977 was of visiting her with Oliver at the Busy Bee Diner. Her knee-length hair, with its mixed strands of gray, was knotted and netted behind her head. A cigarette dangled out of her mouth as she sat at the table with us. She kept looking up, around at the other tables. "I've got to get back to work," she said. "It's your break, Gayle," Oliver said. Then she was up and gliding through the diner, sliding pie plates across tabletops and sloshing coffee into people's cups. She brushed her hands across her white apron, covered with yellow and red stains.

I don't think that Mrs. Laxton ever wore an apron, much less anything covered in stains. Mrs. Laxton brushed back her long hair with one hand when she opened the door to Oliver and me. She always met me at the door, whispering something to Oliver. The Laxtons' house, shaped like a barn, stood at the edge of Snoqualmie, next to the tracts of logging company land. A dairy farm lay below the house and, as the three of us stood on the porch, we could hear the cattle moving through the trees and underbrush. They bellowed to one another. When Oliver drove away, Mrs. Laxton and I watched the Dart's headlights flash over the large white heads of the cattle.

The exterior cedar siding held a light green coating of mold. The Laxtons' house smelled of mildew and alder smoke. Mrs. Laxton led me downstairs. Mr. Laxton usually worked in the evenings, under a metal engineering lamp in the living room of his house. The news played on the TV.

He didn't work at a desk, but huddled over the coffee table and drafted illustrations on sheets of paper so waxy it looked as though someone had rubbed them with butter. He didn't look up from his work.

In the basement, as the den meeting began, we were always aware of Mr. Laxton's presence above us, summoned through hisses to be silent and sudden warnings not to shout. My den was six children strong. Lance, Greg, Keith, Dayle, Willie, and myself. When I came into the basement, Keith and Dayle nodded their heads. "Hey." I sat in a chair. They sat together on the couch and whispered to each other. They wore the same badges and the same ribbons. They wore every article of Cub Scout issue they could get their hands on, but because they always did things together, they had earned the same merit badges.

We were working on map skills. Keith held an atlas in his hand and would whisper a capital to Dayle, who would try to guess the state. "Baton Rouge," he whispered.

"Louisiana," I said.

"I'm not talking to you," Keith said.

In the den, I occupied the lowest position. I knew this because anyone else could call me the easiest insults, like *lard-ass*, or *fathead*, or *shitsucker*, things that were vulgar, but didn't require much thought. When they started going, even Willie wouldn't protect me. While I sat waiting for Greg to come and Mrs. Laxton to begin the meeting, I thought of good insults like *moth ears, flaky face, spaghetti head,* but I never had the knack for coming up with insults that caused my enemies to pause. They were inept, off the mark, without the kernel of closely observed detail that lodged into me like the thin edge of a blackberry thorn. One day after I had observed that my eleven-year-old belly hung slightly over my belt, Greg said I had a cottage cheese gut, and I felt my face redden. I spent the rest of the den meeting plotting how I would lose weight and build a muscular stomach and one day casually take off my shirt and have the ribbed stomach of a strongman.

As Greg came down the stairs, we heard someone step-ping down behind him. I laid down my graph paper. Keith and Dayle stopped in midlaugh. Keith closed the atlas. Lance stood up and looked around the room as though he were looking for a hole to jump into, somewhere to go. Mrs. Laxton put out her cigarette.

"Hi kids," Mr. Laxton said. He stood in the center of the room. He wore a white Arrow shirt. The sleeves were rolled back, exposing his large forearms. Hair sprayed from under the cuffs. He clasped his arms across his chest. "I have some things to teach you children," he said. "Lance, get the box."

"What box?"

"The one under my bed upstairs."

While Mr. Laxton was the scoutmaster and we had been coming to this house for several months, he had never addressed us before. Now, he stood before us and started to speak. He told us about God and how He had created the world in six days, how the earth was only six thousand years old. He told us that mankind was doomed to judgment and destruction because of Eve's betrayal in the Garden of Eden.

"Aldous," he said. "Tell me how old the world is."

"Around four point six billion years old."

"Come again?"

"Four point six billion."

"Dead wrong," he said. He snapped his lips. "Six thousand."

"There was a people in the beginning, and then He wiped them out with a flood because they were a bad people. You know about Noah? The Flood was God's judgment. God wanted to destroy His wicked creation. And He did it with water. It floods every spring in the Snoqualmie Valley. You wonder why that is? Have you ever thought that God was punishing us every spring for the winter's wickedness?"

He paused and leaned over the table to pick up Lance's Scout book. He slapped the book on the table.

"We need to have some real learning here; our children must understand why they need to be in something like the Cub Scouts and uphold the American way."

"Dear, this is not 1941," Mrs. Laxton said.

Mr. Laxton didn't say anything for a minute. He just looked down at his wife. We all watched him, waiting to see what he would do. He stood at the base of the stairs on a landing, so he towered over us, even more than he normally towered over us. His mustache throbbed with each gust of his breath "It's 1977, twenty-three years before the end of the Millennium and, already, ignorance rules an organization where young men once understood the values of our society. Every year, the Flood in this valley gets worse and, every year, we draw closer to the real hellfire of Judgment. Even you little men without your full powers are already slipping into damnation. It starts small. How many of you little cretins pull on your puds?"

The den looked at each other. Greg stared flatly at us and Keith and Dayle looked as though they were about to laugh. Willie kept staring at Mr. Laxton. We ended by looking at Willie. "You can tell," Greg said, "that Willie's strangled a few chickens in his day."

"I don't," Willie said.

"Guilty as charged. I always thought your hands kind of smelled funny," Greg said.

Lance returned from upstairs carrying a box that must have weighed as much as he did. He set it down. Mr. Laxton pulled five palm-sized New Testaments from it, handed one to each of us, and then he gave each of us a pamphlet describing each venial sin and its punishment.

He rubbed his mustache as we paged through the flimsy newsprint books. Multicolored pictures showed locusts, famine, and the devil—with horns and forked tail—offering blond boys with their hair parted down the middle, rolls of film, magazines with women's faces drawn on them, and condoms. The next picture showed them drowning in a river, or burning into a skeleton, their bones silhouetted in the flames.

"Read these. Don't bring the meaningless Scout books. We will start with my Old Testament and read through till we finish. Read your New Testaments during the week. Make sure each of you has them at school. Greg, if one of these jokers doesn't have it on them, call me."

"Aldous, make sure that you and your family find a suitable place to go on Sundays."

He left. We sat there and Mrs. Laxton pulled out her Virginia Slims. "Okay kids, a cigarette each." She passed the pack around. Greg drew out two. "Only one, Greg."

"I won't smoke," Lance said. "Cigarettes are bad for you. I don't want to get hooked."

"Your choice, Lance," Mrs. Laxton said. "But you've got to take one anyway."

He drew one out of the pack and laid it across his palm. I held the thin cigarette in my fingers. She passed around the lighter. When I held the papery stick in my mouth, I lit the end and then drew the smoke into my mouth. I watched Greg suck the smoke into his mouth and grunt and then suck more smoke and grunt. His cigarette burned quickly. He smiled lazily and leaned back into the couch. The smoke filled my mouth as though I had just licked a blackened chunk of firewood; then the smoke hit my lungs and I tried not to cough, but spit it back out. Greg rolled his eyes at me. "If you can't handle yours," he said. "I sure could use it."

"He'll smoke his," Mrs. Laxton said. "Don't smoke them quickly. Smoke them slow and learn something useful."

If aliens were to find one of our wind-up rockets, if they found a Scout book with elaborate directions explaining the rubber-band torsion that powered the rockets, would they assume that torsion was a dominant force in our world? They would not, I'm sure, know the things we live with, they would not know about fossil fuel, nuclear fuel, about the decisions people made long ago that we live with now.

I don't know why I made certain decisions when I was a child. I made them based on the assumptions of a person who was only four and a half feet tall. I recall opening the tall wooden door of the shelter we were sleeping in in the Quinault Valley. I looked through the dusk-filled pasture. The rain fell down and everything caught the faint blue light. I knew that Mom and Oliver and Dad had gone into the forest and I thought that they had left Jake, Adrian, and me behind because there was something in the forest that we weren't allowed to have. I didn't know, really, what it was, but they wanted it more than us. I didn't think we compared to much of anything. "Come on," I told them.

I helped Adrian tie her boots. As I did that, Jake held his hand outside. "It's dark and raining." "Come on," I said. The things I recall are like cast-off bits of personal archaeology, and only reveal hints of what I was really feeling and thinking then.

I woke in the middle of the night and stood up, kicking a Lego across the floor, and the sound immediately made me know that I had already heard the sound that night. Jake wasn't in his bunk. He had climbed down and kicked a Lego and I woke up, but then went right back to sleep thinking he was just going to the john. Maybe he had gone to the john, but he hadn't come back to the bedroom. Some time had passed between him climbing down and me waking up, but it wasn't a lot of time because I hadn't really gone back to sleep. I knew then I should be a little bit scared. I walked through the kitchen. The light emitted a thick, gnarly hum and glared down on the sink, making the aluminum glitter and the counters look really still and harsh. In the middle of the night, the stray crumbs and the nicks in the Formica looked like something someone had arranged. I opened the door and let in the smell of outside, the odor of the mucky lawn, rotting bamboo leaves, the sweet smell of flowering fruit trees. The dusk wind had stopped moving the trees. I could hear the distant sound of voices coming from the rhododendron bush Oliver and Jake had come out of when we had been playing hide-and-seek. That was the stupid trick we would play on other people, Jake and me, we would let them hide and then we would leave them in their hiding spots waiting for us to uncover them. And I had been left in my spot. I had been left in the bottom bunk and now here they were talking about Adrian. I wasn't invited, I guess, because I was the one who had made her what she was now. Jake didn't think she was dead. But he told me that he didn't think she was alive either. Then what is she? I asked him. He didn't answer me. A flickering light came out of the bush. I couldn't go there.

I went back to my bed and closed my eyes, but I couldn't go to sleep. I pulled the covers over my head. I pulled the scratchy part of the blanket up. Usually, when I pulled the covers up because it was cold, I would have the soft, silky margin of the blanket lying over my nose. But, to keep out Sasquatches or the dead, I thought I had to have my eyes covered by the blanket and my nose pressed into the scratchy part. I waited and I waited and must have finally fallen asleep, because I woke again when I heard the springs squeak in Jake's bunk. I could smell him, and he smelled like smoke and wax and dirt. I don't know why, but I was able to really go back to sleep then, once I knew he was back in the bunk. In the daylight, I told myself as I fell asleep, I would go and look at the bush and see what was there.

When I woke, I didn't remember even waking up and going outside. I should have gone right then and looked but I didn't remember to or I didn't want to remember. I don't know now how long it took me, except I do know I didn't go for a long time.

Because I live with the results of decisions I made years ago, I remain responsible for them. I would like to believe that I could find absolution in only having been a child. But when a child kills another child, he has still destroyed someone and that person will never really exist. An absolute result means absolute responsibility.

I often imagined, looking at the last photograph of Adrian, that she and Jake had changed positions. Sometimes she stood closer to me in the image and sometimes he did. In looking at it now, I saw that I was in the middle of fussing with Jake. Adrian wasn't even paying attention to us or to Oliver taking the photograph. Oliver had been in the picture in a tricky way but I couldn't remember how. I looked into the bushes to see if I could see him. Dad stood behind us. Mom looked at whomever took the photograph; she was the only person really looking at the photographer.

I coaxed Mom to take me to the Sears in Bellevue, about fifteen miles away. At the Sears, in the Boy's section, they had every piece of the uniform and all for reasonable prices. I made Mom buy Cub Scout shirts, belt buckles, patches, and pins. I wanted to spread awards and decoration over my uniform until I had to have my own "work uniform" and "dress uniform." In the uniform, I felt that I clearly belonged to a community of boys who I could be like. I rolled a yellow handkerchief with a cub bear printed on the back and fitted a gold clasp around my neck. It was decorated with a corn cob. I wore clothing decorated with easily recognized icons, the same ones the other boys wore.

Of all the paraphernalia I had then, all I have left years later is a handful of pictures of me walking in a parade. I marched with my hands curled into my corduroy jeans, and Mr. Laxton walked beside the troop. His hand was cupped to his face, at once pushing his mustache away from his mouth and acting as a megaphone. He yelled— *left—left—left.*

My face appeared startled. I remembered listening for the harsh rise of the "L," and planting my left foot hard into the pavement. The trick to marching was not to watch the people around me, but to listen to the cadence and remember the beat. But I always cheated and watched the person walking in front of me, and so I was always a step behind.

A few days after he had narrated the history of the world, Mr. Laxton appeared at our living room window. Jake and I were home alone even though Oliver was supposed to be there. He had left after what he had said was an emergency phone call. In the darkness, Jake and I mistook Mr. Laxton's rapping on the windowpanes for branches bouncing against the shingles. The day had been clear and windy. As dusk fell, the wind picked up until the cedar trees started to heave back and forth, dropping their branches into the stand of cottonwood and alder across the street. He stood outside the living room window looking at us. Jake jumped from the couch. He pulled the curtain closed, scattering the curtain pins. "What is that? What is that?" I turned off the television and the blue glow it had cast on the wall died. I watched the picture swirl into a small dot and fade.

"Let me in," Mr. Laxton said from behind the door.

"No one's home," I said.

"Aldous, I'm coming in. It's Mr. Laxton."

I opened the door, and the cold air from outside filled the room. The smell of propane from the tank at the bottom of our yard gushed around him. Mr. Laxton stood in the room. His cheeks were burnished red and his ears glowed. I could tell Jake was afraid. He held his left arm to the side of his body, rubbed his elbow, and watched Mr. Laxton's feet.

"Where is Mr. Bohm?"

"Dad's at work," I said.

"Oliver?"

"He's out."

"As I suspected," he yelled. "I've caught them red-handed." He sat on the couch. Jake moved to the corner of the room. He turned on the light in the kitchen. He left the room and turned on the light in our bedroom, and in my parents' bedroom, and the bathroom. He turned on every light in the house.

Mr. Laxton stared out the window at the black shapes of the naked maple trees. Their branches picked at the sky. Then the living room light snapped on, and we could see ourselves reflected in the window. I stood looking at the three of us. For a moment, I could see Jake standing by the wall switch, and then he was gone. Mr. Laxton looked straight into my eyes. His face seemed loose and hung around his reddish eyes. "I gave him the winning rocket," Mr. Laxton finally said.

"What?" I asked.

"I gave him that rocket so that he would leave her alone. I want it back."

"I don't know where it is."

"Tell him it's mine." Mr. Laxton laid his palm across his nose and sighed. His fingers worked his eyebrows. As his hand slid back against his side, he pressed his index finger into his mustache as though he were fixing on a fake one. He looked at me for a long time. "You people don't get it, do you? She's my wife." Then he turned and left.

The bus arrived Sunday morning at the normal bus stop, but unlike a normal morning, I was the only kid standing on the roadside gravel. Mr. Laxton had told me that if I wanted to remain in his troop, I would have to go to Sunday school once a month. I told Mom because I knew Dad would forbid me to go. She asked if it cost anything. "No," I said, but I didn't know. The bus was blue instead of yellow. I climbed the steps, waiting to be asked for fare or payment of some kind. The driver was a wizened old man who smiled at me and said, "Get on board this spirit-train, son." I jumped up the stairs and found myself in a crowd of older kids I didn't recognize. I didn't have to pay. A kid sitting next to the driver scooted against the window and smiled at me. The other children on the bus looked at me without the frowns or the blank stares that I was used to on the school bus. I slid into the seat next to the kid who had scooted over. "My name's Peter," he said.

"Bohm," I said. "Aldous Bohm." He smiled again and turned to stare out the window.

The bus driver hollered, "Hey kids, what are we going to do with this little light of yours?" The kids started to sing and clap to a familiar cadence. I didn't know the words.

This little light of mine, I'm gonna let it shine
This little light of mine, I'm gonna let it shine
This little light of mine, I'm gonna let it shine
let it shine, let it shine, let it shine

I tried to stare out the window, but Peter kept looking at me. "Don't you know the words?"

"Should I? I don't even know the words to 'Midnight Rambler' by the Rolling Stones and that's my favorite song."

"You should pretend to sing," Peter said.

"I can't sing," I said. "I used to try singing all the time when I was a kid. I would make up songs and then my Dad caught me and he started to laugh. He said that's the worst, crappiest noise he ever heard. So I stopped singing."

"Shhh," an older boy said from behind us. "You two had better sing."

Peter started to sing along and I opened my mouth and mouthed the words, moving my mouth like everyone else's, but I felt as though the soundtrack hadn't been synchronized.

Finally, the bus came to the top of a gravel driveway that circled up a hill overlooking pastures and the distant line of the Snoqualmie River. The kids hurried out of the bus and lined up in the parking lot. The older kids stood in one group and the younger ones in the next and, finally, I stood in the last group of the youngest children. Fiberglass Quonset huts lay around the parking lot. The bus driver climbed back into the bus and drove away, leaving us standing in our little groups.

I drew my sneaker through the gravel of the lot. I looked around at the other kids. They each had their own blue backpack plastered with silver-dollar-sized buttons that read, "Here Comes the Sun," or "Jesus Loves You," or "Snoqualmie Bike-a-Thon 1976." I swung my lunch box and bit my lip. I looked around for Peter, but he wasn't in my group.

Four men in black suits walked from behind one of the huts. They didn't look at us, but walked into the middle of the parking lot and said, "Come on." Each group marched into its Quonset hut. Inside, the hut was set up just like a school classroom: the same short desks, the same plastic chairs, a chalkboard with the alphabet written out on top. The only difference was that the Quonset hut had scenes from the Bible painted across the ceiling. In each of the pictures, bearded men in robes gestured to each other. In one, a cloud split open and a hand reached out. The lightning symbol had been painted under the cloud. I spent a long time looking at the ceiling and, finally, the instructor tapped my desk with his hand. "And hello, young man. Sorry to disturb your reverie, but you should introduce yourself to the class."

I looked around the room and found that all the kids my age were staring at me. I recognized a few of them from school, but they were the kids who hung out at the swing during recess and I didn't know them. "Bohm," I said. "Aldous Bohm."

"It's great to meet you, Aldous," the teacher said. He sat on a desk next to me and started talking about the beginning of the world. He asked the class questions and everyone, except me, raised his hand. The teacher could call on anyone and the student would continue the story from where he had left off. It went on and on and I didn't know what to make of it.

"Aldous," the teacher asked me. "What did God do with Adam's rib?"

"He gave it to the farmer in exchange for some fresh vegetables?"

"What farmer?"

"The farmer of this garden we've been talking about."

A bell buzzed so loudly that I thought it was a fire drill, but the teacher smiled around at the class. He stood up and pulled his slacks out from his legs. The other kids grabbed their backpacks and filed out the door. I followed them. I didn't know where we were going. The parking lot filled with the children and they milled around, collecting in knots of people. The teachers stood in a group by one of the huts and smoked. I couldn't tell which hut I had come from. I wandered the lot looking for Peter, but just when I saw him, a buzzer sounded again and the kids ran back into the huts. I ran toward Peter's hut. I recognized one of the children from my former class, but I found myself in a hut full of the oldest children. These kids had the start of facial hair. They whispered to each other until the teacher came through the door and they were quiet. He looked around the room and then opened his desk. He took out a bundle of pencils and a stack of papers. He handed them to the first kid and he handed it to the next. Finally, the pile of limp, mimeographed sheets slipped past my table. I found that I had a test. It was multiple choice, but how was I supposed to know what Jesus did with the loaves and fishes?

No one noticed that I was in the wrong group, and when the test was over, after the next buzzer sounded, I followed everyone to an outdoor shelter where they all took Tupperware lunch boxes out of their blue backpacks. They sat in groups. I sat by myself with my lunch box and, as soon as I finished my sandwich, I packed up everything and started the walk home.

In an effort of self-edification, I started carrying the Bible with me all the time. I tried to read it, but it was easier to just quote the Ten Commandments. We had to deliver them at the den meetings, like the Pledge of Allegiance. I told Oliver that he was going to Hell. I listed the Ten Commandments and I told him all about the Hell I had read about, with its lurid glow of flames just hot enough to torment him forever but not hot enough to destroy him.

"You are committing adultery with Mr. Laxton's wife. Everyone knows. You will go to Hell."

I told Oliver this while eating dinner with Dad and Jake. We ate roast beef sandwiches made from beef Dad had brought home from the kitchen where he worked. I told Dad that he had stolen and that he would go to Hell while I was in the middle of putting my mouth around the sandwich. "Dad," I said matter-of-factly, "Thou Shalt Not Steal, and that means that you will also go to Hell. In Hell they say the devil has a barbecue and he roasts people all day long. In Hell, the devil has a bonfire and he burns the clothes off people all day long. I know; I've seen the pictures."

Oliver started to laugh. Dad grabbed my sandwich. It slapped against the back of the garbage bag. Jake stopped eating. He spit a mouthful of food onto his plate. Dad, Jake, and I watched Oliver laugh. He laughed until tears began to form at the edges of his eyes. The noise made a soft wheezing hiss and that was it. It sounded as though he were forcing a hairball out of his throat.

"You're going to Hell," I said again.

"Go to your room," Dad said. "I don't want to see you."

As I left, I knocked my chair over. I made a face at Jake. I tried to make a spectacle. My face felt as though someone were running hot water through it. Once I got into my room, I opened my window and jumped outside. My shoes sunk into the muddy trench behind my bedroom and I ran up to the ruins of the barn that stood in the forest just above our house. I didn't want to see Dad or Jake or Oliver.

I also savored the moment a little, because I had made Dad respond somehow. I made him respond with my words. He had reacted to me. Dad had stopped chewing his sandwich. He had looked into his plate and his lips had turned white. It seemed like a victory for me, once I was sitting in there. Mom had put some old wooden lawn furniture in the barn. The walls of the barn had rotted off so that the wall posts rose like columns to the roof. Moss draped over the rotting roof. The forest around our house had once been cleared for a farm and, now, young fir trees had begun to return. Slugs crawled across the surface of everything. I picked them off the seat and sat alone in the woods. I savored my righteousness as I listened to the birds call in the forest and the raindrops fall from the maple branches. Even though I hadn't eaten much of my dinner, I felt comfortably full.

I could see the house below me, and smoke rose from the chimney. I didn't want to go back to the house. I wanted to sit quietly in the forest and not do anything. I would ponder. From my coat pocket, I removed the New Testament Mr. Laxton had given me. I flipped through it. I heard the swish of ferns and plants moving, and I knew someone had followed me from the house. I placed the book under the chaise cushion. Oliver climbed into the old barn. He sat on the floor with his legs folded under him.

He didn't say anything for a long time. I could hear him breathing in and out. I started to get mad, because his soiled presence was wrecking my peaceful righteousness.

"I think sinners should repent," I said.

"Sure you do," Oliver said. "You know, I was chaplain's assistant in the war. Catholic. Raised a Catholic, just like your Dad. I was in on the whole thing, so you telling me that kind of crap doesn't really bother me. Well, it doesn't bother me in the way I think you'd like it to bother me. It pisses me off that Mr. Laxton has brainwashed you and you don't even know it. But I don't really care about sin. Your Dad does, though, he's a real fan of sinning."

"He has to repent."

"He can't. He's atheist. He's an atheist who believes in sin. It's sort of a waste."

"You need to repent."

"I don't. I know how these things work. Nothing happens to people who do whatever they want. They just get to do whatever they want. Whatever you've been told, you need to remember that this place is very old and a whole lot of life has happened that God doesn't know anything about."

In the spring of 1978, I realized I would never get beyond the rank of a Cub Scout in the Boy Scouts. At the last pack meeting in the winter, the Scouts held a meeting to promote the older Cubs to Boy Scouts in a ceremony called "The Arrow of Light."

When the first part of the pack meeting ended, we gathered around a makeshift stage of lunch tables. Astroturf

coated the tabletops. Keith and Greg were going to be promoted, and Willie sat next to me.

He tried to make jokes with me. He whispered, "So
who's the clown in the blue zoot suit?" when all the boys
wearing their uniforms stepped onto the stage.

"Look at the nose on that guy," he said, talking about
Greg. Greg and Keith stood with the other boys, and I
thought they looked somehow imbued with mystical
power. They had been chosen to undergo a rite of passage
while I sat in the audience.

Each boy stepped into the spotlight, the so-called
Arrow of Light. I suppose that it must have been meant to
be God's ray shining down on the chosen ones. When
Greg stood forward, he repeated the words that the scoutmaster fed to him. I could hear a slight quiver in his voice;
I didn't think it was stage fright, but the power of the
incantation that he spoke. He said each word slowly and
spoke each sound.

We all sat, witnessing Greg recall the words. He stood
in profile to the light, and then turned suddenly to face the
light when a shape beside him whispered something to
him. The light turned his face white and bleached his hair.
His eyes sparkled as though they were made of marble and
had been polished to a fine luster. I think he believed for a
moment, when the light shone down on him and he moved
from the circle of young boys to the older boys, in every
word Mr. Laxton had told us about the way the world was.

He believed in each moment of the universe as narrated by Mr. Laxton. He believed when the light shone on him that a God existed that would protect him and that he would grow up to be happy. In the space of time that Greg recited the words, I think everyone in the room also spoke them and maybe believed them. I could hear us all breathing more or less on the same intake and exhale. Except Oliver, of course, who breathed on our exhale, but then he depended on our standard to act in opposition, and for that moment we were all connected and it didn't matter what we believed.

In the spring it flooded. The bus drove on a raised road through fields covered with standing brown water. The water covered everything up to the small hills. In a few places, stands of trees rose out of the brown plain. Farther from the road, the surface of the water reflected the sky in sepia tones. The water flowed across the road and the bus would rush through it, the parting water spraying into the rippling water. Sometimes, we passed a house that seemed to float in the water.

Mom started to get phone calls. The first caller said she was concerned about my "spiritual growth in such a desolate household," and volunteered to take me to church with her family.

When Dad found out, he stamped around the house and then he said, "No, it's finished. This is Free America. We can believe whatever the Hell we want. There is no way in Hell you will go to this thing again."

"What thing?"

"This Cub Scout shit," he said.

But they had already decided that I didn't really fit in. Maybe Greg had turned me in and told them that I couldn't think of good insults. Maybe the number of easy merit badges I had compared to the difficult achievement badges flagged my file and I was kicked out. Mrs. Laxton drove her car into the driveway just as I came home from school one day. I turned off the after-school cartoons. As I opened the door, Oliver climbed out of the attic.

"Amelia," he said.

"Hi, Oliver," she said. She held her purse in her hands. "I was just dropping by to tell Aldous some bad news. I don't think it's a good idea if he continues to come to the den meeting at my house."

"Then we'll see you at the pack meetings," Oliver said. He smiled and leaned against the door. I felt the loss of intimacy between my uncle and her. They didn't whisper.

"No," she said. "It's been decided that it just wouldn't be a good idea for Aldous to attend any more meetings." She pulled her purse up into the crook of her arm and turned to leave. "Bye," she said without looking behind her.

One spring night, I woke and rolled out of the bunk bed. Jake didn't stir from his bunk. I found Lance's torsion rocket and put on my jacket. I hiked until I came to the edge of the rushing floodwater. In the darkness, I could hear the bulk of water sliding over the floor of the valley, like a steady groan. Above the dark river, a few clouds hung low to the flowing water, catching the light from Snoqualmie. I wound the propeller, set the hull of the rocket into the cold river, and let it go. The propeller turned and carried the missile into the darkness. I imagined somebody finding the rocket far downriver and thinking that it was some sort of toy boat. Really, they probably wouldn't know what it was. They would lift the object out of the water and marvel at its strangeness, not knowing that it had really been Oliver's only trophy.

Sixteen

Willie and I were isolated from the parks and the back-yards of the children in Snoqualmie. We lived at the end of the road, far past the asphalt cul-de-sac where the cruising high schoolers turned around. The rutted gravel road wound through stands of second-growth timber along the North Fork of the Snoqualmie River. But for a time in the summer of 1978, Willie and I didn't notice or care that we lived far beyond the other children's yards.

Willie, Jake, and I always rushed home from school so that we could draw. We fought to drink from the garden hose. Our thirst needed to be filled like an inflatable swimming pool. Dripping wet, we stumbled into the kitchen to paint. We drew abstract-expressionist finger paintings. We did watercolor landscapes. We used crayons and then used the iron to make the surface flat. Art filled the kitchen and overflowed in glaciers of masking tape and construction paper and butcher paper into the living room. Mom selected one picture every day from each of us. She hung the pictures on the brick wall Dad had built behind the Franklin stove.

When Dad stopped going to work in the morning, he and Oliver started filling the kitchen with smoke in the long afternoons. After school, Jake, Willie, and I rushed into the house, but Mom sat knitting or reading in her corner watching Dad and Oliver talk. We sat on the porch, waiting for the dusk so Dad would leave for his graveyard shift at the Red Diner. As soon as he left, we took over the kitchen table with paints and brushes and paper. Willie stayed at our house far past the time he should have headed home. The dark forest scared him. Finally, his stepmother would call, and he would run as quickly as he could toward his house.

Then Willie and I started to play at his house, a rambling structure perched on the edge of a gully. A small stream gurgled in the depths of the hollow. In the kitchen, we looked through the tops of the cedars; it looked as if his house were built in the trees. On the other side of the house, the forest of gigantic Douglas fir stretched over the roof. The house smelled like an old campfire; the floorboards creaked; adults had to duck to pass through the doorways; the house seemed to have been built long ago exclusively for the use of children.

Willie had truck magazines. He knew everything about eighteen-wheelers. When he grew up, he wanted to drive his own rig, like Bandit's friend from *Smokey and the Bandit*. We read Willie's magazines and drew pictures of trucks. While we played in his room, a long rectangle carpeted with thick orange shag, his fifteen-year-old sister, Wilma, would tell us to shut up. "I'm studying." Stairs rose through the middle of Willie's room, ending in Wilma's room. The door had been removed and Wilma had hung a bead curtain from the frame. When Wilma ran up the stairs, she rushed through the beads, flipping them behind her. They jostled for a long time. I always stopped whatever I was doing when I heard Wilma rushing up the stairs. Her arms, flashing to part the beads, the sparkle of her frosted pink lipstick, and her long, swirling hair made me feel a little sick. Though she was only in front of her door for an instant, I had her features memorized. Sometimes, I played in front of her door and tried to peer through the beads into her room.

"What are you doing?" Willie said. "Get away from her door. She'll kill you."

"Why doesn't she have a door?"

"I can hear you two talking about me," Wilma yelled from her bedroom. She burst from under the beads. Willie and I sprawled onto the top step. She stood above us. I looked up her thighs to the curve of her breasts. She squatted down and I scooted away from her. "You two perverts better not talk about me," she said. When she leaned down, I noticed that even through the titanic pack of makeup, I could see small red pimples speckling her cheeks and forehead. She smiled at me, spreading her thin lips. The metallic pink glittered in the faint hall light. Her hand brushed my face and then she cupped my chin. She squeezed. "Because if I find out about it, I'll slice off your balls." She jumped up and the beads swirled around her, clicking and sighing as they jostled against each other.

Willie chuckled. "Witch."

"She has got quite the temper," I said.

Wilma was out of her bedroom and had me pinned. She grabbed my crotch and squeezed and pulled so hard that I felt as though my testicles were going to snap. I howled and then Wilma pushed me back and tickled my rib cage. The edges of her chewed fingernails left red welts. I felt I might pee my pants. "Just keep your mouth to yourself," she said.

In the aftermath, I lay on top of Willie's desk.

Willie sat on the floor by the desk. He read a magazine. Through the open window, I could hear the birds calling in the trees. A breeze shook the maple leaves and came into the room. I was covered in a film of cold sweat. "Do you think she'd do that again?"

Willie chuckled. "She will if you pay her."

"How much?"

" 'Bout a hundred," he said in a fake drawl.

"How old is she?"

" 'Bout a hundred."

"How old is your mother?"

" 'Bout a hundred. But she's not my Mom. She's just a woman Dad married. She plays the fiddle and drinks whiskey. Wilma says she's the devil but we still have to call her Mom."

"Where's your Dad?"

"At work. After it's dark, Mom will give you a ride home. Her name is Rosaline. My Dad, he has the same name as I have. People sometimes call him Big Willie."

"Then you're Little Willie?"

"Shut up." He socked me in the ball of my shoulder.

Rosaline drove me home. The Minipis' driveway skirted an orchard. The late spring dusk lit the blooming fruit blossoms, making the entire stand of trees glow. "It's just lovely," Rosaline said. Petals had fallen off and they covered the ground. She drove slowly past the trees and told me to roll down my window. The scent of the grove filled the car. The limbs of the trees twisted into the knotted canopy of crossing branches, leaves, and flowers. A few of the trees supported branches that had been slipped into their old trunks and secured with rope and tar. "See those branches," Rosaline said. "Big Will and I grafted them there. Our orchard is almost seventy-five years old. It's one of the oldest orchards in the valley. Five years ago, Big Will and I moved here, and this orchard and the entire farm were in danger of being bought up by Weyerhaeuser. These trees would have been cut down. Now we're here, making the old trees grow fruit and giving them new sap." She stopped the car. "I just love being next to these old trees. They've provided life to so many people over the long time they've been here." She looked at me and I stared past her at the trees and the gigantic piles of blackberries that looped up into the maples beside the pasture and then beyond to the ranks of Douglas fir. Even though the pasture stood in the fading light, all round it the forest had been dark for hours.

"It's nice," I said. I imagined that the bears didn't come out of the forest to eat the fruit in the Minipis' orchard. Our orchard, filled with stunted, blackberry-covered trees, attracted the bears in the autumn. They stumbled through the bushes, drunk on the rotting apples and pears. The Minipis' orchard seemed safe enough to sleep in at night.

Rosaline started the car up again. She wore a burgundy flower-print dress with white lace around the collar and cuffs. Pewter cuff links glittered in the light from the windows. A few strands of exceedingly fine hair, so thin that part of the stray strands seemed to disappear and reappear in the air, slipped free from her bun. Her nose was large and looked like a man's. Her lips were thin and red against her pale skin.

She pulled into our driveway, to our small house, with its stand of runt fruit trees. Mom opened the front door, wearing an apron and her rubber gloves. "Hey," she said.

"Hello," Rosaline said. "I'm Mrs. Minipis, Willie's mother."

Mom looked at me and then back at her. "Did Aldous break something?"

"Oh no," Rosaline said, "hardly." She laughed to herself, a quiet noise that sounded like coughing. "It's dark. I just wanted to bring Aldous home. And drop by and say hello. Hello."

"Thank you for bringing him home."

"No trouble." Mom and Rosaline stood in the dark yard for a second. I watched the moths flock from under the eaves of the trees and dance around the porch light.

"Please, come inside. Would you like a cup of coffee?"

Rosaline sat on our couch, looking at the paintings Willie, Jake, and I had painted. They covered the wall behind the stove and a few had turned a little brown from the heat. Mom made coffee. "Cream?" she asked from the kitchen.

"Black, please, with a little honey if you have it. The kids' paintings look good."

"Yeah?" Mom carried the coffee and sat in the chair next to the couch. She looked at me sitting at the other end and frowned a little. I smiled at her.

"Willie told me," Rosaline said, "that you were a painter and that you were showing him the craft."

"I don't know much about it."

"The paintings look good. Whatever you're telling them is working."

"Really?"

"Oh yes," Rosaline said. "You should teach painting. I mean, look at that top row. They're really good. And to tell me that a twelve-year-old had done them. I would have never guessed, except that they're behind the fireplace."

"I'm only ten," I said.

"See," Rosaline said. She smiled at me. "Only ten. You know developmentally that ten- to thirteen-year-olds have the most hang-ups."

"Especially if they're Aldous," Mom said.

"I'm not retarded," I said. "I do good in school."

"Do well," Mom corrected me, and rolled her eyes.

"Willie told me about the big painting you did of a trestle? I'd like to see it, if you don't mind."

Mom slid from the counter, where she had been leaning. "He told you that? Well, you're going to be disappointed. But you can look at it if you like. It's in the bedroom. Please excuse the mess." They stood at the far end of my parents' bedroom. My parents' bed, a gigantic frame Dad had found at an antique mall in Sultan, took up most of the room.

"Nice bed," Rosaline said. "It sure is big."

"Fifty bucks," Mom said. They squeezed between the foot of the bed and the wall, stepping over a cardboard box full of books. Rosaline almost fell, but grabbed onto the bed frame. "Sorry," Mom said. Mom often did this, and it embarrassed me even then. She would apologize for anything she had that other people liked or she would tell a story about how worthless this thing really was. She had a reddish stone ring in a silver setting that people often admired, asking her whether it was real. "Oh no," she said. "It's glass. It's nice, isn't it? But it's a fake."

"Oh, yes," Rosaline said. She stood under the window that looked out over our backyard at the hillside pasture of our neighbor. "Willie was right. This is a very, very nice painting. It's a shame that the bed is in the way."

"Now you're obliged to say something nice," Mom said, "After undergoing the gamut of getting to the other side of the room."

"No. Really, I'm very impressed." Rosaline began to make strange clucking noises. "It's great. It's just excellent."

The painting covered most of the bedroom wall. It showed a trestle where Mom had hiked with Jake and me almost every day for a month. We had our own place on the old gravel levee where the rusted tracks ran. Mom would walk around the trestle, stand on the trestle, constantly drawing, making watercolors and paintings, sometimes off in the forest and sometimes closer to the trestle.

She had made this painting in the old root cellar, before Dad had kicked her out of the space, filled it with black potting soil, and started growing his plants. There was something oddly unstable about the trestle, though. It looked as if it might fall at any moment, even though all the supporting timbers seemed solid. The light of the painting was a dramatic dusk light with a far-off intensity of color, but closer to the trestle the colors were cool and already in darkness. The view was from the base of the trestle, down in the stream gully that it passed over. I could see through the girders of the timbers to the sky, with a moon just visible through the cedar trees. Each time I looked at the painting, I could never decide if it was morning or evening.

Standing closer to the painting, I could see the impact of Mom's brushstrokes. Long forceful trails of splattered paint ended in tight knots like tadpole bodies. The trestle itself was composed of strong, short brushstrokes layered and stacked, while the cool colored shadows in the trees and the shape of the gully were in smoothly applied colors, lacking any sign of having been placed on the canvas, leaving the heavy trestle to float unstably in space.

Over coffee, Rosaline told Mom about her fiddle playing. She played with two other people at weddings and at parties. Mom used to play the violin when she was growing up. The violin sat at the back of the coat closet; dust and fine splatters of paint covered the case. "Let me have a look at it," Rosaline said.

"No. It's okay where it is."

"How long has it been since anyone has touched it?"

"Not too long." Mom stood up and filled both of their coffee cups. She turned to me and topped off my cup of Kool-Aid with coffee. She sat and said, "Okay. A long time."

I sipped my coffee and Kool-Aid, then went into the kitchen to dump it into the sink. I went to the back of Mom and Dad's closet and dug out the heavy violin case. The scales of the hide-covered case felt rough and cool against my hands. Rosaline held the dusty case on her lap. Frowning when she opened it, she slid her hand under the violin and lifted the smooth wooden body from the case.

"It looks a little ill," she said. She held it up to her chin and plucked the strings, then brought the bow across the instrument. A strange, discordant howl filled the living room.

"See," Mom said. "You have the right kind of body for it. Your arms are long and thin. My arms are stubby and fat. Your fingers are obviously strong. Mine are curled from slinging coffee."

"Oh, quiet." Rosaline giggled. She played with the top of the violin and then played a scale. It was less discordant. "I think you need new strings, but this is a nice instrument. You should practice again."

"I don't think I have the frame for it."

"Who told you that?"

"No one." Mom took a sip of her coffee. "Just my music teacher and the first guy I lived with."

"Asses," Rosaline said. "You have a very nice frame and that has nothing to do with playing the violin, or anything else."

"He didn't complain about my frame when we were in the middle of it."

"Who didn't complain?"

"The guy that I lived with." Mom took a sip of coffee. "Or my music teacher, for that matter."

Rosaline laughed and Mom smiled as she sipped more of her coffee. Rosaline played a song on the violin, keeping time with her foot tapping on the floor. It slid along and I was uncertain if she was just tuning the instrument or if she had started the song. And then she began to sing.

> *Walked up Ellum and I came down Main*
> *Trying to bum a nickel just to buy cocaine.*
> *Ho-Ho, honey, take a whiff on me.*
> *Take a whiff on me, take a whiff on me,*
> *And everybody take a whiff on me,*
> *Ho-Ho, honey, take a whiff on me.*

When Rosaline finished, she snapped the violin away from her neck and made a silly face at Mom.

Mom and I clapped. "Great," Mom said. "Can you teach me a song? Would you like some more coffee?"

"Thanks, no," Rosaline said.

"With a touch of Bailey's?"

"Well, that sounds like a different matter."

Oliver threw open the door. When he saw Rosaline, he leaned against the door frame. He hadn't shaved for a few days, so his hair grew in a thin goatee. He wore a pair of black slacks, a loose-fitting white shirt that was open a few too many buttons, and his wire-rimmed glasses. He paused at the door for a second. "Hello," he said.

"Hi," Rosaline said. "You're Paul?"

"Oliver. Paul's brother. I don't believe I've been introduced."

"Rosaline Minipis. Willie's stepmother." She offered her hand.

Oliver leaned down to give her a hug. He picked her up out of her chair and held her for a second, then set her back away from him and stepped back to look her up and down. "You're too young to be Willie's stepmother."

Rosaline seemed amused. "You'd be shocked, I'm sure, to find out how old I am."

"Can we get you anything? Beer? Coffee?"

"Gayle's nudging my coffee with Bailey's right now."

"Really?" Oliver said. He looked away and then he ran into the kitchen. "Give me some, give me some," he said. Rosaline and I looked at each other as he skipped outside to the ladder up to the attic, a tall glass of coffee in one hand. His charge shook the entire house.

Mom and Rosaline talked into the evening. And when she left, Mom said, "Well, she doesn't like us." I didn't understand. I had listened to them talk, watching Rosaline lean toward Mom when they laughed. And I realized that adults moved in mysterious spirals around Jake and me. Rosaline hadn't said that she didn't like us. She had smiled when she left and said, "I'll make sure Big Will and I return your hospitality real soon. I look forward to seeing you again. You'll have to sample some of our blackberry wine." Mom picked up Rosaline's coffee cup and poured the remains down the drain and washed the dishes.

That night, after Mom and Dad went to sleep, Oliver sat up with me at the kitchen table, and we put together the puzzles Mom had received for Christmas, pictures labeled: *The Mill Pond, English Garden, Mountain Meadow.* Mom had never built the puzzles and, as the fresh pieces came undone, a brown powder coated our hands. We stacked the finished puzzles on top of one another, like finished work. Together, we developed a quick system. We built the straight borders around the edge and then worked with the different colored areas. I worked sky blue and forest green. Oliver worked water blue and ground brown. We could have been professionals. He asked me questions and he drank coffee. To all his questions, I said, "I don't know." I didn't.

"Who is Rosaline? Who is Will? How old is Willie? His mother is? Have you ever seen Rosaline naked? What is her breast size? Her waist size is _____, fill in the blank."

Willie's parents had a sauna. Willie and I sat in it with towels wrapped around our waists. Our skin became sticky and damp. It turned luminous. My head cleared and felt like a tight cedar box. The room was lined with cedar. Willie lay back and closed his eyes, but I became bored after awhile. I felt like I was sitting in someone's lungs.

"When will we be done, Will?"

"When we feel better."

"I feel worse, Will."

"You will feel better, Bub, then we can go, Bub." But I felt worse and worse, and finally I felt like all the fluid in my body had been squeezed out onto my skin, where it pooled and evaporated. My blood was getting thicker, and my skin was becoming coated in brine. I was turning to salt.

Watching the cedar lining in the room, as I became dizzier and dizzier, I thought the grains of wood started to swirl and rush. "I'm done," I said, "I feel better." The walls blacked, and then faded back in with white flashes.

When we stepped outside, into the musty hallway between the sauna house and the house, I smelled the alders and maples in the forest, a mix of mildewed wood, rotting leaves, and wood smoke. The floor of the hallway was littered with leaf pulp, branches, and dog tracks. Bits of wood stuck to my feet.

Oliver loved the sauna. He winked at me when he would go up to the Minipis' house to use the sauna. "I think I'll pay Big Will a visit."

He and Will would sit on the porch, overlooking the dismal gorge, drinking wine. Will brewed his own wine from blackberries. He bottled the wine in old green bottles and stacked them in a storeroom below the sauna. Oliver told me, once when he was smoking with Dad, that if he finished two bottles with Big Will, they would start on the third, and Big Will would drink almost all of it. Then Will would start to nod and fall asleep. Oliver would go into the sauna and Rosaline would meet him there and they locked the door.

Oliver and Dad returned from a fishing trip empty-handed on the day we first had dinner at the Minipis' house. They tossed the fishing poles into the broom closet. Oliver stomped upstairs to beat the typewriter. Dad abused the lawnmower, kicking it to make it start and slamming it against the boulders bordering the lawn. When Dad finished, he stood in the kitchen, drinking from an aluminum mixing bowl filled with tap water. Fragments of grass leaves coated his white T-shirt. He stood with his legs apart and lifted the bowl up as he chugged the water down. Oliver sat at the table holding his mug of water, watching me watch Dad. "Your Dad's a big drinker," Oliver said.

"Sure is," I said.

After they had showered, they stood in front of the bathroom mirror, shaving and putting on cologne from the green glass bottle. They waited on the porch for Mom to bathe and dry her hair with a gigantic hair dryer that sounded like a vacuum cleaner tangled in shag carpet. Dad wore a pair of white jeans and a blue denim shirt. His face was tan and he seemed at ease with himself. He chuckled as he and Oliver passed a joint back and forth.

Jake and I sat on the porch with them, looking at the dusk begin to fall, listening to the birds go crazy in the dark forest. The smell of the mowed grass floated up into the air. One of our cats sat under the blooming fuchsia. The large pink flowers drooped into the freshly cut grass. Already, a few blossoms had wilted and draped in the carpet of bleeding hearts that grew in the rockery Dad had built with the stones he had carted out of the Snoqualmie River. The gray cat shifted back into the shadows, its eyes catching the last of the day's light. Each iris was a faint smudge of yellow. The cat flicked its tail from under the bush and vanished into the underbrush.

When we arrived at the Minipis' house for dinner, Rosaline opened the door quickly. She wore a long black dress she had ironed so often that the creases had worn into the cotton fabric. "Come in, I can't chat, I've got supper on the stove. Come in, Big Will will get you something to drink."

Big Will came down the stairs, holding onto the banisters. Behind him, a stained glass window filled the hallway with the orange sunset and the sparkling, red light of the stained glass. Tumbling down the steps, Big Will plunged into Dad and Oliver. "It is excellent to have company," he said, turning to Mom and hugging her and inadvertently enclosing my uncle and Dad in the span of his arms. He clasped them to his gigantic stomach. I looked past their shoulders at his bloated face. His skin turned crimson from the strain of squeezing my parents. Each feature was stuck into the loose flowing fabric of his face. He released Oliver and my parents and strolled across the Minipis' gigantic kitchen, stopping for a second to drop a slice of bread into his mouth as quickly as I could swallow an aspirin. He stopped in front of his cabinet of wine bottles. "Surely I can get you folks something to drink while Rosaline finishes cooking?"

He kept talking as he poured glasses of wine. He talked about playing the bass fiddle, which he did for a living. "I am not a little man among fiddlers," he said. He ushered Mom and Dad and my uncle out of the kitchen where he said Rosaline was "Doing her magic thang." He gestured my parents into two medieval-style chairs in the living room.

While we waited, Willie took Jake and me upstairs and I said, "Jake doesn't think my dead sister Adrian is dead. Do you, Jake?"

"She's not dead. Who killed her, if she's dead?"

I didn't have anything to say to this because I knew what he thought.

"I've never met anyone who has died," Willie said. "What was she like?"

"She was my sister," Jake said. "How do I know what she was like? What's your sister like? You might tell me something now. But then if she died, you'd say something different. She is still alive, but she can't come into the house because Aldous killed her."

"You're weird," Willie said. Willie sat back on the steps and looked up at the naked bulb over the doorway. "If she's dead of course she can't come into the house. Dead things rot. Flies come and lay maggots in them and then the maggots eat all of the fat and muscle and intestines and so forth. They eat everything until the dead person is just bones. A mold or something eats away the cartilage. That's what holds together the bones. I've seen dead animals along the road behind the house. A raccoon gets hit by a logging truck and its belly gets bloated because it is rotting and then so many maggots eat it that it makes a buzzing noise and then it is just a little bit of fur and bone and some wild animal found that and took it apart. Didn't last more than a week. Your sister, if they buried her, probably lasted longer. How long ago did she die?"

"Doesn't matter," I said. "They burned her."

"They did not," Jake said.

"They cremated her."

"That doesn't mean they burned her."

"That's what it means. They took her body and then

burned it and then gave Mom the ashes and she dropped them in the Snoqualmie on the way home."

"I don't remember that."

"We all did it," I said. "It was right before we came home. They stopped on the bridge and we all got out."

"We didn't do that," Jake said. "We couldn't have done that. Because Adrian isn't ashes."

"Dead is the opposite of alive," I said. "If you don't think she's dead, you don't know what death is."

"Who killed her if she's dead? Jake asked. "When you kill someone, even if it's by accident, that is wrong."

"An accident is if you run a stop sign and hit someone or get drunk and hit someone."

"You don't have to drive a car to kill someone," Jake said. "I know what death is. It isn't goneness but worse. It's the same as wereness. A stone is dead and a stone doesn't ever change, no matter what it does."

"Rivers and ice wear stones down," I said. "Every rock comes from a bigger rock."

"You aren't listening to me," Jake said.

"I don't know what you are saying. It doesn't make any sense to me."

"Me neither," Willie said.

At the dinner table, Willie, Jake, Wilma, and I sat at one end; the parents sat at the other end. Wilma didn't look at us while we ate. She had on a black dress, a bead necklace, and her frosted pink lipstick. She sat next to Dad and kept talking to him. Willie nudged me and nodded at his sister.

At the end of the table, Oliver kept Big Will laughing, a deep stomach rumble that vibrated the glasses. Rosaline covered her mouth while she laughed. When Oliver or Mom made a joke, Rosaline leaned across the table and touched them on the shoulder. Mom hoarsely coughed and laughed with her mouth full, which set off another roll of laughter. We passed around the dish of corn on the cob. We passed around the bowl of noodles. Big Will walked around the table splattering spaghetti sauce onto our plates and saying little things to each of us. "Sauce of a saucy woman," he said to Rosaline. "A ladle of spaghetti for a dandy dude," and so on, around the table.

Wilma leaned back in her chair to look up at Dad. Jake could hardly handle the pitcher of grape juice. He handed it me. I filled up my cup and passed it to Willie. Willie accidentally set it down on the table. "This," Dad said, "is the best meal I have ever eaten." Rosaline blushed and looked down at the table. "Thank you," she said. What she didn't realize was that Dad, after sharing a joint with Big Will in the living room, was ready to proclaim the exalted taste of burnt macaroni and cheese. "This food, I don't want to call it food, because many, many lesser things are called food—McDonald's sells food. But this, this meal before us, is composed of something, while nourishing, yes, that exceeds the taste of anything else I have ever tasted. I will attempt to describe: a spicy sauce filled with savory chunks of meat floating in a stringy fiber of *succulent* noodles. I see you laugh at the word succulent, but these noodles," and here Dad pulled a long noodle from his plate and stretched it wide, then snapped it into his mouth, sucking in the two free ends, "this noodle is succulent."

Wilma dropped the pitcher of grape juice on Dad's white pants. Dad jumped away from the table. Rosaline gasped. "Wilma!" Mom started to laugh. She fell against Oliver. "It's okay, Paul, honey. It just means you're not a little girl anymore." Big Will frowned. He looked at Rosaline, who had started to smile. Dad dumbly stood away from the table. The grape juice looked red against his crotch and spread away from it as though his penis had exploded.

"I'm really sorry, Mr. Bohm, let me get a towel." Wilma rushed into the kitchen.

"You're going to need to take off your pants, honey," Mom said.

"Take it off!" Oliver said.

"You can wear one of Big Will's pants. Wilma, this is your fault. Will you help Paul get his business sorted?"

"Yes, Mother," she said, returning with paper towels bunched in her hand.

"Don't take that tone with me," Rosaline said. "It's your fault. You shouldn't be so clumsy. How many paper towels is that? They cost five cents each. That must be a buck's worth of towels."

"The pitcher is heavy," Jake said.

But no one listened to him. Wilma and Dad went into the kitchen, and Oliver asked for seconds.

"But I just gave it to you," Rosaline said.

"I can never have enough, and anyway the noodles are so succulent."

Big Will and Rosaline laughed, I thought gratefully, because Big Will smiled and started to tell a story about an accident that had happened to him at the fiddle play-off in Sumner, Washington. "Now, in Seattle, they have contests worth some dough, but in Sumner, that's where all the old-timers go to show their tricks and strut. I can clean up in Seattle, but I go out to the Sumner event and that's it then . . ." Big Will told a long story about an old fiddler who had once been famed for the speed with which he played his fiddle. In the middle of the competition, it became apparent that his old dexterity just wasn't there. Everyone drank pints of beer. During the break and under the pretense of cleaning up, the old fiddler cleared away his competitions' pint glasses and heated them in the kitchen's oven. As everyone sat down to continue, the old fiddler said, "A toast," and he grabbed his glass. The other players grabbed their glasses and flung the pints across the room. They burned their hands on the hot glass and blisters formed on their fiddler calluses. The old fiddler won the contest because he was the only one who could play.

Dad returned wearing a long denim skirt with a poodle sewn onto the front. "How do you like my dress?" he said. He sat at the table and looked at Oliver. "Mighty fine," Oliver said.

"Where are your pants, honey?" Mom asked.

"They're in the kitchen sink. I couldn't get the stain out."

"Is your food hot enough?" Rosaline asked.

"Yes. It's excellent," Dad said through a full mouth. He kept eating.

"Will was telling us about playing the fiddle. He and Rosaline are going to play us something," Gayle said. "What happened to Wilma?"

"Mmm?" Dad asked. He looked up from his plate.

Mom jumped out of her chair. "I think I need another joint." Rosaline followed her into the living room and they sat down on the sofa. "I have an upset stomach," Mom said.

"It's the wine, that's all." Dad sat next to her, flouncing his skirt. Everyone laughed because they thought they could see his penis. I thought that I saw his underwear on backwards. I looked around at everyone else laughing, but they had stopped and were licking their lips. Oliver hand-

ed the joint to Big Will, who squinted and drew in a
mouthful of smoke and handed it to Rosaline, who sat
between Big Will and Oliver. Rosaline smiled and passed
it to Mom and Dad, who sat on the couch together, oddly
looking like a couple. And so it went around and around
the room, while Rosaline and Big Will prepared their
instruments. Big Will began to play his fiddle and Rosaline
sang in a quick twang. Oliver jumped up and had me
twirling around the room. Willie and Jake and I danced.
Dad and Mom danced. The room spun, and we flew
through the flat, blue layers of smoke, tripping and falling
onto our elbows and then around, ducking and dancing.

> *And it's ladies to the center and it's gents around the row*
> *And we'll rally round the canebrake and shoot the buffalo.*
> *And we'll shoot the buffalo, we'll shoot the buffalo,*
> *We'll rally round the canebrake and shoot the buffalo.*

Dad spun into the middle of the room, screaming, "Shoot
the buffalo!" His skirt flew up, showing that his underwear
were not only on backwards, but that the front of them,
stretched taut over his butt cheeks, were stained with a
sponge-cake crust of pink lipstick. But I realized then that
Big Will wasn't even looking at Dad, but at Rosaline, who
was sitting next to Oliver. Oliver had his hand on her knee
and she had just leaned away from him. Her eyes were
closed and her lips were pursed.

The fiddle stopped. No one said anything for a second as Big Will stood in the middle of the room. Marijuana smoke swirled around the room in a dense cloud at chest level, flat-bottomed and rising in fuzzy shafts. Hair curled around his eyes and fell into strands behind his neck. I thought he was going to fall over. He stood swaying. "I'm sick of it, sick of it. Sick. You two touch and fondle each other right here in my house. In my house. I'm sick of it."

"You act like we're having sex," Oliver said.

"You are. In front of me. I'm sick of it."

"We are not," Oliver said.

"Just get out, get out of my house." He pointed at Oliver with the hand holding the fiddle bow. "Out," he said, and he left through the bedroom door. The smoke clouds, stunned by the slammed door, flurried through the room, mingling corkscrews of fumes around Jake and me, and then slowly began to settle.

"So . . ." Oliver said.

"The night was winding down anyway," Mom said.

"I suppose so," Rosaline said. "Too much to drink."

"Too much," Dad said.

We left, and drove down the steep hill by the goat pasture. Overhead, the dark clouds rolled over the dark valley.

———

Somehow my friendship with Willie had drawn my entire family into his family. For a while we fared well enough. But when it was done, so was my friendship with him. He was a grade older in school, and I sometimes saw him in the play yard. He was the last of the kids who would talk to me, and I found that I no longer really spent much time with the children my own age anyway. My life was starting to really shift away from the world that kids talked about at school. Oliver would begin playing drums at two o'clock in the morning. Dad disappeared for three weeks in the mountains and returned with a flour sack full of quartz crystals. Mom worked graveyard shift at the Busy Bee Diner and drank her bedtime coffee with us as we ate breakfast to go to school. Sometimes, I wondered how things had come to this. I thought maybe Oliver had made this happen or maybe Adrian's death made this happen. I wanted to find something that had made it happen, so that I could maybe do what I wanted to do and have friends and be like everyone else.

For a while, on the bus to school, Willie and I rode next to each other, but we slowly ran out of things to talk about. When your Dad has slept with your best friend's sister, when your uncle has slept with your best friend's step-mother, how many times can the two of you rehash the plot of *Smokey and the Bandit?*

The Garden for the Sight Impaired

Seventeen

As I paid for a single-occupancy room in a San Antonio motel, the lobby windows painted with stick-figure reindeer and an amorphous, red Santa Claus, I thought of the motel as a place Mom would appreciate with its storable stacks of rooms, its Astroturf-carpeted hallways, and the Coke machines plugging the bottom of the stairwells. An ice machine ran on change and a dollar bill feeder. The fact that *motel* came from the words *motor* and *hotel* efficiently streamlined together reminded me of Mom's lesson about the economy of the traveler: Don't own anything you can't fit in your pockets.

"Single occupancy?" The motel clerk crushed out her cigarette in an ashtray that said "Party in Corpus Christi." She lifted her yellow fingers out of the ashtray coated with a layer of ash, twisted the particles into a little ball and dropped it back into the bowl.

"Yes," I said. Renting a room to do it for the first time seemed a little finicky to me. I had heard Oliver, Dad, and Mom tell stories about having sex for the first time in the backseats of cars parked on a back road, in the lot of the Hoquiam Elk Lodge, anywhere they could park long enough. And I had never rented a room before. I was certain I would blunder some form of procedure, sign the wrong line, say the wrong thing, and then she would be on to me and want to know if I was of age, if she was of age, if both parties consented, if money was changing hands. I was certain she would want to know what was going on. The manager glanced at me, making a quick circuit over my body, and pressed the keys into my hands. "Check out time is ten-thirty." She curled her yellow left-hand fingers to scratch behind her ear as she turned back to the page of her *People* magazine.

I met Janet in the stairwell next to the Coke machine. Janet grabbed my hands and said in a low voice, "You chickened out, didn't you? You didn't get the room."

I pulled out the plastic disk with the room number on it and a small brass key attached with a chain. "Come on, let's go," I said, relieved to find that my voice, at least, sounded sure of itself.

I walked up the outside stairwell. In the cool air, we heard cars sloshing through the damp highway. A scaffolding of steel girders supported each flight of steps out and away from the motel wall, away from the motel's structure of cell-like rooms. We stepped off the girders onto the Astroturf-carpeted terrace lined with twenty doors. A slanting, metallic stick-on number marked each door. "A fine establishment," Janet said.

"Cost-conscious," I said.

The room looked like the kind of place used for sloppy drug use, the kind that, in my mind, required rubber tourniquets and broken skin. The radiator issued a heavy, damp heat. The moisture held the set-in odor of dried blood as stale as Fort Sam's phlebotomy training room. A misshapen queen-sized mattress with an orangish chenille bedspread lay on a plywood board supported by a two-by-four frame. Urn-shaped lamps, one cracked and artfully glued back together, tottered on thin wire-lattice nightstands. A thin, chipped crack ran over the wide black surface like a zipper. Brownish sprays on the wall along the bed added a random element to the monotonous floral wallpaper. Four quarter-sized bolts secured the TV to the top of the cabinet and a wire bike chain looped under the bolts to a screw on the remote. Oliver used to say, "You get what you pay for." He'd raise his arms and say, "Free!"

"Well, well, well," Janet said. She set her bag on the edge of the bed. She lifted the sheet on one corner and took a whiff. "The linen smells clean. And looks clean. Should we assume that it is clean?"

"What else can you do?"

"Wrap ourselves in cellophane?" she asked. "Let's examine the bathroom. That should give us some clues."

A strip that looked like a Miss America pageant banner indicated that the toilet had been sanitized. "Well, the toilet is ready for safe sex," Janet said.

I realized then that I had forgotten to buy condoms. When Janet had asked me if I really wanted to stay in the barracks, she had said, "Wouldn't it be better if we just found a cozy, cheap hotel to spend a couple of days in, before we go back to our parents' houses and our first adult Christmas?" I had said that I thought it would be better, although I didn't know if I could live without green wool blankets. As soon as I got back to my room, I had written a list of supplies on my official Army stationary, writing condoms right over the Army logo, and then toothpaste, breath mints, cologne of some unobtrusive but pleasant scent, boxer shorts—nice ones—a belt, Tic Tacs, and new shaving blades. But at the store, after walking up and down the aisles picking out my things, I stopped and realized I still needed the condoms. I decided then I should buy them at a 7-Eleven or something because I didn't want to stand in line with the sunny orange or green package showing its bright, vampires-are-rising sunset and the couple embracing for the upcoming night of unproductive fornication—which is the only kind of sex I wanted. I couldn't allow the cashier to zip the box through the scanning laser, to see among my M&M's and Irish Spring soap that I was also purchasing twelve uses of individually wrapped latex condoms, effective, if used properly, against pregnancy and AIDS and other STDS. Twelve doses of intimate contact.

Janet brushed back the curtain to the shower and looked at the stall. A ring of cleaner with some hair clotted the drain. "This is where you get clean, among other things; unfortunately, we can't stuff the room into it." Janet caught her reflection in the mirror and swept her hair from her face. She turned slightly to the left and stuck her chin out. This motion unlocked a series of actions. She adjusted her breasts with a quick shove of her hands and bit her lips, then rolled them out. She smiled at me and looked back into the mirror. "What do you think?" she asked me. I thought the image in the mirror was wrong, a little off. Her left eye drooped a little and she had wide, dark bruises under her eyes that she had tried to hide with makeup, but in the hard light of the heat lamp and bank of vanity lightbulbs, they only looked deeper. "Well?" she asked.

"I like you."

"You think I'm pretty?"

"You're great," I said.

"But do you think I'm pretty?"

"Yes," I said.

"I wouldn't know what you were up to if you didn't."

She slid open the plastic slider in the vanity with a snap. The enamel inside had peeled and lay in little flakes on the shelves. Rust burns spread through the interior. "Nice enough," Janet said. "We can pretend it's clean."

"But really it's dirty," I said.

Her eyebrows knotted and she frowned. She glanced at me standing near the toilet, looking at my shirt and belt, at my creased pants and shoes. "Nice belt."

The hangers, looped around the crossbeam, crackled against the wall as Janet brushed them back against the closet wall. "I've always wanted these hangers for my own bedroom because then I would always have a hanger." Janet stood on her toes and blew a cloud of dust down from the top shelf. She coughed and buckled over and fell down on the floor.

"Janet?" As I ducked into the closet, Janet jumped out from the side and hit me in the head with a purple bag. "Get out of my closet, you fiend." She jumped down on the bed. "Look what I found." She held a child-sized purse, bunched around a drawstring.

She was staring at the bag and not looking at me and not adjusting her hair or biting her lips, and I felt relieved because we had this bag, this project, to examine and we didn't have to think about the first moves toward sex. I had no idea how to begin. We were here in a motel room, the bed was ready. But to just say, "How about we screw?" was beyond me, and Janet didn't seem to be in any hurry to get

naked or make me naked or even to kiss me. I began to wonder if I was assuming things. So much of what I knew about
this entire procedure came from male anecdotes, books, and
the movies. I thought maybe I was assuming too much.

She sat down with her legs spread on the floor and
dumped out the contents of the purse onto the carpet: a
silver-dollar-sized compact, metallic purple lipstick, a used
TWA ticket for San Antonio, a rubber glove full of quarter trinkets from the twenty-five-cent machine in front of
a grocery store. "Who do you think this belongs to?" Janet
asked. There was also a black rubber change purse that
puckered open when Janet squeezed the sides. Plastic bags
stuffed the pocket. One bag held a knot of marijuana;
another bag contained six slices of small paper. The last
bag had a packet of Zig-Zags. At the bottom of the purse,
Janet found a set of keys attached to a metal tube. She displayed the items in two neat rows and lay the purse to one
side like the geological curiosities displayed at the Rock
Chalet at the Snoqualmie Pass. The strange gathering of
items also reminded me of the odds and ends Oliver had
been carrying on him when he killed himself. The police
gave them to my father and he brought them home in a
brown paper sack and left it on the coffee table for weeks.
Sometimes, I would take Oliver's things out and lay them
on the table and try to piece together what had happened.

"These are the person's keys," Janet said. "And this is
mace. So, my guess is whoever left this here didn't plan to

leave it here. That's as far as I'm guessing. But still, I wonder what happened?"

"They were probably arrested," I said.

"They could have been killed or something, too," Janet said. "Whoever had this purse wasn't very old. Something happened to them suddenly and they left their keys and their marijuana behind."

"Their rubber glove and their dope," I said.

"What's wrong with dope?"

"I didn't say anything," I said. "But what is this?" I held up the plastic glove. I pulled out a flattened purple Roman playing a lute and standing on a flat base a capsule filled with a viscous, glow-in-the-dark green blob a plastic eagle attached to a key ring a plastic yellow Tyrannosaurus Rex and a dozen other supermarket trinkets. "These things don't really tell you anything about her," I said. "Why would she walk around with a glove full of these things?"

"Maybe someone gave them to her? You know, her boyfriend. Or her big brother or something."

"What does the name on the ticket say. What's the date?"

"Jasmin Clay, November eighteenth, 1986," Janet said. "So the ticket is only a month old."

"That sounds like a tombstone," I said. "Name and date. We do know the purse belonged to her now. What else do you think we'd know about her? I guess nothing, really, because these things tell you the same thing about this person as the furniture in this room tells you about the people who live here."

"Well, we live here," Janet said. "Her ticket is from Florida."

I asked. I pulled the rubbery thing out of its capsule. It stuck to my fingers with thick, glutinous tentacles. I threw the blob at the urn. It clung to the smooth surface and then rolled down the side into the lattice side table. It slid through a hole, leaving a tentacle to cling on the wire. Finally it slipped down onto the carpet.

"Now it's going to have hair all through it," Janet said.

"I don't think that there's anything we could leave that would tell future tenants of this room about us. I mean, even if we wrote a letter and hid it and someone found it, what do you think they'd make of it? They'd think this person was going to kill themselves. They might call the police. And that would be that. They would have done their duty, but they wouldn't have understood anything about me. Once we leave this hotel room, that's going to be it. We're going to be as gone as if we had never even been here."

"Are you saying coming here is meaningless?"

"No," I said. "It means something to me." I wondered now if she thought this, or if she was putting words in my mouth to see how I would react.

"Then what *are* you saying?" Janet asked. She rolled off the carpet and sat against the wall.

"I just think we don't know, that's all. The things in her purse are interesting, I guess. But we can't tell anything about the person who put them in the purse anymore than we can tell what a person is like from their interior decorating. People buy what is cheap, or what is in style, or what the stores stock. Our little purse owner didn't make any of the things in the purse."

"A person chooses the things they own," Janet said. "I think you can tell a lot about someone who owns a Morris chair and antique furniture and original art on the walls as opposed to someone who has Metropolitan Museum of Art prints on the wall and used office furniture," Janet said. "It really means something."

"One person has money and the other doesn't."

Janet scooped all the things together and dumped them into the bag. "How did you get to this? How long have I known you?"

"What?"

Janet sat on the edge of the bed. "My parents are just like yours," she said. "I joined the Army just like you."

"I didn't join the reserves," I said. "I joined the active Army, so I could get a start on things. I didn't join the Army so that I could get college money or whatever. What kind of car does your Dad drive?"

"What does that have to do with anything?"

"Did he buy it because it was cheap? Because he wanted to get from one place to another?" I asked.

"See, you have to admit that you're thinking he bought it for the other reason. Because of his personality. You can tell the personality of this woman because of the things in her purse," Janet said.

I asked again, "What kind of car does your Dad drive?"

"He drives an old Cadillac."

"A vintage Caddy? Restored, I assume."

"Well, he had it painted. I suppose your Dad drives something from the '70s, one of the generic cars, like a Nova, or a Fairlane, or a Duster or something. The kind they always use for car chases in the movies and they drive off cliffs and bridges and blow up."

I lay down on the floor while Janet said this. I looked under the bed. Dust bunnies lay in a wide swath under the middle of the bed. "I don't know," I said.

"I was just having fun," Janet said. "I'll put the purse back. I just found it, that's all. I didn't kill her."

"I'm sorry," I said, I climbed onto the bed and grabbed my book. I'll just lie down here and read and when I look up I'll be fine."

Janet jumped away from the bed and twirled around. "Here we are," she said. "Relax." She turned on the lamps and the overhead light in the main room and unzipped her bag. "Aren't you going to make yourself at home?"

"Yes," I said. I sat on the bed and took off my shoes. The mattress sank like a half-deflated life raft. I lay the spine of the book on my chest and started to read, listening to Janet unpack, to the snarl of zippers opening and closing, the buttons snapping, all kinds of noises. "Excuse me," she said. She walked over the bed. "This bed is quicksand," she said. Her socks were off. She wore long underwear under her jeans. The lace anklet brushed my nose as she stepped past me. "Hey, you almost kicked me in the face."

"Well, watch where you're lying," she said. I turned over and put my book on my face, breathing in the comforting smell of library dust and paper. I wished she would say something about us being here together in this room. When I looked up, Janet was fiddling with her Walkman at the table. "My tape's stuck," she said. Her things lay sprawled over the room, her jacket over a chair, one of her shoes in the middle of the room, the other one by the door. She had strung red and white ribbon around the top of the room and hung a card of Santa Claus over the bed. "Merry Christmas," she said. She stood away from her tape and grabbed a package from the top of her pile of loose luggage.

"I didn't get you anything," I said and felt my throat turning dry."

"Open what I gave you, it's only a small thing," she said. "Wait a minute." She turned off the overhead light and wrapped some of her red crêpe paper around the lamp, and it cast reddish strands of light up over the ceiling. "There, that's better," she said. I sat on the edge of the bed. She sat down next to me, turned slightly toward me. Her hair had slipped over her face. I brushed it back and then looked at the package she had given me.

It felt like a book. It was wrapped in gold paper. I unwrapped the paper and a small board book came out. *Girls Are Girls and Boys Are Boys: So What's the Difference?*

"Do you think I don't know?" I felt like I was floating in the humid air in the room. A cold drop of sweat started to leak from my hair.

"You idiot. Open it up."

Four condoms marked the page. *"Boys aren't Girls and Girls aren't Boys,"* I said. "I usually don't see most books advertised, 'Condoms included.'"

"Or boys and girls included," Janet said. Janet pushed me back onto the bed and kissed me.

For what seemed like both a long time and not a very long time, Janet pressed her lips against my face. I wanted her to kiss me on the lips, but she wouldn't after the initial kiss. The first kiss left a trace of her lipstick on my lips. It tasted oily and sweet like rose-flavored candy. She left a small puff of air on my skin as she faintly kissed my cheek. And then she pressed her warm face into the crook of my neck.

As she kissed me, she pressed her body into me. Her hip bone jammed into the soft tissue under my stomach and above my groin. I shifted back and her weight pressed down on me and I felt as though we were slowly sinking below a bath filled with Mr. Bubble.

Her hair covered my eyes, drifted over my face, exposing the ceiling above her, the tiles faintly browned toward their edges, and the ceiling lamp covered with the black bodies of flies caught in the dish. I closed my eyes as she pressed my shoulders down. And then she kissed me again.

I opened my eyes and her eyelashes brushed my eyelids. Even though I could see the small marks on her skin, the mole under her left eye had a barb of hair sticking out of it, the fine fibers of her facial hair looked like a powdery glow over her whole face. I felt as if I was in the shadow right next to her skin, like the astronauts passing around the moon, from the day into the night.

It bothered me a little, as I felt her teeth drag over my lips, that I really couldn't see anything, I could only feel the exhalation of her breath and listen to her slight directions. "Sit back," she whispered. I felt suddenly swallowed by her in the soft bed and her body on me, but I didn't want to move or stop anything because I wanted it to go on and on, and then she laughed. "Well," she said. "Did you shave today?"

I sat up. My neck felt hot. The vein running alongside my Adam's apple throbbed. The room looked washed-out. The sheets bunched around us. Janet's shirt was partially unbuttoned. I could see the white strap of her bra against her collarbone. "I could shave again," I said.

"Could you?" she asked. "Because you're sanding my face off. I think I've got rug burn."

"Should I shave right now?"

"No. Just let me recoup," she said. She sat on the edge of the bed "Let's smoke it," she said.

"Smoke what?"

She leaned over and grabbed the papers in one hand

and the baggie in the other. Rolling back, she sat with her legs crossed. "Let's smoke this and then have sex."

"What are you doing? You don't know what this is."

"It's marijuana." She said. "Hashish."

"Quiet," I said. I jumped off the bed and looked out at the hallway between the window curtain. No one walked outside; cars were still moving steadily on the highway. The window had fogged a little and felt cool against my face. I let the curtain fall back and felt myself back in the warm, damp room. It was shadowy and the lamp cast red arcs of light. Janet fumbled with the paper and came up with a loosely curled paper. Her joint sagged and dropped fragments of dope as she tried to hold it up to her mouth, and then it came completely apart. "It's more difficult than you think," she said.

"Have you smoked this before?" I asked.

"Someone has always had it already rolled. Could you try, maybe?"

I took the Zig-Zags and grabbed the book for a flat surface. I creased the paper and then placed crumbs in the fold as if it were a tiny burrito; pulling tight on one edge, I rolled the paper into a compact straw. I wrapped the ends and licked the length of the joint, tasting the paper and then getting fragments of dope that rolled out to the top of my tongue, and I couldn't help myself, but I cleared with a pinch just like my father used to. It was a fluid motion, as familiar as tying my shoes, and it brought back a kind of faded memory of watching my father teach Oliver how to roll a joint. I handed it to her.

"How, Mr. Bohm, do you know how to do that?"

Which was what I was afraid of as soon as she had said she wanted to smoke. My front of normality was about to be blown.

"I've seen the movies," I said.

"I've seen a lot of movies," Janet said, "but I couldn't just do that. Which movie?"

"*Cheech and Chong.*"

"This is perfect," she said.

"Why do you want to smoke now? Doesn't that make you not feel anything?"

"Like Novocain?"

"How do you know what you are feeling is not just the drug?"

"You know, for a guy who rolls a joint like that, it sounds like you've never smoked before."

"I have never smoked anything," I said.

"For me, it makes me feel nice. It makes me feel more alive. It makes me see things in a different way. It's fun. I don't know. It sounds stupid to describe it. I just like it."

She sat cross-legged on the bed. She licked her lips and then leaned forward and kissed me again. She sat back and then lit the tip of the joint. A rich, familiar odor suddenly filled the room. She leaned forward and handed me the joint. I sat next to her, holding the burning paper. Smoke twirled up toward the ceiling. "Don't you want any?" Janet asked.

"They tested us. They'll probably test us again before we get released."

"It'll be out of your pee in a week."

"I guess I'd like to try it if you say it's good, but not right now."

"That's all right," she said. "You don't have to have any. I'll put it away. Just let me have another toke. 'Kay?" She took another toke and grunted, tried to poke it out like a cigarette and left it to smolder.

After she put the stuff back into the baggie, she put that into her backpack. She turned around and smiled. "You roll the next one, too." She leaned forward and slowly unbuttoned her shirt. For a while, she stood in front of the chair with her buckle cutting a little into her stomach; then she unbuckled her belt, unzipped her fly, and eased her pants down her hips. She wore underwear with little flowers over it. She quickly slid these down over one leg and then stepped out of them, just wearing her bra. When she removed her bra, she sang a little "Ta-Da" and then giggled. She walked across the room and I worked back into the bunched bed. "Hey, come back," she said. "Take off your clothes. Or I'll have to tear them off."

I lay in the middle of the bed, hardly able to move. Janet grabbed me and then crawled up my body. When she reached my head, she started to laugh. "What are you afraid of?"

"I don't know."

"Well, relax."

She was just over my head and her breath had that loamy smell of marijuana like ferns and fir needles. Her hands spread over my body and it was different than how she had been touching me before, because now her fingers searched and probed my skin. The tips of her fingers lingered at my belt, running along the edge and then over the raised design on the outside of the buckle. Her nails clicked on the surface. Janet sat up, looking at my zipper. "Zippers are like teeth," she said. "Your penis is the tongue."

"My penis is not a tongue," I said. "It doesn't have any taste buds."

She started to laugh. She coughed and then kept laughing. After the laughing started to slow down, she bit her lip and stared into my eyes. "Sorry. Laughing fit."

"How much did you have?"

"Don't do that," she said. "I get paranoid. When you speak like that it makes me think all kinds of things. You need some."

"I really don't want any."

"I can get everything set up." She looked at her bag. "Maybe. I mean, if you really want to."

"No, I don't want to," I said.

"Come on. Yes you do. Here I am."

"I thought we were going to have sex, not get stoned."

"We are," she said.

"I can't," I said.

"I haven't done something wrong, have I?" she asked.

"No, not at all." I tried to kiss her.

"Eee," she said. "Your face is sharp." She grabbed my chin and then ran the palm of her hand over my chin and neck, letting her fingers trail behind her. She brushed my face the way someone might run her palm over the surface of a wall. "Razor sharp."

She unzipped my pants and pulled apart the flap on my underwear. I lay back. My penis lay as limp as a collapsed push puppet. Janet sucked the head into her mouth. In the warm cavity, I felt the length start to harden. She coughed and started to laugh. "I'm Frenching your zipper tongue."

"Please stop," I said.

"How come you're not excited? You do like me?" She leaned over on all fours. "Come on," she said.

I grabbed my pants and hurried into the bathroom and locked the door.

The room felt like a time machine, with its overheated warmth and the cool rain outside. I sat down on the tub and looked into the mirror at myself. Oliver's favorite pastime when we were waiting in the city was to watch couples. He would make noises as they walked that matched the rhythm of their stride. Every couple had a different style of stroll. A heavy couple would have a casual glide; a young couple might stop sporadically and gesture. Oliver provided the soundtrack, making farting noises with the side of his mouth or rolling notes from a circus organ in a clear, high-pitched voice. And inevitably he said, no matter how old or how oddly dressed the couple was, "Everybody does it."

Janet knocked on the door, three shallow taps. "Aldous?"

"Yeah?" I sat on the toilet with the lid down, my head on my hands.

"Are you all right?"

"I'm breathing."

"Why is the door locked?"

"Because right now you remind me of my uncle."

There was a long minute of silence. Finally, she said, "I'm sorry. I shouldn't have smoked any without you smoking it. I thought you baked."

"I don't smoke it."

"Why not? It's fun. Come out here and have some. You'll like it." I opened the door; she was wearing a thin blue nightgown. "Come on out here and talk."

"I'm not smoking anything."

"You don't have to smoke anything."

I lay back on the bed and stared at the ceiling. In the month after I had arrived at Fort Sam Houston, I had found myself waking up just before dawn with vivid images falling away from me. Every time I woke, I had the over-whelming, sick feeling that I had failed to do something. One incident I half remembered: I had walked down the polished barracks hallway, past the snoozing breezeway guard and out into the warm, Texan night, which seemed all the more dreamlike because it was the end of October.

I had walked until I came into the middle of the dusty red running field where I had lain down and looked up into the swirling stars and thought about the things I should be doing. Around me, locusts rubbed their legs together in their constant, rhythmic music. The image of me, as a child, trying to wake up Adrian in the middle of a forest kept coming back to me. Jake stood behind me, his hands so cold that I could only see them as smudges of blue flesh through the thick drizzle. He grabbed the backs of my arms as I prodded her. "Will she wake up?" he asked. I imagined that if I could wake her up, everything would get warm, the rain would fall back, and a hot sun would slip out of the cold, dusky rain. I probed her and her white lips pursed. "I'm sleeping," she said. "Sleeping. Sleeping. Sleeping." Closing her eyes, she pulled at the damp moss, spiders scurrying from under the ripped fibers, and used it as a pillow as she slipped away.

Jake sat on the gigantic, fingered tree roots. He leaned up against the gray trunk. Mist gushed through the pine boughs, scattering drops over the black mud puddles that covered the path. The wind suddenly felt warm and I felt the forest breathing around us. I wanted to lie down next to this girl and plunge into the deep, cool sleep, like a drop from a hot summer wind into a river pool, where the water would fill my ears with green weight. I sat on the tree next to Jake.

I jumped up, my boots slipping into the mud, water spilling into my socks. "Please," I started to yell into the Texan sky. "Please wake up." I had found myself fully awake, my feet covered in the floury dust, standing in the middle of the field without any shoes.

I didn't know how to tell Janet about this. I didn't want her to become frightened of me. And something about this sleepwalking incident, or whatever it was, filled me with an intense feeling of guilt. As I talked to Janet, she patiently leaned against the wall and smiled at me. I wanted to stop speaking and gently pull her nightgown off, but I was afraid she would start screaming. She would scream and pull away from me, sticking her fingers into my eyes.

I told Janet that my mom liked motels.

"Now you're getting weird," Janet said. She held the black plastic change holder and pulled out the baggie with the squares of paper.

"Whenever my brother and I went to Seattle with Mom, she would visit hotel lobbies and my uncle would turn up," I said as I watched her slide the pieces of paper out onto the bedspread.

"Just like that?" Janet asked.

"Just like that," I said.

"At least someone has had sex in the history of mankind," she said. "Now, what do you suppose these are?"

Eighteen

We stood in the middle of a field and Janet said the world was symmetrical. It was. The tops of the trees rising above the roofline were aligned; it looked like someone had mapped the exact spatial arrangement of everything. We walked through the grid, marveling at the complementary colors. I kicked the leaves in the gutter and the rust-colored scales and the small round spots, like eyes, made the leaves seem like undulating flatworms.

"Let's go in here," Janet said, and we walked into the lobby of the San Antonio Botanical Gardens. I had to make the silver, shining turnstile bar rotate and I found myself in a lobby. Some people stood by the desk. A large wedge thing was on the desk, a cash register built from cream-colored plastic. I imagined that if I ran my hand over it, it would be rough, and in the space of the cracks I would feel particles of dirt. Janet stood behind me. She looked at the television screen that showed an elderly lady in a baggy dress, cream-colored like the cash register. She leaned into the thick green plants, maybe more yellow than green, holding round drops of water. One of the people by the desk said something loudly enough that I heard the voice. It was a woman's voice. "She wants us to pay," Janet said with her woman's voice. The two voices didn't sound the same to me.

I had difficulty paying. I wanted to ask how much, but I thought the blood wasn't hooked up to my mouth. I placed a green five-dollar bill on the cream-colored plastic. For one piece of paper, she gave me a handful of warm metal bits. I put them in my pocket to look at later. They felt heavy. They felt so heavy that when I walked, I had to limp.

"I didn't want these," I said to the cream-colored plastic.

"You can go in," the woman's voice that wasn't Janet's said.

I walked out of the building onto the back of a giant green cat. The thick hair grew up like grass. A Japanese pagoda rested where the back of the neck was. A pool of brackish water, filled with swimming gold coins or carp-fish, I couldn't tell, rested where the mouth of the cat should have been.

I followed Janet through the botanical gardens. We found ourselves on a patio edged with thick, rounded cement walls. On the edge of the wall, plaques with Braille writing were bolted down. Numerous hands had worn the nubs of Braille into silvery caps of metal. I ran the tips of my fingers over them. Leafy plants, examples of almost every type crowded the beds: basil, oregano, parsley, mint. Janet and I closed our eyes and buried our faces and our hands into the plants. We learned about the world as if we were blind; I was Braille-illiterate and flashed my eyes open to see the plant that gave the prickly sweet sensation of evergreen.

Janet and I moved our way through each of the plants. I held her hand, feeling the knot of her fingers, the calluses she had developed from cleaning her M16 in basic training. I smelled the shampoo she used, some generic brand with a powerful wash of floral and chemical oil. It was a relief to return to that odor after I had been swimming in parsley, the green stalks sticking to my chin, the heavy leaves cloaking my eyelids.

We made our way from the garden to an outdoor amphitheater. From there, we wandered to the top of a hill along a spiraling trail. We climbed into a gazebo and from the gazebo we could see the layout of Fort Sam Houston, we could see the Tower of the Americas downtown. At the top of the hill, we felt the wind racing across the sky, circling us, wrapping Janet and me together.

We wandered through the city and, suddenly, I had stepped into Oliver's world. Sitting on a bench in a city park above the Riverwalk, looking at a weathered brass statue, a bust of a bus driver or something from the 1920s, I took Janet's hand in mine. Her hands felt huge and warm and as though they were encased in a mesh of wire. I ran my thumb along the point of her index finger and brushed her knuckles. "What are you doing?" she asked.

"I was going to say something." We watched a crowd of people walk the Riverwalk. They were trying to remember a Christmas carol, all of them drunk and staggering. They burst out in a long refrain, "Nöel, Nöel, Nöel." A man staggered up to the edge of the canal and yelled, "Splash!" "I was going to say that," I said to Janet.

Janet lay her head back on the bench. "Do this."

I lay my head back and looked up into the plain blue of the sky. Way above us, a few birds circled. They were distant specks. They must have been way up in the sky. Around them, the city unfolded and turned around.

"This feels so familiar," I said. And the sensation did. The remarkable clarity of everything. Even its sudden intensity felt like a return to a state I had been in before, as if the tape machine of my senses had its heads cleaned.

"What feels familiar?" Janet asked.

"This sensation." I waved my hand at the world around us. "This is how I remember things before he died. Before Oliver died. Before he stopped being himself."

"You think he was feeding you acid?" Janet asked. She seemed horrified. It seemed televised, as if she were acting. I wondered as I sat there if she had learned that expression from TV.

"Come on," Janet said. We wandered down the street.

"There's a Sasquatch following us, well, following me," I said.

"That's impossible," Janet said. "Sasquatches don't live in Texas."

"Good. Then it must just be a guy in a bear costume."

"Where do you see him?"

"Around."

We came to a comic book store with skateboards in the windows and a mural of a gigantic black-haired woman with spiders painted all over her face. "See," Janet said. "You thought Bigfoot was following us, and here's a giantess pretending to be a storefront." Janet walked into the woman's mouth. A thudding guitar noise came out of her mouth, a sort of sonic indigestion. We paged through the comic books. Above the racks of comic books, in a thin, glass case, faded *Star Wars* figures stood at attention. I found myself transfixed by R2-D2. I was amazed by the familiarity of his little face. He was just a wedge of plastic. Someone had managed to sell millions of these bits of plastic for the huge price of $3.50 at a time when a Matchbox car had cost less than a dollar. I remembered as a child being afraid of turning R2-D2's head because it made a thin, tinny noise. Of all the figures I owned, R2-D2, because of his fragile paper diagramming, had remained my favorite. My figure had lost its paper and its head had fallen off. Telling me not to cry, Mom had held me. "We'll get you another one." Oliver didn't understand. "The manufacturers created the movie so that they could unload that stuff," he said. "Teams of designers created the face of R2-D2, using the facial scanning patterns of children. The big blue eye draws the child's attention and the small eye with the upturned triangle above it gives it a cute, vulnerable look, and then the capper, the red dot of the nose, summoning the memory of that hit sensation, Rudolph the Red-Nosed Reindeer. They couldn't go wrong. The shape of R2-D2 plays on the primal nesting instincts of children, the egg. I'm sorry, Aldous, but you've been duped."

Standing in the store, looking at the faded R2-D2, almost completely out of the context of my childhood, I felt an odd sort of yearning to hold the figure in my hand and also to burn the store down.

An old man in horn-rimmed glasses sat on a stool behind the cash register. He wore faded blue jeans, a plaid shirt, and tattered Converse tennis shoes. He pushed the glasses back up his nose when I stood in front of the cash register. "How much for the R2-D2?"

"Come again?" The man looked past me at Janet. Janet ran her hand along the long Plexiglas casing that held the figurines.

"That little crappy wedge of plastic, next to C-3PO, Han Solo, and Chewie, how much does he cost?"

"He's not for sale. But I think we might have another one. Do you want a used one, or one still in the packaging?"

"I don't want a used one." I said it like I thought he was nuts. "Are you trying to unload junk on me?"

"No. It'll be forty-five dollars."

"Okay." I pulled out my wallet, but all I had was a twenty, a ten, three dollars, and six nickels. I handed him all this. "Here."

"Thirty-three bucks and change? The price, my friend, is forty-five." He tapped a sign on the glass counter. Someone had written in very neat handwriting, "Absolutely No Haggling."

"It's all I have," I said. "Can't I have it?"

"Tell you what. You can have a used one, and I'll throw in a Luke Skywalker and a Han Solo."

"You will?"

"Yes." He went into the back room. Eventually he came back with a small bag. Inside were three tissue body bags. I undid them and I found R2-D2, Luke Skywalker, and Han Solo. I held the three of them in my hand. Looking at their worn faces, I felt as if I had just come home. I felt hot tears fall down my face.

"I'm glad you like them," the man said. He handed me a napkin.

"Thank you," I said.

Janet saw me standing at the counter. "Come on," she said.

"Do I disgust you?"

"Come on." She took me by my hand. Outside, I saw

that the Sasquatch had moved across the street. He squatted inside an azalea. As we walked back to the gardens, I saw him sneaking behind us. Every time I turned around, I saw him hide. He would step into a store. He'd slip into a bus shelter. He'd turn into an old man walking behind us. "Stop looking behind us," Janet said. "You're scaring me."

"We're being followed," I said. "What do you suppose he wants? Maybe he just wants to apologize for breaking my window. It's been a long time. You'd suppose everyone would have forgotten about it now. I've forgotten it. Do you think he'll ask for forgiveness?"

"I don't suppose that he will," Janet said. "But he has come all the way here to see you."

"I don't have anything to offer him. Do you think he'd like my Luke Skywalker? I held the two figures up to Janet. "Do you think I'm more like Luke or more like Han Solo?"

She looked at them for a while. "You are a Luke Skywalker," she finally said.

"Oh no," I said. I didn't know what to do. I had tried to change. I had tried to be Han Solo, like Oliver wanted me to be. And now I had just become Luke Skywalker. "Han Solo was never a virgin," I said.

At the gate to the San Antonio Botanical Garden, we showed our old ticket stubs and walked to the field to lie down in the middle and stare up into the sky. "It seems big," Janet said.

"Yeah," I said. "The world is fucking huge."

———

I woke with a headache that felt like someone was playing a saw blade and jug band inside my temple. Hot
slashes of sunlight cut across the room, illuminating a
misshapen green wool sock, a boot with its laces tangled
around its long, black tongue, and the contents of a
McDonald's take-out bag, napkin, ketchup packets,
straw, and a plastic knife, scattered almost artfully over
the worn motel carpet. I wasn't able to see anything in the
gashes of darkness.

The way the entire room had been divided into stripes
was confusing to me. It was like a billboard with leaves that
rotated to three different ads. There was the room in darkness, the room in complete sunlight, and the room as I
actually saw it. I stumbled out of the bed and attempted to
pour myself a glass of water. I sat at the wobbly dinette table
and drank the brackish tap water. Janet lay sprawled in the
bed. I tried to say something to her, but I couldn't remember
what it was, so I crawled back into the bed and somehow
managed to turn down the jug band in my brain that
huffed notes on massive, blue glass bottles.

Janet and I lay on the bed. We didn't want to go back to
the barracks where we couldn't be together and would have
to kill time until we took the cab to the airport to go home

for winter break. We didn't even talk about calling each other once we got home. We crumpled up bits of my notebook paper and threw them at the table. We were trying to see who could get to the farthest corner. The person who landed the paper at the very tip of the farthest corner was the winner. My paper balls skimmed the tabletop and fell to the carpet. Janet's ball landed close to the edge, but still left a wide margin. "You have really bad hand-eye coordination, don't you?" she asked.

"Oh yes," I said. And then I landed a piece of paper just beyond hers.

"Damn," she said.

"Can I ask some questions?" I asked.

"You're trying to distract me."

"Don't you feel sick at all?"

"Now that's personal. I think I can handle that. I feel utterly sick. I drank some water and had some complimentary motel aspirin."

"That works for you?"

She threw another piece of paper and it knocked my paper off the table. "I'm the winner," she said. She lay back. I leaned against the wall and looked out the window, over the matted knot of telephone wires, neon signs, and traffic lights, at a cemetery. The cemetery started right next to the motel. A tall chain link fence ran around the edge of it. Barbed wire ran around the top of the fence. At the end, a small stone shelter stood, with a pointed, round roof. A bright red flag fluttered from a pole on the rooftop. "Do you think they're trying to keep people in or out of that cemetery?" I asked.

"What?" Janet asked.

"Barbed wire," I said. "I don't think I should have done it."

"What?"

"Taken the LSD."

"There's nothing wrong with it. It's low in cholesterol. It doesn't have any sugar."

"It makes me feel like I'm a hypocrite."

"You aren't one," Janet said. She opened the window and a cool draft blew through the room. She picked up the crumpled paper, sat on the bed, and put her arms around my shoulders. "You had a good time?"

"Yes. But it's illegal."

"So's jaywalking."

"I don't jaywalk."

"But you don't think jaywalking makes you bad person, do you? How about speeding? If you drive sixty in a fifty-five are you a bad guy?"

"Why do you do drugs?"

"I don't *do* drugs," Janet said. "I have taken some drugs in my life."

"Why did you join the military if you take drugs?"

"First, I'm an Army Reservist. That's not really joining the Army. After this training, I'm done with active duty, unless there is, like, a complete mobilization, in which case it's World War III, and it doesn't matter what I'm doing. Second, I joined so that I could pay for student loans."

"Where would you like to go to school?"

"I wanted to go to Columbia, starting this fall. I wanted to go someplace that was old. I have this fantasy of being on a campus in the 1950s, with men who are maybe ten years older who have gone to World War II, and before that, they maybe worked really weird jobs because of the Depression. Their parents are from all over the place, and they hang out after school in a bar and I'm one of their girls. In this fantasy, I do all the beatnik stuff. I wear a black turtleneck and blue jeans. My hair is cut in a shoulder-length bob, and I smoke cigarette after cigarette while these slightly older men talk. Instead, I'm probably going to end up in some community college."

"We'll meet back here in this room when we get back, won't we?" I asked.

"Of course," Janet said. She lay her body across my lap.

"We are going to, won't we? Because, sometimes people make promises and then they leave and things change because they aren't with that person anymore."

"Don't go neurotic on me," Janet said.

"Whenever Mom said to my uncle, 'You're driving me crazy,' he said, 'short drive.'

Janet rolled over and kicked the blankets onto the floor, and then she pulled the linen sheet over our heads. She lay on my chest and rubbed my morning beard with the ball of her hand. "Have you shaved this morning, Private?" she asked.

"Why do you like me?" I leaned over her and peered into her eyes.

She squinted them. "I guess the reason I like you is because you were the last in line at the drug testing, which seemed like you were up to something you shouldn't have been. And you caught me doing something naughty."

"Why do you take drugs?"

Janet pulled the linen sheet around her, like a sari, and then sat against the wall, with her arms wrapped around her. She left me lying on the bed, naked, and the cool breeze flowing through the window gave me goose bumps and reignited my headache. I staggered off the bed as I listened to Janet. I took three aspirin and drank a glass of water, refilled it, and handed the glass to Janet. She drank the whole glass.

"I take drugs because it makes me think about things. I'm into 1960s' psychedelia. Does it mean I want to make drugs a part of my life? Probably not. I mean, you've seen the kid who came to school stoned. In middle school, there was this kid that used to come to class smelling to high heaven of pot. He sat across from me in Earth Sciences. We all knew him, but no one spent any time with him. I remember he'd been on the baseball team of one my boyfriends in the fifth grade. He'd been really good. This kid would play shortstop, and whenever any ball rolled past him, he'd snap it with his mitt and toss it directly to first base. Almost every time the first baseman snagged the batter out. And here he'd been in my seventh grade science class and he couldn't even remember his name. So of course I don't want to make pot or anything else a part of my life.

"But one time I was on LSD and I realized that my parents were going to have a divorce and they hadn't even told me. It was summer and I was seventeen, just hanging out in the garage playing with some Play-Doh and some of my toys from when I was a kid. I had dressed my Ken doll in a green Play-Doh bodysuit and one of my Cabbage Patch Kids had hooked electrodes up to his Play-Doh skin and was electrocuting him. And I realized that the Cabbage Patch Kid was really Mother, and the Ken doll was really Father. I had even made a Play-Doh mustache for Father.

"Mother believes that dreams are true. She believes that they tell us things we know instinctively to be real, but are having trouble thinking about. And taking LSD, for me, is like, I see things in a different way and it can help me in a strange sort of way see things more clearly. Really, of course, it's because it's so much fun. The big incentive is that everything becomes really, really entertaining. I spent all day playing with Ken and my old Cabbage Patch Kids, and it was fun.

"Pot does sort of the same thing for me, but I don't do either of them that much. I think the only reason that I do them, here, in the Army, is because they are completely not allowed. If they didn't allow me to brush my teeth with Aquafresh toothpaste, I would go out and buy ten tubes of Aquafresh toothpaste."

"I wish I could do that," I said.

"You can't," Janet said. "You're such a conformist."

"I try to be," I said. "But I always forget to do little things. I never realized that we were supposed to iron our BDUs. Since they're called Battle Dress Uniforms, it seems stupid to iron them. But Sergeant McCormick chewed me out for not having a crease in my pant leg."

"You try to make sense out of stuff like that," Janet said. She rolled over onto her side. "That's what I don't understand. I'm going to sleep again."

I thought drugs were something that did something to my parents and that anything I couldn't explain about them was because of the drugs. Why did Oliver and Dad lose the Dodge Dart on the North Fork Road? Why did Oliver run into the forest and live in a hollow log for three weeks? Why did my mother kick Oliver out and then let him come back? The drugs made them do it. But with the lingering LSD headache, I realized it wasn't really the drugs. It was something else, something inside my parents that made them act as they did.

Janet and I didn't talk on the way to the airport. She looked out her window and I looked out mine. I held her cool fingers in my hand and rubbed them as though I were lighting a fire with a stick twisted into kindling. "Ouch," she said. She pulled her hand free. "My circulation must be shot." The aftermath of a snowstorm had left slush on the road. Stray chunks of dirty ice lay in the median and on the shoulder. Cold air pounded through the cab driver's open window and the rear heat ducts blew scalding air into our ears. The mix of frigid and hot air eddied around our legs. I kept glancing at Janet to see if she would look at me.

She stared out her window, her head nodding. Occasionally, she sniffled and brushed her nose with the rim of her index finger. When she had first started to get sick, she had bought a package of Alka-Seltzer cold medicine and, because she couldn't find a cup, stuffed all the packets except one into her jacket pocket, filled the seltzer box with water out of a drinking fountain, and drank the mixture as quickly as the tablets dissolved. When she was finished, she crumpled the package and tossed it into the trash.

Bumper stickers and menus covered the cab's dashboard: *Moon Palace, The Hero Sandwich Source, and Josie's*

Chimichangas. A spike of smoky quartz hung from the rearview mirror and reflected the cool winter daylight. A border radio station played Spanish ballads I could barely hear in the windy backseat. "Jorge," written with a green marker on a piece of yellowed masking tape, covered the name on a plaque that started, "Your driver is." When the Caprice stopped at a red light, Jorge turned all the way around and asked, "Do you mind if I smoke?" He lit a match and threw it out the window. "Would you like one?" He turned around in his seat and looked at both of us, then offered Janet the pack. "Sure," Janet said. "You want one, Aldous?"

"No thanks."

"I don't want one, then."

"Go ahead, take one," Jorge hadn't been watching the road. The Caprice drifted into the curb, crushing ice. The hubcaps grated against the sidewalk. "Okay," I said. "I'll take one, but can everyone watch the road, please." Janet slipped her index and forefinger over two cigarettes, and held them up for me to choose. I held it by the spongy filter.

We sat in the backseat holding our cigarettes. "Do you have a light?" Janet asked me.

"I don't smoke." I stuck the unlit cigarette into my mouth and sucked. It tasted like paper.

Jorge leaned back and blew his smoke out the window. From the back of the seat, I could examine the carefully manicured orb of Jorge's black hair slicked with a rose-scented pomade. "Excuse me," Janet asked him, "Do you have a lighter?" He said no, but he flicked out a matchbook from his breast pocket and smiled at us in the rearview mirror. He peeled one of the matches out one-handed and folded the book into his palm to light the match head on the rough, black surface of the meter. The match flame caught his thumb. "Christ," he said, and dropped it. The car swerved and fishtailed as it slowed down. A truck behind us lay on its horn, a deep blast that sounded like a ferry whistle.

"That's pretty tricky," Janet said. "But maybe you could just let me have the book."

"Naw," he said. Jorge leaned forward with his elbows splayed over the wheel while he used both hands to strike the match. The wheel swayed back and forth between his elbows. The match lit and he started to turn to light Janet's cigarette. She leaned over the seat to meet the flame halfway. But the truck behind us lay a steady note on its horn and sped around us. The driver yelled out the window, "Drunk! Get off the road."

A gust of diesel exhaust washed into the Caprice and snuffed the light. "Christ," Jorge said and rolled up all of the windows. He tore the last match out of the book, scratched it over the rough surface of the meter and lit Janet's cigarette. She breathed the smoke in and sat back in the seat, looked back out the window, then exhaled.

"Thanks, Jorge."

"No problem," the driver said.

"Excuse me?" I whispered to Janet.

"You don't smoke," she said.

"I might as well, since I have a cigarette."

She took my cigarette, propped it in her mouth, and sucked the red ember at the end of her cigarette; smoke leaked from the corners of her mouth. I hadn't smoked since I had a cigarette at Mrs. Laxton's house.

"Are you two in love?" Jorge looked back and forth at us in the rearview mirror.

"Love is a pretty harsh word," Janet said. "I think we're in heavy like."

"In the old days, they just said love," the driver said. "I've been married for twenty-two years next Friday."

"Congratulations," I said.

Janet rolled her eyes and took a drag.

"Love," the driver said. "I like my wife's friends. If I loved them she'd cut my balls off. I love my wife."

"Sorry to hear about it," Janet said.

"What's wrong with like?" I asked. "I like, like."

"Like is sort of pre-love," Janet said. "It's just not a sure thing."

"And love is?" I asked.

"It's supposed to be."

Lunatic on the Grass

Nineteen

On the day before Halloween in 1978, Oliver came home from Seattle with a job as the lunch grill cook at the Deluxe Tavern on Broadway. He came home wearing his hair in a ponytail and his food-splattered, double-breasted white smock as evidence. "I'm a changed man," he told Mom. They sat at the kitchen table drinking coffee. Mom left the door open to hear the rain falling through the browning maple tree leaves. As we ate our hamburger patties and canned peaches, we listened to Oliver tell us how he had found his job. "It's all in how you look. I sat down at the bar and started to work in my journal, just minding my own business, not even thinking I would wind up working there, sort of getting into what I was doing, when I overheard the cook telling the manager that they couldn't get anybody to come in. It seems their regular cook had just plain not shown up."

"I didn't know you were looking for a job." Mom poured coffee for my uncle and herself and uncovered a plate of scones. Jake reached for one and she tapped his hand. "After dinner. Oliver, what would you do with something like that? You're happy upstairs. You're doing what you want to do, more or less."

"A man has got to work," Oliver said, "and get paid. Remember that, boys. I'm a changed man. I'm done staring into the wool of my navel. I will work and I will earn a paycheck. When I heard their cook hadn't showed up, I spoke up and said, 'I can cook. I don't have any plans this afternoon. It'll be an honor,' just like that and I was in the kitchen cooking. I work four days a week, six thirty in the morning until two in the afternoon. I'm a chef now." He smiled and ate a scone in three bites and took a swallow of his coffee.

"Aldous and Jake. I will purchase for you, out of my savings, money I was keeping for future living expenses, one commemorative gift each. Remember this for future decisions. Not wanting to work is the worst reason not to work. A person is never too busy to work. What would you like?"

"I want a bear mask," Jake said. "For Halloween." On one of Mom's expeditions to Seattle, we had wandered through Ye Olde Curiosity Shoppe on the waterfront, an old wharf warehouse filled with odd seafaring artifacts, Wild West curios, and North Pacific native art. A shark hung from the rafters; whale harpoons lined the walls; an illicitly buried corpse named Sylvester, mummified in the Southwestern desert, sat in a glass case; the whole place smelled like Puget Sound brine, kelp, and wood smoke. A ceremonial bear mask carved out of cedar hung on the back wall. "That's me," Jake said when he saw it. "That'll be me."

"I made up my mind a long time ago not to let Jake and Aldous go trick or treating," Mom said.

"Mom, *free candy*," Jake said each word carefully.

"It's too dangerous. They're putting razor blades in the apples and rat poison in the chocolate chip cookies. It used to be a small town and we were surrounded by friends, but now we're stranded among dog-owning, .22-shooting strangers."

"Jake, the candy is not free. How much would this bear mask cost?" Oliver asked.

"He wants the Indian one from the curiosity shop," I said.

Jake looked at me, but he didn't say anything because I could tell he wanted to wait to see Oliver's reaction. From there, he would know if he had a chance at getting the mask.

"This is my money," Oliver said. "I can't afford to get Halloween candy with an ancient artifact."

"It's only from 1833," Jake said. "It's not ancient."

"For the price of it, I'll buy you a box of Milky Ways," Oliver said.

"I don't like Milky Ways. I want to go trick or treating."
I could tell Jake was going to pull his baby trick where he
wouldn't cry, but tears would start to come out. He took a
drink of his water, then made a silent sob and the tears
started to roll down his face. "I just want to see my friends.
Tomorrow is dress-up day and everyone will have a costume except me."

"How about a normal bear mask that you can wear to
school tomorrow?" Mom said.

"That'll be okay," Jake said. He smiled and wiped his
tears with the back of his hand, his showiest move.
"Thanks, Oliver."

"Gayle," Oliver said. "I'm out of gas. Can I borrow
twenty bucks for gas to put into the Dart?"

"Now, this is a mask," Oliver said. He held the smooth
sheen of Darth Vader's shark-faced head up into the
fluorescent light of the store. "Don't you want to scare
someone?"

"No," I said. "You can't scare anyone with a plastic
mask. I want to be a good guy like Peter Parker. You know,
with superpowers to help humanity and a cool costume."

"Why aren't you dressing up like Mark Hamill, then?"

"You said he was stupid. Spiderman isn't stupid. He's a
photographer and a mutant and he's got problems like normal people."

"Spiderman is generic," Oliver said. "Who wants to be an ordinary superhero?"

"I do," I said.

"They don't have a bear mask like the one in the curiosity shop," Jake said. "I want a mask like that one."

"You can't have that one," Oliver said. "Why don't you be the Wolfman?"

"He's not a bear."

"How about if we buy Wolfman fur, and I make you round ears?"

"You'll make me bear ears?" Jake asked.

"And we can get you plastic claws and you'll look like a bear."

"All right," Jake said, "But only if I look like a real bear."

In the morning, I put on my blue corduroy pants and red T-shirt, then slipped on the bright red and blue web poncho. I admired myself in the bathroom mirror. I turned to my profile and then back to full front, looking into my eyes, sunk behind the eyeholes. I did the splits and flicked the underside of my arm like the comic book. Who couldn't like Spiderman?

"Dad, how do I look?"

"Freaky," he said.

"I'm Spiderman," I said. "I'm a good guy."

Oliver looked up from the morning paper. "Eeek," he screamed. "You're terrifying!"

At school in the Spiderman costume, I felt hidden and brave. Instead of quietly walking through the halls to recess behind the other children, I hurried down the hall with the kids who wanted to be the first outside. I shoved them and shouted for them to get out of the way. I burst onto the playground and took over the tetherball court. I vanquished all the other players until Gina Lansing started to play. I tried to draw the game out as long as possible. But Gina, dressed as Olivia Newton John from *Grease,* slammed the ball around the metal pole. As she leaned into the ball and pulled back, the straight flex of her arm, its sheer smoothness, made me lose track of where I was. She smashed the ball around the pole and I lost.

Greg, Gina's current boyfriend, waited on the sidelines. He wore loose blue jeans and a tight T-shirt, his long hair slicked back on his head in a ducktail, like John Travolta from *Grease.* He looked like a thug. "Aldous," he said. "Get your devil-worshipping butt out of here."

I flicked the underside of my wrist at him. "Webbed."

"Get lost, freak." He shoved me. For a moment, I didn't know what to do. I slid on the damp grass. As soon as I had my feet, I jumped back at Greg. I hit and fell into him as I slipped again on the slick grass. Greg stumbled onto the tetherball court and slammed into the pole. A deep, full gong spread through the playground under the low drizzle. Greg leaned against the pole for a second, heaving in and out. I looked around the play field and everyone had stopped playing. They just looked at us. Greg stood away from the pole and shook his hands loose. Someone yelled, "Fight!" and kids from all over the playground started to congregate around us. In the distance, Big Bird wobbled through a crowd of superhero-masked children. Rabbits, zebras, hobos, and firemen mobbed the tetherball court.

Greg stood away from the pole and spit into the grass. "You're really ready to get trashed, aren't you?"

I didn't wait to answer. I ran to the monkey bars, peeling out in the mud, and Greg chased after me. I climbed onto the bars. Animal heads circled us. Monkeys, squirrels, and a man jumped away. Greg stood at the bottom and yelled, "Bohm, you're a chicken."

I stood up on top of the monkey bars and looked over the heads of the plastic-masked children at the highway and the brownish mass of the Snoqualmie River. The low rain clouds covered everything else. In the distance, a maple tree stuck its branches out and, beyond that, everything was damp mist. I wanted to tell them how strong I was and how weak Greg was, but they all knew Greg could break every bone in my body. He belonged to the Boy Scouts. I had been kicked out of the Cub Scouts. He had Gina Lansing as a girlfriend. I had spurned even Angie. My classmates clotted around me as though I were a thorn stuck in their hand and they were going to get rid of me, they were pushing me up out of the playground and into the sky. I don't know what happened then. My mud-covered tennis shoes squealed and I felt myself rolling through the air. I clipped Greg's shoulder and he spun into the monkey bars, where he smacked his head and then tumbled between the rungs. He fell back onto the grass, his hair coming loose from the hold of grease, exploding into a shower of strands. His head whipped back and smacked into the grass. Greg just lay still and I sprawled in the mud, long, sticky grass hairs covering my costume.

The Recess Lady burst through the ring of children. "What is this?" She grabbed me and pulled Greg to his feet. She marched me to the principal's office. I watched Greg and the Recess Lady stomp down the hallway to the nurse. I sat on the bench where the offenders waited for their judgment. Whenever I had seen kids sitting on the bench, I had not looked them in the eyes; instead, I had hurried past the bench to my classroom. As the classes came back in after recess, they all passed me. No one looked at me until Lance and Willie stopped in front of me. Lance wore a buccaneer's outfit. "Way to go, asshole."

"Yeah. Good fucking job," Willie said. Willie wore blue jeans and his blue sweatshirt and hood.

"After school, your ass is grass," Lance said. "No one is going to care what we do to you. If we stab you and drag you back to your house, people will just think your old man did it. So we'll see you later."

"Yeah, later," Willie said. I waited for some sign from

Willie acknowledging our former friendship. All he did was look at the hall floor and turn quickly away as he followed Lance.

I had never been in the principal's office before. I sat in front of his desk while Mr. Jones worked through some paper. Almost every inch of the polished wood reflected the light from the windows. Through the windows, I could see over the small garden that the librarian kept, the tall, withered stalks of foxglove standing among evenly spaced wooden poles. Mr. Jones' desk rested directly in front of the window, but he faced the door. I thought this was strange, because I would face the other way if I had a desk in a room with a view like his. I would spend my day staring out across the river, toward the mountains, watching the clouds pile and flow toward the east. "Mr. Bohm," Mr. Jones said. "I don't think I've seen you here before. Is that correct?"

"You haven't," I said.

"You haven't, sir," he said. "Really someone should have taught you these things. You address your elders and superiors as *sir*. That is the correct way of doing it."

"Yes," I said.

"Yes, what?" I could faintly see his face because the light fell around him and into my eyes. I thought he might be joking, but his voice seemed so neutral and carefully modulated that I didn't know what to do.

"Sir," I finally said.

"*Yes*, sir." Mr. Jones worked through some more paper-work on his desk.

"Right," I said.

He looked up when I spoke. He spent a minute looking at me. "Where do they dredge up kids like you? Don't you know any civilities?"

"I didn't do anything."

"Sir," he said. "I didn't do anything, *sir.* Now, Mr. Bohm, you've been in a fight. You've never been in a fight before. So you shall be suspended for the day. Your uncle has agreed to retrieve you."

"Good," I said.

"This will not happen again."

"Greg started it."

"Another occurrence will not happen. Now go outside and wait in the hall."

I stood and the principal turned back to his work.

Once I was in the hall, I walked out of the school and stood under the flagpoles and the totem pole, waiting for Oliver. I pulled my Spiderman mask back over my face and sat with my legs crossed at the base of the totem pole, pretending that I was one of the figures. I closed my eyes and dozed off. A clanging noise woke me. I opened my eyes and saw the Dart parked in the Bus Only zone. Black vapor spewed out of the muffler. I jumped into the car. "Go. Go before anyone sees us." I glanced at the dark class-room windows and I worried that the children inside would look up and see Spiderman climbing into the wrecked getaway car. I looked longingly back at the kids sitting at their desks hunched over their pale blue, wide-rule paper, working out the alphabet or writing stories, counting the minutes until school ended and they could go trick or treating. Oliver whisked me away from this center of normality.

"How's your job?" I asked Oliver.

He smiled at me and said this was his first day off in a long time and that he felt great. "Thank you for asking. My job's great. I'm great. And life is great." He didn't look at me while he said this; he just held the steering wheel and glared at the road.

Oliver had gradually stopped doing things with Jake and me. I felt a growing panic that he would no longer keep up the bargain we'd struck after Adrian died. He no longer kept everyone balanced and, in fact, had begun to throw things out of whack. I could not understand, then, how things had been before Oliver had come. In many ways the problems we had now seemed more to do with Oliver than with Adrian's death. For a long time, I believed that Oliver was a sort of consolation prize for what I had done, but gradually I began to wonder if Oliver's arrival had been as responsible for her death as what I had done.

And one day toward the end of October, Oliver told me, "Adrian wants to talk to you." As soon as he told me, I knew he wanted to take me to the rhododendron bush. I had been waiting for him to ask me. It had been an unvoiced conversation, me asking him when I could go and him saying not now and finally I had just about forgotten about the rhododendron bush. I didn't want to go, anyway. And then he asked me.

"Are you making fun of me?"

"She asked to see you. She has already seen Jake."

"Is that true?"

I could see when I looked at Jake he believed that she had. His lips looked blue from the fluorescent kitchen light. He just shook his head to say, yes, that's true.

"Are you making this up, Jake?"

He shook his head no.

"We had her ashes," I said.

"I do not dispute that," Oliver said. "She came back."

"How does a person come back?"

"I suppose the dead come back all kinds of ways. Sometimes they are stuck between worlds," Oliver said, "and then all you can see of them is their shadow and at night their shadow looks almost transparent. Most people call that a ghost. Sometimes they are just a presence. They can hear and see you, but all you can see of them is a feeling of unease, like something isn't right. In Adrian's case, she walked."

"She walked?"

"She found herself on Hood Canal and began to walk home."

"Why didn't she call home?"

"She said she couldn't remember the number."

"How long has she been here?"

"Do you want to see her or not?"

"I don't know."

"She will be very sorry that you won't come out and see her."

"Why doesn't she want to see Mom and Dad?"

"Who says she hasn't seen them?"

"You mean I'm the only one who hasn't seen Adrian? She has been here the entire time and I haven't seen her?"

"You said it. Not me," Oliver said. "Will you come to her?"

"Should I bring her anything?"

"She likes hot chocolate."

While I boiled the water kettle on the range, Jake stood at the window and stared into the forest up the hill. "It's raining. She doesn't like the rain," he said. When the kettle hooted, I poured the boiling water into the mug and quickly mixed it before it lumped up. I added a little milk, the way Mom had shown us to make it look like milk chocolate and to fix the taste of the mix. Oliver examined the cup, nodded, and then led us up the hill to the rhodo-dendron. He stepped through the branches. Jake stepped through the branches. I put my hand over the lip of the mug to keep out spiders and leaves and I stepped into the bush. A hallway had been cut into the bush, tall enough that Jake and I could walk without stooping. Oliver stooped ahead of us. In the heart of the rhododendron, a big, room-sized space had been cut and decorated with the old pieces of furniture I thought Dad had thrown away. The floor of the bush room was all crispy old leaves and faded petals. A ring of Adrian's toys circled the outer edge of the room where the bush started to clump up, and at the very top of the room, I could see out to the stars. Oliver lit the candles and the bush filled with light. The candles burned in places on the ground heavy with old wax, or in holders dripping long stalactites of white and red wax. The plant had started to flower and the thick purple flowers hung inside the bush. As soon as the candles started to flicker, moths came to dance in the flames of the candles. They caught on fire and emitted a sputtering hiss. Adrian's old changing table lay under a sheet of lace. Around the base of the table, Adrian's old stuffed animals lay in a gigantic heap. They had become swollen and damp from being in the bush. A white powdery fungus covered them. And then I saw that there was a body or a shape like Adrian's body on the table. I could see the remains of her old best dress coming out from under the lace. In the gradual and growing light, I saw that Adrian's body looked a little puffy and funny.

"What is wrong with her?"

"She came back from the dead," Oliver said. He sat cross-legged in front of her and turned up his palms.

"Is she happy to see Aldous?" Jake asked.

"She wants his gift before she answers," he said. "Sit down."

I sat down with a crunch in the dry leaves. And Jake sat down beside me. I wondered if indeed this was her and that her death had been a bad mistake and she had been lost at the hospital or something. I had never seen her body. The newspaper said she died, but maybe they were going off what the hospital said.

"She didn't die?" I asked.

"She wants your gift," Oliver said.

I sat down next to Jake and Jake took my hand. His hand was damp and it kept twitching.

I set the drink down in front of Oliver and then closed my eyes.

I heard a rustling noise.

"She says," Oliver finally said, "thank you."

When I opened my eyes, Oliver was sitting exactly where he was before. His eyes were closed. The mug of hot chocolate was empty.

Adrian actually drank the hot chocolate. This was my initial thought. She had come back from the dead and had drunk the hot chocolate in front of me. In the candlelight, Jake looked at me. His face was wet with tears. He was trying to say something and at first I thought it was *the cardboard's plenty* and then I realized he was saying *the cup is empty*. But there was something in Jake's desperation and

Oliver's smugness and the detail of their altar to Adrian that made me wonder just how much this was something Oliver was playing at and Jake wanted to believe in and so he played along and how could they play at something like this?

"Can I see her?" I asked.

"You can't see her unless she asks to be seen," Oliver said.

"Adrian, how did you like the hot chocolate?" I asked.

"She thanked you," Oliver said.

I leaned forward and Oliver reached down to grab me, but instead of grabbing me he knocked me into the pile of soft and dampish plush animals at the base of the changing table. It tipped over and the lace over Adrian's body slipped off. It wasn't Adrian, but her large stuffed bear dressed in her nice dress. Like the other stuffed animals, it had begun to rot. Blooms of fungus covered its eyes.

"That isn't Adrian," Jake cried.

"It represents Adrian," Oliver said. He stood up and stomped around the bush blowing out the candles. "How could I find her when they burned her body? That is impossible, son." When he had finished blowing out all of the candles, he said, "This is the best I could do." He left us in the dark bush.

Mom came home and Oliver didn't tell her anything.

"You're going with us, aren't you Mom?" I asked. "When Jake and I go trick or treating?"

"You have been forbidden to go. It's too dangerous. How do I know you aren't going to eat candy that someone has dipped in arsenic?"

"I won't eat anything that doesn't come in a tightly wrapped package."

"People bake homemade cookies mixing Hershey's chocolate chips and slug bait."

"I don't want homemade cookies."

"Come on, Gayle, I already bought them their masks," Oliver said. "It's their right as children."

"Please. I want people to see my Spiderman costume, and Jake would be so disappointed if he didn't get to wear his bear costume. Come on."

"You two better eat a good dinner."

"Yes," I said.

Jake smiled and said, "Trick or treat. Give me some candy."

At six thirty, as the last of the light began to fall, we walked down to Snoqualmie. A procession of ghosts, plastic masks, bats, witches, and ghouls walked on their short legs through the city. Mom pulled my mask up. "Stay in the line and when you get to the last of the houses, come back. I'll be in the cafe."

"Aren't you coming with us?"

"Why?"

"Don't you want any candy?"

"No. Of course I don't."

"You won't be able to have any of mine," I said.

"I don't want any."

"I'll let you have some of mine," Jake said. "If you change your mind."

After only two cul-de-sacs, our bags were loaded with candy. We walked up to a large red house and the woman who opened the door screamed, "How cute! A clown!" She gave Jake two actual Snickers bars. She gave me a Butterfinger and closed the door. The night stretched out before us, long, profitable, and gluttonous.

Jake whispered to me. "Are those kids mugging people?" Greg, Lance, Dayle, and Willie stopped on the other side of the street. Willie held a small child down in the bushes and Greg rummaged through the kid's bag. "Give it back to him," Lance said. "He still hasn't hit the red house. They're giving out full candy bars. Let him go and then we'll get them, too."

"I think so," I said to Jake. We tried to walk briskly past them on the other side of the street. When Dayle started to sing the theme to *Spiderman,* Greg pushed the kid they had mugged back into the bushes.

"Hey!" he yelled. "Peter fuckhead Parker, come here."

"Jake," I said, "You should run."

Jake ran. But Willie took off after Jake. Dayle and Lance grabbed me by my arms.

Greg smashed his fist into my face. My mask crumbled and ripped where his knuckles connected with my jaw. My teeth flashed red-hot and then my entire face felt like a big bruise. "Don't you think you're too old for trick or treating?" he said.

Headlights lit up the street and Greg and Dayle pushed me into the bushes. A '57 Chevy stopped. "Hey, you punks!" someone yelled. Standing in the bushes, Greg forced me to my knees. He held me by the back of my neck. I still held my candy. Something flew past us and shattered against a tree; then a half-full beer bottle landed in the dirt next to us. "Hey, big score," Greg said to his friends. "Could you get that? My hands are full."

Suddenly the bushes were full of shadows much larger than us. They grabbed us and yanked us into the street. "What's this?" a man said. He sat on the hood of the idling Chevy. I recognized him as one of the high school guys who came to our house sometimes. He had a thin mustache and a loose-fitting silk shirt loosened to the third button and a gold chain. The gold glittered in the faint light. Another high school guy held Willie. "It looks like you fuckheads have been caught trying to steal little kids' candy. I think you should hand it over." He took the stuffed bags away from Lance. They had Jake's and my bags. "Is this yours?" he asked Jake. Jake nodded. He handed it back to him. "Here," he said and handed mine back to me.

"Hey, man—you're Bohm's little kid?"

"Yes," Jake said.

"How old are you?" they asked me. "You shouldn't try to be getting candy. You think your old man would give us a break on a lid? Seeing as how he doesn't have to go the expense of buying a coffin and burying you. You should tell your old man that Steve O'Grady rescued your ass and maybe he could give me a break?"

Mom met us at the corner. I had straightened out my mask, so she couldn't see the bruise on my face. My mask just had a little hole. "So, did you two get a load of candy?" Mom asked.

"Sure did," I said.

When we came home, I took off my Spiderman costume and Jake his bear ears. We dumped our plastic bags of candy onto the living room floor. The candy mounted up in splotches of red and white wrappers. Mom leaned over the piles, her hair whisking over my plastic mask. I swept the mask off my face. Unused to my peripheral vision, I sat in the middle of the floor looking out of the corners of my eyes. Oliver and Dad leaned into the room from the kitchen where they had been smoking and playing Monopoly. Oliver pointed at my feet. I looked down and saw the odd, reverse image of the cracked, upside-down Spiderman mask.

Mom sorted through the piles, pulling out ripped, wrapped candies, pulling out fruit, pulling out anything that conformed to the list of dangerous things kids brought back from strangers' houses. As she sorted through the candy, she pushed it into a stack behind her, and Oliver squatted down and started to eat it. Dad leaned over his shoulder and muttered something and, soon, they both squatted down, eating and eating and eating and stuffing the wrappers into their pockets.

Mom took a whole wrapped Butterfinger bar that Jake had wanted to save.

"I wanted that."

"It's been tampered with," Mom said. "It's dangerous."

"You're still going to eat it."

"Hey, chocolate," Dad said when I unwrapped a bite-sized Hershey's chocolate bar. "Chocolate would sure be good right now. Do you think we could have some?"

Oliver stood in the door. He waved his hand at me. "I invested in this haul, you know. I bought the mask that earned all this."

"I can spare some," Jake said. He handed out a handful of his candy to Dad and Oliver.

"Thanks, kid," Dad said. Oliver and Dad returned to the kitchen table. For a long time, Jake and I were alone in the bedroom. We sorted our candy and then began to count it. Finally, Jake and I went to the bathroom to brush our teeth and go to bed.

When we came back, Dad and Oliver were sitting on the bottom bunk of the bed quickly sorting through the candy, leaving sours and Lemonheads. They had mixed both Jake's and my bag together. "What are you doing?" Jake screamed. "You mixed up the candy. Aldous always eats his up. That isn't fair."

"I'm telling Mom," I said.

"Don't," Oliver said. "She mustn't know. Or I'll tell her about your fight at school."

"You won't."

Oliver chortled and made a devil's face. He jumped to the middle of the room and did a belly dance; pulling up his T-shirt he exposed his white, flat stomach and deep belly button. "Oompa Loompa, Doopity Doo. I'm giving you a chocolate factory, Charlie." Dad and Oliver left, leaving Jake and me a pile of gumdrops, sour licorice, and hard candy. We heard them in the kitchen, cooking hamburgers and complaining about the lack of chocolate. "Man, you ate it all."

"You did," Oliver said.

That night, I snuck through the wreckage of the living room. Dad lay behind the sofa wearing my broken Spiderman mask. Oliver curled in a tight ball on a single square of the sofa in a nest of candy wrappers. I crawled onto the kitchen counter and slowly inched open the cabinet drawer. I

heard a crunch and then, "Oh, fuck, man," and Oliver
stumbled down the hallway, through the kitchen, and
turned on the bathroom light. A Snickers wrapper stuck to
his foot and he shuffled back and forth until he gave up
and leaned against the wall to lift up his foot and pull it
off. Oliver stood over the toilet for a while and looked at
himself in the mirror. I could only see the back of his head
and a sliver of hair falling over his face. He turned his face
to one side and then smiled. "A lobotomy would do your
eyebrows some good," he said, and pressed his whole palm
to the mirror as he pissed into the toilet. I stood still,
waiting for him to see me, but he flushed the toilet, flicked
off the light and, on the way back to the living room,
stopped in the middle of the hallway.

I eased the two-pound bag of C&H sugar down from
the top shelf. I squatted on top of the counter and set it
down, then I climbed down and eased open the kitchen
door. I glanced back into the living room. Oliver lay on the
couch and was sleeping again.

A faint mist of rain coated the Dodge Dart and dripped
from the cedar tree. My naked feet burned in the frosty
grass. When I finally reached the car, goose bumps covered
my skin even though a burning sweat dripped from my
eyebrows. I twisted the silver gasoline cap out, leaned
down, and then realized that I should use a funnel or something because I'd get sugar everywhere. I left the sugar
under the back tire and walked back up the driveway. Our

house stood small under the shadowy height of the cedar tree in the front yard and the cottonwood that held the hill up behind it. Around us, the dark clouds and trees covered miles and miles, except for the faint glow of the cattle light just behind the crest of the hill. The car connected us to the rest of the world. Now, in the middle of the night, I was aware of how far away we were from everything; even our neighbors' lights were far enough away that they were just faint blue lights flickering through the rustling trees.

Oliver sat at the kitchen table when I came back into the warm kitchen. "Hey, Aldous," he said. "Would you like something to eat?"

"No, thanks." I slid open the drawer with the spatula, cheese graters, and mixing spoons.

"I just needed something creamy to settle the old stomach." He sat straight back in his chair, his hands on his knees. He squinted at me and then nodded his head. "What do you think about me being a chef?"

"I think it's great." I found the white plastic funnel.

"I will make a gigantic cheesecake, a fucking gargantuan cheesecake when I get up there into some fancy restaurant with waiters running in and out of the kitchen and a big bull on a spit getting turned around and around over an open pit. Everyone will just eat my cheesecake and then be like, 'This is beautiful.' They'll go, 'Who's that back there making this stuff? Sandro fucking Botticelli?'"

Oliver stood up. "Well, good night, man." He set his

dish on the bottom of the sink. He grabbed me by the sides of my head and kissed me on the forehead, a long sucking kiss, and then released me. Oliver turned, settled down on the couch, brushed the cheese crumbs out of his mustache with a pinch of each of his hands and fell back asleep.

The door waved open and banged against a stool, knocking it back. Oliver stirred and turned over onto his side. I started to close the door and then remembered that I'd left the sugar outside by the car. For a moment, I realized that I was just going to let Oliver get away with it. Outside, holding the funnel in one hand, I didn't even think of the monsters in the bushes. I didn't feel the invisible beasts with huge, ingrown toenails suddenly closing in on me. Instead, I walked steadily through the drizzle to the Dodge Dart and emptied the bag of sugar into the tank.

I woke when the Dodge Dart rattled and backfired a sharp sound, followed seconds later by its echo. Oliver yelled. He slammed the kitchen door on his way in. "Paul, the car is broken."

"No, it's not," Dad said. "The oil's just been changed. Try it again."

I pressed my hand into the cool wall, waiting for Dad

to go out to the car and find evidence of the sugar. Maybe it had crystallized in the gasoline and long branches of precipitated sugar grew out of the tank over the dirty green license plate and dripped down the battered bumper.

I heard the mumble of Mom's voice.

"It won't start, Gayle," Oliver said. "If it doesn't start, then I don't have a job. I need that job."

"No one is asking you to work," Mom said as she came into the kitchen. She turned the light on. The teapot hummed a rising pitch as she filled the kettle with tap water.

"I have to get to work."

"If the car won't start, then the car won't start. You can find a better job anyway."

"I've looked. I was meant to have this job. I've tried to find a job and I can't except for shoveling cow shit or washing dishes. Nobody'll take me."

"Paul will get the car started. But Oliver," Mom said, "Why do you want to work? You've been busy in the attic. Do you want to leave us?"

I rolled over and stuffed my head under my pillow. The pocket of air pressed between the bulk of the pillow and my bed grew warm, then hot, but I lay still, wanting to fall asleep until everything had ended, until Dad fixed the car, until Oliver drove away.

I didn't fall asleep. Instead, I lay in the bed sweating and waiting and, when the teapot started to whistle, I slipped out of bed. The cold linoleum floor numbed the soles of my feet. I sat at the kitchen table where Mom poured the boiling water into coffee cups and smiled at me. "Early morning?" she asked.

I sat down at the table. "You still have a half hour before you have to wake up. Are you all right?"

"I'm fine," I said. The open door waved back and forth in the damp wind. Dad had the hood open and then he stood up and slammed it shut. "Damn it. Fuck it," Oliver yelled. He grabbed one of the rockery stones and threw it through the windshield of the car. Dad just stood in front of the car and watched him. "What in the hell did you do?" Then Oliver turned to Dad and said, "You don't want me to have a new job. You just like me the way I am, don't you? Well, I don't have to comply." He walked down the driveway, across the road without looking both ways, and disappeared in the elephant ears on the other side of the road.

Twenty

As the apples dropped in the stunted orchard and rotted in heaps in the November drizzle, Oliver didn't come back from the other side of the road. The meat of the apples turned soft and leaked into the spongy, mossy ground. The sweet pulp soaked into the soil, leaving behind the light husks of the apple skins, rattling with seeds and stems. The light, rust-colored shells blew into the ditch. The trickling runoff carried the shells into the stream and they disappeared. The autumn wind left the driveway coated with the fragrant cedar tree needles. Jake and I woke early to eat our breakfast and leave the house before Dad woke. We wore our hats and jackets buttoned up over our schoolbooks so they wouldn't get wet. We played on the playground before the start of school and we played on the playground after school, long after the other kids had gone home and the soccer team had practiced out on the muddy field. We finally slunk home, our faces red from the cool air, and sat down at the kitchen table where Mom sat drinking coffee.

Weeks after he had gone, not even coming back for a slice of cheese, Oliver came back. He stood in the pasture behind our house singing, *The lunatic is on the grass*, from the album he and my father listened to when they were so stoned they couldn't move. It had drifted into the special section of the record collection reserved for the albums they didn't want to tire from listening to over and over again. They sprawled in front of the stereo on their backs looking at the ceiling, muttering, *wow wow wow*. On his return, Oliver's voice came through the bathroom window and faintly through the closed back windows. Mom turned off the kitchen light. We went back into our bedroom to see him standing in the middle of the pasture, naked, with one hand clasped over his chest as though he were belting out the national anthem. He sang the few words he really knew of the song over and over again. The song on the album had sound effects and the tune itself had an almost chantlike repetition. Oliver's skin looked faintly blue under the cattle light.

> *The lunatic is on the grass.*
> *The lunatic is on the grass.*
> *Remembering games and daisy chains and laughs.*
> *Got to keep the loonies on the path.*

When he finished, he walked down to the house and knocked on the front door. He shoved his face up against the glass. "Let me in, I'm starving," and Mom opened the door. He had been leaning on the door and fell into the room. My guilt and anger about dumping the C&H into the Dodge Dart tank returned. I had wanted somehow to get at Oliver, and instead I had helped him make himself a sort of martyr. He seemed different, but it was hard to tell exactly what was different about him because it looked as though he had been living like an animal for two weeks and this was bound to make a person look different. He seemed unfazed by not having seen anyone for two weeks. I wondered if he had been cheating somehow. Mom gave him some leftover spaghetti she warmed in a saucepan. While he waited, she poured him some water, but he refused to drink it in a glass and drank it out of a bowl. He sat on the floor and ate with his hands. He looked at us, and instead of smiling or laughing at our expressions, he frowned. "What is it? Am I doing something wrong?"

"No," I said.

He smelled like dirt, but not like a dirty person, not like an unbathed person. He smelled like soil, like the pungent and almost pleasant odor of earthworms and roots.

"Do you remember the moths? Not the white moths. The wood moths?" Oliver said.

"Yes," I said.

"I found them. I slept where they sleep, in a hole in the ground."

His breath smelled harsh, like the rim of an empty butter tub forgotten in the back of the fridge. Thin scratches wrapped around his body. Blackberry twigs and thin thorny vines lay tangled in his chest and pubic hair. He had grown a short beard, and it actually made him look younger, because it covered up the acne scars on his face. After he ate, he asked if he could lie down, but he wouldn't lie on a bed, instead he lay on the carpet in the living room near the fire and muttered, "Thank you, Gayle. Thank you. I'm sorry." He didn't want to take a bath and, in the middle of the night, the pasta and red sauce made him sick.

We woke to the steady beat of Oliver chanting. It filtered through the house, more of a vibration than an actual noise. Oliver stomped on the attic floor and continued to chant. "Hey Oh, Hey Oh, Hey Oh," Oliver chanted. Jake and I brushed our teeth and stumbled into the living room. We were half awake. I closed my eyes. I could hear Oliver above us, tapping the walls with his fingers. Outside, a wet wind brushed rain against the house and kicked the branches and fallen sticks together.

Dad slept on the living room rug where Oliver had gone to sleep the night before. An afghan covered him. He didn't seem to mind that the kitchen door was open. A thin haze hung just above the trees, and under Oliver's chanting we could hear water dripping from the gutter.

Mom smiled at us even though she didn't look as if she wanted to smile. She wore her work uniform. "I can't have this in my house," Mom whispered. "Where are you and Jake going to go today?"

"Nowhere," I said.

Mom shoved a five-dollar bill into my hands. "You two should walk down to the store and buy something for lunch and then go to the park. I'll be home this evening, okay?"

"Okay, Mom." I looked at Jake. He stood at the foot of Dad. Jake looked at me and showed me the palm of his hands, like, "What do you do?"

We came home later that afternoon, having killed most of the day bumping around Snoqualmie. We went to the park that overlooked the river and swung on the swings, jumping off at the top of the arc. Finally, we walked back home, along the paved road and then along the muddy road, until we finally came back to our house.

Mom was washing dishes in the kitchen. She still wore her work uniform, but it was now singed and smelly from her shift at the Busy Bee. Oliver was still upstairs chanting. Dad was asleep in the bedroom now. Finally, he stumbled out through the living room, through the kitchen, into the bathroom, leaving the door open where we could hear him at the toilet gagging and spitting.

I realized then that the chanting had stopped. It vibrated in my ears long after it had actually stopped. Oliver swung the door open, letting in a blast of cold, damp air.

"Close the door, it's cold," Mom said.

"Yes, ma'am." Oliver closed the door, leaving himself outside. He knocked.

"Come in," Jake said.

Oliver came in and he wore his old clothes, but they hung on him now. He had cut his hair sometime during the night, obviously by himself. He had shaved his beard. Dad was asleep now.

"Let's go, boys," Mom said.

Oliver stood on his chair when he saw her. He jumped over the side, knocking Mom's book onto the floor. "Give me those keys. You're in no condition to be driving."

"I'm in much better condition than you ever are," Mom said. "You seem to have gotten over your retreat into the woods. What have you been taking?"

"LSD, speed, and pots of coffee," Oliver said. "I'm so gone that everyone must have such a blazing contact high that they're in no condition to do anything." He grabbed Mom's hand. "Give me. Give me. Give me."

They struggled over the ball of Mom's fist until the keys scattered over the ground, then Oliver kicked the bunch and they jangled into the living room. Mom and Oliver ran after them. The late daylight came in low through the trees and slanted through the windows. Jake and I sat on the chairs in the kitchen. I noticed, then, that Oliver had hung a papier-mâché figure from the door arch. It had been painted purple and looked like an old man with hooves and a single horn rising crookedly from his knotted brow. Mom and Oliver grunted in the other room, and then Oliver thumped against the bedroom wall. We saw him land near the doorway. He looked at us and then stood up, brushing himself off.

"Fine, Gayle. You can have the keys, but you might need this one." He held up a key. He walked into the kitchen and opened the tool drawer. Dad kept the wrenches, screwdrivers, and saws in the bottom drawer of the kitchen cabinet. Oliver pulled the drawer out and then clamped the key in a wrench. Then he took up a hammer.

Mom stood in the doorway. "No you don't," she said. She took a step toward him, as if she were testing him. Oliver swung the hammer in the air at her, missing widely. "Stay back!"

"I'm fixed," Dad said. He came out of the bathroom with a towel wrapped around his neck "What's going on?"

"Give me my key," Mom said.

"Where are you going?" Dad said. "You're leaving with Oliver? So that's it? Gone, just like that. With my fucking brother." Dad stumbled away from the door; he sat at the table. "Go away," Dad said.

Mom noticed Jake and me sitting at the table. Jake had his hands folded neatly in his lap. I sat on my hands. They felt numb.

"Christ," Mom said. "Jesus fucking Christ, why do you do this in front of the children? It's obscene."

"Come here my boys, my delightfully deformed clones," Dad said.

Oliver smashed the hammer down against the wrench and the tip of the key zinged through the kitchen window. The noise of the metal shard zipping through the glass filled my spine with water. I pulled my hands from under my butt. They were bright red and the denim of my jeans was imprinted over my hands. The windows didn't shatter. Instead, the flying key left an inch-wide hole in the window.

"Oh, cool," Oliver said. He climbed up onto the sink and ran his finger around the hole in the pane.

"Excuse me," Mom said. She sat at the table. "Oliver, get off the counter. Get off the counter and sit at the table. I think it's time we had a rational, calm discussion about what's going on here."

Oliver didn't say anything. Dad looked at Mom. "I don't think it's a good time, Gayle." He shook his head. "We're kind of fucked up right now."

"Kids, go to your bedroom."

We slinked into our bedroom and sat on the bed. Because there wasn't a door to the bedroom, we could hear everything they were saying. I suppose it made Mom feel better that we weren't in the same room.

"Don't you care," Mom said, "what you're doing to our children?"

"I'm not doing anything to them."

"It was fine when they were small. But they're both going to school now, and certain things have to be taken care of."

"There is an entire world inside the glass," Oliver said, "Come here! Here's me, and there's you and you."

"Both of the kids need new clothes."

"What about the clothes we got them for Christmas? Look Gayle, I agree. Hell, Christmas was almost a year ago. We can find them some jeans and stuff at Thriftmart. Not right now though, because, if you haven't noticed, Oliver's fucking out of his mind."

"Oliver? Are you out of your mind?"

"No. I'm fine. I'm busy right now, but I'll join you two in a minute."

"We should talk about this some other time," Dad said.

"When?" Mom asked him. "You two are fried. You go to work half-sizzled and then drop on the drive home. By the time you pull into the driveway, you're halfway to the Yukon."

"That's what having a house is for."

"This house is not just a pot shed."

"Oh, Mrs. High and Fucking Mighty, as if you don't do it too. You're up there with the best of them. I never did this in the sixties. I'm just trying to catch up."

"I think we're a little too old for this."

"Hypocrite. This is my house. I can explore myself in it, you fucking cold bitch."

"Get out. Get out of my house," Mom said.

"And where should I go? This is my house. I paid for it."

"We," Mom said.

"Come on Paul," Oliver said. "I can tell when we're not wanted. A woman gets a little dick—wam-o, bam-o, thank you mam-o—you're out on the street. The way of the world. But you're not going anywhere, missy. Your damn key to the kingdom is broken." He slammed the door as they left.

Mom locked the doors and the windows. She put chairs in front of the doors, jamming them under the handles. She completely sealed all entrances. Jake and I came out of our bedroom. "Come and sit with me," she said.

We sat with her on the couch. I lay against her side and felt her breathing; each inhale pushed me back and the exhale drew me closer. Jake looked through the windows at Dad and Oliver standing outside on the front lawn. Dad went to the root cellar and came back with a wine bottle and the tin pill case. They walked over the road and into the dark forest.

"You two all right?" Mom asked.

"Yeah."

"Good, let's see what's on TV." Mom told us that Dad and Oliver were sick now and would be better in the morning. "Well, they'll be really sick in the morning, but everything else will be better."

Much later, wrapped in blankets and sitting in the blue light of the TV, I twirled fabric around my fist and pulled the satin edge of the blanket back and forth until it started to hurt. When Mom turned on the living room lamp that threw light against the windows, I saw the flicker of Oliver's cigarette in the dark trees. In the middle of a sun-lit commercial for Jell-O where a family in a park sat eating huge piles of food and the women stood in front of them with a plate of molded gelatin, a bright fire jumped up in the patch of elephant ears across the street. Oliver and Dad and a hundred other shadows hunched away from the fire and then it faded down, until it was just the light of a lantern, the light of a candle, the light of a Bic lighter. It wasn't anything, but we knew they were out there still. Much later, Mom leaned over my bed. Her necklace caught the fluorescent light from the kitchen. She smelled like dish soap and Camels, and she kissed me on the smooth shelf of skin between my eyebrows and hair.

"Do you hear that outside?" Jake asked. "I can hear them saying, 'Tell us, is this not so?' "

"What do you mean?" I asked. I listened carefully, but all I could hear were the boughs outside rocking in the breeze and Mom washing in the bathroom and then the snap of the light switch. Dad and Mom talked in the living room. "He's pretty screwed up." And Mom saying, "He'll cool off." The fluorescent over the kitchen cast its atonal light into our room all night, throwing sharp shadows behind the scattered blocks on the floor and Jake's play barn, the rigid bodies of plastic cattle, wooden horses, and tin sheep. Sometimes, I woke in the middle of the night and I would walk out to take a drink of water from the sink, and as I drank, I would examine the avocado Dad kept in a mason jar on the windowsill. It had two spindly toothpicks holding the egg-shaped seed over the water. For a while it had grown hair in the portion submerged underwater and these roots had gathered little bubbles and then they grew a faint moss, and now it just sat under the fluorescent light.

"Can't you hear it?" Jake asked me.

"What?"

"Tell us, is this not so?"

"Jake, you're scaring me. Shut up." I lay in bed planning my escape. My pants and shirt lay draped over the end of the bunk. I didn't need shoes. I heard it then, the sound saying, "Tell us, is this not so?" I listened for the noise maybe of a cottonwood limb brushing the side of the house or, beyond that, the distant sound of a calling voice. At first it was so faint I didn't know if I really heard it. "Help," and then it was louder, "Help me! Please, Good Lord help me," and then again much louder, a shriek, and I could no longer hear the soft, plaintive scrape of the branch saying, "Tell us, is this not so?" on the windowpane or tar roof.

The front door cracked open as suddenly as an eggshell. The back of the chair Mom had placed against the door wedged under the doorknob. The legs of the chair bit into the floor and squealed and then the door snapped shut again. Mom's running footfalls rumbled through the living room and she shoved the chair back up against the door. She propped sections of an old broom handle between the window frame and the stile. She shouted outside, "I'm calling the police!" But Mom didn't even pick up the phone. She just sat in the kitchen smoking cigarette after cigarette under the fluorescent light.

She went into the bedroom and I could hear her talking to Dad. "Wake up, Paul. Oliver is threatening to kill himself."

I could hear Dad's low grumble. "What do we do about it? I'm asleep."

"He said he had a knife. I need you to go out and quietly talk to him and don't wake the kids."

Dad said really loudly, "I am not getting out of bed. I am sleeping. Everything will be cleared up in the morning."

"He was gone for two weeks. Don't you think it's unlikely to clear up in one night?"

"Yes, but I'm tired."

The window in our bedroom exploded, sending slivers of glass over my top blankets and through the plastic toys on the ground. Small bits of glass ticked against everything in the room. Flecks of glass and droplets of sticky fluid caught in my hair.

"Shitolla," Jake said. I thought that was funny. I don't know why, but I started to laugh when Jake said that. Jake hopped out of the bottom bunk, yelping as his feet slid over the shards of glass and scattered Lego blocks. He left dark, wet footprints on the pale kitchen linoleum.

What seemed like a hair-covered creature, a monster, drove its triangle-shaped shoulder through the broken pane of glass. I was struck by how small it was—this real monster—how little the arms were, how stringy the muscle was, how normal the hands looked. The hands weren't claws, or twisted clumps of cruelly hooked fingers, but a small, soft-looking fist with a few rings on the fingers. Blood flowed across the arms and splattered through the room. The small head at the end of the long neck swung out into the shadows behind the house and its howl filled the room. And then I realized it was Oliver. My first thought was that this was some game.

Mom came into the room wearing Dad's rubber fishing boots. She scooped me out of the bed. I was too heavy for her and slipped out of her arms onto the floor.

The howl went on and on.

Oliver's knife flashed into the room, snapping the curtain rod. The drapes fluttered down. Oliver worked his way through the window. I felt Mom's cool hands touch the burning skin on my face. "Come on, honey," she said. She pulled me into the kitchen.

Jake stood by the front door with his hands in his jeans pockets, still barefoot. His lips were pursed and he stared at the notes on the refrigerator. "These are old," he told Mom.

"What?" Mom asked.

"These notes are old. Nobody reads them."

"Come on," she said and she pulled us outside. We ran after her. Jake and I climbed into the backseat and looked back at the house as Mom started the car. The smell of gasoline filled the car. Oliver lurched out of the house. He stood on the porch.

Mom backed down the driveway. Oliver cut across the lawn and threw his knife. It missed the car, glittering as it passed through the lights, and then disappeared into the salmonberry bushes. Mom backed the car up and Oliver bumped into the side of the car. He tried to climb up onto the trunk, but just bounced back into the ditch and Mom drove.

"Mom, what about Oliver?"

"What, honey?"

"Shouldn't we get him?"

"Honey, that was Oliver."

"He's in the ditch," Jake said. "Do you think he'll be all right?"

"What the fuck do I care if he's bleeding to death in the ditch?" Mom said. "He tried to kill us. He's an angel dust snorting freak and he should be put in jail so that he can't kill the last of my children."

But all that I could think about as we drove away was my uncle in the ditch. My uncle in the ditch, bleeding from the cuts after breaking the window and broken bones from running into the car. "Mom, turn back, Oliver could be dying."

"Don't we wish," my Mom said, and Jake and I had nothing to say to that. We just listened to the Dart roll along i-90.

Mom drove until Jake and I woke in the morning. Jake and I looked at our frazzled hair and I picked the hard motes of sleep from my eyes. Mom's hair was slick and greasy-looking and her eyes floated in a shadowy pulp of skin. She smoked cigarette after cigarette and blew the smoke in exaggerated blasts out the window. She ran her hands over her hair. "What would you guys like?" she said to Jake and me.

Jake and I didn't know what to say. He looked at me and then glanced out the window. I lay back against the warm leatherette seat and felt the hot sun stream over me. The moving car, the daylight, felt safer, but underneath I felt an empty gulf widening and spreading and clearing out the bottom-line safety that I had always felt.

Mom stopped in a busy shopping center. We looked at the parking lot, at the people walking into the Happy Grocer, at the shopping carts full of food, at the trucks and cars on the highway, speeding to and from wherever. Mom stood at the phone booth, dialing and then listening to the receiver.

Finally she came back and said, "No one's answering. What would you two like?"

"What do you mean, Mom?" asked Jake.

"Yeah?" I said.

"What kind of *toy* would you like?" she said.

Our hair stood straight up from sleeping in the car. We both bought Fisher-Price action toys—the Shark Hunters, a boat with a shark included. We drove to Aberdeen and visited Mom's grandmother. We walked on the beach and looked at the clouds. We didn't know, really, where we were. And we were unaware of time. Sitting on the beach, we built gigantic sand castles. We built them as large as we could, digging a huge hole in the middle and piling the sand on the outside. And then we laid streets and balconies into the center of the castle. We built houses, towers, buildings. In the center of it all, we built our house, a small building with a sloped roof.

We had spent as long as we could at my grandmother's house. Jake and I still spent as much time as possible on the beach. Mom held long conversations with Dad on the phone. Finally, things were arranged and we were on our way home. On the way, Mom stopped in Seattle and we took a room in one of the hotels where we had spent hours in the lobby. But it was something Mom couldn't enjoy.

In the lobby of the downtown hotel, surrounded by heavy marble mantels with sparkling brass grates over the fireplaces, surrounded by plush easy chairs and couches with buttons the size of silver dollars, served by waiters who would silently approach her and fill her cup with black coffee hot enough to burn her tongue, Mom was no longer comfortable. Jake and I sat on the sofa, our hands folded over our laps, looking outside at the dark streets and watching people hurrying away from the Bon Marché with bags hanging into the damp sidewalk.

Finally we came home, but it was no longer the same. My uncle had disappeared. Jake said he had been kidnapped by the Sasquatch and carried into the forest. The windows were fixed. The house was clean and smelled like bleach. But under that, I could still smell the mold and the fungus. Dad stood in the kitchen when we came home. "Hi, honey," he said to Mom. He hugged her. Jake and I stood by the counter while they embraced, holding each other for the longest time that Jake and I had ever witnessed. I hoped, as they rocked back and forth, that they would never let go of each other.

Twenty-one

Nine months after Dad kicked him out of the attic, Oliver killed himself in the parking lot behind his apartment building. He gassed himself while drinking Absolut vodka mixed with Western Family orange concentrate and listening to a tape of *Magical Mystery Tour*. He left a note, but hadn't been able to get beyond the first word. He started with "Dear," on the first page of a tablet of onionskin typing paper. The paper under the word was ragged from repeated erasing.

His friend Leroy, sounding abnormally calm and even sober, called to deliver the news. I set the phone on the counter and stepped into the dim living room. Dad sat next to his stereo, with a ring of LP sleeves circling the base of his short stool. He removed his headphones and grumbled as he snuffed his roach in the tin ashtray. "The telephone," I said. He followed me into the kitchen and I handed him the receiver. Dad wiped the palm of his hand on his beard and looked at me, then looked at Jake, who was eating cereal at the kitchen counter. Jake's slurping noise filled the kitchen. Dad's knuckles turned white against the orange handle of the phone. He cracked the receiver onto the green Formica counter, walked outside, leaving the kitchen door open and the phone to beep and beep. He started the Dodge. The starter, half-broken, caught in a jarring ring, but finally the car hacked, started, and Dad backed it down the driveway. Jake and I left the phone on the counter for a long time until we realized Dad wasn't coming right back. Jake held the phone to his ear. "Hello?" he asked, and then set the receiver back into the cradle.

Mom wore a string of fake pearls and a hairnet to my uncle's wake. She smelled like the lobby of a department store. She wore a black dress, which was against the convention of Oliver's friends. They wore rainbow tie-dyed T-shirts to all occasions. Mom's dress had three sections and the end segments flipped up as she walked. She looked like a flapper, and I didn't understand the look because I had seen gangster movies and Mom didn't fit in with women who carried hip flasks, danced, and knocked men down flights of stairs.

Dad wore a plaid work shirt he had last worn chopping wood the weekend before. He and I had stood in a frigid forest clearing, tossing hunks of alder wood into the back

of a truck Dad had borrowed from Leroy. Sitting behind
Dad on the way to the wake, I could smell the sawdust and
gasoline embedded in his shirt.

Jake knotted his fingers in his lap, then undid them and
then folded them back up again. His face was white from
having spent all night jumping out of bed to make sure the
window was closed.

My Uncle Oliver's wake took place in an old church, in
north Seattle, in a neighborhood I'd never been to, and to
my knowledge he'd never been to. My parents parked in a
gravel lot between a VW bus and a school bus covered in
painted handprints. Propped into the front hood of a Ford
truck, a small black flag fluttered in the rain.

I fingered the Coke bottle lighter that Oliver had stolen
from Dad and then given to me the last time he had come
to our house to visit. When Dad had found his lighter
missing, he had started calling antique stores and second-
hand stores to see if he could find a replacement. It
looked like a miniature Coke bottle and opened in the
middle. The words "Enjoy Coke" had worn away to a few
flakes of white paint from the million times my uncle and
father had lit and relit the dying nubs of joints. The
objects Dad and Oliver used in the process of smoking
gained an importance that the other things in our house
couldn't have. The round tray where Dad rolled his cigarettes was forbidden to Jake and me. When Dad slid the
tray under the couch in the living room, even the couch

became off-limits. So when Oliver handed me the lighter, I whispered to him, "Does Dad know you have this?"

"Sure," he said. "But don't tell him anyway. Okay?"

"Are you crazy?" I asked him. When I asked him if he was crazy, Oliver would do something to prove that he was crazy. Once he had burned a hole in his hand, and then when I started to yell, he started to laugh, even though his skin had boiled and part of it had even turned black. This time, Oliver just knocked me over and pulled out his dentures and gummed my ear until I started to cry. He'd lost his teeth from exposure to Agent Orange in Vietnam. But when he stopped, I still had Dad's lighter and Oliver didn't ask for it back. When he left later that day, I didn't know what to do with it. Now I wanted to give it back to Dad, but I had to wait for the right moment so that when I gave it back to him, I wouldn't get in trouble for holding onto it for so long.

When we stepped out of the car in the parking lot, Mom leaned back against Dad and he moved out of her way. She stumbled backward in her thick heels and slapped her hand on the splattered car hood. As we walked through the hallways, I looked into dark rooms I assumed were Sunday school classrooms and I could see the short desks with blue pipe legs. The windows had crisscrossed wires through the pane to make them break-proof, which seemed like an important thing in a building that was supposed to hold my uncle's memories. The windows were narrow and tall like arrow slits in a castle. If the glass shattered, then it would stick together in the mesh of wires.

Even with the safety-glass windows, I still couldn't fit my uncle into this place. The halls smelled like bleach, an odor I couldn't associate with Oliver. He reeked of incense and grape juice, thick and loamy, unwholesome and too ripe. The smell came from the wine he drank and, as he got more and more drunk, he started sweating this smell. The odor filled Oliver's attic. The church, its relative cleanliness, the order of the desks in the dark rooms and the safe windows, were not things that belonged to my uncle.

We walked up a narrow staircase and came into a large meeting room filled with people in tie-dyed clothes, long cotton skirts, and blue jeans. The noise of whispering people filled the room with a thick buzz, with no distinct words or voices, just the presence of Oliver's friends.

A stage ran along one side of the room and the rest of the room was paneled with thin, long boards over an orange padded wall. Yellowish linoleum covered the floor. As we started to walk through the room, I saw that I didn't know any of the people. It seemed not very many knew Dad or Mom.

Dad stood in the middle of the room, looking for family or someone he could recognize. The people milled around, oblivious to him. They were oblivious to us, Oliver's family. On the wall, someone had pasted pieces of poetry, pictures, and a story my uncle had written onto thin, colored cardboard. The 'a' character in each of the typewritten sheets stood slightly out of line from the out-of-whack typewriter in our attic. Through the PA system, I could hear the Beatles. They were just at the threshold of hearing, but still they sounded a little too festive. Mom found a group of vague friends to stand next to. My brother and I became part of everyone else.

I followed the line looking at the artifacts; it felt like walking through a traveling exhibition—a circus's collection of exotic animals—snakes with peeling skin under hot lightbulbs, ostriches in cages lined with molding straw, and crocodiles missing teeth. I listened to the people chuckle at the punch line of short poems. A woman snickered while reading the short story. She wore a broad black hat and a black single-piece dress and had dyed black hair.

Finally, someone spoke and said that he was about to deliver a speech and would like us all to share memories of Oliver. Dad looked at him and stood, but the man on the stage turned back and said, "I have something I've written, and I would like to share it with you now, in a moment when one of us has passed." The lights dimmed and the man spoke with a low voice, half singing a speech he had written. Some people nodded. The woman in the black hat muttered, "Hah," and started to cry.

I sat with my hand in my pocket, opening and closing the Coke bottle lighter. The man on the stage held the paper clenched in his hands so that the sheet folded at the top and bottom. His sentences came out and out and I didn't understand anything. Finally, he finished and folded the sheet with his speech into quarters and put it in his breast pocket. Everyone politely clapped. "Mom, is this a show?" Jake asked. A woman with sandy hair and long bony fingers stood on the stage and told us all that it was all right. "Hug each other," she said, "Hug, hug the person next to you." The people in the rows behind us wrapped their arms around each other. Their sobbing sounded like a hundred rags whipping the windows. Dad put his fist to his forehead and looked at the ground. Mom put her hand on his shoulder. She leaned into his ear and whispered something, but before I could read her lips, a woman grabbed me and started to sob. Her hair fell over my face, and I could feel the sharp strands on my skin, and I thought, it must be painful to have a head of hair so sharp. Her breath was thick and fruity, like rotting strawberries. Tears streamed from her face. Whimpering, she rubbed the two lines of her lips back and forth. I wished then that Oliver was alive and there because he would know what to do to counteract their carnestness and then it wouldn't matter that we didn't know anyone.

Oliver was dead, but we got his car, an old Ford station wagon with wood paneling. The paneling on the outside had stripped back and peeled as if the car had burned in the sun. Dad received a package of what they called his effects. I pictured a tackle box filled with special powders and vials that Oliver had used to become funny, or sad, or whatever. Love potions and so on. But Dad didn't get Uncle Oliver's spells; he just picked up his broken eye-glasses, his wallet—a worn wedge of brown leather that looked like the heel of my foot—all the items Oliver used until they wore away like his teeth and his breath. Oliver hissed before he used his car to kill himself. He hissed when he walked. "What's wrong?" I had asked. "I'm using my breath up," he had said, shaking his head.

My parents didn't say anything about why Oliver had killed himself. All that Jake and I knew was that he had put a section of garden hose from the muffler into the back of the station wagon, and drank a mix of orange concentrate and vodka. My parents seemed to assume that the reason he killed himself was self-evident.

I slipped the Coke bottle lighter into the grocery bag filled with Oliver's old stuff, so Dad could find it.

As the winter turned into spring, Jake, Dad, and I would go out to the vegetable patch at night with slim knives to kill the slugs. We would shine our flashlights into Oliver's car. I expected to see something in the darkness like the spirit of my uncle pretending to kill himself again and again. But the car was dark and nothing could be seen behind the thin, scattered spouts of light from our flash-lights. Maybe Oliver was dead already when he came to live with us, but we didn't understand it. I figured Jake was correct about death in that death wasn't forgetting. Death was being the same forever and ever, never getting older, never changing. The moon was dead. The footprints of the astronauts, a memory of their passing, still lay on the lunar surface. On Earth, though, even boulders eroded to rocks, to pebbles, and to sand, then washed out in the ocean. Jake whispered to me that he thought he saw something in the car. He said he saw a T-shirt, an undershirt, something, white moths fluttering around the steering wheel.

Toke

Twenty-two

On the 737 away from Janet and Texas and back toward Seattle, I witnessed my first ten-gallon hat. It rested at a slight angle on the head of an elderly man in front of me. He stooped under the luggage rack to dip his head to take it off. He kept the hard felt hat on his lap during the entire trip. For the three months I had been in San Antonio, the Center of Texan Culture, I hadn't seen a single cowboy hat.

I fell asleep in the recycled, dry airplane air. I woke when I felt the pitch and roll around Puget Sound on the approach toward Sea-Tac. I glanced out the window at the early morning light spilling over the Cascades. The plane rumbled over row after row of small houses with yellowish grass in the backyards in an area of Seattle no one ever talked about. On those cartoon maps of city businesses, the ones where the businesses who've paid to be included have huge signs that stick up almost as tall as Mount

Rainier, this area of the city is never drawn. Fastening my seat belt for the approach to Sea-Tac, I realized I could barely recall how I had spent most of my days during my six months in the Army. Everything I remembered had been compressed.

Jake had once told me he was going to get a gigantic, garish tattoo. "You'll hate it when you're thirty-five," I had said.

"I'm taking revenge on my thirty-five-year-old self."

"But it's still you you're taking revenge on."

"I'm not thirty-five," he'd said.

I wondered if my brother would remember getting the tattoo, or would he wake up one morning when he was thirty-five and catch a glimpse of the dark green shadow on his back and, with growing disgust, step up onto the rim of the tub to examine himself in the vanity mirror?

I had been afraid of talking about Adrian's death for so long, I wondered if Mom or Jake or Dad would remember anything themselves. I knew my choices led to her death. Adrian's death led to my uncle moving into the house. I can't imagine what life would have been like without him in the attic. But his life in the attic had led, inevitably, to his suicide. If she had lived and if he had lived and if Mom had not left—if and if—if I do not answer for what I have done, how can anything be the way it should have been? I changed everything by chasing after Mom and Dad and Oliver that day.

I was nervous about seeing Mom and my stepfather, Harlan, at their house. Mom referred to the place she lived now as if it were both a physical and spiritual place, as if after having left my father she had ascended to another world. She talked about her new place without any of the straight-shooting frankness she had prided herself on during her marriage to my father. She didn't swear or make jokes about being poor. She associated herself, I guess, with authority, with people who had enough money.

Once, just after she had moved to Seattle, she took Jake and me to dinner in Bellevue by ourselves without Dad. She picked us up outside the middle school in her new blue Civic, maneuvering the car between the idling school buses. We rode through the Snoqualmie Valley the same way we used to visit Seattle. She acted as though she had been gone for a long time, although she had only been gone a winter. She sighed and said that she had always loved it out here. We drove under the sycamore trees that hung over the road near the old lumber mill, the same stand that Mom and Rosaline had helped save from the saw when a road crew was increasing the road width. Mom parked the Civic at the edge of the Minipis' orchard and powered down the windows by using the control panel in her armrest. We breathed in the odor of rotting fruit and mud and wood smoke. "Sometimes it's nice here," Mom said. "But sometimes you just want to be in a warm, clean place."

At dinner, we ate fish and chips on white platters and drank Coke from glass tumblers. Jake loved the copper burnished tables and knocked his knuckles on them. The place floated on a wharf in the middle of a marina in Lake Washington. Young men in sweaters filled the bar. Older couples quietly ate at the copper tables under the hurricane lanterns. I felt incidental to the subdued voices of the other diners, to the waitress who noted our order and tucked her blue Bic ballpoint pen behind her ear, even to Mom, who kept asking through the meal, "Well, what do you think?" She wanted to know if we'd consider moving in with her if she rented a house in Seattle. But Jake and I quickly forgot the question as soon as the waitress asked us if we would like pepper in our salads. "Why do I want that?" Jake asked. Hearing Mom ask us to live with her was as if she was asking us, "What do you think about my life?" And Jake and I didn't know, because it didn't feel like our life. It was her life and far outside of Snoqualmie.

"What do you think?"

"I think it's a nice place," Jake said. "Can we come here again?"

"You can come here all the time," Mom said. She stared beyond us, at the choppy water and the crews on the wharf furling the sails up as everyone packed things up for a spring storm.

We only saw her apartment in Seattle the Christmas after she moved. She picked us up on Christmas Eve and we ate dinner at another restaurant. We sat in the middle of a dimly lit room next to a huge white column, and men wandered from table to table laying out wrapped baskets with a hot loaf of bread on a scalding slab of marble. "Is this for us?" Jake asked Mom. "You didn't order this." Jake was afraid to order and had Mom ask for his fish and chips. That Christmas Eve we returned to Mom's apartment, up an elevator. Jake asked her if she ever just rode the elevator up and down. She stood directly in the middle of the elevator, her arms crossed, her weight spread out over both her feet. Jake and I watched rented movies on her new VCR. We fell asleep watching Christopher Reeve's *Superman*, stopping where he returned to his ice-encrusted Fortress of Solitude. I wondered, as I finally lay back on my bunched-up jacket on the couch, why Superman didn't build a more comfortable place to live? If I was Superman, I'd have big easy chairs, and bear rugs, and a fireplace where I'd burn entire trees. I'd be warm and comfortable. I woke in the middle of the night, the way I had at Oliver's apartment, to the sound of car horns and traffic on the street, and I thought that only my father remained with us and that both Oliver and Mom had finally abandoned us.

That spring, a year after Mom had left, she married Harlan Boggs in a private ceremony, too private to include Jake and me. She moved into his house on Queen Anne

Hill. That Christmas, she went to Hawaii. We received by mail, in a box full of stale popcorn, two professionally wrapped Fisher-Price fire trucks and a Christmas card that she signed, "Merry Christmas, from the Boggs." These gifts were to the children that we no longer were. Jake and I and my father had suddenly become a part of her past, belonging to the time before Oliver's death.

At Sea-Tac, I didn't know whether Mom or my father would pick me up. I passed the stewardesses who said "Happy Holidays" down the row of departing passengers. Faint light from the gray clouds fell through the portholes on the entrance ramp. Bumping through a crowd of people who smelled like soap, flowers, or deodorant, I excused myself and hurried through the busy hallways. I paused as the escalator carried me down to the baggage claim. People were disorderly and talked and wore anything they felt like, instead of standing in rigid formations. People faced each other, even though people had to face up the down escalator.

My duffel bag lay at the base of the luggage chute like an overstuffed weeble-wobble. I heaved the weight onto my back and waited near the entrance of my flight gate in case someone showed up late to pick me up. Family cars—Mercedes, Cadillacs, Skylarks—pulled up and older men with white hair shifted luggage from dollies into the spacious, carpeted trunks turning their pale faces red. They smiled as they opened their doors and closed them, sitting with their families beside them and then they were gone. I waited until I knew no one would come.

A cab dropped me in front of the return address on Mom's letter. The house sat on the south slope of Queen Anne Hill, overlooking the city where rain washed over the Sound and watered the office towers. I dropped the duffel bag on Mom's front steps. Two cement lions reclined on the brick walls bordering the walk. Someone had started to paint them white, leaving off in splotchy patches toward their backs. Mom's yard looked as if someone mowed it every day, reducing the grass to a flat plush surface like a green bathroom rug. Even the cedar tree that sat in her front yard was secured behind a plastic border guard to keep the acidic leaves at bay. I knocked on the metal door. Finally, I heard someone walk down the front steps. Mom cracked the door open. "Hi," she said.

I raised my eyebrows, but I didn't know what to say. "Here I am" didn't seem right. Nothing seemed right.

"I just came in for Christmas," I finally said. "I didn't want to sit at Fort Sam, so I came home. You don't mind?"

"You should've called."

"I wrote," I said. "I wrote a few weeks ago. You said I could come." At Fort Sam Houston, I wrote her a letter every two weeks telling her all about myself and the things I had been thinking about. Long letters, twelve or thirteen pages of cramped handwriting. She sent me a packet of postcards and photographs with a small note, "Miss you,

Mom." She spelled out *you*, as *y-a-h*. She had gone on a cruise from San Francisco to Tijuana. The postcards came from San Francisco, where she had gone to visit some of her new husband's friends. She included pictures of herself and her husband involved in deck things, shuffleboard, leaning over the side rails with a sunset exploding behind them while they leaned into each other, a huge tropical moon dipping into the wake of the thirteen-story cruise ship.

I looked at the man and saw a man who looked like my father. I figured I would turn out, eventually, to have the same stooped shortness, the developed gut, the skin as leathery as a carrot left in the fridge. He looked directly at the camera, his smile exposing slightly yellowish teeth.

"You almost missed me," Mom said. "I was just on my way to work. We have a guest bedroom upstairs. There's something to eat in the refrigerator. Help yourself. I'll be gone until seven or so. Harlan should be back around eight."

She led me up the stairs. The house smelled like lavender and the hallways were clean and warm and light. It didn't feel like her house. It didn't have the closed-in smell of mildew and wood smoke and coffee grounds. When I opened the bedroom door, I found it decorated with a yellow comforter that coordinated with the pine green carpet. "Thanks," I said. The window overlooked a yard with a stained wood deck and black lattice lawn furniture. An empty bottle of Jack Daniels sat on the table and a cigar lay seated in the rainwater-filled ashtray. "Goodbye, honey," Mom said from downstairs. "It's good to see you."

When the door closed, I lay on the bed and pulled off my shoes. After I showered, I looked through the house trying to find some sense of how Mom was doing. In the kitchen, I found a freezer full of microwave meals and a bar stocked with whiskey in glass bottles, whiskey in plastic bottles, and whiskey in black bottles, a cornucopia of whiskey. I filled a coffee cup halfway to the top with whiskey. When I tasted it, I swallowed hard and spit into the sink.

A lack of noise and action emanated from the orderly Queen Anne yards. The neighborhood sat on the highest ground in Seattle, separated from the traffic and businesses by a half mile, all round, of steep streets and green belts. Edged by methodical gardeners, every single lawn as far as I could see lay cropped close to the sidewalk like the lawns of the officers' houses at Fort Sam. I left the house and walked through the idealized Seattle neighborhood. Between the trees, the gray morning light fell from the Cascade Mountains. I could see clouds in the distance at the same level of the street and a glimpse of lower Seattle. Mom had escaped to Queen Anne, the Avalon of Seattle suburbs, safely removed from the hum of street traffic. When I came to the edge of the old sidewalks, the palatial Victorian houses with towers and spoke banisters tumbled down the steep hillside to the grid of the Seattle Center and the sky-scraper skyline.

I didn't feel as though I belonged to the city anymore. I jogged down the south Queen Anne steps into the apart-ment buildings and the small offices on the Denny

Regrade. Where my father had worked at the Red Diner, Westlake Mall was being built. A bookstore occupied the same airspace that had once been the roof of the Red Diner. The cooks had once squatted next to the aluminum, mushroom-shaped duct caps, filling the air with marijuana smoke and faintly audible blues. In the street below, a man in a suit stopped the flow of foot traffic while he yelled something into his mobile phone. The motion of the city seemed foreign now. The changes in decades had worked out as a change in geography.

I didn't know if Jake lived in Seattle. I saw aspects of him, in the kids sitting in front of Westlake Center, in the disinterested and self-important rush of a boy dressed in a flannel shirt and white-long-johns-under-shorts. He brushed past me, through the glass doors onto the street. I followed him. His hair, shaved in back, dyed black so often that it seemed as brittle as dry moss, cascaded from the top and down the side of his head and across his shoulders to his elbows. He walked past the Convention Center and behind the tall, uneven brick wall of the Paramount Theater. He strode down an alley. I followed him, aware of our footsteps echoing on the surface behind the buildings. He stopped at a security door on an empty street. It snapped shut behind him as he ran up the steps. At the wooden door inside the gate, he glanced back at me. But my eyes were on the six earrings that studded his ears and nose and eyebrow. He slammed the door. The door had been painted so often that the molding's contours had been evened out and reduced.

Mom came home before Harlan. She wore a turquoise skirt, a beige sweater, and square earrings and smiled when she saw me. "Aldous. You got a hair cut." She raised her eyebrows and asked if I would like a drink.

She poured us two whiskey and Diet 7-Ups and sat down on the couch with me. Mom started to prep me about her husband. "Harlan is not a tolerant person. He is mean. Just like my husbands always are. He is more interesting than your father. He likes to meet people, so he'll ask you a lot of questions. He and I get along pretty well. I'm sure you and he'll get along. No one else gets along with us as well as we get along with each other. We'll see."

My stepfather and I squeezed each others' hands as hard as we could. He grinned; I grit my teeth as he folded the sides of my hand. I squirmed free. "Back from the basic, eh?" he said. He stood in the entryway of his house with a briefcase and an umbrella my father would never own. Dad always lost his umbrella. Harlan wore his gas station jumpsuit that was too big in the shoulders and too small in the waist.

"Nice to meet you," he said. He hauled himself up the stairs and huffed, "Sit, make yourself comfortable, make yourself at home."

I looked at Mom; she looked around the hallway at the dust-free bookcases full of leather-bound editions of

Dickens, Melville, and Tolstoy. She must have used a maid now, because the house was cleaner than my commanding officer's office. "Sit at the dinner table," she said and clicked her high heels as she walked into the kitchen. I sat at the table, feeling out of place, until Harlan stumbled into the room with sweatpants on. "Hey, get you a drink?" he asked as he opened the cupboard above the sink and dropped a plastic two-quart high-impact-resistant whiskey container onto the counter.

"Sure," I said. He poured out three water glasses with square sides and prism bottoms and clinked ice cubes into the whiskey. Mom set the plates and some food she had been heating in the microwave onto the table. Harlan sat down at the table, smelling the food with audible sniffs. "Damn fine cooking, Mom. Nothing like a home-cooked meal, what do you say, A.?"

Dinner was very spartan, five sprigs of broccoli she'd boiled into mushy green follicles, a gray lamb chop, and a dollop of whipped potatoes. Mom sat in a chair where she was busy fishing the ice cubes out of her drink. She tossed them into the sink. She caught me looking at her and she smiled. "The water was fucking up my drink."

Harlan laughed. "You gotta have a woman with a sense of humor." He stood and leaned over Mom and wrapped his arms around her. She crouched under him, sipping from the square glass.

I slammed the whiskey down.

After dinner, Harlan moved us into the living room, lit with two lamps that gave out a faint, orange light. I heard the ice jostle in Harlan's drink as he sat down in an easy chair in front of the picture windows. We could see the houses across the street, and then the Seattle skyline. "We're having a great time, aren't we, Aldous?" Harlan said. "I don't know why your mother didn't bring you around before. It's always nice to know you have family you can stand. So tell me, A., what are your plans?"

"I don't know. It depends on where I get stationed."

"I own two gas stations."

"I know," I said.

"Being a business owner is a lot of work. It's not running the business that's difficult. Hell, that's just like showing up to work. Everybody can do that. Everyone's got to get paid. It's the involvement with the other people—the involvement in what do they call it—the community. That's a bitch."

"I bet it is," I said.

"Have you met Chris?"

"No, I don't think so."

"Chris is my oldest son. You can treat him like a brother. He'd like that. He's a real driven boy. You'd love the guy. He runs my gas station on Aurora. You should talk to me when you get back and we can see what kind of job I can get you."

"Sure," I said.

"I miss the military life. You know, A., I was in the

Marines." I couldn't see him in the dark living room. I heard him swallow his drink. "Waking up early. I'm sure right now you can't stand it, but in a couple of months you'll be like, hell, I'd give anything to just live life like I did in basic training. Don't you think?"

"You're right. I wouldn't be able to stand it."

He chuckled. "Good one, A. What would you like to do tonight? Would you like to take the car out?"

"No. That's all right."

"I have some football tapes. Seattle vs. everyone."

"No. No thanks."

"Another snort?"

"Sure," I said.

"I would've stayed in the Corps, but there's not much money to be made in philosophy," he said. He stood over me with the plastic whiskey bottle and poured it straight into my glass. Mom appeared out of the shadows with her glass cupped in both hands. She smiled at Harlan; he looped his arm around her waist and they stood in front of me, swaying back and forth. "The real world," Harlan said as he topped off Mom's glass, "doesn't have rules. It doesn't have any rules. In the real world, that's where my mettle has been tested."

"Which world is that?" I asked.

Mom squinted her eyes at me, an expression she flashed, when I was a child, at Oliver and Dad. She squeezed her eyes as if her eyelids were voodoo symbols of my lips do not use them, she meant. But Harlan was in no danger of noticing that I had spoken.

"You can take a man out of the Corps, but not the Corps out of the man. I got the best training of my life during those fourteen weeks of basic. Nothing," he spit, "nothing like having the hell beat out of you for a man to learn about life, about being strong. In the end, it's just endurance. Doesn't matter if he can run faster, speak faster, work faster, think faster, because he's gotta work longer. Know what I mean?"

"Sure," I said.

"So what do you do?"

"I'm a pharmacist tech."

"In the Marines?"

He looked at Mom. She sat on the edge of a chair in the orange light under one of the lamps. She looked at him and said, "He's in the Marines, I thought—"

"The Army," I said.

"Army," he said. "No offense, then, but good luck to you." He stood up. He shook my hand. "I can't eat with you." As he left, he muttered low enough and loud enough that we could all hear him, "Pussy-wussy man."

When he left the room, I stood up. My chair slipped back and I didn't stop it from rattling the linoleum. I found my legs like I did jumping to attention. I assumed position. I held my back straight and loose and pressed the arc of my thumbs to the creased seam of my jeans.

"He doesn't mean anything by that," Mom said. "He's just dragging out his dick." Mom sat against the table. The fabric of her blouse spread out in ivory waves. "Sit down, honey. Say something. Talk to me."

"You don't know what branch of the service I'm in."

"You're in the Army. We just established that. Harlan's a good guy. He looks after me. Pride's his problem. Everyone's got something wrong with them, and if he thinks too much of himself, that's better than not thinking enough."

"I'll get out of your house tomorrow," I said. I leaned over and kissed my mother on her forehead. I'd never done this before, and her forehead smelled like baby powder and had a leathery feel like an old belt. She flinched and leaned back into her chair and wrapped her arms around herself.

"Why did you do that?"

"Where was I, Mom?"

"What do you mean?"

"What city have I been living in for the last six months?"

"Why are you doing this to me now?"

"Do you know?"

"You're in the Army. That isn't in any one city, is it?" She blinked at me and then stood up and collected the plates from the table, and I helped her load the dishwasher and left her in the kitchen as she mulled over my question. "Why should I know something like that? This isn't a fucking trivia game."

In the morning before I left, I gathered up their gallons of whiskey. I displayed them all on the table, the frosted glass, the thick and round plastic carafes. I poured them into the black and rusted half-circle of their barbecue. The bottom filled with clear fluid. A plume of heavy fumes lifted up like gasoline. I went inside and found a Sorry Charlie's matchbook from a drawer stuffed with birthday candles, expired coupons, and bottle caps that read "Sorry. Please try again." I threw a match from the other side of the porch and the fluid popped and slowly burned around the rim of the barbecue, a blue flame until the paint caught on fire. I found the fuzzy envelope with the faded handwriting on the outside. "For Dear Oliver." Was this my grandmother's handwriting? I didn't even need to pull out the photograph to see it, although I wish I'd taken a look at it because I've forgotten already exactly how everyone stood at the Quinault trailhead. Did we all look at the camera unaware of what would happen? There were clues, I'm sure, in how Mom looked at whoever took the picture. I didn't remember now if Dad or Oliver took the photograph. Dad or Oliver stood behind us, I remember that. I tossed the envelope into the middle of the flames where it blackened and then burned with a blue flame, and the crumpled mass fluttered into the air.

Twenty-three

The house my father had moved into after my parents' divorce lay hidden at the end of a valley under Rattlesnake Ridge. At the edge of his property, the Cedar River watershed started. Signs posted on the trees warned trespassers that they were not only in danger of being prosecuted, but that their presence would destroy the supply of fresh water to Seattle. We stood in the third-floor room where Dad watched TV. Below us, two floors stood empty and cool. Pale forest light fell across the hardwood floors. From the ceiling, leafy green plants hung from wire racks. Their leaves had dried and crumbled.

Dad lived in one bedroom on the top floor. He told me, as we watched *Buckaroo Banzai* for the third time, how he had fields of marijuana hidden in the watershed. "It's not as bad as it may sound," he said. "They," he meant the government, "have allowed entire miles of forest to be chopped down. At the river source, just below Mirror Lake, the entire source valley for the Cedar River has been mutilated. So what if I plant an acre or two? So what!" He laughed and leaned back into the chair. He watched the movie. The blue light filtered through the gray smoke onto his face.

I slept in an extra bedroom on the third floor. There wasn't a bed, just a petrified sofa that had been in the house my parents lived in before their divorce. I walked outside to clear my head, afraid that I had spoiled my blood for drug tests just being in the same room as my father.

Dad had begun to collect edible and semiprecious objects out of the forests above his house. For the Christmas meal, he cooked a turkey seasoned with his favorite mushrooms. He called them ah-ah 'shrooms because he didn't know their name and when he had first discovered them, he had been stumbling down a steep slope attempting to get around cliffs. "They aren't poisonous, or even, alas, syllabicates," he said. He smiled and lowered the platter of turkey, smothered with layers of the slimy, dark troll ears of mushrooms. He poured a glass of milk from the carton on the table and tilted the bottom of the carton at me. "Would you like some?"

"Water is just great," I said. I tried to halve a mushroom with my fork, but a stringy internal fiber held it together. Dad brushed his beard into his shirt and tied a plaid napkin around his neck. He lifted a forkful of mushrooms and rolled his eyes. He chewed noisily and murmured, "Mmmm. These are delicious, don't you think?"

"Sure. Sure," I said.

Dad coughed and clutched his neck. His face turned bright red. Tearing his napkin away from his neck, he half stood and then sprawled onto the floor. One arm broke his fall and the other twisted behind his back.

I knocked my chair down. Leaning down beside him, I could smell the close odor of him, the syrupy cloud of marijuana, smoke, and dirt. He twisted his face around to look at me. Sprawled in that position, his face had turned a bright red, and he started to laugh.

I jumped away from him.

"You don't get it, do you?"

"Hilarious," I said. I sat back in my chair. Dad sat in his chair and brushed his shirt smooth. He took a long drink from his milk. He started to chuckle again. "You never got anything."

"I was stupid, I guess." I closed my eyes and stuffed a whole mushroom into my mouth. The greasy fabric of the mushroom filled my mouth and I started to gag. I swallowed into a solid gag and I found that the mushroom clogged my esophagus. It felt as if someone had shoved a plastic cap directly over my windpipe. Dad cut his mushroom into little bite-sized chunks. I told myself to settle down. My palms started to sweat and I felt the weave of the cotton tablecloth. I needed to throw up. I clutched my glass of water. I felt the cool glass at the tips of my fingers. And then a complete numbness overwhelmed my entire body.

My shoulders ached, and Dad crouched over me. His face turned red again and several buttons on his plaid shirt popped open. My entire body felt filled with Novocain. My legs lay under the table and I vaguely made out the sideways sprawl of my chair.

"Smart," Dad said. "You win, now don't you? I pretend to get poisoned and you have to really poison yourself."

"Poisoned? You said these things were safe."

"I said that they were as safe as eating a hamburger at McDonald's," Dad said. "Which is practically safe, I think. You don't think twice about eating there, do you? You've been eating somewhere and quite a lot by the looks of it." Dad clasped my hand and helped me to my feet. My legs didn't hold. Dad grabbed one of my elbows and looped his arm around my waist and lowered me to the floor. "You can get up when you're ready," he said. He sat back at his place and began to eat.

"So, how's the Army?" he asked me.

"Just a minute," I said. I leaned up and put my hands on my knees. My body still felt odd, and I just sat on the floor, breathing in and out, looking at the underside of the table and listening to my father chew his mushrooms. When I finally righted the chair and sat at the table, I said, "I wrote you a letter."

"A letter. How come you didn't call?"

"I don't like telephones," I said. I preferred writing a letter because when I said things on the page, I could imagine people responding exactly as I needed. On a telephone, I had to deal with the fluctuations in the person's mood. Dad's voice would lengthen into a long drawl late in the evening, after it had been knocked out of alignment by a six-pack of Rainier and a joint. In the morning, his voice would be tight and he would quickly get off the phone.

"Come on," Dad said. "Why don't you use phones? It's because you don't want to talk to me."

"Why wouldn't I want to talk to you?"

"Obviously you don't like talking to me."

"I'm here, now, talking to you."

"Not really. You're jumping under the table. I don't think that counts for talking to me. You're not even eating the food I cooked for you. Don't you like it?"

"I almost got poisoned, Dad."

"That's bullshit. You choked. Is my food not good enough for you?"

"Now I'm here, enjoying the turkey that you've cooked, and we're talking. See." I put a piece of the turkey into my mouth, even though it tasted like someone had marinated the meat in potting soil.

We sat in the room for a long while, looking at each other and preparing to say something. Finally, Dad began talking about a trip he had taken a few weeks before to the hot springs on the middle fork of the Snoqualmie. He tapped out his pipe into his tin ashtray and leaned back in his chair. He found a match and lit his pipe using the Coke bottle lighter recovered from Oliver's effects. The familiar motion of my father's hand as he swiveled his wrist up in flicking the flint, as if the lighter was much longer and heavier than it really was, brought back a stream of memories of the beginnings of my father's dinner table stories. He was telling a tale to Mom after dinner and Mom was pouring homemade wine from an old bottle. Dad was speaking to friends from the Red Diner as Jake and I were clearing the dinner plates and Corningware saucepans. As we wrapped leftovers and washed dishes, the smell of weed and the rhythm of my father's stories filled the kitchen.

Dad's voice had always remained the same, although physically, Dad changed drastically from year to year. In some photographs, he looked like a loser 1960s rebel, still caught in sock-hop styles—ducktail and a blue plaid shirt. A few years later, he appeared in all the photographs without his shirt on. He was emaciated, his arms were as thin as pipe cleaners, and his belly was taut over the extension of his belly button. His facial hair and hair length grew through the late seventies. This was how I remembered him. At one party, he wore old jeans, leather sandals without socks, and wire-rimmed glasses. His mustache jutted from under his noise, an affection of *Sgt. Pepper*'s era John

Lennon. And then a year later, on a hiking trip to the top of a mountain, he stood with his arms raised directly into the air, clean-shaven, the long loop of his ponytail trailing in his shadow and, behind him, the heaps of mountain peaks fell back into a bluish haze.

I found in that cache of photographs, one taken at the Enchanted Valley trailhead of all of us, Mom and Oliver stood to one side and Dad stood behind us, caught getting into position. He had left the camera on the hood of the Dodge Dart. Adrian stared into the camera abstractly and Jake and I stood next to her, oddly looking around the same age as Adrian. I put the photograph in my pocket.

Listening to him begin another tale, he revised himself again. When my father talked about his future, he talked about himself as had always appeared to himself, as a twenty-two-year-old man with a young wife and young children.

Dad and I went to the end of the Middle Fork Road and came to the flooding river. It wasn't as bad as he said it would be. We found a fallen tree to walk across, and then we were in the forest where the moss hung from the trees. Finally, we came to the cabin. It was empty. Dad and I walked up to the hot springs and swam in the water.

We floated in the dark, hot belly of the mountains, and I wondered if I could talk to my father about the things that had happened when I was growing up. "Dad?"

"Mmm?" He floated back into the darkness of the cave, swimming on his back.

"Who do you think killed Adrian?"

Farther in the cave, he lit a candle, and the entire cave exploded in the light. Small and large quartz veins caught the light and filled the cave with sparkling flashes. "Whatever has happened in the past, I don't much care about, because here I am in the only perfect place on earth."

I floated in the dark water for a moment and dunked under the surface, holding my entire body suspended in the hot water. I had always believed that the death of Adrian was something that deeply affected my father because he rarely mentioned it. Dad's obliviousness had eroded everything like the water of a deep, slow river. I rose out of the hot water and, outside, rain fell in the cold woods. All around us, the forest was silent and muddy, and without thinking of the long trip here or the long trip out, everything seemed perfect. I believed then that I understood something about my father: he existed in the single moment of the present. This moment never existed for me. I anticipated the future with sweating palms and a dull ache at the pit of my stomach. As soon as the present slipped into the past, I regretted it with an instant nostalgia. But for my father, days were not anticipated or regretted. They just happened. He didn't have any clocks inside his house. The clock on Dad's VCR flashed 12:00 forever.

I swam to the lip of the cave, listening to Dad splash around behind me. "Dad, who do you think killed Adrian?"

The cool outside air rose goose bumps on my shoulders. I looked through the caves of the cedar tree boughs across the river, and, for a moment, I looked directly into the face of the man in the red plaid shirt. He stared into me with blank spaces where his eyes should have been and then he was just the shadows between the trees. This was the forest where Adrian had died and I knew after all I had said, and as far as I had come, I was back in the forest feeling rain on my face, back where I had started, back to the end of the earth, where my father lived in a constant flux of instant after instant. "No one killed her," he said. "She died of hypothermia."

Dad dropped me off in the parking lot of a bakery on top of Queen Anne, unwilling to drive me down the block where Mom lived. "Just being up here is bad enough," he said. "I don't need to see her house." We ate donuts and drank coffee in his truck, sitting in the parking lot looking at the people coming out of the bakery in their jogging suits with bagels and coffee. I walked back and up the steps into the house, found the key Mom had told me to find under the terra-cotta pot full of soil and the coils of long-dead flowers. I held the key in my hand and looked around at the empty neighborhood. The ferns planted in the beauty bark stirred in the wind. I put the key back under the pot and left. I could get a cab to the airport myself.

Before I left, though, I walked across Seattle, back down Queen Anne. Mercer still carried a steady stream of cars on their way to work on the Eastside. While much of the city had changed, there was the underlying odor of moldy cedar tree needles and Puget Sound brine. I felt like an intruder from the city's recent history. The past had receded so quickly that even something as recent as my memory of riding the bus last year out to Seattle Center from Snoqualmie and watching the retired men in their bolo ties and polished shoes fox-trot with the women in turquoise scarves and flared square-dance skirts seemed to belong to the jumble of past events going back to Mom leaving Jake and me in Oliver's Murphy bed apartment and Dad carrying an armload of groceries—eggs, flour, and oil—into Oliver's last, cold studio apartment to find him lying on the floor tangled in loose newspaper and stained bedspreads.

Oliver had worked at Andy's Diner off and on in gradually diminishing roles. At first, he worked as a night cook before he disappeared on a binge. He returned to work as a prep cook in the mornings until he disappeared again. No one knew where he went, and when he resurfaced, he was intermittently employed as the dishwasher or janitor, or finally, as a casual laborer. He resurfaced the gravel parking lot. He didn't like the work, but was thankful to be getting any money, and since he was getting paid by the hour, he took a lot of smoke breaks huddled with his pick and shovel under the tangled cedar tree shrubs.

I had come back to Seattle, I think, to absolve myself of guilt. Janet had identified it for me, like some foreign body or hostile and quickly growing skin growth. I didn't even know I felt it while I lived in Snoqualmie. I thought the feeling of things done wrong came with the rain and the evergreen trees. I imagined guilt worked more like a mineral problem and that somehow I could pass it like a kidney stone or have it cut out. I was born a boy with brown hair and brown eyes, and I transposed letters, and I had killed my sister and finally my uncle. I am right-handed and wear a size nine shoe. As a child, I didn't ponder the consequences of my actions or even consider that time could last as long as it did. I felt at the mercy of events. Things happened to me. I didn't feel I had any influence on the outcome.

As I walked across town, the dampness of the sky soaked my coat. The hard pavement and my civilian shoes raised blisters on my heels. My sweater held a sheen of light moisture by the time I had worked my way over the one-way streets. I walked up Denny to Capital Hill, taking my jacket off and keeping it folded over my arm. A steady cool flurry of droplets washed down around me out of the sky, neither actual rain nor humidity nor low, flat clouds. Late-morning walkers filled Andy's Diner, talking softly to each other. The odor of scorched eggs and scalded coffee filled the place. Everyone drank bloody beers and ate eggs with salsa. I sat down and ordered myself a plate of scrambled eggs and coffee. This was the Seattle I had left behind.

I paid for my breakfast and walked to the reservoir behind Broadway, across the street from the crumbling structure of the Oddfellows Hall. Oliver's midseventies Murphy bed apartment had a bay window overlooking the intersection of Pine and Broadway. My uncle could stumble out of the Comet Tavern and walk a block, cross the street, two flights of stairs, and lay himself out in his wall bed. Drizzle coated the reservoir benches. The drizzle stopped and the sun tried to burn through the gray haze. The shadows of the pedestrians trickled across the slick pavement.

I took out the photographs in my jacket pocket, the photo of us at the trailhead before those last couple of days. Adrian was actually almost as tall as I was in the picture. But I hardly remember her now. The clearest thing about her was her absence afterward. I remembered repeating after Oliver, "Good Monster, God damn," as he snapped the picture.

I stopped to watch the children play at the wood chip-coated play yard at the far side of the park. One child had just fallen out of the swings and was crying, holding his hands out stiff to either side of his body. He walked around in tight circles while the other children kept on playing. The kid waiting his turn in line at the swings climbed onto the swing the other child had just fallen out of. It occurred to me then that these kids were older than I had been when I went into the Quinault Valley.

At the intersection of Pine and Broadway I stopped. Across the street, a new QFC stood where Oliver's building used to be. I wanted to stand where his apartment had been, so I walked into the entrance on Pine and came into a bakery. Glass cases filled with donuts and birthday cakes replaced Oliver's bookcases. Aluminum chairs and tables with crumpled-up napkins sat under the window where his old sofa used to sit.

I imagined Oliver coming home from the mountains, tired and half-stoned. He would want to eat the cakes, but he'd be confused because he couldn't find the stairwell up to his apartment. He would stagger down the line of cashiers zipping items over the laser-eye beam and think, "Shit, I thought I was stoned, not frying." Where his apartment should have been, among the piles of apples with little stickers on each one, I came to a pile of furry round kiwifruit and I couldn't imagine what Oliver would think of them. Sasquatch testicles, a gigantic heap of abominable snowman ball-sacks? I picked one up and held it. One of the stock boys hosing off the spinach watched me until I put it back in the heap.

Twenty-four

I pressed my nose against the rocking glass porthole as the plane jostled down onto the San Antonio runway. The tires broke through the wispy clouds and lowered down onto the early morning grid full of aligned orange lights and bounced on the damp pavement. I followed the line of passengers up the ramp, past a bleary-eyed father with a coffee cup in one hand hugging his returning daughter. Men in blue jumpsuits drove groaning floor-buffing tractors down the empty marble concourse. A cold, damp wind flapped the international flags outside. The sun lit the horizon in a long silver line, bleeding light up into the faint clouds and then guttering pricks of stars. I tried to make out where Fort Sam might sit in relation to me with the frigid wind in my face, but I could only figure which way was east. I had left a thick, Southern humidity and returned to this. Nothing seemed the same.

A cold snap had hit San Antonio the last week of December. Hunks of ice lay on the lawns. Frost grew in the shadowy crook of the gutter and sidewalk. Icicles hung from the palm trees around the barracks. The yellow, wind-beaten grass looked like unwashed hair. I hurled my duffel up onto my shoulder and marched into the barracks. The CQ's chair sat butt-down on the desk, the legs sticking up, with a thin spiderweb arching from one leg to the other. A water-stained sheet of paper had been taped on the door. The ink letters ran in teary streaks. REPORT TO THE MAIN CQ TO ACCESS BARRACKS. I jostled the handle to the No Females Allowed door. It was locked. The No Males Allowed door didn't budge either.

With a growing sense of alarm, I crossed the empty parking lot. I'd expected the base to be full of life, of soldiers marching, of students in the barracks highlighting their study notes for the final skills test at the end of the month. Instead, I didn't even see a cockroach. Icicles cracked in the faint sunlight.

A specialist wearing crumpled BDUs and toothpaste-speckled glasses sat at the desk listening to headphones. He stood when he saw me. "What do you want?" He said this in an overloud voice, loud enough that he could hear himself over guitar chords and the fossilized hoots of a mob in bleachers.

"I'd like access to the barracks, Specialist."

"What?" He paused the tape. I repeated myself.

I had to go through all of the steps of getting my bedding again, but this time alone and without standing in line. The Specialist handed me a plastic package with a green wool blanket and another with my pillow. My back ached. He opened the door to the barracks. "They won't be unlocked until Friday," he said.

"How am I supposed to get in and out?"

"You don't have to be here until Monday morning," he said. "If you're here now, it's your problem."

I went through the barracks. A film of dust coated the blankets. Mold grew on the windowsill and frost coated the upper edge of the window frame. I stuffed my duffel bag in my locker. I swept the surface of the bed with the palm of my hand and lay down. I stared up at the wire mesh under the upper bunk and fell asleep. I woke sometime later. The room was the same. I went out into the hallway and it was empty. The sun came in through the common room window, laying long warm light across the buffed floors. I crossed through the second-floor breezeway. The second-floor female door was unlocked and I entered their barracks. It was just as quiet as the male side. I found my way to Janet's door, counting out room numbers. I knocked and then put my hand on the door because the sound filled the hallway. I listened at her door and to the barracks and then I checked her door. It was unlocked. A Christmas tree shed needles all over the floor. The room smelled like a pine forest. A dank, rotting smell came from the desk. They had a fishbowl. A goldfish, no longer orange but green, floated, adhered to a flat, floating island scum of mold. I dumped it into the toilet. The mold skin clung to the empty fishbowl rim. I rinsed it under the hot tap water and shook it and the mold peeled off and splashed. I flushed again, but the tank hadn't refilled. I stood in the empty barracks in Janet's empty bunk room listening to the cold water fill the empty white tank.

I heard someone say *fuck* and skid down the hallway. Someone slid into the female second-floor common room and down the hallway. "Janet?"

Something whizzed by and then Viscount slid down the hallway in his socks and gray Army sweat suit. He held a window-shade rod, and a red Super Ball rolled back from the end of the hall. He swung like a golfer knocking the ball against the cinder block, against the ceiling, ricocheting off the floor and against the ceiling again.

"What are you doing over here?"

"What are you doing back from the Yukon?"

"Am I the only one who's come back?"

"Yeah," he said. "Like how many hours do we have until class starts again?"

"98 hours or something like that."

"If I went home I wouldn't be back until 97 hours from now. Unless it was the Yukon. I understand they don't have timepieces out that way."

"You stayed here?"

"This is my home now," he said. "I'm in the Army now, son. But if I lived somewhere else, I wouldn't come back until I had to."

"Have you seen McGrath?"

"He's free to go and come back at the very last minute, so I don't think so. The only people I've seen are Sandy Comstock's parents."

He threw the ball against the far wall and it ticked against it, the floor, the ceiling, and the floor again.

"Did you see her? Did you see Sandy?"

Viscount leaned down and caught the ball. "I did not, but she's still here. She stayed on base all break too. I tried to see her the week after Christmas. I wasn't allowed. Family only. They were looking for her in her old bunk room and then along I come playing golf and I don't think they were too happy."

"What happened to her? Where is she?"

"Psycho ward. She's nuts, man."

He handed me the window-shade rod. "You should play. It'll do you a world of good." He threw the ball against the far wall again and instead of bouncing against the floor it flew back toward us. I swung and missed.

"What did you do on your break?" Viscount asked me. "I went home. You know how you leave something behind or think you're leaving something behind, but it's all you can think about once you leave it behind and you think everyone back home is thinking about you as much as you are them and then you go back and you realize they haven't been thinking about you for maybe ten years?"

"I guess." He leaned down to pick up the ball, and then he dropped it for me. I hit the ball and we followed it down the hallway and he picked the ball up and we walked up to the third floor and then he pulled a ladder down and we climbed up and were on the roof of the barracks. There were beer cans lying around. "Shit, I got to clean up before McGrath comes back." He sniffed an upright can sitting against the wall. He jostled it. "There's still some beer in here." He took a drink and smiled and then offered the can to me. "It's practically full."

I waved it away.

We leaned on the upper edge of the railing and looked up at the pale blue sky and the faintly etched clouds. Viscount had heavy wrinkles I hadn't noticed before running from the edge of his mouth down to his jawline. His lips were really red and his skin was this sort of luminous, even transparent, waxy color. He wore his thick, wire-framed aviator glasses that had the support beam lying across his nose.

"How come you didn't go home, I mean to your real home?"

"I told you, I don't have a home anymore. As soon as I set out in the world, I left it all behind me. This is my home now. Here," he tried to hand me his beer.

"No, thanks," I said.

"All right, I'll down it," he said.

"Cheers," I said.

"Did I tell you," he said, "I learned the riff to 'My Generation?'"

Sunday evening, I sat on the cold steps waiting for Janet, pretending to read while I watched the soldiers come back. They stepped out of their cabs wearing civilian clothes and walked with limp civilian struts or hunched peacetime slumps as they hurried past me. They looked around at the barracks and at the other stunned faces of the returning soldiers and shook their heads. "Does this place ever look cheerful?" one female asked.

"Compared to home it could. It could be cheerful," I said.

She stopped and adjusted the weight of her suitcase strap. "Was I even asking you? Who are you, the barracks rat?" The trainees no longer looked anything like the trainees ushered off the basic training buses.

After the sun set, after the washing machines started to throb, after six soldiers in gloves and their BDU caps lined with the green arctic insert began to play volleyball on the frozen sand court, Janet still hadn't jumped out of a cab. I knocked on the female door until someone came. "Is Janet Wahl back?"

"Who are you?"

"I just want to—"

"—let me check." She closed the door and didn't come back.

I woke early and went running through the streets glazed with black ice. My breath came out in big round clouds. When I came back to shower before muster, I found Janet on the front steps. She wore a University of Wisconsin sweatshirt and threadbare blue jeans. She jumped down the steps. I didn't expect her to. She hugged me before putting her cigarette out. I really hadn't thought she'd do that. She dropped ashes on the back of my neck and I didn't mind.

"I'm sorry. I'm tired. I didn't want to get back until the last possible moment. If I fall asleep in formation that will make McGrath's year." She leaned forward and put her forehead on my forehead and said, "It is nice to see you."

"I came back last week."

"Home can't have been that bad."

"I went back to my parents' houses. I didn't go home."

"I am way too tired and you're getting sweat on my forehead." She leaned back. "I have to go eat some coffee grounds."

In formation, Janet stood in her spot. Instead of occasionally looking over her shoulder at me or turning around and showing me the back of her tongue, she swayed in her spot and stared up at the faint cirrus clouds in the frosty blue sky.

Slush covered the sidewalk from class. No one had walked on it yet. Heavy, dime-sized flakes whirled down from the fuzzy clouds. I could hear tires whirring on the damp pavement. The snow crust made a crunching noise as Janet and I left tracks behind us, black and bleeding water, on the sidewalk. I looked behind us as soon as we reached the road, and the tracks had already started to fade and then disappear. Janet and I stood there watching our tracks vanish.

"Come on," she said. We slipped our way up the hill, peeling out on the steep slope. At the top, we crossed the parade field. Janet climbed up into the bleachers with a roof, really built to keep out the sun—it was just a latticework, and snow fell through and lay in tiny, neatly arranged piles, until the snow had accumulated enough on the roof that it had plugged the holes.

"Do you think it will collapse?" I asked.

"How much snow do you think they're going to get in San Antonio?"

We swept a spot clean and sat down and looked out over the PT field. The snow fell in long waving arcs, and maybe three hundred yards away we couldn't see anything except the snow coming down. The ground was warm enough that the snow turned slushy when it landed.

"Sometimes in Minnesota," Janet said, "it's too cold to snow. They say that the Arctic pole is really desert based on the amount of precipitation that falls."

"Water everywhere and not a drop to drink."

She scooted over to me and leaned against me. She smelled slightly of stale smoke and the wintergreen mints she chewed to cover the smell. In six weeks, Janet would wake up in her bedroom the way she had the summer before. That summer, I had woken at five to bike down to the feed store to work. I didn't even imagine then sitting here now with Janet. Next summer sitting here with her would seem just as implausible. If it seemed unlikely, even though we both sat right next to each other on a bench, how likely was it that she would understand anything that had happened to me? How then could she understand about Adrian? Dry leaves rattled in the crawl space under the bleachers. Janet's hair tangled in the wind. Janet shifted a little toward me and slid her hand up my sleeve and grabbed my forearm. She ran a finger over the ridge of the scar I had from basic training. I'd attached my bayonet backward and, trying to secretly and quickly remove and reattach it before the drill sergeant noticed, I sliced a long gash into my arm. The drill didn't believe me. "Those things are so dull, they can't even open an onionskin envelope. Did you stab yourself, Private?" I kept thinking as the drill shouted, HE isn't going to make me knock out push-ups on a bleeding arm. That was before I knew better.

"What happened?" Janet asked. "What happened to your arm?"

"Nothing," I said.

"I didn't want to come back here," Janet said.

I wanted to tell her that I wanted to see her, but I also didn't want to force her into a situation where she had to tell me why she didn't want to come back. It was a military base. What was there to like about chrome floor-buffing machines, formations of Army Rangers, and saluting the endless stream of medical officers we ran into in the Academy of Health Sciences?

She leaned over and kissed me. Her face pushed me back and the shock of the kiss almost knocked me down between the slates of the bleacher. Her lips were cold and her breath felt warm and then puffed out over my face. She pulled back. "I really didn't want to see you again. As soon as I saw you, I didn't want to go home."

Janet took my hand as we left. I held her hand and didn't know what it meant to be holding hands; there were rules against PDAs and this was a PDA and I didn't exactly like PDAs, but then I liked Janet making any kind of display of affection, even a public display. However, it was also in the middle of a whiteout.

"Do you want to go back to the barracks?"

"What else is there to do?"

"We could get a room."

"We could," I said.

So we did. It was a little boxlike room with a slightly musty smell of rust and chlorine from the air conditioner, and Janet smiled at me and then we took off our clothes.

She accepted me and I accepted her and we lay in the bed accepting everything, several times.

After graduation, Janet and I left early Saturday morning in an old Dodge that she had bought for four hundred dollars in a San Antonio used car lot. We didn't stop until we were outside Texas. We ate lunch in Las Cruces, New Mexico, and then drove Highway 25 to Albuquerque, and then for miles and miles to Flagstaff. I don't remember much about the drive. For long miles of road, the sun glanced off the asphalt. Frost coated the cliff shadows. Above the highway, the sky never broke.

Finally, we came to a small motel and wooded place in the middle of the desert. Flat, undisturbed desert stretched away all around the motel. The motel itself was built on the summit of a small hill covered with stunted pine trees. I could only hear our jeans rubbing on the stiff vinyl interior as we slid out of the car. A distant bird called over and over again.

I knew when I told her about Adrian she would understand now. I wanted to tell her.

We sat in our room, and I felt as if I had finally come to a place that had never known mold; there was a clearness to the place, and I felt as if my body had finally started to dry. We started a fire in the small fireplace, and soon the room was hot. Janet and I lay on the covers of the bed. "Where do you suppose we are?" Janet asked.

"I don't know."

"What are you thinking?"

"I want to tell you something."

"What is it?"

I lay my head on her stomach. She placed her hand on my temple. My head rose slightly with each breath she took. The lamp hardly lit the room and so the fire cast fuzzy flickering shadows over the wall behind the bed. A framed, black-and-white photograph of a hacienda with a Model T Ford parked in front of it hung from the wall. When Janet's breath came out, my head went way down into her and the bedsprings creaked. "Dad," I said, "began to dig the dam behind the house the summer I was nine, the summer my sister Adrian died, the summer Uncle Oliver came to live in the attic . . . "

When I woke in the morning, I jumped away from the bed the way I had in basic training. Janet murmured something and reached her arm through the depression in the mattress where I had slept. She turned to the wall, curled up, and fell asleep. I poured hot tap water into my plastic Texaco mug and spooned in several heaps of instant coffee. I decided to go for a long walk in the desert before Janet woke.

A bluish glow lit the eastern sky and a faint light filled the desert. I walked over the loose soil. It spit out from behind the balls of my feet. I kept the small hill behind me, because in the desert there weren't any variations in landscape. There was nothing to place me in relation to the sky, to the earth, to where I had come from. Each section of land looked the same as the other, and the sky overhead held a monochrome flatness that didn't alter with the rising of the sun. For an instant, I felt a wave of coldness, the sensation I always associated with deep, clear pools under spruce boughs.

Sometimes, walking on the bank of a fork of the Snoqualmie, the river paused in a deep cache of stone. Through the clear water, I couldn't see to the bottom because the forest shadows rippled over the surface. I would stare into the water as it washed by, each ton drawing the heat from the rocks. And if I had plunged into the river, it would have quickly drawn the heat from my blood until I was gray and mottled like the round river rocks. I always tried to see Adrian in the water. I believed she had been carried away by this elemental force after she had died, and that she lived now in a pool of water somewhere in the woods. Staring into the black depths of river water, I could see her white arms, an apparition summoned through the monotony of passing water, through the constant stare into the river depths. Her lips were green and she smiled at me and pulled herself back to the bottom of the river, among the speckled trout and worn stone.

She was a little girl, unfamiliar with yellow salmonberry branches and green, star-shaped salmonberry bush leaves tangled in her hair. She'd been with me the entire time, and would be with me in the desert, Germany, wherever. I turned back to the hill in the distance, with pine trees growing up to its crown, where Janet slept and waited for me.

Also available from Clear Cut Press:

The Clear Cut Future
edited by Clear Cut Press
CCP 000 / 528 pp. ISBN 0-9723234-1-4
With color and B&W illustrations
$12.95

This anthology maps the territory of interest to Clear Cut Press, more or less. Among the contributors are writers Stacey Levine, Charles D'Ambrosio, Emily White, Rebecca Brown, Robert Glück, Pravin Jain (a former Enron executive), Casey Sanchez (a fish slimer), painter Michael Brophy, and photographers Robert Adams and Ari Marcopoulos.

Ode to certain interstates and Other Poems
by Howard W. Robertson
CCP 001 / 184 pp. ISBN 0-9723234-2-2
$12.95

From 1995-96, Eugene, Oregon, poet Howard W. Robertson worked as a long-haul truck driver in the eleven Western states and British Columbia, an experience that inspired the thirteen-part title poem in this collection. In 2003, he was awarded the Robinson Jeffers Tor House Prize for Poetry.

*Occasional Work and Seven Walks from the
Office for Soft Architecture*
by Lisa Robertson
CCP 002 / 274 pp. ISBN 0-9723234-3-0
With color illustrations
$12.95

Since 1996, poet Lisa Robertson (*XEclogue, Debbie: An
Epic, The Weather*) has used the Office for Soft Architecture
as an apparatus for lyrical research focused primarily on
Vancouver, B.C. This collection of essays considers such subjects as public fountains, pleasure-grounds, bridges, gardens,
office towers, suburbs, shrubs, restaurants, and motion.

Denny Smith (stories)
by Robert Glück
CCP 003 / 268 pp. ISBN 0-9723234-4-9
$12.95

These new stories by the author of *Margery Kempe, Jack the
Modernist,* and *Reader* use events in the life of their author,
such as burglary, sex, reading, conversation, humiliation,
child raising, and porn, as a ground for the expansion of
empathy and intellect. Self-absorbed, the stories are also
profoundly communal. Michel Foucault esteemed Glück
as one of the world's finest writers about sex.

Core Sample: Portland Art Now
edited by Randy Gragg and Matthew Stadler
CCP 004 / 416 pp. ISBN 0-9723234-8-1
With color illustrations and DVD
$15.95

Core Sample was an artist-initiated, citywide exhibition of contemporary art that took place in Portland, Oregon, in October 2003. This catalog documents Core Sample's methods and results and serves as a practical guide to the mobilization of noninstitutional cultures and a reflection on the worth of such projects. With essays by Lynne Tillman, Lawrence Rinder, Cecilia Dougherty, and Peter Culley.

Orphans (essays)
by Charles D'Ambrosio
CCP 005 / 238 PP. ISBN 0-9723234-5-7
$12.95

Eleven essays from the award-winning author of *The Point and other stories*

Frances Johnson (a novel)
by Stacey Levine
CCP 007 / 270 pp. ISBN 0-9723234-6-5
$12.95

A new novel from the PEN Western Fiction Prize-winning
author of *Dra__* and *My Horse and other stories*, this is the
story of a woman living in a small town in Florida who can't
decide whether or not to attend the town dance.